Black Widow

Black Knights Inc: Reloaded

JULIE ANN WALKER

To my fellow Americans. We are fighting for the soul of our nation. In this battle, we cannot lose sight of our principles. Honesty, integrity, and accountability are fundamental to democracy.

Remember that right is better than might.
And love must always trump hate.

People shouldn't be afraid of their governments.
Governments should be afraid of their people.

—Alan Moore, V for Vendetta

PROLOGUE

Red Delilah's Biker Bar, Chicago, Illinois

Sabrina Greenlee had worked at Black Knights Inc. for nine months.

That was precisely eight months and thirty days longer than any stretch of sustained happiness Hewitt Birch had ever known.

From the back booth, he watched her laugh at something the bartender said. No matter how hard he looked, he couldn't find the shadows that once clouded her eyes. Couldn't find the horror that once haunted her pretty face.

She was better. Brighter. Healing.

A spring flower that had shoved through the frozen ground of her grief and trauma. Fragile yet fierce. Ripening. Resilient.

Sabrina…

Named for the Roman river goddess.

Fitting, since she had the grace of a gentle stream and a laugh as clear and sweet as a babbling brook. Plus, she had a pull on him no mortal had ever managed.

It was wild how his life had shifted since she'd come to Chicago. Once, he'd been content to hole up in the old menthol cigarette factory-turned-motorcycle shop, nose buried in a book, satisfied to let the outside world fade away. Now? He found himself out among the unwashed masses because she'd grin that Sabrina grin of hers—all sparkling eyes and mile-wide mouth—and say, *It's Friday night.* Or Saturday. Or Tuesday. Didn't matter, really. *"Let's go have some fun."*

And damned if he could say no. He didn't want to say no, because just being near her made him happy and—

"You look like hammered shit," Boss said from across the booth, dragging Hew's gaze away from the river goddess.

"Ayuh." He glanced at the big, black Garmin Tactix on his wrist and scratched his beard. "Took longer than usual for the insults to start. Ya feelin' okay, Boss?"

"If I were insulting you," Boss countered, the gray in his spiky buzzcut catching the overhead lights, "I'd say something about you crawling out from your cave near the Earth's core to join us tonight."

Hew cocked an eyebrow.

"You know." Boss shrugged a bowling ball-sized shoulder. "All that heat and pressure explains why you're so antisocial."

"You're one to talk." Becky smacked Boss's arm. "When's the last time we came here?" She gestured at the peanut shell-strewn floor and the three well-worn pool tables. Red Delilah's was a holy Mecca for guys who liked leather, chrome, and machines that rattled their bones. "Two months? Three?"

"When you said the girls were with their aunt and uncle tonight, I figured that meant we'd be using our spare time for a little…" Boss wiggled his brows. "Not coming *here*."

Becky rolled her eyes. "Like having our daughters home has ever stopped us from a little…" She matched the eyebrow wiggle.

"It stops us from doing it on the kitchen counter," Boss argued. "Or on the living room couch."

"You mean the kitchen counter where we make our kids' food? And the living room couch where they sit to watch cartoons?"

"There's such a thing as bleach, you know."

"For the couch?"

"No!" Boss threw up his scarred, wide-palmed hands. "For the kitchen counter." His grin turned wolfish. "We can just throw a blanket over the couch."

Becky gave him a playful elbow, then turned to Hew. "As you can see, *my better half* has no business giving you grief for being a homebody. I had to twist his arm nearly out of its socket to get him here tonight."

Boss's sigh was drawn out and long-suffering. "I'm just saying, we could've stayed back at the shop and had a couple of beers around the fire pit instead of being forced to listen to other people's music."

Boss craned his head toward the jukebox near the front door. Someone had spun Katy Perry's "Firework." It was a bold choice considering the usual mix heard inside Red Delilah's tended toward classic rock or outlaw country.

"It's too hot for the fire pit," Becky declared, pulling a root beer-flavored Dum-Dum from her pocket. "Shove this in your mouth," she said after handing it to her husband. "It'll give your tongue something to do besides complain."

Boss grumbled but dutifully unwrapped the lollipop. Then, he pointed the round head of the sucker in Hew's direction. "Your report to the higher-ups said the mission went as planned. How come the shadows under your eyes tell a different tale?"

"Just 'cause a mission follows the plan doesn't mean it went smoothly," Hew muttered as he shifted uncomfortably at the thought of just how *un*smoothly things had actually gone.

"Bad intel? Bad equipment? Or both?" Boss asked.

"Intel was fine," Hew informed him, his tone bland.

Boss nodded in understanding.

Frank "Boss" Knight had been the head of the original twelve-man crew at Black Knights Inc. Like the current six-man team, the OG covert defense firm guys had taken their orders from and reported directly to El Jefe himself, the president of the United States. But the change in leadership at the White House had resulted in a change in BKI's active-duty roster.

The new madam president had wanted to form her own clandestine, fast-response team, made up of men loyal to *her* and not the previous administration.

Enter: Hew and his five teammates.

"So how bad was it?" Boss asked, using his tongue to swap the sucker from one bewhiskered cheek to the next.

"The Bell 412 the RIB gave us was a friggin' pile," Hew lamented with a distasteful twist of his lips. "I didn't expect their best, but I'd hoped for more than a Huey held together with duct tape and dreams. After we rescued the hostages, we made it twenty klicks from the Boko Haram base before she started fallin' apart midair."

Becky's eyes widened. "Jesus."

"Ayuh." Hew nodded. "I was prayin' to him and anyone else listenin'. It was sheer luck I could bang a uey and limp us over the border into Nigeria."

"Sheer luck and a hell of a lot of skill, I imagine," Boss interjected.

"Brought us down in what Graham called a *hard landin'.*" Hew made air quotes. "More like a controlled crash. Light on the *controlled.*"

"Navy SEALs." Boss grinned broadly, referring to Graham Coleburn… and *also* himself since he'd once sported the Budweiser. "We're nothing if not kings of understatement."

Hew grunted and took another pull from his beer. He was bone-tired. His ears still rang from the systems malfunction warnings that had blared through the cockpit. And the twenty-six-hour trip home, squirreled away in the belly of a big G17 Globemaster cargo plane, had been anything but relaxing.

And still…

The second he'd walked through BKI's front door to see Sabrina leaving for Red Delilah's, he'd dropped his duffel and followed her like a goddamned golden retriever.

"Don't say it." Becky's voice yanked his attention back to the present. The diminutive motorcycle designer shook a finger at her husband's nose.

"Didn't even open my mouth." Boss blinked innocently. *Too* innocently.

"No. But your face is speaking volumes."

The couple made an incongruous pair. Becky was tiny and beautifully elfin in appearance. By contrast, Boss was huge and burly and looked like he'd gotten tangled up with a weedwhacker at some point.

Hew flicked a curious gaze between them. "What did I miss?"

"Let's get *your* opinion on this," Becky declared. "What do you think is the appropriate length of jail time for the heinous crime of leaving wet towels on the bathroom floor?"

"According to her"—Boss hooked a thumb—"the answer is a life sentence."

"Hooks are on the back of the door *and* next to the shower. You have a wealth of options, and yet—"

"In case no one's ever told ya," Hew interrupted their argument. "It's annoyin' as hell bein' the third wheel in your Hallmark movie. Where's my damn backup?"

He looked back toward the bar and…immediately sat up straighter.

A short, stocky guy with a cleft in his chin rubbed a finger over the back of Sabrina's hand.

His first thought was…*Would you look at the sack on this friggin' guy?* His second thought was to rake his gaze over the man with so much force that he was surprised the douchebag didn't feel it.

From the top of the man's salon-styled superhero hair to the bottom of his handmade Italian loafers, he had *silver spoon* written all over him and *giant asshole* written on top of that.

Preparing to rise from the booth and rescue Sabrina—she was bound to attract a few bugs when she lit up a room the way she did—Hew blinked in astonishment when Mr. Short and Shiny slipped an arm around her waist. Instead of Sabrina feeding the fucker her knuckles, she smiled at him. Actually *smiled* that too big Julia Roberts smile. And as if *that* weren't enough, she then proceeded to catch her bottom lip between her teeth and give the dickwad a flirty wink.

Becky saw Hew's distraction and followed his line of sight. "Oh, look, babe!" She elbowed her husband. "Martin's here."

Martin.

The name rang in Hew's ears like a death knell. He couldn't hide the disdain dripping from his tone when he demanded, "Who the fuck is Martin?"

"The guy Sabrina's dating," Boss answered easily.

"*Datin'*?" He swore he could hear the squeaking slide of his testicles retracting into his body. "Since when is Sabrina datin' someone?"

"Since two weeks ago," Boss supplied, blissfully unaware that Hew was fantasizing about walking over and punching the unsuspecting Martin in his soft bits. "After you guys left for Africa, she got on one of those dating apps. Matched with Martin right away."

"They really hit it off," Becky added unnecessarily. "It's a good sign, I think. Means she's feeling better, more settled."

"I was worried about her for a while there," Boss agreed. "Thought she might never—"

Boss and Becky continued to talk, but Hew couldn't hear them. Not because the bar was filled with the jukebox's music, dozens of conversations, and the *crack* of pool balls. Oh, no. He couldn't hear them because the blood rushing between his ears was as loud as a jet engine.

"He's too short for her." The words were out of his mouth before he could stop them.

"Not when you stand him on his piles of money," Boss joked.

Hew pinned his fellow Knight with a hard look. "What's that mean?"

"He runs some fancy-dancy hedge fund, drives a Mercedes, and has a sailboat docked at the Chicago Yacht Club. That more than makes up for his vertical challenges." Boss cocked his head and narrowed his eyes at Hew. "What's with the face? Why are you looking at me like I just popped naked out of a cake?"

"That's some mental imagery I could have done without." Hew tried to wipe his expression clean.

Tried and failed, if Boss's next words were anything to go by. "Are you… *jealous?*"

That had Becky's head snapping around. "Wait a minute." She pointed at Hew's nose. "I thought you two were only friends."

"We *are*," Hew insisted through a jaw clamped so tight it was a wonder the words found a way past his teeth.

If he had to put a label on things, he'd say they were *best* friends.

He'd told Sabrina things he'd never told anyone, even his social workers. And she came to *him* for comfort when the grief over her brother's death and the nightmares of what that fuckface Eddy Torres had done to her got to be too much.

Their individual traumas had formed a mutual bond between them. She'd become his safe space. And he'd become her emotional scaffolding, giving her the strength and structure to pick up the pieces of her shattered life and start building something new.

"She's not ready," he insisted with a hard shake of his head. "She's still got healin' to do."

Becky watched Sabrina squeeze Martin's bulging bicep. "She sure looks ready to me."

Hew's chest suddenly felt like he'd swallowed a box of fireworks. And that sustained happiness he'd experienced for the last eight months and thirty days?

Gone.

CHAPTER 1

Black Knights Inc., Goose Island, Chicago

Eliza breezed into the TV room, a lotion bottle in hand. "If I leave my favorite hand cream in the half bath downstairs, will it remain unmolested? It's expensive. And I don't want you guys using it for… other purposes."

Sabrina Greenlee hid her smile behind her can of sparkling water.

Welcome to Black Knights Inc., she thought. *Home to elite operatives and leather-clad degenerates. They can dismantle a two-ton bomb before breakfast and spend the night debating lotion etiquette.*

Arranged around the space on the third floor of the old menthol cigarette factory were the men and women who'd opened their homes and hearts to Sabrina when she'd had nowhere else to go and no one else to turn to. Some were her roommates there at the shop. Others were coworkers who'd moved out of the old brick building to live with their significant others.

Speaking of the significant others…

Hannah Blue was a computer whiz working for the D.O.D. Grace Jackson and Julia O'Toole were both FBI agents employed at the local field office. And when you added the Black Knights, basically the real-life versions of Tom Cruise in *Mission: Impossible*, Sabrina couldn't help but sometimes feel she was living inside a spy novel.

James Patterson, eat your heart out.

The television was tuned to an episode of *M.A.S.H.*—Graham Coleburn's choice, no doubt. But the volume was muted so that she couldn't hear Hawkeye's words. Bowls of popcorn filled the hands of half the room's occupants, and the scents of salt and butter overpowered the smells that usually permeated through the three floors of the shop: grease, molten metal, and automotive paint.

"I'm looking at *you*," Eliza pointed to Graham while Fisher, her fiancé, dragged her down to join him on an adult-sized beanbag chair. "You don't have an amorous outlet other than your hand, so I figure you're the most likely culprit to engage in lotion molestation."

"Please." Graham gave an almost imperceptible shake of his head while his big body took up every square inch of the large, leather La-Z-Boy shoved into the corner. "Just 'cause I'm not datin' anyone in particular, that don't mean I gotta tug my own pug."

"Speaking of pugs," Frank "Boss" Knight said as he bent over the pool table at the room's far end. His wife, Becky, eyed his ass appreciatively. "Didn't Sabrina catch Eliza doing something interesting to Fisher's pug right before you all left for Cameroon?"

Sabrina winced when every head in the room swiveled in her direction. "Don't." She pointed a menacing finger toward Boss's craggy face.

"Sorry." He shrugged, but he didn't look the least bit contrite. "It's too good not to share." He turned to Fisher and Eliza and announced, "She saw what the two of you were doing to the treadmill."

"Not *to* the treadmill," Sabrina was quick to clarify. "*On* the treadmill. We should hang a Do Not Disturb sign on the gym door, by the way."

"Saw what? What did ya see?" Graham demanded, his green eyes shining with prurient delight. When Sabrina refused to answer, he turned to Boss. "What did she see?"

"Our sweet Sabrina was woefully short on the details," Boss admitted with a sorrowful shake of his buzzcut head. "She just said I should wait to work out because Fisher and Eliza were in the gym using the treadmill together."

"If the lady throws her legs over the handrails," Fisher explained, "it puts her in the perfect position to receive—"

"Fisher!" Eliza slapped a hand over his mouth.

"But…is the treadmill *movin'*? Like, are ya walkin' while also…" Graham made a motion with his big hand.

"This is no longer a conversation," Eliza groaned. "This is a hostage crisis."

Graham's tone was serious, but he was clearly biting the inside of his cheek. "I'm just tryin' to make sure I have the correct mental picture. Was the treadmill on or not?"

"*No*," Eliza hissed. "There was no motorized movement. We're not *weirdos*."

"That's debatable." Graham shrugged noncommittally.

Eliza's invitation for the big former SEAL to shove it where the sun never shone was issued and ignored as Graham turned his attention to the doorway.

Hewitt Birch stood briefly on the threshold before sauntering into the room with Peanut, BKI's onsite feline mascot, doing figure eights around his jean-clad legs.

"What about him?" Graham pointed an accusatory finger at Hew as Hew dropped onto the sofa beside Sabrina.

He brought the smell of the outdoors with him. Hot pavement and wind-lashed freshness clung to his T-shirt thanks to his motorcycle ride home from Red Delilah's. Underneath all that, though, she could detect a hint of his cedar-and-sage aftershave.

She would always associate that smell with everything that was good and kind and *right* in the world.

The cushion sagged under his weight, so her shoulder slid into his. When he touched her, she wanted to curl into him like Peanut curled into a sun-warmed patch of floor because he was like the sun. Big. Steady. Warm. And with a gravitational pull that had drawn her to him from the beginning.

"What about me?" he asked around a mouthful of yogurt while lifting an eyebrow that matched the color of his short beard. His facial hair was two shades darker than the thick mop on his head.

"He's flying solo these days." Graham pointed at Hew but looked over at Eliza. "Shouldn't ya give *him* the hand cream lecture too?"

Eliza glanced at Sabrina. But the look was so fleeting that Sabrina had no idea what it meant and thought maybe she'd imagined it.

There was no reason Eliza should look her way when discussing Hew's amorous impulses. Everyone knew she and Hew were only friends.

Not that she hadn't tried for more. In fact, for a while, she'd dropped enough hints to form a breadcrumb trail straight into her panties. But either Hewitt Birch was so slow on the uptake that she would have had to reach down his jeans and grab his balls to make him realize she was open to the idea of them exploring something beyond friendship, or he'd intentionally ignored her overtures.

Since Hew wasn't an idiot, she'd had to accept it was the latter.

She'd been disappointed, of course. But having Hew as a friend was a far cry better than having him as nothing at all. So it'd been three weeks since she'd batted her lashes at him or slid him a smile meant to entice.

"I'm putting this lotion down in the half bath." Eliza held up the bottle to show Hew what would heretofore be off-limits to him. "It's expensive. I don't want you single men using it for alternative purposes."

"Speakin' of utilizin' things for alternative purposes," Hew said casually in that delicious Mainer accent. "Thought I heard something 'bout you and Fish usin' the treadmill for activities other than exercise. Remind me to take a pack of sanitary wipes the next time I head to the gym."

"We're better off hosing the whole place down with bleach," Sabrina quipped. "I still have plenty left over from when I had to pour some into my eyeballs after I caught them in flagrante with the cardio equipment."

Hew chuckled. And the sound made her stomach dip like she stood on the roof of one of the city's skyscrapers.

Fisher lifted a contradictory finger. "What Eliza and I were doing qualifies as exercise. It certainly got *my* heart rate up." Eliza smacked him on his chest. "And are all social media gurus as snarky as you, Sabrina? Or did we just get lucky when you arrived on our doorstep?"

Before Sabrina had landed in Chicago, the Black Knights hadn't known they needed someone to run their social media accounts. But within four weeks of taking over the job—the least she could do to repay them for her upkeep—she'd shown the Knights what they'd been missing.

Using every ounce of know-how she'd gleaned from ten years in the business, she'd taken Black Knights Inc. from a well-respected chopper shop known to the ultra-wealthy inside the custom motorcycle community to a household name.

Because of the photos and videos she posted to Facebook, Instagram, Bluesky, and TikTok, not to mention the YouTube channel she'd started, everyone who was anyone now wanted a custom BKI creation.

"We're all this snarky," she informed Fisher. "It's dark times on the internet, and we who must enter into the abyss tend to find humor where we can."

Fisher snorted, and the gang splintered into little knots of conversation since it appeared all the tea involving Fish and Eliza and the treadmill had been well and truly spilled. Sabrina used the noise as cover to sneak a surreptitious look at Hew.

Since they'd returned from the bar, something had seemed slightly off with him. She might have thought it was her introducing him to Martin. But Hew had been nothing if not polite.

I mean, she thought back now, *he was polite* after *he stood up and made Martin wince like every man winces when presented with so much…Hew.*

At six feet two inches, Hewitt Birch loomed. Broad-shouldered, square-jawed, with dark green eyes and hair that lived somewhere between red and brown, he looked like a younger, hotter version of Sam Heughan. Add a gym-sculpted body and an ability to focus like a predator stalking prey, and no wonder Martin's first reaction had been to flinch.

To his credit, though, Martin had recovered quickly.

Probably because Martin was wildly handsome himself. His jet-black hair was cut by someone who knew exactly how best to frame his face. The cleft in his chin gave Superman vibes. And a personal trainer had honed his body to physical perfection.

Plus, he was smart as a whip, rich as Croesus, and…for reasons she was still a little confused by…he seemed to really like *her*.

So why didn't I go home with him tonight when he asked me to? she wondered.

They'd been on a handful of dates, and she *liked* him well enough. She was certainly attracted to him—*because who wouldn't be?* But when he'd whispered that invitation, she hadn't been able to tell if the flutter in her stomach was anticipation or fear.

Ever since Eddy Torres had tortured her in the back room of her brother Cooper's place, the thought of sex felt…foreign. Stomach-churning, even. Terrifying?

She'd lost more than her only sibling back in Charleston last fall. She'd lost the part of herself who laughed easily, flirted freely, loved her body, and let others love it too.

She liked to think she'd been healing since then, though. Working through the trauma. Meditating and reading all the self-help books and even attending a weekly online support group. With the Black Knights' help—with *Hew's* help—she finally felt ready to get back in the saddle.

So why did I freeze when the moment came?

She didn't know. She *needed* to know. Because Martin was a good man, and if she wasn't ready, she shouldn't lead him on.

"I'm going for a drive," she blurted, setting her half-full can of sparkling water on a coaster atop the coffee table.

Hew's head came up. A deep line formed between his eyebrows. "What do ya mean?" His glance slid to the big window. "Why?"

"I have a lot on my mind and do my best thinking in the car."

Her new-to-her Prius was her sanctuary. With the music on, road ahead, thoughts untangling mile by mile she could almost convince herself that she was back to normal.

"It's rainin' cats, dogs, and every other animal ya can imagine." He nodded toward the rivulets racing down the glass.

"I'm not made of sugar. I won't melt."

"I'll come too." He started to stand, but she blocked him with a hand.

"No. The whole point is peace and quiet. Besides, the last time you rode with me, your knees were practically touching your nose. I kept picturing a head-on collision where your kneecaps ended up in your skull."

His frown deepened, eyes going almost black. "Ya might still have enemies out there."

Enemies. Right.

A chill raced down her spine and made her shiver.

What a strange thing it had been for her to have *enemies*.

Before her brother got mixed up with a Charleston cartel, before Eddy Torres changed the course of her life, the only *enemies* she'd had were the mean girls in middle school who'd teased her mercilessly about her hand-me-down clothes and dime-store shoes.

"Eddy Torres is dead," she said with a decisive dip of her chin. "And the cartel's kingpin and top lieutenants are behind bars. It's over. I'm safe."

The FBI agents in charge of her case had *assured* her the danger to her had passed and she could resume her regular life.

"But it's dark out."

But it's dahk out.

That accent—lord help her—it always made her melt. It was *almost* enough to make her let him come with her. But she needed to think. And if there was one thing that was impossible to do with Hew near, it was think.

"I adore you for worrying." She smiled softly. "Truly. But I'm fine. Even in the rain. Even in the dark."

She blinked, a little surprised—and a whole lot proud—to realize she meant it.

She *was* fine. For the first time in months, she felt like herself. Like maybe what had happened to her back in Charleston was simply a chapter in her life and not the whole damn book.

Fifteen minutes later—and after more arguments from Hew that she handily batted aside—she cruised past BKI's gates, waved to Toran Connelly on security duty, and turned right into the night.

Rain whispered against the windshield as she navigated the city streets. Ella Fitzgerald crooned "Dream a Little Dream." And her thoughts unspooled in a long ribbon of questions.

Am I ready to take a lover?

Can I be with a man without panicking?

Is it fair to Martin to even try if I'm not sure?

She was so caught up in her own ruminations that she didn't see the black van slip in behind her. Didn't notice it match her speed.

Didn't realize she was followed out of town.

CHAPTER 2

White Pigeon Road, Lake Geneva, Wisconsin

Out on the forgotten stretch of country road in bumfuck Wisconsin it was all deep shadows and slick pavement. Rain pattered against the windshield, soft as satin, steady as a heartbeat.

Vivian Drake sat in the passenger seat of the rented cargo van, legs crossed, gloved fingers resting loosely on the pistol in her lap. She didn't need it yet. But it was comforting nonetheless.

Like silk sheets, she thought with a sly grin.

"Where the fuck is she going?" asked the man behind the wheel.

He was tall and muscular. His eyes were a little too close together, but he had a good head of hair and a cock that was as thick as a Coke bottle.

His real name was Mark Kessler. His code name was Hummer. A moniker he'd earned by driving a Humvee straight through a barricade in Mosul. Twice.

He'd been drunk both times. So when he'd signed on to work with her, she'd had two stipulations. One, he couldn't imbibe on the job. And two, when she wanted a quick fuck, he had to give it up.

"Who knows?" She shrugged. "But she's doing us a favor. We're hell and gone from any CCTV cameras. We'll snatch her with no one the wiser."

"Yeah." Hummer nodded. "And then we gotta hump it all the way back to the city."

It'd been two days since he'd popped the top on his last beer. They hadn't known when a mark from the big, hulking factory building would present herself, so they'd wasted time staking out the joint. Two days without a drop always put Hummer in a temper.

Not that his foul mood rubbed off on Vivian. Quite the opposite. She'd cash in on it later, after they had the woman locked down.

Hummer in a temper was one hell of a fuck. All anger and energy and drive.

"Let's give her another mile or so," she murmured. "GPS says we should be coming up on some woods. The trees will give us cover to stash her car."

Hummer grunted and refocused on the road. The rest of her team shifted restlessly in the back of the van.

"Let's just do this already," came a nasally complaint.

"Shut your face hole, Kurt," she snapped without turning because she'd recognize his voice even in a crowd. He refused to get his deviated septum fixed, and it always sounded like he was suffering the world's worst head cold. "Unless…" She grinned. "You need Momma to get you a pillow? Maybe a soft blankie?"

Kurt was sensitive about his height—five-five if he stretched and stood on tiptoe. Nothing pissed him off more than being treated like a kid.

She couldn't hear what he said in rebuttal, but doubted it held much wit since his mental stature matched his physical one.

They rounded a bend, and she spied the thick copse of trees she'd seen on the map.

"Almost time," she told the boys in the back. "Stay loose."

"Hard to stay loose when your spine's been fused to cold steel for the last hour and a half," Vance muttered, referring to the hard metal flooring in the cargo hold.

Vivian turned in her seat. She knew what Vance saw when his blue gaze met her gray one. Like slate or steel, her eyes had no warmth, only weight.

"What a bunch of whiny babies. Amazes me that I've ever considered fucking any of you. Although, in my defense, the thought only really crosses my mind when I've got a belly full of tequila."

Silence. Then, a short chuckle from Deke. Code name: Diesel.

The man was nice enough to look at. Big, strapping, and still had most of his original teeth. But she'd read his rap sheet, which was enough to keep her away from him even after a pitcher of margaritas.

She turned back toward the windshield, watching the trees flash by in blurs of black and gray. As it often did when the hunt neared its climax, her mind slipped to the one who had hired her.

Code names were as common as coercion in her line of work. And her current employer went by Bishop.

Like the religious clergy or the chess piece?

She wasn't sure. If she had to guess, though, she'd say he was named after the game of strategy and tactics. Bishop was wily. Deliberate. *Careful.*

They'd spoken only a handful of times. And he always masked his voice. But even still, something in his tone made her uneasy.

He was too calm. Too composed. Too… *emotionless.*

Not that she wasn't used to dealing with cold, calculating sorts. Anyone who hired her wasn't likely to be a wilting lily. But even those who needed her for wet work usually displayed *some* kind of reaction. Some excitement, some nervousness, some impatience.

Bishop?

Nada.

Colder than a fucking corpse in a meat locker.

It didn't help her unease that he knew things he shouldn't. Movement orders, the identities of covert operators, the names of people and places not written on any piece of paper or hidden on any hard drive in the basements at Langley.

He was government. That much was obvious. Someone near the tippy-top would be her guess.

And *that* was dangerous.

People at the top ate those beneath them.

"Get ready," she told the men, narrowing her gaze on the Prius. It crawled along the dark road like a pale blue insect. So harmless. So unaware.

"Say the word." Hummer's thick hands tightened on the wheel.

She leaned forward as if she could inhale the moment. The seconds right before the action reminded her of the lead-up to orgasm. All the tension. All the anticipation. That *ache* for satisfaction. "Now! Ram her into those trees!"

Hummer stomped on the gas, and the van's engine roared as the tires ate up the asphalt.

Vivian nearly moaned at the rush, at the spike of adrenaline and the giddy leap of her pulse.

When Hummer slammed the van's front bumper into the car's rear one, metal collided with molded plastic with a satisfying *crunch*. Tires screeched. The little car fishtailed once, twice. But the pretty brunette at the wheel couldn't regain control.

When Hummer slammed the brakes, the crew in the back cursed as they slid across the cargo space. But Vivian? Her attention never wavered.

She watched the Prius skate off the road. The mud slowed it, just like she'd hoped. It clipped a few branches on the shorter trees before smashing into the thick trunk of a larger tree with a dull, perfect *thud*.

She threw her door open before the van came to a complete stop.

CHAPTER 3

Black Knights Inc.

"**W**hat do you love most about being a soldier?" *Sabrina angled her chin toward Hew but fixed her gaze on the fire pit. The red-orange flames danced in her pretty brown eyes, reminding Hew of melting chocolate.*

"Notice I didn't say 'airmen,'" she added, with a self-satisfied grin. "Airmen are Air Force. Soldiers, even the ones who fly helicopters, are Army. Oh, the things I've learned in three months."

Three months.

A mere ninety days.

In some ways, it felt like she'd just arrived. In others, like he'd known her forever.

When the Lake Michigan wind wasn't sharp enough to slice through their clothes, it had become their custom to sit out by the fire pit after dinner. There was something mesmerizing about a fire. Something ancient and fundamental. The dancing display calmed the senses and soothed the synapses.

That's what Sabrina needed. Calmness. Safety. Security.

He'd been doing his best to see that she got all three.

When he'd stayed quiet too long, her expression grew concerned. "Sorry." She winced. "Was that too personal? I mean, I get how enlisting in this kind of work might be something you don't want to talk—"

"The thing I like most about bein' a soldier is makin' a difference," he cut her off. "And what's this bullshit about too personal? I thought we'd established nothin' is too personal between us."

He started ticking things off on his fingers. All the things he'd come to know about her in the three months she'd lived at Black Knights Inc. and took on the role of his best friend and confidante. "I know ya got your first period at twelve, and 'cause your ma was a mother in name only, ya thought you were bleedin' out." He sat back in his Adirondack chair. "I know Travis Parker was the first boy to kiss ya. Although I like to refer to him as Little Shit, on account of him catchin' your lip with his braces."

"He came at me like I was a pail of chum and he was a shark."

"Ayuh. And when he made ya bleed, instead of apologizin', he told the whole middle school you were the worst kisser in the history of kissers."

A small smile played on her full lips. "He really was a little shit, wasn't he?"

"And I know what happened the night Cooper was killed." That stole the smile from her face, so he quickly switched gears. "And you know how I used to run to the Portland Head Lighthouse to get away from my foster homes and group houses. I told ya all about how I'd stare out at the ocean and dream about growin' wings so I could fly above it all."

"And I know how you spent weeks trying to find the perfect paint for your motorcycle," she murmured. "That very specific gray/blue color that matches the Atlantic off the New England coast. I know you named your bike Freedom because that's what it represents to you. A means of escape."

"See?" He spread his hands. "Nothin' is off-limits with us, right?"

"Oh, I don't know." She slid him a sly look. "I bet there are a few things you're keeping to yourself. Like the blonde at the bagel shop across the street."

"What blonde?" he asked, all innocence.

"The one who desperately tries to get your attention every time we go there," she said, her South Carolina drawl softening the edges of the words.

The first two months she'd been at BKI, she'd kept herself inside the compound. Since Eddy Torres's death, though, she'd started venturing out—never far, and always with Hew in tow.

The bagel shop was one of their regular stops.

"Don't know what you're talkin' 'bout." He took a pull from the beer bottle resting loosely between his gloved fingers.

"You are so full of shit," she said before throwing back her head and laughing.

He gaped at her.

He'd seen her grin. Heard her chuckle a few times. But her grief had eclipsed any real laughter, and this? Oh, this was as real as it got.

And it was the sweetest thing he'd ever heard.

She pointed a gloved finger at his nose, eyes dancing. "You'd have to be blind to miss her signals. She's like one of those airport people. The ones with the orange flags?" She flailed her arms like she was directing a Boeing 747 into Gate B12.

"Ayuh," he allowed with a dip of his chin. "But that doesn't mean I'm interested."

"Why? You don't like big boobs and gobs of cornsilk hair?"

Instead of answering, he lobbed his own question. "Let's say I did take her up on it. How would she feel 'bout you sneakin' into my room three, four nights a week?"

He'd meant it as a joke. But the way her teasing smile faded told him it had landed all wrong.

"I'll stop," she said quietly.

Fuck.

He didn't want her to stop. The best sleep he got was when she crawled beneath the covers, still cool from the air in the hallway, and warmed herself up by curling against his back. Him—six foot two, two-ten, trained to kill. And her—one-thirty soaking wet, and yet holding him like a shield against the dark.

He opened his mouth to tell her as much. But she kept going before he could get a word out. "Or you could just tell her the truth. That we're only friends. Nothing more."

Hew lay sprawled on his back, one arm folded beneath his head, as he replayed the memory while staring at the dim lines where the bricks of his walls met the mortar between them.

He liked the idea of brick walls, soaked in years of stories, steeped in a thousand memories. They were permanent. *Enduring.*

He hadn't experienced much of either in his life. That is, until he'd come to Black Knights Inc. and, for the very first time, understood what it meant to be part of a family.

Turning onto his side, he buried his face in the extra pillow and imagined all the times Sabrina's head had lain right there. Right in that very spot.

He'd convinced her after that night by the fire pit that he welcomed her after-hours visits. That he was honored to help chase away her nightmares. That their friendship wasn't the reason he hadn't gotten the barista's number. But even so, her visits had become fewer and farther between.

It'd been nearly a month since she'd slipped through his bedroom door, her luscious brown hair a tangled halo, her dark eyes bleary with sleep and shadowed by the vestiges of bad dreams as she grabbed the stuffed toy from atop his dresser and climbed into bed beside him.

He breathed deeply, imagining her sweet smell lingered even though he'd changed his sheets since her last visit.

Why would it remain? he thought. *To remind me she's past the point of needin' me?*

The idea rankled, hitting a place inside him he hadn't realized was sore.

Of course, he shouldn't *want* her to need him. He shouldn't *want* her to be haunted by nightmares that dragged her from her own bed and sent her running into his. But hell if her midnight visits hadn't been the best thing to ever happen to him.

And he *missed* them.

Missed the way she hooked her knees behind his. Missed the way she spread her fingers over his ribs and murmured barely there nothings against his neck. Missed the heat of her breath and the softness of her breasts against his back.

Sabrina, the river goddess.

She didn't know it, but her ethereal sweetness, her delicate vulnerability, had knitted his broken pieces together. Pieces he hadn't even realized needed mending.

And now, she was dating. *Dating.*

Not that he begrudged her happiness. Not that he expected her to remain a nun. And certainly not that he didn't *want* her to move past the hurt and the horror that had kept her trapped inside BKI and inside her own mind.

But it's too soon. She's not ready.

As her friend, he *hated* the thought of her pushing herself when there was no reason for—

Are ya sure that's all it is? The unwelcome question zipped through his mind, and he clenched his jaw so hard his back teeth creaked.

Instead of answering, he reached for his watch on the bedside table. Depressing the side button made the face glow blue.

Almost 6 A.M.

Seven hours since she left.

Any other guy might assume she'd snuck in while he was out cold. But Hew slept with one eye open and both ears cocked. A pin dropping was enough to rouse him from stone-cold slumber.

If Sabrina had come home, he'd have heard her footsteps. Heard the tiny whine of her door hinges and the rustle of her sheets.

Seven hours since she left, he thought again. And his brain spooled out a series of horror reels.

Her, stuck behind the wheel because her car lost traction on the wet roads and plowed into a tree. Her, desperately trying to escape her Prius as it filled with water because she missed a curve and drove into one of the many small kettle lakes that dotted the countryside outside the city. Her, broken and bleeding and *needing* him and—

Another thought stabbed into his brain with the destructive force of a Ka-Bar.

Martin…

What if she'd gone to see Martin?

An image of the charming bastard with his perfect hair and even more perfect smile emblazoned itself in Hew's mind's eye. He was reminded of Martin's possessive hand at the small of Sabrina's back in the parking lot at Red Delilah's after they'd paid the tab and made moves toward home. Reminded of the blush on Sabrina's cheeks when Martin had leaned in to kiss the corner of her mouth.

Hew had pretended not to watch the couple's exchange as he slipped on his motorcycle helmet. But behind his visor, he'd read Martin's lips.

"Come home with me tonight."

Sabrina had made excuses, and Hew had heaved a sigh of relief.

But what if she changed her mind? he thought now.

What if, right at this very moment, she's curled up against that fuckstick's back, her nose pressed to his neck, her fingers ghostin' across his *ribs like they used to ghost across mine?*

He squeezed shut his eyes, hoping to stop the images that poured through his head. But that only made things worse. On the backs of his eyelids, he could actually *see* her there, in Martin's bed, her pale skin contrasting with Martin's and—

The door hinges squealed. He shot upright. "Sabrina?"

But it wasn't her. Peanut sat in the threshold, his gray fur as black as a shadow in the darkness, and his silhouette looking as round as a soccer ball.

"Shit." Hew scrubbed a rough hand over his face and told himself to lie back down. Go back to sleep.

Sabrina was a grown-ass woman capable of making her own choices.

Himself was a traitorous bastard, though. Because himself whispered, *Ya could always check to see where she is.*

All of them had trackers on their vehicles in case of theft or in case emergency services needed their exact location. It was a safety measure, not a spying measure. And yet…

He tossed back the covers. After pulling on his jeans, he assured Peanut, "It's not 'cause I'm jealous. I just need to make sure she's okay."

The cat slow-blinked and then lifted a leg behind his head to bathe his fuzzy butt. Hew couldn't help but feel that it was the feline version of calling bullshit.

The rain had picked up during the night. It spat angrily against the windows of the old brick building, and the low *hiss* was why Hew didn't hear Graham until they nearly plowed into each other at the bottom of the stairs that led from the second floor to the third.

Graham held a half-eaten turkey leg in one hand. The other jumped to his chest in startlement.

"Lord a'mighty." His north Georgia drawl echoed through the quiet of the building. "Ya don't sneak up on a guy who carries a gun. I mighta dropped the hammer on you, Birch."

Hew smirked. "Ya packin' heat in your Fruit of the Looms, Coleburn?"

Graham had a habit of walking around shirtless even in the middle of the day. In the cold light just before dawn? Hew counted himself lucky the chowderhead had thought to put on boxer briefs before raiding the fridge.

"Jet lag's got my circadian rhythm more twisted up than a snake in a shoebox," Graham admitted with a scowl of annoyance. "You?"

"Maybe," Hew answered evasively. "Woke up and couldn't get back to sleep. Heard from Sabrina?"

"Why would I?"

"She's not back, and it's not like her to stay out all night."

Graham's unconcerned shrug irritated Hew. The man's words were even more annoying. "Maybe she decided to go to her boyfriend's house."

"She doesn't *have* a boyfriend."

"No?" Graham tilted his head. "Boss and Becky said she—"

"She's been on a few dates with the guy. That doesn't make him her *boyfriend*." Why was Hew's vision turning black around the edges?

"Right." Graham held up his turkey-leg-free hand in surrender. "Sorry. Her *lover*, then."

The black around the edges of Hew's vision started crackling with lightning.

Graham chuckled. "You should see yourself. Your eyes are bugged out of your head so far, ya look like a horny toad tryin' to shit a chicken bone."

Hew wiped his expression clean. "I've got no idea what you're talkin' about."

He heard his own accent turn the word *idea* into *idear*. New Englanders had a haphazard way of dropping the R sound off some words and adding it to others.

Graham rolled his eyes. "From the moment Sabrina Greenlee walked through that front door, you've been calf-eyed over her."

"You want to try that again in English? Instead of whatever possum-wranglin' dialect that was?"

Graham shook his head sorrowfully. "What's that one singer say? *Forgive my northern attitude?* Y'all spend so long buried in snowbanks up there, even your jokes come out frostbit."

"Is it the jet lag that's turned you into a Chatty Cathy?"

"Nice try changin' the subject." Graham smiled knowingly.

"I don't know what the subject is anymore. Noah Kahan? Chicken bones? Calf's eyes?"

Ignoring him, Graham said conversationally, "Ya know what? I'm ninety-eight percent sure ya don't wanna have this conversation right now. But I'm one-hundred percent sure I don't care. You're crazy about Sabrina. But for whatever reason, ya don't have the sac to face it. Why is that?"

"Doesn't matter what *I* feel." Hew ground his jaw. "Because *she* doesn't like me for anything more than a friend."

"You ever asked her?"

Graham was off in his percentages. Hew *one-hundred percent* didn't want to have this conversation.

"I don't need to. She's made it clear in a thousand different ways. And the fact that she's datin' some chowderhead who could've auditioned for a role as a Munchkin back in the day is the clearest indication of all."

Graham blinked. "Sabrina's lover has dwarfism? Boss and Becky didn't mention that. Not that it matters, but it's just interestin' and—"

"*Stop* usin' that word."

"Which word? Dwarfism? I think it's the correct terminology and—"

"*Lover*," Hew hissed. "It makes me want to blow groceries."

"Well, how would *you* describe the guy Sabrina's screwin'?"

Hew had to shove his hands deep into his front pockets to keep from wrapping them around his teammate's throat. "Sabrina isn't screwin' him."

Then, he remembered she might very well be screwing the bastard right at that very moment and that he'd come downstairs to see for himself if she was.

"Ah." Graham rocked back on his heels. "Now I get it."

Hew was hanging on to his patience by a thread. "Get what?"

"Why you're headed over to the computers." Graham hitched the turkey leg toward the bank of monitors and blinking towers that were daisy-chained together to form a supercomputer capable of performing tasks Hew couldn't begin to understand. "You're gonna spy on her."

"It's. Not. Spyin'." Each word was uttered through a jaw clamped down like a steel trap.

"No? What would *you* call it then?"

"Checkin' to make sure she's okay."

Graham snorted, and Hew took that as a period on the conversation.

Turning on his heel, he marched toward the bank of computers. After pulling out a rolling chair and, he was prompted for a password and typed in 60065. It was the numerical representation for *boobs*.

Ozzie—BKI's own hacking genius and one of the original Knights—had a sixteen-year-old boy's sense of humor.

As Hew brought up the tracking program, he glanced over his shoulder to find Graham standing a few feet away.

"Ya goin' to stand there gawpin' like a jackass at a clambake, or ya goin' to come help?" he muttered.

"I'm worried when ya see Sabrina over at her boyfr—" Graham stopped and tried again. "Lov—" He caught himself a second time and finally settled on, "I'm worried when ya see Sabrina over at the Munchkin's house, your brain will explode. I really don't wanna wash gray matter out of this shirt. It's my favorite."

Hew rolled his eyes at the sight of Graham hooking a thumb back at his bare chest.

A few keystrokes later, a glowing red dot showed on a 2D map. His chin jerked back when he didn't recognize the road's name. He used the mouse to expand the map until he saw the state line and the distance Sabrina had traveled.

It wasn't unusual for her to cross over into Wisconsin. The scenery was far more serene there. And the lack of traffic on the winding roads afforded her the ability to concentrate on her thoughts instead of her driving.

What *was* unusual was that it looked like she was stopped in the middle of nowhere.

"The fuck?" He leaned closer to the monitor.

"What?" Graham strode forward.

"You think Martin lives in the woods in Wisconsin?"

"Who's Martin?"

"The Munchkin."

"Right." Graham bent over Hew's shoulder and hit several keys that switched the map from 2D to 3D. "Huh," he muttered as he straightened. "Looks like she's parked inside a stand of trees. The only structure nearby is a farmhouse. And that's half a mile away."

Fear grew in Hew like a malignancy as he pulled his cell phone from his pocket. He scrolled to Sabrina's contact information, hit the button, and held the device to his ear.

It rang.

And rang.

When her voicemail picked up, he cut the call as broken glass filled his lungs. It shattered up into his throat, making breathing impossible as he stared hard at Graham's now concerned expression.

"Something's wrong," he wheezed.

CHAPTER 4

Sabrina woke slowly and felt like she was swimming through Lowcountry muck after a hurricane. Nothing felt firm. Nothing felt real. Everything was soft, quiet…

Except for the pain that thumped mercilessly inside her head.

Her skull was too small. Or maybe her brain was too big?

She also had a crick in her neck like she'd slept with her head bent at a ninety-degree angle.

And what the hell is wrong with my tongue?

Why was it coated with something fuzzy?

She tried to swallow, but her throat was as dry as parchment paper left out in the sun.

She needed water. And Tylenol. And more water. And probably some more Tylenol. But the thought of moving made her break out in a cold sweat.

She shivered.

And that hurt too.

Everything hurt.

Why does everything hurt?

Screw it, she thought. If everything hurt, there was nothing to do but grit her teeth and do what was needed.

Tylenol.

Water.

In that order.

Girding herself, she opened her eyes. Or...she tried to. They didn't cooperate. Her eyelids were sandbags soaked with rain. It took everything she had to pry them apart the barest crack. Just enough for her to make out a soft, gray light.

She tried to focus. Tried to get her bearings. But her vision floated, and her head spun as terrible nausea churned in her belly. And *Jesus!* The throb inside her skull was worse with her eyes open.

Did someone spike my drink at the bar? Was I roofied?

She lifted a hand to press it against her forehead, to massage away the fog and the pain.

No, she didn't.

She *tried* to. She couldn't.

Her arm was leaden, immobile.

Am I lying on it?

Nope. She wasn't lying at all. She was upright. Sitting.

But why was she sitting? *Where* was she sitting?

Panic slid into her cognizance like smoke under a door. The haze inside her head was no longer soft and quiet. There was a heat to it now. A *burn* that spread down her neck and chest to smolder in her belly.

Where am I?

She blinked and tried to clear her vision as scraps of memory bubbled up through the soup of her semi-consciousness.

I was driving, wasn't I?

Yes. I was driving and thinking about Hew. Thinking about Martin. Thinking about my future and then—

She remembered bright lights. Remembered the *crunching* sound of metal. Remembered a scream.

My scream?

Yes. Definitely hers. And then there was fishtailing. Sliding. Trees. She definitely remembered trees.

I crashed!

Her breath caught at the memory of the big oak looming in front of her car's hood and her helplessness in avoiding it. But *why* had she crashed?

Had she hydroplaned? Had a deer run into the road and—

No.

A black van. There'd been a black van. It had surged up behind her, advancing, swerving, clipping her rear bumper.

She'd fought to keep control of the Prius. She could still feel the wheel in her hands, that first list sideways as her wheels lost traction with the roadway, the fear that gripped her as she careened toward the trees.

Except…she hadn't crashed.

Or, she *had* crashed, but not really. It'd been more like a fender bender with the big oak. Her airbag hadn't even deployed. But the silence that followed had sickened her. Sickened her and terrorized her, because when she'd tried to move, she couldn't. Her seat belt had seized up.

Her fingers had been as useless as wet spaghetti noodles when she fought with the buckle. But then…finally…freedom!

She'd pushed open the door, shoved out of the vehicle into the soft, misty rain, and turned to run, but—

The woman.

Sweet baby Jesus, the woman*!*

Dressed in black, platinum hair streaming behind her like a banshee.

Sabrina had barely had time to register the blonde's intent before she sprang forward and landed on Sabrina.

Sabrina had opened her mouth to scream again, but the cry had died in her throat when she felt the sharp pinch in her neck. A pinch and then warmth and then…

Nothing.

Just blackness. Just a void of sight and sound and memory.

Now, the blackness was fading. And abject terror rushed in to fill the space it left behind.

She tried moving her hands and couldn't. Tried moving her feet and couldn't. She was bound to a chair, ankles secured to the legs, wrists cinched tight behind her back.

She willed her eyes open further, and the light drove into her brain like a spear. All she wanted was to close her lids and return to the void, to the soft nothingness.

But she couldn't.

She had to take stock.

She had to think.

Being careful not to bring too much attention to herself, she glanced around and realized the space she was in was enormous. Hollow. *Old.*

An abandoned warehouse, maybe?

No, she decided. *Some sort of factory or plant.*

Hulking, rusting machinery sat like mechanical dinosaurs on the rough, concrete floor. She didn't have a clue what the beasts might have done back in the day. Now, they rotted with the passing of time.

The soft light of a new dawn painted the filth in pale streaks of gray and grit. Brick walls, stained and crumbling, wept with mildew. The multipaned windows were now just jagged teeth where rocks, wind, or the steady march of years had shattered the glass.

The air was fetid with the smell of neglect and—

Sabrina saw her then.

The woman. The blonde. The Banshee.

The bitch who dosed me with who knows what?

She stood in the shadows at the edge of a shaft of light, a specter pulled from some terrible nightmare. Her black clothes fitted her frame like armor. Her platinum hair was slicked back from a face sharper and crueler than any Sabrina had ever seen.

But it was also…beautiful.

Beautiful like an oleander is beautiful. Like a poison dart frog is beautiful. Allure mixed with venom, she thought.

Breath catching, pulse thundering, Sabrina knew she'd been here before.

Not *here,* here. But in a situation like this one. Where the person standing before her smiled as they approached.

But it wasn't a smile of kindness. It was a smile of malice.

A smile that said they looked forward to hearing her scream.

CHAPTER 5

Black Knights Inc.

"**H**ew." Graham Coleburn kept his voice low but firm. "Brother, you'll wear a hole clean through that floor if ya don't quit that pacin'."

It was like watching a lion prowl its cage.

Or, Graham corrected grimly, *like watchin' Mama when her stash ran out, twitchy and strung out, eyes wild for somethin' she couldn't get.*

"Why don't ya come sit?" Graham pulled a chair out from the conference table, motioning like he was coaxing a skittish colt into a stall.

Hew didn't even glance his way.

"It's takin' too damn long." Hew raked a hand through his hair until it stuck up at the temples like devil horns. "I should be in the air, on my way to her."

Eliza, perched on the table's edge, tried for calm. "Wait until we hear back from the police. Then, if we need to, we'll all go."

Fisher padded barefoot toward the coffee tray, pulling a hoodie over his head as he went. He poured himself a mug, then raised an eyebrow at Graham.

"Yeah," Graham agreed with a nod. "Pour me one, too. Jet lag's fixin' to catch me by the throat." He'd been up half the night, but now all he wanted was to crawl into bed.

The gray light through the tall windows looked weak and tired. Dust motes drifted on the beams, but they were lusterless and lazy on this rainy morning. Outside, though, the city was waking up. A garbage truck groaned, somebody shouted for a cab, and tires hissed over wet pavement.

Such different sounds from the ones he'd grown up with. Birds trilling, bugs humming, chipmunks chattering under the porch of the old clapboard house in Rabun County.

Rabun County…

It'd been twenty years since he'd set foot back there.

Where does the time go?

But he knew. It'd gone to BUD/S training and jump school. It'd gone to missions and mayhem, blood and guts. And then, it'd gone to building a life in Chicago, to becoming part of the Black Knights Inc. family.

He took the mug Fisher handed him with a nod of thanks, grateful for the bitter burn of the coffee. It was harsh enough to strip paint, hot enough to cauterize wounds, and intense enough to wash away old memories.

"Should I call in the others?" Fisher asked. "They'll want to know Sabrina's missing."

"We don't know she *is* missing," Eliza stressed. "She might've pulled off to sleep. It could be one big misunderstanding. Besides"—she caught Fisher's wrist and checked his watch—"they'll be here soon anyway."

After the popcorn party, those who no longer lived on-site had loaded up and headed home. But thanks to the siren's call of Eliza's fresh-baked pastries, they usually strolled in again before seven a.m. to grab breakfast.

The sudden buzz of Hew's cell phone shattered the momentary quiet. Everyone froze as they stared at the former Nightstalker in expectation.

"Wisconsin area code," Hew rasped, peering at his phone's screen with an expression that was a sick cocktail of hope and dread. Like a man waiting to hear if the doctors would give him a clean bill of health…or a death sentence.

They'd called the Wisconsin highway patrol an hour earlier, requesting a welfare check at Sabrina's last known location. During every slow, painful minute since, Hew had bucked and bristled like a mule with a burr in his saddle.

Now, his voice snapped like a whip when he thumbed on the device and barked, "This is Hewitt Birch."

Graham didn't need to hear the other end of the conversation. The immediate devastation in Hew's eyes told him everything he needed to know.

Sabrina hadn't pulled over for a nap. This wasn't some big misunderstanding. Hew was right. Something was wrong.

"What about tracks?" Hew demanded, jaw clamped down so tight that Graham could see the muscles' striations under his short beard. "Any sign she walked away?"

Graham's gaze slid to the windows. Rain painted the glass in racing rivulets.

Too wet, he thought. *If it's this bad over there, even if she did leave tracks, they were washed away in seconds.*

He watched Hew rest his cell phone between his shoulder and ear so he could resume pacing. "Is it possible she hit her head on the steerin' wheel and wandered off into the woods in a daze?"

Hew turned back to the three waiting near the conference table and shook his head. Covering the mic with his palm, he repeated the information he'd been given. "She crashed. But not bad. No airbag deployment. No blood. No sign of a struggle."

"Well, that's a relief," Eliza whispered.

But Graham wasn't so sure. The knots in his gut told a different story.

They had been so confident that Sabrina was safe to go about life as usual. Sure that the heat from Charleston and the cartel had cooled. But maybe—

"What about her phone?" Hew asked. "Is it with the car or—" He didn't finish the question. It was clear the patrolman was already answering and Hew shook his head for the benefit of the others listening. He covered the mic and whispered, "They found it on the ground beside her vehicle."

"Goddammit," Fish muttered.

Graham said what they were all thinking. "She wouldn't leave her cell. Not on purpose."

Before anyone could respond, the shrill ring of Boss's office line cut through the air.

Four pairs of eyes snapped toward the hallway and the closed door where the head of BKI spent the majority of his days.

"That phone never rings this early," Fish said, though nobody needed telling.

Sabrina? Graham wondered. *Would she call the shop instead of callin' one of us?*

Eliza whispered, "Maybe she didn't realize she dropped her cell when she got out of the car. Maybe she walked to a house and borrowed a phone. Our cell numbers aren't listed anywhere. So if she wanted to contact us, she'd have to call the shop's landline."

That's all it took to break the spell.

"I'll have to call ya back," Hew told the patrolman and then the four of them took off down the hall, legs pounding, hearts in their throats.

But Graham had a sneaking suspicion…

Whatever's waitin' on the other end of that line, it's not good news.

CHAPTER 6

Ten million dollars.

That's what the woman demanded. *Ten million dollars* for Sabrina's life.

A burble of laughter threatened at the back of her throat. But it wasn't humor. It was incredulity.

Incredulity and a heavy, sinking feeling of dismay.

Black Knights Inc. might look rich on paper. Some of those custom bikes sold for six figures. But there wasn't a lot left over between the factory upkeep, property taxes, and the employees' salaries.

None of the Knights had ten million dollars lying around. And even if everyone pooled their funds, cashed in their IRAs, sold their vehicles, and liquidated their assets, Sabrina *still* thought they'd come up short.

Especially with a deadline of midnight.

Not that the Knights wouldn't try. Of course they would. They'd bleed themselves dry to bring her home.

But there was no way. She didn't *want* there to be a way. She didn't *want* to be more of a burden than she'd already been.

She shook her head to imply as much. But the blonde ignored her as she continued to outline demands into a device that changed the sound of her voice before transmitting it through the phone's microphone.

Sabrina leaned forward until the zip tie bit deep into her wrists. She desperately wanted to hear who was on the other end of that call.

If she could catch a snippet of Hew's voice, if she could just for a second hear that deep baritone and that rough Mainer drawl, she'd have the courage to keep from losing her shit. To keep from melting into a puddle of terror and self-recrimination.

But the Banshee—that's what Sabrina had come to call the woman—was too far away for Sabrina to hear the other side of the conversation. And a hard hand grabbed Sabrina's shoulder to slam her back in her seat.

She winced when the move made the pain pounding in her head radiate down her neck and across her shoulders. Whatever they'd dosed her with had left behind one heck of an aftereffect. It was like the flu of the century and the world's worst hangover had gotten together and birthed a baby in the bowels of hell.

But she would not whine. She would not whimper. She would not give these *assholes* the satisfaction.

Instead, she lifted her chin and glared daggers up at the man.

Or, rather, she glared daggers a *little* way up at him. He was short, with a stubby little nose and beady little eyes. He reminded her of the trolls from fairy tales, ugly, disproportionate, and stupid-looking.

To make matters worse, when he leaned close and hissed, "Sit still, bitch," his breath smelled like something had crawled down his throat and died.

She wanted to pull her face away from the foul-smelling hole in his, but she gritted her teeth and held her place. Then, her attention was diverted when the Banshee headed in her direction across the dirty, cracked concrete floor.

The woman was incredibly fit. With each efficient step, her muscles rounded her shoulders and bunched her thighs. But she managed to be extremely feminine, too—curves in all the right places.

"Tell your friends you're alive." The Banshee shoved the phone near Sabrina's face as the four men gathered around Sabrina's chair in a semicircle.

She'd noticed they instinctively moved closer to the blonde whenever she came near any of them. It was like she was a magnet and the men were metal. And Sabrina hadn't missed the various looks of lust and longing in their eyes when they stared at the blonde.

Whoever the Banshee was, she was in charge. And it was clear she used sex—or the *promise* of sex—to stay in that position.

"Do it!" she snarled, her blood-red lips pulling back to reveal teeth that were too white, too perfect.

Veneers, Sabrina decided, even as she shook her head in refusal.

She would not be a part of this ransom demand. She absolutely *would not* put the Black Knights in the position of having to sell everything to race to her rescue.

It wasn't the short man who gripped her breast in a cruel fist. It was the biggest of the lot. The guy who had a face like a tank, all solid and square and mean-looking.

"Do it," he snarled. "Do what she says."

When Sabrina only shook her head again, he twisted her tender flesh until tears sprang unbidden to her eyes.

"One sore titty will be child's play compared to what I'll do to you next if you don't fucking open your mouth and do as you're told."

Shame, hot and cloying, flooded into Sabrina's system. It wasn't just from the pain, but from her own weakness.

Reminded of all the ways Eddy Torres had tortured her, knowing she couldn't survive another assault like that, she couldn't hold on to her bravado. She broke.

"I'm here!" she yelled, hating the catch in her voice. Hating the smell of her own fear. Hating the hot tracks her tears left on her cheeks. "I'm alive! But don't give her anything! They won't—"

Pain, white-hot and inescapable, slammed into her cheek, snapping her head back on the stem of her neck with enough force to rock the chair beneath her.

It was so sudden that, at first, she didn't know what had hit her. Didn't have time to cry out or wince. She could only blink stupidly as agony bloomed, as she felt her heartbeat in the teeth on the left side of her jaw.

When the stars stopped exploding in her vision, she saw Tank Face flexing his thick fingers and grinning in satisfaction.

He had been the one to slap her. And she was lucky he hadn't broken her cheekbone. He had fists like ham hocks.

Fuck you! She wanted to scream as she tasted blood, felt the split in her skin directly over her cheekbone and the warm trickle that leaked from it. But that would only give the bastard more of what he wanted.

More of her fear.

More of her indignity and shame.

Instead, she smiled. *Wide.* Knowing it looked macabre because her teeth were coated in blood.

He blinked in surprise, then revulsion, before turning away to watch the Banshee with hot, covetous eyes.

The woman played with the zipper on her form-fitting top as she continued pacing and spouting instructions to the Black Knights. The move looked inadvertent, but Sabrina knew it was intentional.

Maybe I should start calling her the Succubus instead, she mused. *She's a demon sent to lead these wicked men straight back to the sulfurous pit they clawed out of.*

She used Tank Face's distraction to spit out the blood in her mouth. She hadn't aimed at his big combat boots. But she hadn't necessarily *not* aimed at them either.

He grimaced at the wad of saliva and congealing plasma that splattered on the black leather toe of his boot. When he lifted his leg, she thought he might kick her and clamped down her jaw against the scream that threatened. But he simply shook off his shoe as he glared at her with enough fury to mottle his skin red.

"You want another?" He balled up his fist, knuckles gleaming white.

"Cut it out!" the Banshee shouted, having finished the call. The woman's phone glinted like a weapon as she shoved it into the front pocket of her skintight tactical pants. The smile that crept over her face was sleek and cruel—a raptor's grin—when she announced to the group, "It's done. Now, we get ready."

Get ready for what? Sabrina wanted to demand.

None of her abductors wore masks. They weren't worried about her IDing them. And if they weren't worried about her IDing them, they had had no plans to let her leave, even *if* the Black Knights made good with the money.

So what was the play? Why had they taken her? And what did they plan to do to the Black Knights when they came for her?

The woman's voice was serpentine, her S's overpronounced. "So, my sweet, soft thing. I see you've gone and made Diesel mishandle you." She tsked. "If you value that pretty face, you'll make sure you behave from here on out."

Diesel. A nickname? A last name?

"Why should I?" Sabrina snarled, her heart slamming like it was trying to break free from the cage of her ribs. "You're not letting me leave this building."

The words hung in the air. A verbal punch of defiance. A *nanner-nanner-boo-boo, I know more than you think I do.* But also, there was a part of her that hoped maybe…*maybe*…the Banshee would contradict her.

The woman only smiled again. And there was nothing in her eyes. No malice. No humanity. Just a swirling gray abyss.

Sabrina's stomach churned, nausea rising like a high tide through the marshlands. Despite the heat and humidity gathering inside the abandoned building as the rain let up and the sun rose steadily into the sky outside, goosebumps peppered the flesh over her arms.

She could hear the rushing blood in her ears—a drumbeat to drown out the scuttle of rats and the faint, echoing drip of water from the sagging roofline at the far end of the space.

I've been here before, she thought again. *Not* here, *here. But here with people who have no intention of letting me live.*

She had survived the last ordeal. Her brother hadn't, but *she* had.

Something told her she wouldn't survive this one.

Making herself sit up straight—or, as straight as her restraints would allow—she lifted her chin and mirrored the Banshee's cold, careless stare.

If this was the end, she refused to let them see her fear. She refused to give them any more of her tears.

CHAPTER 7

Lura Dougherty sat at her desk, reading over the speech the president was due to give to the United Steelworkers later in the week. Being raised by a mother who went to debutante school meant Lura's posture was ramrod straight.

Well, that and her post in the West Wing, where slouching garnered a side-eye from the Marine who stood guard outside her door.

The AirPod in her right ear hummed with Sheryl Crow's "Soak Up the Sun." Her left ear remained empty because she had to be ready to hop to when her boss barked orders like a drill sergeant with a headache.

Leonard Meadows, the White House chief of staff, refused to use the intercom on his desk, preferring to shout from the adjoining room.

And preferring to see me scamper in with tablet in hand, she thought with annoyance.

The whole shouting thing was just one of her boss's many quirks. She'd learned to tolerate almost all of them. The only one that still made her want to take a sledgehammer to his head was when he acted like he was doing her a favor every year when she actually *took* the two weeks of vacation she was due.

She put in for the leave months in advance, made sure her temporary replacement was up to speed on the chief of staff's calendar of events, and left him a three-ring binder chock-full of anything and everything she could think of regarding potential questions he might have. And *still*, the day before her vacation started, he would look at her over the top of his reading glasses, sigh heavily, and say, *"I suppose I can do without you for a fortnight."*

Fortnight? Seriously?

Who was he? Some British colonel in a BBC miniseries or—

Clunk. Snick.

The sounds caused her to lift her head and pull the AirPod from her ear. Sheryl's voice shrank to a tinny murmur in her hand.

She knew that little *clunk-snick* by heart, even though the door connecting the chief of staff's office to the Oval Office was rarely used.

Her boss preferred to enter the Oval through the main entrance, insisting it was the *proper* way to meet with the president of the United States. But, occasionally, when Madam President wanted to pay a visit to her right-hand man and not have it clocked by her secretaries, her body man, or the three Marines posted outside the Oval's windows, she used the connecting door.

And every time she did, Lura's ears perked up.

She couldn't help it.

She was nosy by nature.

Blame it on being Southern. Blame it on growing up in a small town where everyone was into everyone else's business. Or, hell, blame it on reading too many Judy Moody books in elementary school.

She set aside the printed speech and her AirPod, wondering, *What sort of international intrigue is afoot now?*

She knew she shouldn't eavesdrop. It was probably illegal to eavesdrop on the president. *Treasonous even?*

But, like always, her boss had left the connecting door ajar. Just enough to tempt. And through that tiny crack, quiet murmurs reached her ready ears.

"They say they want ten million dollars."

Eliza Meadows. Leonard's daughter. Her cool, crisp voice was unmistakable. Even coming through the speakerphone, it reminded Lura of freshly washed linen and expensive pearls.

Lura had worked hard to ditch her north Georgia drawl, but she'd never mastered the elegant, East Coast intonations that came naturally to Leonard and Eliza Meadows.

Not that Eliza was haughty or stuck-up. Quite the contrary, she was warm and surprisingly funny. But she had so much innate poise, so much Jackie O grace, that Lura couldn't help feeling like a buttered biscuit compared to Eliza's champagne brunch.

"And they've only given us until midnight to come up with it," Eliza continued. "We were hoping—"

"Let me stop you right there," Leonard Meadows's voice cut across his daughter's words like a sharpened letter opener. "If you're calling to ask for money, we can't help you."

Why do Eliza and the Black Knights need ten million dollars? Lura wondered. And then her mother's favorite phrase ran through her head. *Curiosity killed the cat.*

Lura reached for her AirPods. Fiddled them between her fingers. But she didn't plug them in.

She *should* plug them in. A *good* assistant would plug them in.

Shooting a quick glance toward the hallway door, she half-expected the uniformed Marine to burst in and accuse her of subversion or spying or… *whatever.* Just last year, a junior aide had been reassigned to the Department of Agriculture because she'd had a bad habit of listening in on meetings she wasn't part of.

Alas, Lura's inner Nancy Drew won out. Per usual. And Lura held her breath to make sure she didn't miss a word that was said in the next room.

"We thought it might come from the same pot you pull the men's salaries from," Eliza said.

Leonard Meadows's response was immediate. "That line item in the president's budget is fixed. We can't take out an additional ten million without drawing attention to ourselves."

Lura bit the inside of her cheek. Her boss didn't bend. Not for governors. Not for Congress. Not even for his own daughter.

Lura had never really understood the relationship between Leonard and Eliza Meadows. Lura's own dear daddy still called her pumpkin and kissed her forehead as they said their tearful goodbyes whenever she had to fly back to D.C. after a trip home. In contrast, Leonard Meadows spoke to

Eliza as if she were another subordinate, keeping her at a professional arm's length.

"Dad…" Eliza tried again, her voice softening. "Please."

"This has nothing to do with *our* side of the equation." Again, the answer was clipped and concise, leaving no room for argument. "It sounds like maybe all this recent social media coverage has caught the attention of someone trying to make a quick score. Or maybe the Charleston cartel played the long game and finally made their move on Miss Greenlee. Either way, the motorcycle shop's responsible for figuring things out, not me or the president. I'm sorry, Eliza, but—"

Click.

Lura flinched. Eliza had cut the call.

Without saying goodbye.

Not that Lura blamed the poor woman. What was the point of wasting time on a farewell when Leonard Meadows wasn't going to help, and when the clock was ticking?

Lura loved her job in the West Wing. She loved the fast pace and the importance of everyone's efforts. She loved how she sometimes got to add her two cents to the president's speeches since she came from "common folk" and knew how to talk to the masses.

But her boss was a hard man to work for, a hard man to like. And that was just god's honest truth.

There was a beat of silence from inside the chief of staff's office. Then, "Is there really no way we can help them?"

Lura liked President Sandra J. Stevens. More than that, she admired the woman.

Madam President was as brilliant as all get-out but still humble enough to know she didn't have all the answers. Most importantly, though, Sandra Stevens had the gumption to stand up to the nation's enemies, both foreign and domestic. And *that* was why she'd been reelected for a second term in a landslide.

"It's too risky," Meadows said flatly. "The oversight committee would flag that cash transfer in a matter of days, if not hours. We can't hazard that kind of exposure."

"I have personal funds," the president insisted. "I could—"

"No." The word came fast, sharp. "You know your personal banking is scrutinized as closely as your professional banking. And before you ask, because I recognize the look on your face, *my* personal banking as your chief of staff is scrutinized, too. I can't dip into my personal wealth to help them. They're going to have to figure this one out for themselves."

Lura's throat went dry even as her palms began to sweat.

She knew where the Black Knights could get their hands on ten million dollars without attracting the attention of the oversight committee.

But you should take a page from the book titled: Stay In Your Lane, A White House Survival Guide *and keep sitting right where you are*, she told herself. *You know anything else is beyond dangerous.*

She hadn't *meant* to read the memo from the president that had been sandwiched between policy files and speech drafts. She hadn't *meant* to point to it on her boss's desk and ask, *"What's this about a mission gone wrong and an unofficial extraction team?"*

Lord, remembering the look on the chief of staff's face that day nearly made her toss her morning coffee, even now, three whole-ass years later. After explaining what she'd seen, Leonard Meadows had sworn her to secrecy with an icy promise of dire consequences should she not keep her trap shut.

And they hadn't spoken of it since. *She* had tried not to even *think* about it since. But now…

It's my patriotic duty to help if I can. Right?

Or maybe her patriotic duty was to pretend she was deaf and dumb. Maybe a *good* assistant would mind her own damn P's and Q's and—

Better to beg for forgiveness than ask for permission.

That was one of her father's favorite sayings. And it was enough to have her shoving to a stand.

Her knees were Jell-O, her throat was dry. But she managed to work up enough spit to swallow stickily as she crossed the short distance to the thick oak door that separated her office from the chief of staff's.

She was fully aware that by doing what she was poised to do, she could be placing the last nail in the coffin of her career. But she'd been raised never to turn a blind eye to those in need. And it sounded like the Black Knights were in need indeed.

They only have until midnight.

Before she could second-guess herself, she rapped her knuckles against the wood.

"Come in, Lura," her boss called at once, sounding impatient. He *always* sounded impatient.

Her heart chugged like a freight train inside her chest as she pushed on the heavy wooden panel. After stepping fully into the room, she closed the door behind her with a soft *thunk*…a sound different from the Oval's door. But it still felt portentous. *Final.*

Leonard Meadows's office was everything anyone would imagine it to be. Leatherbound books lined mahogany bookshelves. The lemony scent of furniture polish lingered in the air. And the chief of staff's desk was piled high with files and paperwork, one desktop, one laptop, and a cluster of coffee mugs because the man consumed caffeine like water.

Meadows sat at his desk in one of his bespoke three-piece suits, his arms crossed over his chest. President Stevens stood beside him, looking powerful in a gray pantsuit with an American flag pin stuck through her lapel.

Lura opened her mouth, but the words dried up in the back of her Sahara Desert throat. She licked her lips with a tongue so dehydrated she could feel her individual taste buds rasping against her skin.

"Well?" her boss prompted. He didn't abide hem-hawing or hesitation. "What is it?"

Lura took a steadying breath and met the gazes of the two most powerful people in the country—maybe even in the world.

She might be the lowly daughter of a small-town mayor in Rabun County, Georgia, but she had an idea. A brilliant, *inspired* idea.

"I know where the Black Knights can get ten million dollars."

CHAPTER 8

Black Knights Inc.

Four goddamned hours!

That's how long it'd been since the ransom call came in.

Hew scraped both hands down his face and blew out a breath that didn't do jack shit to lessen the pressure building in his chest. The air in the War Room on the second floor felt thick and sticky, like aged maple syrup, only without the sweetness.

His boots stomped heavily across the space in ragged, restless strides. And the longer he paced, the more he wanted to shoot something.

*No. Not something. Some*one. *That bitch who made the ransom call.*

He'd start with *her.*

And, ayuh, despite the voice modulator, it'd still been clear that the one making the demands was a woman. Sabrina had confirmed as much when she'd screamed, *Don't give her anything! They won't—*

What? They won't *what?*

Screwing his eyes shut, he heard the echo of her cry, as clear now as it had been then. *I'm here! I'm alive!*

The memory felt like shrapnel in his brain.

He should've *been* with her on that damned drive. Should've stopped her from going in the first place. But he'd swallowed his objections, pushed aside his worry, and done neither. Now, the woman he…

What?

What *exactly* did he feel for Sabrina? Affection, sure. Respect and fondness and tenderness and understanding, of course. But…was there more? Was that fire that filled his heart whenever he heard her bright, babbling brook laugh indicative of something bigger? Was that ache low in his belly whenever she gifted him with one of her mile-wide smiles proof that he—

Don't go there. It's not the time!

Time…

Every tick of the clock on the wall was a hammer blow against his skull. Every second that slipped by was a new inch in the ever-widening gulf of fear opening up inside his chest.

Time…

Just bleedin' away.

"Damnit," Ozzie muttered, pulling out his earbuds and tossing them beside the mousepad. "I can't trace the ransom call. They rerouted it through so many proxies that it could've come from Brazil, Bangkok, or the Taco Bell down the block. I was able to track it through two darknet relays, then a tower in Iowa that's supposedly been offline for a month. But that's where the trail ends."

Hew clenched his fists so tight he could feel his blunt nails biting into his palms. If Ozzie, the best damn hacker Hew had ever met in real life, couldn't trace the call, then the call couldn't be traced. It was as simple as that.

From his office, Boss's voice boomed. "—don't care if it's unorthodox. We need the cash *now*, not tomorrow."

Becky's voice came next, sharp with urgency. "That's not good enough. We need to make this happen *today*. Can't we find someone who—"

Hew tuned them out.

He loved them both. Loved their optimism that they could somehow mortgage the shop to get the money needed. But banks didn't fork over millions without paperwork, protocols, and red tape.

And that took time.

Time they didn't have. Time *Sabrina* didn't have.

And so that left…

Fuck, he had no clue what that left. No one did. But everyone was scrambling to find out.

Grace Jackson paced by the railing, thumbs flying on her phone. Julia O'Toole sat at the end of the conference table, laptop open, typing like her fingers were on fire.

Both were FBI agents. And both had come running to help the instant their BKI partners had put out the call.

As for Hew? Well, his forte was flying and fighting. And for now, there wasn't a damned thing he could do to further their cause of finding Sabrina by taking to the air or greasing his gun.

So, instead, he paced.

And he worried.

And he tried not to let his sense of helplessness and rage grow into an all-consuming apoplectic fit.

Forcing himself to drag in a ragged breath, he vaguely noted the scents of metal grit and polished chrome. They were familiar smells. Solid smells. Generally *comforting* smells.

He found no relief in them now.

Black Knights Inc. wasn't home, it wasn't *whole*, without Sabrina. And he couldn't help but remember that well-known little nugget that said the first twenty-four hours after an abduction were the most critical. After that, the chances of recovery decreased significantly.

We've wasted too much time, he thought bitterly. *Precious goddamn time.*

Time waiting for the highway patrol to do their wellness check. Time bringing the team up to speed. Time debating options. Time trying to convince the president and Eliza's coldhearted father to help.

And all the while she's been stuck out there. Stuck with fucksticks doin' who knows what to—

No.

He couldn't let his mind wander to what she might be suffering. If he did, that valley of fear opening up inside him would become the Grand Canyon. And that wouldn't help anyone, least of all Sabrina.

He flipped his wrist and saw his watch read 10:57. He waited and waited and *waited*, but it felt like an eternity before the seven turned into an eight.

He was going to implode. Explode? He needed a course of action. He needed *something* because his inaction was killing him faster than any bullet ever could.

Grace shoved her phone into her hip pocket and turned to address the room.

"I had a buddy inside the bureau run the prints the local police took off Sabrina's car." When she saw the alarm on some of their faces, she quickly added, "This is strictly off books. So rest easy."

Right. Because saving the world always came with an asterisk at BKI. Now, saving the *girl* came with an asterisk, too.

Instead of doing all this out in the open, they had to do their work where they always did it. In the shadows. They had to protect their covers. Protect the shop. Protect the motherfucking president and her chief of staff because—

"The only prints on the car are hers, yours"—Grace tilted her head toward Hew—"and Martin Massey's."

Hearing Martin's name, knowing the too-pretty bastard had touched Sabrina's Prius—maybe been inside at some point?—made Hew's hands curl into tight fists.

Julia followed up Grace's announcement with, "Paint from her rear bumper's been sent to a friend of mine who works in the local lab. She's running an off-the-books analysis to see if she can narrow down the make and model of the vehicle that appears to have rear-ended Sabrina. Says she'll have something for us in two hours."

Two hours…

Fuck!

Even with the feds calling in favors, nothing was moving fast enough. Then, like a grenade exploding in his mind, the answer to all their problems suddenly presented itself. And he couldn't *believe* it'd taken him this long to think of it.

He hated the idea. He hated everything about it. But it didn't matter how he felt. Because it was Sabrina. It was *for* Sabrina.

Drawing in a slow breath, he released it on a windy sigh and pushed the name out of his mouth. "Martin."

"Huh?" Samuel Harwood said from the rolling chair beside Ozzie. Sam was a former Marine Raider, a native Chicagoan, and the biggest fan the White Sox could ever hope for. He'd been scouring the files on the

Charleston cartel responsible for killing Sabrina's brother in the off chance they'd missed something that had led her to her abduction. But now he stared at Hew quizzically.

"Sabrina's…" Hew's gut turned sour at the thought of speaking aloud the next word. "Boyfriend. Or…would-be boyfriend. Or whatever the hell he is to her."

Billionaire, savior, pain in my ever-lovin' ass.

"He has money," he finally ground out, noting how he said the phrase with the same distaste in his tone he might have used if he'd said *he has mange.*

Boss must've finished his call, because he stepped out of his office and announced coolly, "The more outside influences we bring into this thing, the less likely it is we'll be able to keep the true nature of this place under wraps."

"Ayuh, well…" Hew's voice was low and tight, even to his own ears. "Sabrina's life is on the line. *Our* Sabrina." He didn't say *my* Sabrina. He wanted to, but he didn't. Because it wasn't true. She wasn't his. "So that's a risk I'm willin' to take," he finished firmly. "Anyone disagree?"

There was a beat of silence. The kind that said a thousand things all at once.

"No one disagrees," Fish assured him. "We'll do whatever it takes. But first we need to—"

"Holy shit!" Ozzie's voice suddenly sliced through the air like a thrown blade. Every head in the room snapped in his direction. "I think I may have something."

Hew's heart lurched violently. He was across the room without his boots touching the floor. Bracing his hands on the back of Ozzie's chair, he asked, "What is it?"

Ozzie didn't answer right away. He waited for the others to converge around the bank of computers. Then, "I fed the make, model, and color of Sabrina's Prius into a program I wrote that scours the city's CCTV footage. I asked it to pull all relevant images from last night."

A grid of still photos bloomed to life on the screen. All grainy. All muted colors in the dark of night. And yet…

There she was. Sabrina. Inside her little Prius with its telltale dent on the back quarter panel from the day Hew had taken her to a Cubs game and she had tried to parallel park on a side street with all the grace of a blind moose.

For the first time in hours, something warmed inside his center. It was hope. Big and bright and burning.

"Oh-kay." Sam's voice was skeptical. "So what? We can see her leaving the compound, taking surface streets, and then turning onto Lake Shore Drive. But we already figured that's the route she took out of the city."

"No." Ozzie shook his head, his sandy-colored mad scientist hair waving. "Look *behind* her." He jabbed a blunt-tipped finger at the screen and quickly clicked through four photos.

In two of the images, tucked a car-length back, was a black van.

Unmarked. Unremarkable. Creepy as hell.

"Can you zoom in?" Boss's deep voice was as grim as the expression on his face. "Clean up the images a bit?"

"I'll do my best," Ozzie muttered as he worked his magic until the images grew clearer.

But only marginally.

The van's windows were tinted as dark as hell's midnight. There were two figures visible in the front seats. But both were cloaked in shadows, nothing more than silhouettes.

"Damn," Sam cursed.

"What about the plates?" Hew's voice was low and urgent. "Can ya find a view of the back of the van?"

Ozzie didn't answer. Just pounded the keys again until images raced across the monitor like a high-speed flipbook and—

"Stop there," Hew barked.

Ozzie froze the frame on a grainy image of the back of the van looming ominously behind Sabrina's little Prius.

He could just make out the shape of Sabrina's head through her car's back windshield, and a sick, sour feeling twisted his gut when he realized she'd had no idea she was being followed. Being hunted.

"Running the van's plates now." Ozzie's words were clipped.

Everyone in the room went still. Breaths were bated. Hearts skipped beats. Then…

"It's fake." Ozzie sat back with an aggravated sigh. "A ghost plate."

Of course it was.

"What about the van itself?" Grace asked from across the room. She looked fierce and focused, an FBI agent through and through. "Can you check the make and model? See if we can't narrow something down that way?"

"On it," Ozzie replied, his fingers already flying.

The group watched him work in tense silence. A second passed. Then another and another. Finally, Ozzie scrubbed both hands down his face.

"It's a standard cargo vehicle," he said. "White-label. There are thousands on the road. Could be commercial. Could be private. And there aren't any mods to help us hone in. Trying to find exactly *which* vehicle it is could take weeks."

The warm bubble of hope inside Hew's chest didn't pop. But it certainly deflated.

"Wait a minute. Everyone, be quiet." Eliza lifted a hand, motioning for silence as she pressed her cell phone to her ear. "Who's at the gate asking to speak with me?" She paused, and Hew watched both of her sleek, dark eyebrows arch high over her pale forehead. "Okay. Yes. Send her through."

When she pocketed her phone, her brow furrowed in confusion. "My father's assistant is here asking for me."

"Your father?" Hew said, not daring to dream the chief of staff might have changed his mind about helping them.

"His *assistant*," Eliza emphasized. "What does that mean?"

"Only one way to find out," Boss declared, and the entire group moved as a unit toward the stairs, drawn by the spark of optimism the mysterious assistant's arrival flamed to life.

They pounded down the treads in a thunderous line. And when they hit the cement of the bottom floor, the soles of their shoes boomed around the cavernous space like gunshots as they raced en masse toward the front door.

Eliza was the one to swing it open with a pop and a hiss. And they all watched as a pretty woman in a black pencil skirt hustled toward them. Her blue silk blouse was tied at her throat in a delicate knot. And her mass of red hair was wind-tossed and wild.

There was determination in her heart-shaped face. Unfortunately, Hew noted, there was nothing in her hands.

No giant bag of cash. No handcart stacked with gold bars.

"Lura?" Eliza held the door wide so the woman could step inside. A sheen of sweat glowed over her freckled face. "What in the world are you doing in Chicago?"

"After your call this morning, I caught the first flight out," the redhead explained, sounding as breathless as she looked. "I—" She glanced around. "Good grief! Will you get a load of this place? I mean, I've been following the social media posts. So I knew you all were doing amazing stuff here. But to be standing in—"

"Lura," Eliza cut in, and Hew wanted to kiss her right on the mouth. *And never mind the shiner I'd get from Fish.* Because if *she* hadn't interrupted the redhead, he would have. They didn't have time for a tour. "Why are you *here?*"

"Oh, right." Lura nodded briskly. "See, here's the thing. I know where—"

She stopped again, and it took everything Hew had not to grab her shoulders and shake her like a rag doll.

"Graham Coleburn?" the redhead blinked.

Hew glanced over his shoulder to find Graham standing there with his mouth hanging open and his eyes bugging out of his head.

Now Hew understood what a horny toad trying to shit a chicken bone must look like.

"Lura Dougherty," Graham recovered enough to say lowly, slowly. "As I live and breathe. How's your momma and them?"

Hew had fallen into an alternate universe. One where nothing made sense and no one was in a hurry to change that fact.

Eliza looked between Graham and the new arrival. "You two know each other?"

Hew barely heard the answer, still trying to keep hold of the threads of his sanity so he wouldn't unravel completely. He knew his voice sounded as rough and ferocious as a black bear caught in a trap, but he didn't care.

He didn't care because nothing mattered except finding Sabrina.

"Enough!" he roared. Then, he pointed a finger at the new arrival and demanded, "Why are ya here? And what does it have to do with this morning's phone call?"

Lura didn't flinch. She simply nodded curtly, like she was used to men thundering questions at her.

"Right. So, I know how you all can get ten million dollars."

CHAPTER 9

Location Unknown

Sabrina sat in bed, book in hand, trying to become engrossed in the story of dragons, fairies, and wars between realms. But she'd reread the same paragraph six times and still had no idea what was happening with the plot.

Her mind was too busy working through other *things.*

Namely, her sudden preoccupation with one particular helicopter pilot who hailed from the great state of Maine.

The whole group had celebrated that the last heads of the cartel had been apprehended and tossed in jail by taking Sabrina on her first trip to Red Delilah's. With the danger to her deemed null and void, she was once again free to come and go as she pleased.

You know, like a regular human being.

She should have been dancing a jig. Howling at the moon. Shooting off finger guns.

Instead, she was a hurricane of doubt, spinning with thoughts she didn't quite know how to name.

On one hand, she was delighted to finally see the infamous biker bar. It was everything they'd hyped it up to be. Loud, laid-back, and full of grizzled men in leather. On the other hand, Hew had spent the first ten minutes standing at the bar, all bearded and broad, talking to a pert brunette like it was his full-time job.

From the way the woman had batted her lashes, laid a hand on his forearm, and grabbed his phone to punch in her number, Sabrina half-expected to get an invitation to their wedding next week.

Not that she cared. Not that she was jealous or anything, because there was nothing to be jealous of.

She didn't like Hew that way. He was her friend. Nothing more. Nothing less.

Or at least that's what she told herself.

To her dismay, herself answered back, Are you sure about that?

Yes, *she was sure. Except…*

"Except what?" she asked aloud as she stared at the brick wall across the way.

Hew's bedroom was on the other side of that wall.

Knowing he was a stone's throw away had been a comfort for months. In a world turned upside down by the loss of her brother, the loss of her home, the loss of the life she'd built in Charleston, he had been her one constant. The one thing she could depend on to be there, to give her the strength to pull herself up by her bootstraps and carry on.

She would always be grateful to him for that. For stepping into the shoes of the friends she'd left behind, the brother she'd lost. But earlier…

Something had shifted.

In the air.

In her.

Since coming to Chicago, her feelings for him had been decidedly platonic. After what Eddy Torres did to her, platonic feelings were all she was capable of.

But maybe being out in the world again had nudged her healing a little further down the track. Or maybe seeing how other women watched Hew with hungry eyes had peeled the scales from hers.

*Whatever the reason, she'd looked at him and for the first time she'd seen something more than her confidant and colleague. She'd looked at him and had seen…*man.

A strong, vigorous man with a large, muscular build. A big, beautiful man with luscious hair and a rawboned face. An undeniably sexy man with a high, tight ass and hands that looked like they knew all the ways a woman needed to be touched.

Attraction had slammed into her with a one-two punch.

The first had hit her in the chest.

The second had hit her in the belly.

And ever since they'd gotten back from Red Delilah's, she'd been asking herself…what if?

What if it wasn't just shared trauma that tethered them? What if this thing between them was more? Bigger? Better than—

Speak of the devil.

Hew stood in her open door, his hands gripping the frame above his head so his thick fisherman's sweater pulled up and showed an inch of golden flesh above the waistband of his jeans.

He looked so very…New England-y. Like a lobster fisherman, or a maple syrup farmer, or an innkeeper for weary leaf peepers. So very rugged and outdoorsy. The model on the cover of L.L. Bean.

The social media guru in her imagined starting a YouTube channel featuring him chopping wood. He could do it shirtless…or wearing nothing but jeans and suspenders. She knew she'd have a hit on her hands. A million followers in under six months and monetizing views in under three.

"How was it being out at the bar?" he asked, and she was surprised she *didn't melt into the mattress at the sound of his deep voice.* Out at the bah.

Why is my heart jittering in my chest? It's just Hew.

Except, it wasn't just Hew. Not anymore.

It was Hew like she'd never experienced him before when she'd been too battered and bruised to see much past the end of her own nose.

Her bedroom had always felt so spacious, but now she wondered if there was room for herself along with his broad shoulders, big arms, and steadfast stare.

"It was good." She fought to keep the breathlessness from her voice. *"Weird. But good."*

"Weird how?" He tilted his head, and her eyes tracked up to the whorl of *deep, auburn hair that had fallen over his broad forehead to cover the little crescent-shaped scar there.*

I wonder if his hair feels as soft as it looks? I wonder if it'd curl around my fingers if I ran my hands along his scalp? I wonder if it's warm or cool or—

She shook her head. Not in answer to his question, but to jangle her errant thoughts back into place.

"Weird being around strangers. Weird not expecting someone from the cartel to come crashing through the door. Weird feeling…free." She shot him a teasing look. "Weird watching you flirt."

His expression blanked so quickly it was comical. "I wasn't flirtin'."

"Pfft." She rolled her eyes. "I saw that woman give you her phone number. And I saw how you looked at her when she did it." She gave him a curious once-over. "So no dice with the blonde at the bagel shop, huh? The brunette in the cowgirl boots is more your type?"

"Not sure I have a type, actually."

"Every man has a type, Hew." She tossed the covers off her legs to get out of bed.

Her type used to be the suave and sophisticated sort. Smooth talkers in expensive suits with hard, ambitious eyes. The kind of guys who were so very different from her father or her brother. The types who'd always disappointed her when she realized their pretty packagings hid disingenuous hearts.

Hew was the opposite.

Not that his outer trappings weren't pretty. They were. *All the appreciative looks he'd gotten from the clientele at Red Delilah's proved that.*

But his dedication and loyalty to his team, his quiet consideration, and the kindness with which he moved through life despite his warrior's training, these were the things that made him truly beautiful.

Maybe that was why the thought of pursuing something more than friendship with him scared her as much as it thrilled her. If he ended up disappointing her, she might not recover.

"Where ya goin'?" he asked when she headed toward him.

"I'm hungry. There are still a couple of strawberry scones left over from this morning."

That's what she told *him. The truth was, she needed air.*

Hew hanging onto her doorframe, looking so big and beautiful and…big, had sucked all the oxygen out of her lungs.

He dropped his hands when she stopped in front of him. She breathed a sigh of relief that she no longer had to work to keep her eyes averted from that hint of love trail that disappeared into the waistband of his jeans.

"Sorry." He winced. "Ate the last one five minutes ago."

She faked annoyance. "I should've known." Then, "The lemon tarts?" she asked hopefully.

It was incongruous to see such boyish guilt on such a manly face. "Graham inhaled 'em as soon as we got home. Didn't even chew."

She sighed in exasperation. "Bottomless pits, the both of you."

She could have stepped into the hall. He'd given her plenty of room. But she stopped with her back against the doorframe and her bare toes touching the tips of his socked feet.

Studying his face, she tried to see…something. Anything that would tell her she wasn't the only one to notice the shift in the atmosphere between them.

Could he feel how the air vibrated? Could he smell how her soap mixed with his aftershave to create an intoxicating blend? Could he see how her pupils dilated and her breath came too fast?

"What?" *He blinked down at her.* "Ya wanna punch me in the gut for eatin' the last strawberry scone? Gotta warn ya, strawberry scones on top of beer do not *make a pretty picture when they're revisited."*

Why had she never noticed the flecks of brown in the green surrounding his pupils? And had his mouth always been so luscious, his bottom lip just the littlest bit fuller than the top?

It's now or never, Sabrina, *a voice whispered urgently.* You'll never know if he's feeling what you're feeling unless you put him to the test.

Desperate to reclaim the part of herself she'd lost the night her brother died, she lowered her lids to half-mast and slowly walked her fingers up his chest until she could grab his bearded chin and give it a little shake.

"I know how you can make it up to me," *she whispered in her most seductive voice.*

It was rusty. It'd been a good long while since she'd used it.

Time seemed to stretch and slow as she waited for him to say something. Anything. *But he just stood there, not moving. Barely breathing.*

Oh, shit, *she thought as the tips of her ears heated.* He isn't *feeling what* I'm feeling.

"Okay." *She forced a laugh as humiliation took hold.* "So you're not attracted to me that way. I get it. But you can't blame a gal for giving it the ol' college try."

She shoved into the hall and walked toward the stairs. Refusing to let her shoulders droop in defeat. Refusing to allow her embarrassment to quicken her steps.

Dignity, Sabrina, *she coached herself.* Don't you dare tuck tail and run.

She felt the warm, manacled grip of his hand before she heard his footsteps behind her. He yanked her around so quickly that her hand jumped to her throat.

He looked like a giant with the overhead light haloing his head and casting his face in shadows. "You're an idiot if you think I'm not attracted to ya that way." His voice was soft and low.

Before she could reply, he pulled her forward until she plowed into him. Which was sort of like plowing into a wall of solid concrete.

She uttered a quick oof before he caught her chin, angled her head up, and…didn't slam his mouth over the top of hers.

He stopped with his lips a hair's breadth away.

Her heart stuttered. Her lungs burned. Her nostrils flared because his breath was hot and sweet. It smelled like strawberry scones.

"What's happening right now?" she whispered against his lips, aware of every place their bodies touched. His thighs were hard against hers. Her nipples brushed the unyielding expanse of his chest. And his fingers on her chin were callused and warm without being rough.

"Don't know if I can be gentle." His voice sounded like he'd sent it through the garbage disposal. "I'm starvin' for ya. I've been starvin' for ya. Everything in me wants to devour you whole."

Some of her old gumption, her old moxie, returned. It's what gave her the courage to whisper, "Do it."

That's all the consent he needed. He slammed his mouth over hers like a man whose life depended on him tasting her.

And taste her, he did.

His lips were firm and demanding. His tongue was confident and searching.

It was the kind of kiss that left her with no recourse but to hold on tight. So her fingers gripped his biceps. Her nails bit into his tough flesh as passion, lust, and an aching longing blasted through her in a series of explosions that left her breathless.

Mindless.

Helpless.

His hand fell from her face then, and she whimpered at the loss of his touch. Then she moaned in victory when his arms came around her in a crushing vice as he lifted her off her feet. She automatically wrapped her arms around his shoulders, her hands spearing into his hair.

It was as soft as it looked.

And warm, so very warm as she pulled him tighter. Ever tighter.

She wanted to cry with victory at the proof that he wanted her as much as she wanted him. She'd never felt more complete than she did right then, right there, in his arms. And for the first time in months—maybe years—she didn't feel broken. She felt chosen *and—*

"That woman will fuck the hair clean off your balls."

Sabrina blinked open her eyes and groaned at the pain pounding in her temples, the bite of the zip ties at her wrists and ankles, and the awful crick in her neck that made it feel fractured.

The blood on her cheek had dried to a crust. And hours without water had scorched her throat like someone had poured in gasoline and struck a match.

She wanted to go back to sleep. Go back to the delicious dream that was part memory and part fantasy and *all* escape from her current reality.

Hew *had* come to her room after her first trip to Red Delilah's. She *had* teased him about the brunette and the pastries.

 But that's where things had ended.

The instant she'd stepped next to him in the doorway, the instant he'd loomed above her and his wonderful body heat had wrapped around her, she'd lost her nerve.

There'd been no flirty walk of her fingers up his chest. No suggestive invitation in her eyes or on her tongue.

She'd simply punched his arm and said something inane before scurrying off down the stairs like a complete chickenshit.

"How would you know?" The brusque voice pulled her from her thoughts. Her regrets.

Three of the Banshee's four men gathered around a rusting metal table. It was piled high with weapons that looked like they belonged on a battlefield.

The musky smell of gun oil hung in the air. It mixed with a slightly more chemical tang, and she was reminded of the time she followed Hew to the outbuilding where the Black Knights kept their arsenal.

She'd been overwhelmed by the sight of so much death-dealing machinery then. She was overwhelmed by the sight of so much death-dealing machinery now.

The difference was BKI's arsenal had made her feel safe. This one made her feel like prey.

"I know because I've been there. Done that." The blond man smirked.

"When?" demanded the short guy with the pug nose and the mean eyes.

"After we celebrated the Idaho job. She was knee-deep in Jose Cuervo and all over me outside the bar."

"Bullshit," Pug-nose snapped. "She'd fuck Diesel if she was gonna fuck anyone besides Hummer."

"Far as I can figure," the blond mused, "she refuses to fuck Diesel because he has a bad habit of putting his conquests in the hospital. And she refuses to fuck *you* because you'd have to stand on tiptoe to get the tip in."

The short man pointed a thick, blunt finger at the blond. "Ever heard that old wives' tale about a man's short stature being a sure sign he's packing serious heat in his pants? You know, 'cause all his growth hormones went to his dick?"

The blond guffawed. "You made that up."

"I'll show you."

"I swear to god, Kurt, you whip that thing out and I'll use it for target practice."

The short man—*Kurt* apparently—grinned. The sight sent a shiver down Sabrina's spine.

"I get it." Kurt clicked his tongue. "They say comparison is the thief of joy."

Whatever Blondie's response was, Sabrina missed it. She got distracted by the very *obvious* noises coming from the little room at the far end of the space.

It was walled off from the rest of the open floor—the old manager's office, maybe?—but the door that had once kept the area private had fallen off its hinges. Now, it simply leaned against the outer wall, partially covering its old doorframe, partially leaving the entrance wide open.

Through the breach, she heard the *slap, slap, slap* of flesh meeting flesh. It was a sickly rhythm. Primal. Cruel. Her brain rejected the sounds even as her ears betrayed her and picked up a man's animalistic grunts and a woman's moans of encouragement.

Dear god. In the middle of all this filth, the Banshee and the one they call Hummer are fucking.

Bile burned up Sabrina's throat to sit bitterly on the back of her tongue.

Her revulsion must've been apparent because Kurt, the little troll, sauntered over and gripped her shoulder. She could feel the imprint of all five of his fingers, and his touch made her skin want to crawl off her body.

"You like the sound of that?" His nasally voice was wet with glee as he rubbed the bulge behind his zipper. "I can oblige you with some of the same."

"Cut it out," Blondie snapped, still checking weapons. "We're supposed to be getting ready."

"We're ready." Kurt stepped closer to Sabrina, his crotch inches from her face. "Why should Black Widow and Hummer get to have all the fun?"

Black Widow…

So that's *what they call the Banshee.*

Perfect name, Sabrina decided. The platinum blonde used sex as a weapon, and Sabrina figured she'd also happily eat these men alive.

"Come on," Kurt wheedled. "Look at her. A beaut. Shouldn't we show her a good time… one last time?"

Sabrina wanted to use the only weapon she had at her disposal—her teeth—to rip off Kurt's dick. But she knew the denim of his dark jeans would save him. She'd bruise him at best. And that simply wasn't enough.

"Don't you want to give her a go, Diesel?" Kurt cajoled. "Don't you think you deserve to get some since that bitch"—he hitched his chin toward the small room where the sounds of sex grew louder, more frenzied—"won't give you your fair share?"

Sabrina's heart came to a screeching stop when the man who'd punched her and twisted her breast, the man dubbed Diesel, turned his crystalline eyes on her. They were as blue as an iceberg. And just as cold.

She wanted to shrink away from the brutality she recognized in him. But if he saw her fear, he'd feast on it like the monster he was.

Instead, she shoved it deep and met his chilling gaze head-on. Forcing herself not to be the first one to blink.

"Now, we're talking," Kurt chuckled. "I love a woman with some fight in her. Come on, boys. Let's fuck every hole she's got."

He was still rubbing, rubbing, rubbing.

She could see his erection getting firmer, standing taller behind his fly. The sight made her stomach roil and made those old demons rise out of hell to scratch at her heart until she was bleeding out on the inside.

She knew the depravity of men like these. Knew how much pleasure they took in a woman's helplessness and pain. But this time, she wasn't going down without a fight. This time, she was going to get in her licks.

"You talk pretty big for being such a small fraction of a man," she growled at Kurt.

The muscles of her stomach trembled. But not with fear. With fury. A hot, searing fury that made her flex her hands against her zip ties.

Her fingers ached for a weapon.

Or a throat.

Kurt stopped rubbing to stare at her. The acidic hate in his eyes scoured her brain like a chemical burn. But she just lifted her chin, pulled back her lips, and gave him her best sneer of disgust.

"You bitch." He grabbed her jaw in a painful grip. "I'm going to fuck your ass bloody—"

She braced herself, her spine locking tight and her vision tunneling.

He'll have to unbind me to do it. Be ready. Use your teeth. Use your nails. Use everything that—

"Kurt!" Black Widow's voice boomed across the hollow space, and the mean little man immediately dropped Sabrina's jaw. "I thought my instructions were clear!"

Black Widow walked toward them, adjusting the zipper on her top without hurry, her red lace bra still on proud display. Hummer trailed after her, zipping his pants and looking as self-satisfied as a man strolling away from a good meal.

"What's good for the goose is good for the ganders," Kurt muttered petulantly.

"Aw, poor baby." Black Widow pretended to pout. "Did it make your little dick hard to hear mommy and daddy going at it?" She wiggled her pinky finger as if to indicate the size of Kurt's penis. "Do you need to go into the office and give yourself a hand so you can feel better and get back to work?"

"Fuck you," Kurt spat.

"Oh, no." Black Widow shook her head. "I fuck men. Not boys. When you grow four more inches, *then* we can talk. In the meantime, do as you're told. Bishop is paying us all a pretty penny for this job. So keep your head out of your pants and in the game."

Bishop?

Sabrina filed the name away. Not that she thought she'd have an opportunity to pass it along. But just in case there was a sliver of hope. Just in case, against all odds, she was able to—

"Take your own advice, why don't you?" Kurt snarled at the blonde.

"Because I don't have to." Black Widow studied her fingers as if checking for chips in her manicure. "Because without me, none of you would have work. You'd all be pulling your pork in some no-name dump of a town and doing your forty hours in some dead-end job just so you could have a little extra scratch to get drunk on the weekends and harangue some poor bartender with tall tales of your glory days in the military."

Her words were feather-light. Her tone was scalpel-sharp.

"*I* have the reputation in the field. *I* have the contacts that get us the jobs. *I* say when and where and who." She dropped her hand to pin her soulless eyes on Kurt. "Got that?"

The short man didn't speak. He didn't nod. He simply went back to work with the others.

Sabrina didn't let herself exhale. One, she didn't want to make her relief at Kurt's departure obvious. Two, it was hard to feel relieved when Black Widow turned her attention from the short man to her.

The corners of the woman's red-stained lips lifted ever so slightly, like she was amused by the sight of horny men and deadly weapons and the promise of blood.

Did she reapply her lipstick after her little assignation with Hummer in the back office?

The errant thought was chilling because it was such a casual, everyday thing to do. Or—and this was *more* chilling—did she not *need* to reapply it because she and Hummer never kissed?

The sounds coming from the little room had certainly been primitive. But the thought of sex without the intimacy of sharing breath was downright animalistic.

Slowly, with an almost feline swagger, the blonde strolled over to stand in front of Sabrina.

"You're tougher than you look, Sabrina Greenlee," she remarked conversationally, and Sabrina blanched.

They knew her name.

Black Widow saw her reaction and purred. "Oh, yes. We perused your purse before chucking it out the window somewhere in Wisconsin. You have a South Carolina driver's license. Southern girl, eh? But now you work with the Black Knights?"

Sabrina didn't respond. Didn't blink. Even when Black Widow bent down until their faces were mere inches apart.

"That's okay. You don't need to talk. You can just continue to sit there and act tough." Black Widow straightened. "I admire your tenacity," she went on. "There are too few women like us in the world. Women who refuse to back down to assholes like Kurt."

Sabrina's throat worked around the bile lingering there. "You and I are nothing alike."

The woman's smile sharpened. "So much spunk and spite. Too bad it won't save you."

Maybe not, Sabrina thought. *But it might be enough to screw up your plans.*

She glanced at the broken windows and the glittering glass beneath them. All she needed was an excuse. Something to sell the act.

She didn't have to fake the nausea. Her stomach had been roiling since the moment she regained consciousness.

"Better back up," she warned. "Unless you want what I had for supper last night to end up all over that top."

Black Widow's top lip curled even as she stepped back. "Vance," she snapped. "Find a bucket."

Vance. That was the blond man's name. Sabrina tucked it away with all the others.

"Let her puke on herself," Kurt sneered.

Sabrina gagged, loud and wet. "You'll be smelling it for—"

"Dammit!" A blade appeared in Black Widow's hand like magic. Light hit it just right, making the steel gleam like fangs.

Sabrina barely registered the motion before Black Widow sliced her ankle ties and yanked her upright.

"Take her," she ordered Hummer. "Let her puke in the corner. *Away from all of us.*" She waved a dismissive hand toward the far end of the room.

Hummer grabbed Sabrina's elbow and frog-marched her across the dirty concrete and around the rusting machinery.

Pins and needles attacked the soles of her feet. Her knees ached from having been bent for so long. But she barely noticed either of these things as she pretended to stumble, made another gagging sound, and gasped, "Hurry."

When they reached the end of the room, she spied the piece of glass she wanted and staggered so she could fall against the wall. Catching herself with her shoulder, she slid down the grimy surface until her butt hit the ground and her bound hands could feel for the makeshift weapon.

She carefully closed her fingers around the shard. Then, getting her knees under her, she bent at the waist and made a show of retching like a cat trying to puke up a hairball.

She brought up more air than vomit. But thankfully, there was enough bile left in her stomach to make her performance convincing.

Fear still coiled inside her like an insidious serpent. But now it had a twin spiral of resolve sitting next to it.

She might die in this place…probably *would* die in this place.

But by god, I'm going to take at least one of these motherfuckers with me!

CHAPTER 10

Black Knights Inc.

Graham Coleburn stood at the kitchen island, a jar of Duke's mayo in one hand, a bottle of French's mustard in the other, and a head full of thoughts that didn't have a lick to do with condiments.

Lura Dougherty.

It's a damned small world.

What were the odds someone from his past—his hometown, no less—would show up at BKI with the answer to their prayers?

Considering he hadn't seen hide nor hair of anyone from Clayton, Georgia, in nearly twenty years, they had to be as slim as a sliver.

And yet here I am. And there she is, all grown up and filled out and remindin' me of home in a way I haven't been reminded in a long, long while.

Hell if he knew how to feel about this blast from the past.

On the one hand, she was easy on the eyes, and he was never one to complain when a pretty woman entered his orbit. On the other hand, he'd spent his adult life putting distance between himself and the tragedy he left behind the day he signed enlistment papers in that hot little booth at his high school career fair.

Having Lura Dougherty walk through BKI's front door brought back all that old shame. That old guilt and sorrow.

Home is where the heart is. That's what folks said. But for him…it was where the hurt lived.

"Which is it?" He wiggled the containers in his hands.

She wrinkled her nose from her spot atop a barstool on the other side of the island. He didn't notice how cute the expression was.

Or maybe he did. Just a little.

"Mustard, please. Mayonnaise is oil, vinegar, and egg whites whipped into a white fury. Disgusting." She shivered theatrically.

He made a face like she'd just insulted his granny's cornbread. "How very *un*-Southern of you."

He set the jars aside and reached for the loaf of homemade bread Eliza kept in wax paper in the wooden breadbox beside the fridge.

"I haven't lived in Georgia in fifteen years," she said, winding a strand of that deep red hair around her finger.

It was nearly auburn but not quite. The kind of color women paid good money to fake, but Lura had had naturally since she'd run around in pigtails at Sunday socials.

"Pretty sure everyone back home would say I've turned traitor and become the worst thing someone can become. A *Yankee*," she added with a dramatic widening of her cobalt-blue eyes.

"Ya know what they say about Yankees." He grinned. "They're like hemorrhoids."

She finished the saying with a smirk. "A pain in the ass when they come down and a relief when they go back up."

He cocked an eyebrow. "Noticed ya lost your accent. Most of it, leastways."

That earned him a wide grin, and his hand tightened around the counter's edge because something weird happened to his kneecaps.

Lord have mercy. She was as sweet as peach pie, sure. But that smile? That smile could make a man forget his own name.

"You haven't lost yours," she countered. "It's still as thick as a bowl of cheesy grits."

"Ya can take the boy outta the north Georgia woods, but ya can't take the north Georgia woods outta the boy, I reckon."

He braced for another smile and was mildly relieved when she got distracted by Peanut.

All the womenfolk who lived and worked at the shop had reformed the former alley cat of his wicked ways. Instead of chasing mice and sifting through dumpsters, the tom now spent his days hunting up sunny patches to sunbathe in and haunting the kitchen in hopes someone would toss him a treat.

The cat twined around her barstool's legs, earning himself a cheek rub that had him purring loud enough to drown out the fridge's humming compressor.

The shop was oddly quiet for the tail end of a workday. No whine of metal grinders. No boom of Ozzie's eighties hair bands from the speakers in the War Room. No good-natured insults bandied about as folks went about their various tasks.

Half the group had gone off to support Grace and Julia on their mission to the Federal Reserve Bank of Chicago. The other half was helping Ozzie follow a lead he'd pinpointed on the recording of the ransom call.

Normally, Graham would be right there with the second half, doing what he could to contribute to the endeavor. But as Lura had been tapping away on her phone, looking for flights back to D.C., he'd heard her stomach growl.

The first time, he'd ignored it.

The second time, he'd lifted an inquisitive eyebrow.

The third time, he'd said, *"Your belly's makin' noises like it thinks your throat's been cut."*

After some coaxing and a promise to build her the best roast beef sandwich east of the Mississippi, he'd escorted her down to the kitchen.

His nerves had been strung as tight as a fiddle string all day. Abductions of friends and colleagues and ten-million-dollar ransom demands would do that to a man. But Lura's presence for the last handful of hours had brought about another kind of tension.

It wasn't homesickness. Although it sort of felt the same. It wasn't wistfulness. Although it kind of felt like that, too.

If he were forced to put a label on it, he'd say it was equal parts nostalgia and regret. The kind of feeling that fisted in his gut and twisted in his heart, because every glance her way pulled up memories he'd shoved down deep.

He thought he'd buried the boy he'd been back when he knew her. Thought he'd healed from the hurt that had driven him away.

But with her close, breathing the same air, all those old feelings clawed right back to the surface and proved some things don't stay in the ground. Some things are always right there, waiting to rear their ugly heads.

Lord, what he wouldn't give to go back to the day his mother had her accident. He'd fake an illness so she'd stay home instead of going to work. He'd slice her tires so she couldn't drive. He'd tackle her before she could set one foot inside that textile factory.

What would his life look like now if that fateful day had never happened?

Would he have stayed in Rayburn County? Married a sweet Southern girl who made sun tea and wore daisy-print dresses? Would he have coached football? Taught his kids how to bait a hook and change a tire?

Would his life have been simple? Clean?

Would he still know how to cry at funerals?

He flicked a covert glance across the island as Lura continued to love on the cat, trying to reconcile the girl he'd known, the skinny one with the braces and the knee socks, with the tall, curvy woman who reminded him of Lynda Carter back in her *Wonder Woman* days.

Only this version has red hair, expensive clothes, and flew halfway across the country to tell us how we can "borrow" ten million dollars from the United States' central bank, he thought with a reluctant grin.

His grin faded when an image of Lura dressed in a red Lycra bustier and solid gold cuffs bloomed to life in his mind's eye and riled up a part of his body that had no business being riled up.

Peanut yowled his affront when Lura stopped petting him and straightened to turn back to Graham.

Afraid he might get caught staring at her like a starving man stares at a buffet, Graham busied himself by peeling off a slice of roast beef and tossing it into the corner. The old tom scampered after the meat as fast as his furry, fat legs would take him.

When Graham turned back to Lura, he found her expression thoughtful. Searching.

Searchin' for what? he wondered.

For the cocky jock he'd been back when she knew him? For the boy who'd gone from homecoming hero to self-imposed isolation once his mother died? For the changes all the years since had wrought?

In the end, she didn't say anything. Didn't ask him the question sparkling in her eyes. She simply went back to playing with the ends of her hair and silently watching him finish the sandwich preparations.

He plated her sandwich and slid it her way before wrapping his fingers around his own.

"Thanks." She nodded. Then, she added in a voice as soft as cotton, "I'm sorry about what happened to your mom. I wanted to tell you that then. But you were you, and I was…well…*me*, and I didn't have the courage."

He stopped with the sandwich halfway to his mouth. It would taste like cardboard now. So he set it back on his plate.

"Happened to a lot of folks," he rasped through a tight throat. "Too many folks 'round those parts, especially back then."

"The commonality of it doesn't make *your* loss any less."

He didn't want to talk about his loss. He didn't want to *think* about it, even all these years later. He swerved onto the off-ramp she'd offered. "What do ya mean 'cause I was me and you were you?"

She gave him a look like the answer was obvious and he was just fishing for compliments. "You were the big-deal senior football star. I was the derpy freshman cheerleader who hadn't figured out how to use her mile-long legs. Jenna Albright used to say I looked like a giraffe trying to sip from a pond whenever I did a toe-touch."

He remembered the girl who'd been chased by the boys on the football team, but who'd seemed to him, even back then, to be small-minded and mean-spirited. "Jenna Albright was a chinless snob with a bad bleach job."

Lura bit the inside of her cheek. "Still has the bad bleach job. But now she has weak *chins*. Plural."

He chuckled. "Got big, did she?"

"If she were an inch taller, she'd be round." Lura's eyes twinkled with vengeful delight before she caught herself and shook her head. "Wow. That was mean. I take it back."

"She called you a giraffe," he countered with an indifferent shrug. "I think ya got a right to return fire. And just so ya know, you were never derpy. I may have been the senior football star, but *you* were the mayor's daughter. If you'd talked to me back then, I would've tripped all over my tongue 'cause you'd deigned to lower yourself to the likes of little ol' me."

He expected her reply to be light and flippant. It was neither.

"You were never little, Graham. Not in stature. Not in spirit. What happened to your mother didn't diminish you in anyone's eyes."

Damnit! That feeling was back. That regret mixed with nostalgia that came with too many what-ifs and if-onlys.

He changed the subject again. "So, tell me how ya came up with this brilliant plan of yours?"

She wrinkled her nose—habit, clearly—and he distracted himself from being too charmed by the move by taking a bite of his sandwich.

"Don't count your chickens before they've hatched." She shook her head. "It's only brilliant if your friends can pull it off."

"Concept's solid regardless," he contradicted around a mouthful of bread and meat.

"It is, isn't it?" She grinned, clearly proud of herself. Then she waved a breezy hand. "It's simple, really. A bunch of day-to-day stuff crosses the chief of staff's desk. By proxy, it crosses *my* desk. And when I overheard Eliza talking to her dad this morning about needing cash fast, I remembered seeing a memo about how the Federal Reserve Bank here in Chicago was slated to destroy a bunch of old one-hundred-dollar bills at the end of the month. Figured with BKI's contacts, you all might be able to get your hands on those bills before they went into the paper shredder."

She was right about their contacts. They had more than their fair share. Even still, they'd had to call in enough favors to make a politician blush.

Boss had rung up Lawrence P. Washington, the former police chief, with the ask. Washington had called up an old prosecutor friend and *that* guy had given BKI the name of a justice willing to sign off on a warrant granting permission for two local FBI agents to "temporarily use" ten million in scrap-bound bills. And only after all that had been squared away had Grace and Julia scurried out the door on a mission to pick up the warrant and take it to the Federal Reserve. Fingers crossed, they would return home soon with bags chock-full of bills bound for the burn pile.

"And instead of callin', you flew here because…?" He let the question dangle.

"I *wanted* to call. Told the chief of staff we *should* call to give you guys plenty of time to get the ball rolling. But he's paranoid. He said he didn't want me using the phone. Didn't want any breadcrumbs to lead back to him or the president if this thing you all are dealing with suddenly goes sideways. So, my options were a homing pigeon or a Boeing 747. I figured the latter might be faster."

Smart, pretty, *and* funny?

Lura Dougherty was an embarrassment of riches.

"How'd you end up workin' for Meadows anyways?" he asked around another bite of roast beef, ignoring Peanut, who was back to begging by doing figure eights around his calves.

"Little bit of luck and a little bit of being dumb enough to take the job no one else wanted."

When he cocked his head, she continued. "After college, my dad pulled some strings and got me an internship in the West Wing. I worked my way through the secretary pool, and when Meadows's office manager passed—she was eighty-six, god love her—my name was put forward as her replacement. I *jumped* at the chance to take such a prestigious position." She made a face. "More fool me."

Graham nodded in understanding. "Leonard Meadows has got more quirks than a porcupine's got prickles."

Her grim smile said she didn't disagree.

"What about you?" she asked with a curious cant of her chin. "Everyone thought you'd go on to play college ball. Then you just…disappeared."

His half-eaten sandwich suddenly felt like it weighed twenty pounds. He stared at it briefly, then set it back on his plate.

He hoped she couldn't hear the rawness of his voice when he admitted, "After Mom died, football felt…meaningless. She'd been the one who signed me up for peewee. The one who drove me to the weight room on the weekends and waited in the car for me to finish gettin' my reps in. She was always there on the sidelines…until she wasn't. Until she got too sick. And then when she wasn't, I got mad. So mad at the system and the situation and the sorriness of it all that I figured it was better to take out my anger on America's enemies rather than on friends and family. So when the Navy recruiter shoved a sheet of paper at me and said, 'Sign here,' I didn't hesitate."

She blinked like she hadn't expected him to be so honest.

"Four years enlisted," he went on. "Nine as a SEAL. Five now as a Black Knight." He cocked his head. "Speakin' of which, how the hell do ya know about us? I thought Madam President and Leonard Meadows kept this whole situation we're runnin' real hush-hush."

Lura winced. "I, uh, came across some information I shouldn't have. Then, in typical me fashion, instead of keeping my mouth shut, I asked questions. By that point, the chief of staff knew me well enough that he figured it was better to come clean and swear me to secrecy rather than have me playing Sherlock Holmes in the outer office."

"What's that old saw about curiosity killin' the cat?"

Her sigh was exaggerated. "That's what Mom always says and—"

Pop. Hiss.

Graham took one more bite of his sandwich before brushing off his hands. "That's the front door. Time to find out if your brilliant plan bore fruit."

Lura wiped her hands on the paper towel he'd given her to use as a napkin and hopped down from the barstool. He didn't notice how the move made parts of her jiggle.

Okay, so he *did* notice. But only a little.

Together, they followed the hall to the main shop, where most of the Black Knights had already gathered.

Graham, a head taller than most, caught sight of Grace and Julia and breathed, "Oh, thank Christ."

"What?" Lura asked from beside him, going up on tiptoe. "What do you see? Did it work? Do they have the money?"

He opened his mouth to answer. But just then, the gathered group parted to reveal the two FBI agents.

Both women looked very official in their pantsuits and with their badges hanging on lanyards around their necks. But, more importantly, they looked victorious since they each held an army-green duffel bag loaded down and lumpy with cash. Sam Harwood, a former Marine Raider, and Hunter Jackson, a former Green Beret, held an additional two bags each.

Ten million dollars.

Would ya get a load of that?

"Julia had to do some convincing even *with* the warrant," Grace told the group, her face shiny with sweat even though the sun was well on its way toward the western horizon. Golden rays streamed in through the tall windows, casting honey-colored shadows over the whole shop.

"And Grace had to bat her lashes and flash some cleavage at the old guy running the place," Julia added in her South Side Chicago drawl. "But we got it."

"The catch is, we have to return it in seventy-two hours." Grace made a face. "Or our asses are grass."

"How are we planning to do *that*?" Becky asked the question they were all thinking.

"One problem at a time," Boss declared. "We have the cash to buy Sabrina's freedom. After that's done, *then* we figure out how to get the money back from her abductors."

"Uh, guys?" Ozzie's voice echoed down from the second floor, and that's when Graham realized the mad hacker was missing from the crowd. "You'd better get up here. You're gonna wanna see this."

The alarm in Ozzie's tone was as clear and ominous as a klaxon. In response, duffels were dropped on the floor like they were full of dirty socks instead of stacks of cash.

Graham was the caboose on the train of folks who wasted no time beating feet up the stairs. Which meant he bore witness to half a dozen gasps and curses before he hit the landing and saw what all the hubbub was about.

All six monitors had switched from screen savers to show jet-black backgrounds with bright white letters blazing in the middle of each.

"We are the ears that listen in the darkness.
We are the eyes that witness secret sins.
We are the guardians against tyranny and fascism.
We are Kerberos."

Kerberos...

The hacker collective. Anonymous on steroids.

"Well, shit," Graham muttered, the sandwich in his gut turning to stone.

If Kerberos was reaching out, it meant only one thing.

This wasn't some simple abduction motivated by greedy bastards wanting quick cash. Something was very, *very* wrong.

CHAPTER 11

"**H**ew! Go take a walk!" Boss thundered.

"I'm not your damned dog!" Hew's voice cracked. His hands fisted. His body shook. "I'm not—"

"You're not a dog," Boss cut in, his tone softer but still with that same iron center. "But you're about to go nuclear. And this isn't a launch pad. Go cool off so the rest of us can think."

Hew's pulse was a ferocious thing. It rushed through him in a torrent that made his head pound. Made his vision tunnel. Made him want to give someone a fatal dose of projectile lead poisoning.

"Crunch on this. It'll make you feel better." Becky pulled a cherry-flavored Dum-Dum lollipop from the front pocket of her pink bib overalls.

He took the proffered sucker. Because, *damnit!* What else could he do? It was either that or give in to the urge to break the conference table in half.

Julia, ever the diplomat, said reassuringly, "It's good they contacted us. Now we've been warned and can adjust accordingly."

"Warned," he growled, ripping the paper wrapper off the sucker. "But that's it. If they know enough to tell us this is a trap"—he thrust a finger at the monitors and the screensavers bouncing around their edges now that Kerberos had disappeared—"why the hell can't they tell us *how* they know? Why the hell can't they tell us who or what we're up against?"

"Knowledge is power," Ozzie muttered, scratching fingers through his wild hair. "And power is identity. If they reveal too much, someone might figure out who they are. That's death for them. And the good they do would die with them. It's enough that they gave us what they did. It's more than we had five minutes ago."

Fuck if it's enough! Hew silently raged. Aloud, all he did was grunt.

Kerberos had revealed only: *This is not about money. This is about BKI. Beware.*

And that was it.

Just those three short sentences before…*poof!* The hacker group had vanished. Digital dust. Back into the bowels of the dark web from which they'd sprung.

Sabrina was out there all alone with these…*motherfuckers!* And it had been bad enough when he'd thought she'd been taken for ransom money. To know she'd been snatched because of the Black Knights, because they'd made enemies that didn't have a damn thing to do with her, was more than he could stand.

"I swear to god," he growled. "If they harm one hair on her head, I'll beat the flesh off their skulls."

"Hew." Boss clapped a heavy hand on his shoulder. "You're no help to us like this, brother. We need the cool-headed Nightstalker back. Go do whatever you gotta do to make that happen, yeah?"

A roar of frustration threatened. Hew strangled it until it died a hard death at the back of his throat.

He didn't remember taking the stairs down to the first floor. He didn't remember walking through the kitchen and out through the back door. He didn't even remember stepping onto the patio.

He didn't come back into himself until he felt the pain in the top of his foot from where the laces of his steel-toed boot connected with the arm of an Adirondack chair. The blow sent the chair flying into the air before it crashed onto its side.

"Damn, man. You're slow to anger. But when it comes on ya, it's fierce, ain't it?"

Hew turned to see Graham leaning against the back door's jamb. The evening sun beat down on his head until it felt like his brain was stuck inside a pottery kiln. But the heat in his face had nothing to do with the Fahrenheit.

He was acting like a fool. Unraveled. *Volatile.*

Having seen what lack of self-control and self-discipline did to people, having *suffered* at the hands of those who'd never learned the fine art of restraint, he'd promised himself he'd never be *that guy.*

And yet…here he was.

Fuck!

Closing his eyes, he focused on box-breathing. Then, he carefully righted the Adirondack chair, dragged it out of the sun, and placed it in the shade cast by the patio's short roof.

He should sit. He didn't *want* to sit. He wanted to pace and punch and kick and curse. Which was why he should sit.

With as much dignity as he could muster, he shoved the cherry lollipop into his cheek and lowered himself into the chair.

Graham pushed away from the doorjamb and disappeared back inside.

Gone to join the others now that he's made sure I'm not about to go on a murderous rampage, Hew thought as he sullenly sucked on the sugary treat and stared broodingly at the brick wall surrounding the property's edge. It was ten feet tall and topped by razor wire. A veritable fortress in the middle of the city.

Beyond the wall, he could hear the *roar* of a water taxi as it transported people upriver. Somewhere across the way, a hotel bellhop whistled for a cab. And farther down the river, a jackhammer worked tirelessly, tearing up concrete.

How weird was it that the world outside continued to turn when *his* world had stopped on a dime the moment that ransom call came in?

"Hydrate, brother." Hew looked up to see Graham holding out a cold bottle of water. Condensation had already beaded on the plastic. "Throwin' a hissy fit with a tail on it is thirsty work."

"Christ." Hew shoved a hand through his hair. "What an asshole I turned out to be."

"Nah." Graham pulled a chair up beside him and lowered his bulk into it. "You're just an operator on the edge. That's normal. Guys in our line of work usually end up bein' homicidal or suicidal at some point. I'm just happy you're the former and not the latter."

It was said lightly. But something told Hew it was anything but.

He studied his friend and teammate carefully. Graham Coleburn had always been a closed book, the guy in the corner who preferred to squint and scowl and crack an off-color joke rather than bare his soul.

Now, Hew wondered if all those flippant remarks and taciturn looks hid a deeper melancholia.

"Which are you?" he asked as he pulled out the sucker and swished a glug of water through his teeth and over his tongue. He spat it on the flagstone next to his chair and then poured half of what was left in the bottle over his face.

Good thing I don't have a mirror, he thought, shoving the sucker back into his mouth. *I don't think I'd like to see the thing starin' back at me.*

The façade on the unflappable, ever-composed helicopter pilot had cracked wide open to reveal who he was at his core. A man capable of savagery. Ruthlessness. *Barbarism.*

"I've been homicidal since I was eighteen," Graham admitted with a laconic shrug. "Why d'ya think I became a SEAL?"

"The dress whites." Hew forced a little levity into the conversation, as much for his own sake as for Graham's. "Figured ya liked the look of ice cream man chic."

"That's just a bonus." Graham grinned and then joined Hew in staring out at the brick wall.

"I've seen ya worried before," Graham observed after a little while. "Seen ya troubled and tormented. But I've never seen you like this." He slid a glance Hew's way. "*Beat the flesh off their skulls?*"

Hew closed his eyes. He *had* said that, hadn't he? And more, he'd *meant* it.

"Not that you've ever shied away from doin' what needs doin' to keep yourself and those of us who go into battle with ya safe from all comers," Graham clarified. "But violence is usually your *last* instinct, not your first."

Hew nodded. "I've tried to keep that side of myself in check." He used his tongue to shove the sucker to his opposite cheek. "But I have it in me, just like any other man. Right now, it's slipped its leash and is roarin' so loud I can barely hear my own thoughts. Those fuckers who took Sabrina? I want their heads on a platter, Graham. And I know that has nothin' to do with justice and everything to do with vengeance, but I don't give a rat's ass."

Graham had nothing to add to that, so they once more lapsed into silence.

When the slightest breeze wafted by, it cooled Hew's head enough for him to add, "I'm grateful to Kerberos. But I also want to reach down their throats and pull out their lungs because they didn't give us more."

"They did drop a whole lot of nothin' in our laps, didn't they?" Graham's expression was less than pleased.

"A big ol' steamin' pile of it," Hew declared. Then, he added, "She's out there because of us." The words stuck in his throat like they came with barbs. "Because someone wants to…what? Kill us? Expose us?"

Graham didn't sugarcoat his answer. "Maybe both."

"Well, fuck 'em for draggin' her into it." Hew had to swallow the vitriol that burned the back of his throat like battery acid. "She's innocent."

"That she is." Graham agreed.

And since there was nothing left to say on the subject, Hew drank the last of his water, crunched the last of the sucker, and shoved the stick into the empty bottle before twisting the cap shut.

"You love her, don't ya?"

The question, spoken so casually, punched Hew in the gut. He recovered quickly. Or, at least, he *thought* he did. But his voice still sounded a little hoarse when he answered. "Ayuh. Like I love all you dumb pissahs. You're family. And that's no small thing for a guy like me."

Graham lifted an eyebrow. "Sure that's all there is to it?"

No. Hew wasn't sure. But…

"Doesn't matter." He waved a dismissive hand. "She's with someone else."

And that *pang* in his chest when he thought of her with Martin? He ignored it.

"I want her to be happy," he added simply. Because it was the truth. "And if the Munchkin makes her happy, then he's my favorite person in the world."

He expected Graham to call bullshit on that last statement. So he was a little relieved when the former SEAL said only, "We'll get her back. And then we'll find out who's out to get us."

Hew nodded, although his optimism was hovering somewhere between rock bottom and the pits of hell. "Because the good guys always win in the end."

Graham's bearded chin jerked back. "Do they?"

"That's how it works in all the books."

Graham rolled his eyes. "Too much reading has rotted your brain."

Hew felt the corner of his mouth curl for the first time since he woke up to find Sabrina missing. "Because bein' well-read has *always* led to brain-rot and never to enlightenment."

That was one of the first things he and Sabrina had bonded over…their love of libraries.

He'd loved them because they'd given him a quiet respite from the horrors of his childhood. When things had gotten too bad in his foster homes or group homes, he could always run downtown to the library and escape into the stacks. *Plus, a library card is free.*

She had loved them because she'd used her local library's internet to surf the web, to peruse the social media accounts of celebrities and influencers and dream of a life different from the down-and-out one she'd been born into.

The more he'd gotten to know her, the more he'd come to believe she embodied the best of the heroines in the novels he'd grown up reading. She had Jane Eyre's principles and passion, Elizabeth Bennett's wit and intelligence, and Jo March's courage.

Sabrina Greenlee…

Even her name belonged in a book. So lyrical and light-sounding. Like church bells ringing or song birds singing.

Sometimes, late at night, alone in his room, he would whisper those five syllables just because he liked the feel of them on his tongue. The sound of them hanging in the darkness.

Sabrina Greenlee…

Graham stood and slapped a hand on his shoulder. "I'm headin' back in to see what's what. Ya comin'?"

"Nah." Hew shook his head. "Think I'll stay here for a bit longer."

"Can't imagine why you'd wanna. It's hotter than two rabbits screwin' inside a wool sock."

"You have to stop hidin' your light under a bushel, Graham. A poet laureate, ya are."

The former SEAL chuckled before disappearing inside, and Hew was left to his swirling thoughts, complicated emotions, and the memory of the last conversation he'd had with Sabrina before leaving for Africa.

Eliza had volunteered them for cleanup duty after dinner. They'd been standing side by side at the sink, Sabrina scrubbing dishes while he carefully fitted them into the dishwasher with Tetris-level precision.

There had been an odd tension in the air. He'd known the cause…

"I won't tell you not to worry," he said quietly, stacking two dripping plates into the bottom basket. *"I worry anytime we walk out the front door. Worryin' is natural. But we'll be back."*

Her throat worked over a swallow. "I'm not sure why this time feels different. Y'all have been running missions since the day I arrived. I should be used to it by now. But I…" She shook her head and sent him a sheepish glance. "I know you now. Like, really know you."

He noticed how she'd switched from the plural to the singular. Had she intentionally gone from talking about the Knights in general to him in particular?

And why did the thought of that make his heart skip a beat?

"Oh, yeah? What is it you think ya know about me?"

She smiled that Sabrina smile. So big and wide he couldn't help grinning in return. "I know your favorite comfort food is a whoopie pie."

"Ayuh. And it's not escaped my notice that everyone here needs schoolin' on the joys of chocolate cake and marshmallow cream."

She went on as if he hadn't spoken. "I know your favorite holiday is the Fourth of July."

True. Christmas had always been hit and miss. Sometimes his foster folks had remembered to fill a stocking for him. Sometimes they hadn't. The same could be said for Easter. Sometimes he'd awoken to a basket of sweet treats hidden inside plastic eggs. Most times, he hadn't.

The Fourth of July had been the only holiday he'd been able to depend on. The city celebrated with fireworks displays, and it didn't matter which house or shelter he'd lived in at the time, he could always walk to the beach and watch the rockets burst over the ocean.

"And I know your first memory is of being too cold because your foster father made you sleep in an unfinished basement in the middle of a terrible Maine winter."

This last part, she said sadly. And he was reminded of the rainy afternoon they'd spent together in the TV room.

The crew had gone to a motorcycle show on Navy Pier. But since the feds hadn't yet given the all-clear concerning the Charleston cartel, Hew had volunteered to skip the event and stay home with Sabrina.

It'd been the best afternoon of his life. So quiet and restful. They'd eaten ice cream on opposite ends of the couch and talked and talked and talked *without seeming to run out of subjects.*

Truly, he'd never talked with anyone as much as he'd talked with Sabrina that day.

"And your favorite holiday is Halloween," he said quietly, proving he knew her as much as she knew him. "You and Cooper always trick-or-treated together."

She smiled softly. "Coop was great at coming up with cheap costumes. He could make a toga from an old bedsheet and a witch's hat out of papier-mâché."

"Your favorite comfort food is chicken and waffles 'cause it's what the lady who ran the diner down the street fed you when your parents forgot to bring home groceries," he added. "And your first memory is fallin' out of the tree in your backyard and breakin' your arm. Cooper rode ya to the hospital on the handlebars of his bicycle."

He watched her rake in a deep breath before she shook her head. "We're a pair, aren't we? The poster children for how kids shouldn't be raised."

They were a pair, he mused now.

They'd always *been* a pair.

Copacetic from the jump because they knew what it was to carry the scars from childhood that lived under the skin and couldn't be scraped away.

Suffering recognized suffering.

Like recognized like.

Two storm-beaten ships who'd found safe harbor with each other.

That thought had a flicker of a smile tugging at his lips, but it didn't last. Not when the weight of what was to come in the next handful of hours sat so heavily on his heart.

CHAPTER 12

Location Unknown

Sabrina had never known the sheer agony of thirst.

Sure, she'd been dehydrated. Parched even. But this…

This was something else entirely.

Her need for water had started out in the usual way. A thick tongue that stuck to the roof of her mouth. Dry lips that cracked and threatened to split. A throat that felt raw and hot, like it was sunburned from the inside.

But as the day had dragged on, and afternoon gave way to evening, her need for hydration had gone from discomfort to a clawing torment. She no longer knew if her head pounded from the drug or from her body's slow breakdown as her cells shriveled up like dry sponges.

Despite the heat inside the old building, she was no longer sweating. Her body hoarded the last of its water reserves. Her heart fluttered as it worked to maintain her blood volume. And her brain had been hijacked, her attention narrowed to a single, unrelenting desire.

Water.

Cold Water.

Warm water.

Dirty water.

Any *water.*

She lifted her chin from her chest and stared out the broken windows to the east.

She had no idea how long she'd been unconscious after her wreck or where her captors had taken her. But if they'd brought her back to Chicago, Lake Michigan was somewhere out there. Lake Michigan, with its sixteen thousand miles of shoreline and millions of megaliters of cool, crisp water.

She could drink it all. Just open her mouth and swallow and swallow and swallow until the whole thing was empty and she was filled up.

Drip. Drip. Drip.

Remnants of rainwater falling in through the sagging roof taunted her.

Glug. Glug. Glug.

The vile, violent-eyed Diesel seemed to know her need and took pleasure in tormenting her by drinking loudly from a bottle before pouring what was left of the life-sustaining liquid over the top of his head.

She nearly opened her mouth to beg for a sip. But what few synapses she still had that weren't desiccated to dust reminded her it wasn't time.

Not yet.

Her hands weren't free.

She *needed* her hands free if she had any hope of following through on her plan to take one of these sonsofbitches out.

Dropping her chin back to her chest because she couldn't stand the prurient gleam in Diesel's eyes or the way Kurt wagged his tongue at her, she concentrated on her movements. Slowly, *slowly*, she used the glass shard she'd secreted between her palms to saw at the thick, plastic zip tie binding her wrists.

It was awkward. The edges of the glass were hard to hold onto without slicing her own fingers off. The angle she had to use was far from ideal. And she needed to be ever-so-mindful of keeping her elbows and shoulders from moving too much lest she alert her captors to what she was up to.

She searched for a memory to distract herself from the tediousness of the task. Something absorbing. Something affecting. Something to make her forget where she was and what she was doing and the tearing misery of thirst.

North Avenue Beach, three months ago…

"Let's walk down to the water," Hew said after removing his helmet and raking a hand back through his thick, unruly hair.

His accent curled around the words, missing Rs and all, and had her smiling.

She mirrored his movements, shaking her hair free of the helmet and turning her face into the cool breeze wafting in off the lake.

Spring had sprung with a vengeance, thawing the ice flows in the water, turning the city parks emerald green, and reminding her that, despite everything, despite all she'd lost and mourned over the previous cold, bleak months, life did go on.

Snow melted. Flowers bloomed. Hearts and minds and bodies healed.

When Hew had suggested they take advantage of the beautiful weather, she'd jumped at the chance to climb onto the back of Freedom.

She'd spent months staring longingly at the rows of gleaming custom motorcycles. Marveling at the intricacy of their designs and the power of their V-twin motors. Longing for the day she might know what it was to ride one.

Er…ride on the *back* of one.

She didn't have a motorcycle license. And the thought of getting one sent her into an anxiety spiral because…seriously? Why did each appendage have a different job?

When she'd expressed an interest in learning to ride, Hew had patiently explained how her right hand was responsible for the throttle and the front brake, her left hand took care of the clutch and sometimes the turn signals, her right foot operated the rear brake while her left foot was in charge of shifting gears.

"Wicked wild, right?" *he'd said with a knowing smirk.* "Like tryin' to pat your head, rub your belly, and recite the alphabet backwards. All while doin' sixty miles per hour. But don't worry. Practice makes perfect, and muscle memory eventually takes over."

Yeah. No, thank you, *she had decided then and there.* I'll just be a passenger princess.

And honestly, now that she'd done it, she could say with certainty that being a passenger princess was where it was at.

She could enjoy the view. Feel the powerful machine roaring beneath her without worrying about controlling it. And hang on to the big, broad-shouldered man in front of her.

He pulled a blanket from the compartment on the back of the bike. After walking with her down to the beach, he spread it on the sand near where the water lapped lazily at the shore.

They lay on their backs, hands behind their heads, to watch white, fluffy clouds morph into familiar shapes against a postcard-worthy blue sky.

It was the perfect day.

She was free from the danger that had stalked her. Free from the worst of the crushing weight of her grief.

With Hew's help, her emotional scales were no longer tipped constantly toward despair. She would miss Cooper each and every day, but missing him was no longer all she did. And piece by piece, the walls she'd built around herself after her assault were starting to come down.

She was starting to feel like herself again.

Freedom…

Such a simple word. Only two syllables. But it was packed with power.

Freedom…the name Hew had given to his motorcycle.

She looked at it now, parked just beyond the tree line. A crowd had gathered to gawk, and no wonder. With its blue-gray paint job, hand-tooled leather seat, and gleaming chrome pipes, the bike was a work of art.

Freedom…because that's what it meant to him. Freedom from his past. Freedom to build something that was wholly, uniquely his. Freedom to take off whenever the open road called.

She turned back to him now, shading her eyes against the sun. He had the most beautiful profile. Sharp and masculine. A face hewn from granite.

"You've never said much about your folks," she remarked quietly. "Do you know anything about them aside from how they died?"

The muscle in his jaw flexed beneath the cover of his well-trimmed beard. For a moment, she thought he wouldn't answer. Thought she'd finally hit on the one subject he wouldn't touch.

Then he said, "They were high school sweethearts. Supposed to get married after graduation, but they never got that far."

"So young." She shook her head. "Too young to be taken like that."

He'd told her they'd been gunned down in a mass shooting at a music festival. But he hadn't elaborated beyond that.

"Mom was eight and a half months pregnant with me when it happened. Accordin' to the police reports I read after I was old enough to go lookin', seems like she was one of the last ones shot. Which I reckon is how I'm here with ya now. When the paramedics arrived on the scene, my mom was gone, but they could still hear my heartbeat."

She wasn't sure what she'd expected him to say, but it wasn't that.

Yes, she'd known he'd lost his teenage parents when he was very young. But she hadn't realized he'd lost them while he was still in the womb!

Jesus!

Tentatively, she reached for his hand. When he squeezed her fingers, she bit her lip to keep from sobbing at all the tragedy he'd suffered before he'd ever breathed his first lungful of air.

"My father's body was found over hers," he said quietly. "Guess he tried to shield her. Didn't work, though. She'd already been hit. Paramedics cut me out of her in the back of the ambulance."

Sabrina's breath caught, sharp and jagged. Horror bled into heartbreak until her chest ached with both of them.

She could see it all so clearly. The terrified girl. The dying boy shielding her and their unborn child. The carnage and the mud and the blood.

It took everything she had not to weep. For the young mother who never got to hold her child. For the brave father whose last act had been one of sacrifice and love. For the baby boy who'd entered the world already steeped in loss.

She should say something. But what?

It was all too cruel. Too much. Too awful for words.

"I'm so sorry, Hew," she whispered, because it was all she had.

"Don't be. You weren't the one on a roof bangin' on a long gun and takin' out a bunch of kids just tryin' to have some fun."

"I'm sorry for the world," she clarified, her voice trembling right along with her chin. "Sorry it lets monsters run loose. Sorry it treats orphaned kids like afterthoughts. Sorry for every hug you never got. Every Christmas you spent alone. Every birthday nobody remembered."

"Even kids with parents go without," he murmured, turning to bring his face within inches of hers. His breath smelled of spearmint and sunshine. "You did."

She closed her eyes.

It was true. Her parents had been more interested in getting drunk and high with their other deadbeat friends than raising kids. But she'd had Cooper. And Diana at the diner. And various neighbors who had ensured she had hand-me-downs to wear to school and haircuts when her ponytails got too heavy.

He'd had no one.

"How did you do it?" she asked, gently pulling off his sunglasses to see his eyes.

His expressions tended toward stoicism. But there was always a world of feeling in his eyes.

"Do what?"

"Turn out so…good. Most kids who grow up like you did end up behind bars or"—she had to stop and swallow—"worse."

"Dunno." He shrugged with his eyebrows. "Guess I just don't have the heart for crime."

It was more than that, though. So much more.

Where others offered judgment, Hew offered grace. Where others gave up, he stood firm.

He didn't deny the dark side of life. He'd lived it. Been born in it. Been raised in it.

And still…still he'd chosen the light.

He was…incandescent, she supposed was the word. And she'd spent months warming her frozen soul beside his glow. Looking for it when she felt herself getting lost in the deep black shadows of her own trauma and grief.

Now, she swallowed thickly and turned back to the fluffy white clouds. She couldn't continue to look at him, to see all the hurt and the horror that hid in the shadows of his eyes. It hurt her too much, and she knew he'd stop and comfort her if he understood how close she was to breaking down into a ball of tears and chest-heaving sobs.

And this wasn't about her.

It was about him.

"Didn't you have grandparents who could raise you?" she asked, hoping he couldn't hear the huskiness in her voice as she battled the lump in her throat.

"Ayuh." His accent deepened. "Mom's folks took me in at first. But my gramps died of an aneurysm when I was about eighteen months old. Gran followed not long after of a broken heart."

She slid him a quick look and caught one corner of his mouth twitching.

"At least that's how my five-year-old self remembers the story my social worker told me when I asked her," he explained. "I suspect the truth is, Gran died of a heart attack."

So much death. So much upheaval before he'd even been old enough to learn his ABCs.

"I wish I remembered them." He sighed. "I have some stuff I found online. Obits from the newspapers and such. And about ten years back, I called my *parents' old high school. Asked to have a copy of their senior yearbook shipped my way. I love lookin' at their pictures. They were nothin' but babies themselves. Far too young to be bringin' a baby into the world. But, even still, I like to think I was made in love."*

"You were," she assured him. "Your mother kept you despite her tender age, and your father was found shielding her in the end. That tells me everything I need to know about them. They loved each other, and they wanted you."

It sounded sticky when he swallowed. "I took a lot of comfort in that when I was a kid."

She suspected he took a lot of comfort in that still. But she didn't say as much.

Instead, she asked, "What about your dad's parents? Why didn't they take you in after your mom's folks died?"

"My dad's ma couldn't handle the loss of him, apparently. Went to the grave six months after buryin' her baby boy. His dad hit the bottle hard after losin' both of 'em. Wasn't fit to take in a puppy, never mind a toddler."

"Jesus," she whispered.

"Not exactly a Shakespearean comedy, huh?"

"What were their names? Your parents, I mean."

"He was Thomas Birch. And she was Natasha Smith. Although the yearbook lists them as Tommy and Tasha."

"Tommy and Tasha," she repeated reverently. Together they'd made the most beautiful man she'd ever known. "Will you show me their pictures when we get home?"

"Ayuh. If ya want me to."

"I want you to."

And he had. He'd pulled the yearbook down from the shelf in his closet and opened it to pages that had yellowed around the edges from where he'd run his fingers over them.

Tommy and Tasha had both been gorgeous.

Hew had inherited his mother's auburn hair and his father's square jaw. But more than that, he'd inherited their light.

The teenagers had seemed to shine from the pages of the yearbook. And not just with the glow of youth, but with the brightness of something deeper. Something more fundamental and—

Hallelujah!

She snapped out of the memory when she felt the zip tie give way under the relentless pressure from the glass shard's edge. Every part of her wanted to stretch out the tension in her muscles and joints. Keeping her arms behind her back took all the self-control she possessed.

She knew the zip tie lay somewhere on the floor behind her. But didn't dare look. Didn't dare move.

She couldn't draw attention to herself until it was time. Until she was ready.

Shifting her weight ever so slightly, she winced when the chair creaked. But lifting her chin a little and cracking open one eye showed her captors paid her no mind.

They were having some sort of discussion at the far end of the room. The men were gathered around Black Widow, their faces rapt as they hung on her every word.

Neck or eyes? She thought as adrenaline tried to pulse through her sluggish veins. *Neck or eyes?*

If she went for the eyes, she imagined screams, blindness, chaos. Maybe her captors would panic. Maybe they'd rush her victim to the hospital and reduce their number.

One less gun for the Black Knights to contend with when they get here.

They'd come. She knew they would.

She wished they wouldn't. She wished they'd stay safe and sound inside the high brick walls of the compound.

But they'd come.

Because they were family. Because they considered *her* family.

The jugular, she thought, and imagined stabbing one of the men in the throat. Imagined the shock in his eyes. But no scream. Just gurgles followed by collapse and a pool of blood.

That *too* would deplete the number of her enemies by one.

But her arms felt like they were lined with lead, and her shoulders ached something fierce from the hours she'd spent restrained. She had no strength. Little stamina. And only a small chance she'd actually hit what she was aiming for with enough force to do any real damage.

Still, it was a chance worth taking.

Anything she could do to help her situation, to help the Black Knights, was worth the effort. Even if it came at the cost of her soul.

Uncertainty suddenly gripped her.

Can I do this? Can I take a life?

Guess I'll find out, she thought determinedly.

All this was happening because she'd been dumb enough to hop in her car despite the late hour, despite the rain. Because she'd been so caught up in her own tangled thoughts that she hadn't recognized she had a tail.

It was her duty to level the playing field if she could. She *would* level the playing field.

Which one will answer my call? Which one will come to me, thinking I'm beaten and broken? she wondered as she counted her ragged heartbeats.

Her thumb brushed against the jagged shard. Touching. Testing. Tensing.

Holding her breath, she waited for the perfect opportunity to make her move.

CHAPTER 13

Vivian hated the heat that pressed down on her inside the rusted-out skeleton of the old bottling plant. She hated the dust that hung thick in the air and scraped at her lungs whenever she dragged in a breath. But, most of all, she hated the dread running beneath her skin until her whole body buzzed.

Bishop.

Their current employer was due to call any minute, and she couldn't wait to be done with the whole damn conversation. The whole damn *operation.*

It wasn't just the mechanical pitch of his altered voice that set her teeth on edge. It was the unspoken warning behind every word he said.

Do this for me, or else.

Vivian didn't believe in god. Heaven and hell were myths made up by rich men who hoped to keep the peasants from revolting. But every time she spoke to Bishop, she couldn't shake the sense that she was talking to someone or some*thing* too powerful for its own good.

Creepy bastard.

She'd tried to take the edge off her garrote-tight nerves in the usual way—flat on her back with Hummer between her thighs. And to his credit, he'd delivered. *Twice.* But the warm glow of release had already burned off, and the crawling rawness was back in her blood.

If there hadn't been so many zeros in the amount Bishop had agreed to pay them, she might have passed on the job. She'd learned long ago to trust her instincts when it came to contracts, and her instincts told her Bishop—and everything he stood for—was bad news.

But her crew would've strung her up by her toenails if she'd waved toodle-oo to ten million dollars.

Ten million on top of ten million, she silently corrected. Because Bishop had promised that if the Knights came through with the ransom, she and her boys were welcome to keep it.

"You think he wants them all dead?" Kurt said, sounding like he always did. Like someone had shoved a wad of gauze up his nose. "Or just the hostage?" His face showed disappointment that this last thing might be an option.

Kurt was a bloodthirsty little fucker. Which was usually a boon to the work they did.

But maybe not today.

"Bishop is paying us a pretty penny to do exactly as he says." She swiped a bead of sweat from her temple and flicked it off her fingertips. It hit the floor at her feet, leaving a dark circle on the concrete. "If he says we only body the hostage, then we only body the hostage."

That's *another* thing that bothered Vivian. Bishop hadn't exactly been magnanimous when sharing the details of this op.

All he'd said when he'd hired her was, *"Take one of the women. Hold her for ransom. I'll provide next steps after that's done."*

And when she'd asked if they needed to protect their identities, if his intention was that they release the hostage once the transaction was complete, his exact words were, *"That seems like too much trouble. Killing her is easier."*

So cold. So careless.

Most of the time, Vivian considered those to be positive attributes. But, with Bishop, she had to wonder—

"Back up." Diesel elbowed Hummer. "You smell like dirty sex, and it's making my dick hard."

Instead of retreating, Hummer grinned. "Jealous?"

"No." Diesel flicked a hot, calculating glance at Vivian. "She can't handle me. She's admitted it."

She knew the only things keeping Diesel from doing to her what he did to the other women were his fear of losing the paychecks she brought him and his certainty she'd kill him graveyard dead should he ever try to slip something into her drink.

Because he expected it, because they *all* did, she gave him one of her lethal smiles. All teeth. No feeling.

"Oh, I could handle you," she purred. "I just like being fully conscious when I fuck someone. It's more fun for me that way."

"Your loss." Diesel shrugged his gargantuan shoulders.

"So you keep telling me."

She checked her watch and pulled the burner phone from her hip pocket.

Soon, she'd hear that eerie voice. Soon, she'd receive her final instructions. Soon, there'd be nothing left to do but the doing.

She was ready.

She was *past* ready and—

"I'm hungry," Vance declared, cutting into her thoughts. "And it's still hours before the drop. I saw a Wendy's three blocks back. I'll make a run."

Vance. Cool-headed. Steady. The only one of them she never had to ride roughshod over.

She'd fucked him once. But she'd been too drunk to really remember much about the experience. And he'd never indicated he wanted a repeat of it.

That pricked at her pride. But only a little.

"Walk it," she instructed and watched annoyance flicker across his face. "I know it's hot as hell, but Bishop says the Knights have access to the city's CCTV grid. If they were able to retrace her route as she was leaving the city"—she tipped her chin toward the bound woman—"then they might've zeroed in on us tracking her and have eyes out for the van. It stays parked where it is until this thing is done."

The rest of the group easily rattled off their orders—baconator this, frosty that—and Vance took it all in without writing it down. After he sauntered through the bottling plant's massive steel door, blond hair catching a shaft of light on his way, Vivian returned her attention to the seconds ticking by and the unease growing inside her.

The waiting was always the worst.

Diesel went back to the weapons and gear spread across the table; he liked the feel of steel in his hands. Hummer ambled over to the case of bottled water stashed by the wall. And Kurt strolled purposefully toward their captive.

Because of course he did. He never missed an opportunity to torment.

Vivian didn't know if Kurt had been born a bully or if he'd matured into one once he stopped growing and developed a Napoleon complex. Either way, he was a dickhead. A thorn in her side on a good day and a severe pain in her ass on a bad one. She'd have kicked him to the curb long ago if he hadn't been such a crackerjack shot.

Unfortunately for her, trained snipers—*talented* snipers—were few and far between.

Sighing heavily, she lifted her hair off the back of her sweaty neck. The heat inside the building was suffocating and—

"Water," their hostage croaked. She seemed to be shriveling into a human raisin right in front of their eyes. "Water. *Please.*"

"Water, please," Kurt mocked in an exaggerated falsetto.

"Cut it out, Kurt!" Vivian barked. She had little sympathy for Sabrina Greenlee. But she had less than zero patience for Kurt's bullshit. Especially today. Especially in the oppressive heat that made her brain feel like it was stuck inside a pressure cooker set to high. "Give her some fucking water."

"I got it." Hummer grabbed a second bottle from the pack and cracked the seal on the lid. He ambled toward their hostage in that slow, loose-hipped way of his.

Mark "Hummer" Keslar could be as ruthless as the rest of them. But he was capable of humanity when it counted.

She figured his humanity was what led him to dive headfirst into the bottle when they weren't on the job. He was human enough to be haunted by what he did. By what *they* did.

She didn't quite understand that about him. But she liked it.

Opposites attract and whatnot, she thought. *Plus, he has that Coke bottle cock.*

She felt her phone jangle to life inside her hand before she actually heard it. She ignored how her pulse leapt as she answered with a crisp, "Yes?"

"Everything proceeding as expected?" came the warped, soulless voice.

Before she could respond, a screech pierced the factory's stagnant air like a hot blade through soft flesh. It was a harpy's scream. A wraith's wail. The kind of sound to lift the hairs on Vivian's arms.

Then Hummer bellowed. A raw, shocked roar that made Vivian's stomach bottom out.

The phone was still to her ear when her head snapped around. But she dropped it to the floor the instant she saw what was happening.

Hummer's hand clutched his throat as blood pumped hot and red between his fingers. The hostage was still in the chair, but her arms were free. A bloody smear marked her right hand like war paint, and her eyes were wide. Feral.

Vivian had been on assignment in Wyoming once and had come across a wolf with its paw caught in a trap. The blood on its muzzle had been thick and oozing, but that was nothing compared to the blood on the beast's mangled foot, where it'd been gnawing away its own flesh in a desperate bid to escape.

Freedom at any cost.

That had been the wolf then. That was Sabrina Greenlee now.

"No," Vivian breathed even as she bolted across the room.

Hummer was already on his knees when she reached him, and Diesel wrenched their hostage's arms back behind her back. But it was too late.

The damage was done.

Vibrant blood darkened the front of Hummer's shirt. It gushed between his fingers and spattered onto the concrete in thick, metallic-smelling drops.

So much blood.

Too much blood.

"Don't pull it out!" she screamed when his hand curled around the glass shard protruding from his neck.

But he'd already yanked before she could finish the sentence.

Now his throat gushed like a ruptured pipe. And the sound… *Jesus Christ!* That wet *ffitt-fffitt-ffffit.* It made her knees buckle.

"Hummer!" She slid an arm around his big shoulders, her other hand pressing down hard on his ruined neck. "Hummer," she repeated, trying not to think about the sticky heat running thick and wet between her fingers. "Hold still. I got you."

His eyes, dark and dazed, found hers. There was a question there. And more. There was…

Fear.

He was afraid because he knew. This was the end for him, and her cold, hard heart cracked. Just a little.

He opened his mouth, but it was only a wet-sounding wheeze that escaped, more blood than breath.

"Don't speak," she cooed, easing him down onto the floor, her soft tone at odds with the carnage blooming around her on the concrete like a macabre flower.

The human body held five liters of blood. Hummer had already lost one. And he was losing more with every tick of the clock. Every beat of his heart.

She could lie, tell him it was okay, that *he* would be okay. But she'd never pulled her punches with her men. She wasn't about to start doing so now.

"You've seen enough death to know what's coming." Her voice sounded hoarse before she swallowed and smoothed it out. "It comes for all of us. It'll come for me soon enough. It's nothing to be scared of."

His nostrils flared wide. A single tear slipped from the corner of his eye. Then, he gave a shallow nod and covered the hand she pressed over his throat.

He didn't drop her gaze.

He didn't try to speak again.

He simply accepted, waited, and willed himself to be brave until the last moment.

She didn't know how long they stayed like that. It could've been the span of a heartbeat or the long trudge of an eternity. But, eventually, his pale lips parted on a breathless gasp, and his hand fell away from hers to lie palm-up in the ever-expanding pool of his own blood.

Gently removing her hand from his neck, she watched as the wound pulsed once. Twice. Three times. Then fizzled.

Death rattled his chest.

Muscle spasms rippled through his body as nerves fired for a final time.

His skin blanched before her eyes when the last drops of his life drained from it.

And then…it was done.

Mark "Hummer" Kesslar was dead.

For long moments, she stared down into the rugged face she'd stared up at so recently. The face that had followed her through the last four years of assignments and anarchy.

He'd loved her.

He'd never said as much, but she knew.

She'd loved him, too. In her way. In as much as she was capable of it.

"Sweet dreams, Mark," she whispered, closing his sightless eyes and leaving behind bloody streaks on his eyelids.

Her chest felt tight. Tears burned the back of her nose. But there wasn't time for grief. There wasn't *room* for grief. Not when she was filled with fiery hot fury.

That fucking cunt!

Rising slowly, rubbing her sticky hands on her utility pants, she felt her heart beat with the terrible rhythm of a war drum. Felt the nuclear blast that blazed through her veins and burned away all reason.

Her nostrils flared, filled with the iron scent of Hummer's blood, as she turned and pinned her hate-filled eyes on the brunette.

Her holster was clipped to the waistband at the small of her back. She had her gun out before she made the conscious decision to move. A second later, the safety was off, and her finger was curved around the trigger.

She would have fired had Kurt not blurted, "Whoa there, Widow. We need her alive for the next check-in. Just in case the Black Knights ask for another proof of life."

Blood roared in Vivian's ears. And yet, there was a part of her that heard Kurt and knew he was right.

Her hand shook as she re-holstered her weapon. And when she blew out a slow, harsh breath, her vision expanded to include more than just the square inch of real estate in the center of Sabrina Greenlee's forehead.

"When the time comes to do her"—she nodded toward their hostage, her jaw working back and forth—"I get the honors."

Diesel and Kurt didn't respond. They didn't need to.

"Resecure her hands." Her voice was sharp with the cutting edge of her fury. "And don't feel like you have to be gentle about it."

Diesel didn't hesitate. He yanked a zip tie from his pocket and cinched it tight around their hostage's wrists. Vivian saw the relish in his expression. But the woman didn't flinch. Didn't hiss.

She just stared daggers at Vivian.

In another life, in another situation, Vivian might've admired her for her courage, her ingenuity.

But it was *this* life and *this* situation, and all Vivian felt for the woman was the need to mete out venomous revenge.

She *would* get her revenge.

And she promised herself it would be sweet.

When Diesel stepped back, Vivian stepped forward, hand up and open. Her palm cracked across the woman's cheek, and the sound of the slap was loud enough to echo around the cavernous space. Hard enough to have the chair rocking to the side on two legs before once more righting itself.

"Fuckin'-A," Kurt muttered.

The woman didn't make a sound as a red handprint bloomed on her cheek, half Hummer's blood, half burgeoning bruise. And her eyes? They were still fierce. Still defiant. Still burning with that maddening, unbreakable will.

Vivian grabbed her jaw and bent down until their noses nearly touched.

"I'm keeping you alive until the end," she hissed. "You'll watch them all die first. Smell their blood. Hear their screams. See their final, rattling breaths." She squeezed the woman's cheeks so hard the tendons in her hand ached. "And then I'll kill you. *Slowly.*"

Now fear flickered in Sabrina's eyes. But Vivian didn't feel vindicated.

She wouldn't feel anything until this woman screamed like Hummer had. Until she was broken and bloody and struggling to breathe through a crushed windpipe.

"Black Widow!" The tinny sound of her code name reached her ears. She glanced over her shoulder to where her burner lay on the floor.

Bishop.

Fuck.

Releasing the brunette with a shove, Vivian stalked back to the phone, careful to avoid the puddle of Hummer's blood as it spread out in an ever-widening circle around his cooling body.

"The bitch we grabbed stabbed one of my guys in the fucking jugular with a piece of broken glass," she snarled into the receiver. "So we're down one man."

Silence. Then, "Can you still get the job done?"

"As long as you tell me the job is to kill every last one of them," she spat.

"I don't care about the specifics." The mechanical voice was as cold and emotionless as ever. "Make enough of a mess that the authorities will investigate. The president has pushed her power too far with this group. It's time they, and *she*, are all brought into the light."

"It's done," Vivian promised, her heart a swirling mix of vengeance and violence.

CHAPTER 14

The place was humming.

Not with the sleepy, fluorescent whir of a typical after-hours office. Oh, no. It was the electric buzz of adrenaline running, nerves jumping, and gears turning. The kind of charge that raised goosebumps and warned: *something big is coming soon.*

A huge part of Lura wanted to stay. To see it through to the end. But she'd lingered as long as she dared.

Leonard Meadows had spent the afternoon sending her texts like, *Where did you put the latest report on Palestine?* Then he'd proceeded to spend most of the evening sending her gruff reminders—*yes, text messages can be gruff, especially when they come from the chief of staff*—that tomorrow was a big day, packed with morning meetings with the Joint Chiefs, a luncheon with the press secretary, and the state dinner honoring the prime minister of Japan.

His last text had flat-out demanded, *Come back, Lura.*

Got a seat on the red-eye, she'd hastily typed into her phone. *I'll be in the office at 7 A.M. Per usual.*

She'd waited for the three blinking dots to tell her he was typing a response. But to no one's surprise, they never appeared.

Leonard Meadows didn't show gratitude, even when he'd browbeaten someone into doing exactly what he wanted. *Especially* then.

She paused inside the big metal door that acted as the front entrance to the Black Knights's headquarters. *Blast proof?* she wondered absently as she checked her Uber app and saw her ride was still fifteen blocks away.

A quick search on her phone's traffic map assured her I-90 was clear to O'Hare. Unless the security line was three hours long, she should make her flight no problem and—

"Are you following me?" Sam Harwood turned to look over his shoulder. Graham was three feet behind him in the dark hallway leading from the motorcycle shop to the kitchen.

"No. I try to stay upwind of ya when I can," Graham rumbled in that slow, Southern drawl that reminded Lura of home.

She still dreamed in that accent.

Isn't that strange? she thought. *Or maybe not. Maybe people always dream in their native tongue. And mine is pure Southern Appalachia.*

"*Downwind* of ya, and I'm liable to choke on the smell of brimstone," Graham added.

Sam snorted. "If I'm the devil, what's that make you?"

"God's gift to women?" Graham spread his massive arms wide.

"Pfft." Sam shook his head. "All those growth hormones that flooded your system during puberty did something terrible to your head. It's twice as big as it should be. Too bad more of those same hormones didn't go to your dick, huh?"

Graham, completely nonplussed, threw back his head and laughed. "You know you're talkin' nothin' but shit. You've seen it."

Lura cleared her throat just as both men stepped out of the hallway. When they spotted her standing by the front door, Sam had the good grace to look guilty. But Graham?

He was as stony-eyed as ever.

Even as a teen, he'd had a poker face to impress Lady Gaga. But after his mother died, he might as well have been carved from granite for all the emotion he'd shown.

In the years since, he'd clearly perfected that mercilessly blank mask.

"Did you…uh…" Sam scratched his head. "Any chance you've gone temporarily deaf?"

Despite the seriousness of the situation, the gravity of the entire day, and the solemnity of what would happen next, Lura felt a laugh bubble in the back of her throat.

"I've come to two conclusions today," she told him. "One, you're some of the most impressive people I've met. And that's saying something since I work at the White House. And two," she finished with a tongue stuck in her cheek, "you like nothing better than to cast aspersions on the size of each other's dicks."

Again, Sam looked properly chagrined. "My sense of humor stalled out at age fourteen. What can I say?"

Before she could respond, he walked over and shook her hand. "Headed out?"

"Waiting on my Uber to pull up."

"Thanks for everything. We couldn't've done it without you."

"Something tells me you'd have found a way."

His grin said she wasn't wrong. "You did say we were some of the most impressive people you've ever met."

"And *you* think *he's* got a big head?" She hitched her chin toward Graham, who still hadn't moved from the mouth of the hallway.

"Don't judge me too harshly." Sam shook his head in mock sorrow. "A swollen ego's an occupational hazard."

She laughed as they said their goodbyes. Then, after Sam ambled away, she turned toward Graham.

He crossed the shop's floor with steps both confident and efficient. He'd changed into black tactical pants, which he'd tucked into a giant pair of scuffed combat boots. A snug, long-sleeve Henley accentuated a frame that hardly needed the help. And a sidearm was strapped to his thigh.

The man radiated casual menace.

Graham Coleburn, she thought. *He's gone and grown all the way up.*

When he stopped before her, his shadow spilled over her face.

At five feet eleven, she was used to meeting a man's eyes. But she had to tilt her chin back to meet Graham's implacable gaze.

Way back.

"Sorry we didn't get more time to catch up, Lura." His warm drawl hit her ear like a song she'd heard a million times and would never tire of.

"You've been busy." Her voice was softer than she meant it to be. "All of you have."

He ran a hand through his hair. It was still that same sun-streaked brown that she'd stared at longingly across the cafeteria.

"Understatement of the century." He grimaced. "But also, just another day at the office 'round these parts."

Since the Knights had returned with the money, and since Kerberos had delivered their cryptic message, Ozzie had cleaned up the recording of the ransom call. He'd focused on Sabrina's scream—how it had echoed, how it had rung—and had decided she was being held somewhere big, hollow, and empty.

A warehouse? A parking garage? A storage depot?

Then he'd picked up the distant sound of a train whistle, which had been enough to give the Black Knights something to chase.

Combining the midnight drop deadline with the promise of a phone call at eleven P.M., they'd determined Sabrina had to be within an hour's drive of the BKI compound.

Given all of that, the team had mobilized. Everyone had grabbed a screen, a map, or a laptop. They'd analyzed, scanned, and filtered until finally, after a few tense hours, they'd whittled down the options where Sabrina was being held to six possible locations.

"Six needles in a haystack full of nightmares," Hew had muttered, chewing the inside of his cheek and radiating fury as Ozzie queued up satellite surveillance on all six sites.

Then had come the prep. Weapons had been polished. Magazines had been loaded. Radios had been checked with a kind of ease that didn't belong in the middle of Chicago.

And what had she done through it all, you may ask?

Well, besides answering her boss's texts, she'd mostly stayed out of the way.

That and watched Graham Coleburn more than I'll ever admit to anyone.

"I'll admit," she told him now, "I was shocked to walk through that door and come face-to-face with someone from back home."

His eyes narrowed slightly. "Ya didn't know?"

"Leonard Meadows made it *very* clear I wasn't to go snooping around about this organization." She waved a hand to indicate the old factory building. "It already stuck in his craw that I found out you guys exist. It would have sent him into an apoplectic fit if I'd asked who worked here."

His eyes crinkled at the corners, weather-worn lines that showed the years that had passed and all the sunrises he'd squinted into since the last time she'd seen him. "That must've nearly killed ya, bein' such an inquisitive little thing."

Her eyebrows lifted. "I was nearly six feet by the tenth grade, Graham. I have *never* been little."

He looked her over slowly. Not in a crude way. In an appreciative way that made her stomach flip and her knees go wobbly.

"Always did like tall women." His voice was as soft and as hot as the sand on Tybee Island right before sunset.

Is he…flirting with me? she wondered, feeling fifteen all over again.

Is Clayton, Georgia's golden boy—the homecoming king himself—actually looking at me and seeing something he likes?

Before she could recover enough to fire back something flirty or clever—oh, who was she kidding? Her brain had short-circuited. She couldn't have come up with a pithy retort to save her life—he cleared his throat and stuck out a hand.

"Thank you, Lura." The teasing was gone from his tone. Now, it was all business. "For comin' all this way."

His hand was large and warm. She felt every rough edge of callus against her skin and had a fleeting thought of what it would be like to have those big, square hands skating over her body.

"Glad I could help." She quickly withdrew her fingers lest she actually swoon. "And I'm glad I got to see you again, Graham. I've thought about you a lot over the years."

His gaze sharpened. "Have ya now?"

"Sure." She tried to play it cool with a shrug. "I wondered what happened to you when you disappeared. Now, I know. Mystery solved."

His lips parted, and she held her breath, waiting for…what? What did she want him to say?

But then his attention flicked over her shoulder. "Your Uber's here." He nodded toward the television on the brick wall beside the door. It showed security footage of the front gate.

She glanced around to see a black SUV nosing to the curb next to the guardhouse. When she looked back at Graham, his implacable expression had fallen into place.

"Well," she cleared her throat. "You all be careful out there tonight."

His cheek muscles moved slightly. She supposed it was what passed for a smile. "Careful is my middle name," he said.

"Really?" She canted her head. "I seem to remember it being Alexander."

His eyebrows shot up.

Yes, I remember your middle name, she thought. *I remember everything about you.*

She turned before she could say anything else—anything foolish—opened the door, and stepped into the thick summer night. As the heavy metal shut behind her, a question curled like smoke inside her.

Is this the last time I'll ever set eyes on the legendary Graham Coleburn?

CHAPTER 15

"I think we need to install a Xanax salt lick for times like these," Fisher muttered to his fiancée.

Hew didn't need to look over his shoulder to know they were eyeing him as he paced back and forth across the length of the War Room.

He *had* tried to sit down. But every time he got quiet and still, his brain offered up increasingly horrific mental reels of what Sabrina might be enduring.

Had she been tied up? Beaten?

Was she bleeding? Broken?

Had her abductors left her alone in the dark somewhere with nothing but her fear to keep her company? Or, worse, were they *with* her? Tormenting her? *Abusing* her in ways he—

Stop it! He silently railed at himself. *You're not doin' her any good by imaginin' the worst.*

Pressing a hand to his chest, he tried to relieve the pressure there. It didn't help. His ribs felt too tight for his lungs.

He'd been in plenty of hairy situations. Had dropped friends behind enemy lines, flown into hot zones to pick up wounded brothers-in-arms, and dodged missiles and mortar fire with a chopper full of men depending on him to get them home in one piece. But this…this *waiting*, while

Sabrina was god-knows-where suffering god-knows-what, was worse than anything he could remember.

"Found her!" Ozzie crowed from his spot at the bank of computers.

Those two syllables were enough to lock up every muscle in Hew's body. Then, like they were spring-loaded, they launched him across the room.

"Where is she?" he demanded from behind Ozzie's chair. "Show me."

Around him, he could feel the rest of the Knights gathering. Graham, Sam, Hunter, Fisher. A wall of grim-faced warriors who'd do everything possible to get Sabrina back.

There should've been comfort in that. But there was nothing that could comfort Hew now except for her safe return.

Ozzie zoomed in on an image. Then, he zoomed in again. And again, until Hew was forced to bite his tongue and curl his fingers into fists lest he start yanking out Ozzie's mad-scientist hair by the roots because the man seemed not to grasp how short Hew's fuse was.

"Oz, man, what are we lookin' at?" he finally asked impatiently.

It was clear they were viewing real-time satellite footage, but it was grainy and grayscale thanks to the abysmal light of the moonless night.

"Pretty sure that's the van that followed Sabrina." Ozzie tapped the keyboard with rapid-fire precision, and the image came into sharper focus.

Hew's chin jerked back when he realized Ozzie had zeroed in on the bottom of a wheel. The vehicle it was attached to was parked atop a dirty concrete slab, and only part of its hubcap was visible beneath the drooping edge of a tarp.

Hope bled out of him like air from a punctured lung.

"That's it?" He managed to grit the two syllables from between his teeth. "That's all ya got?"

"I know, I know." Ozzie's fingers began another dance across the keyboard. "It doesn't look like much until you compare it to *this*."

Another image popped up on a split screen beside the first. It was the photo they'd captured off the CCTV cameras of Sabrina and her tail as she drove past the city's limits.

Ozzie zoomed in on the van's front wheel.

"Look." He pointed to a jagged white scratch that ran across the hubcap like a lightning bolt.

It matched the scratch on the hubcap in the satellite imagery.

"Damn good eye, Oz." Boss clapped a hand on Ozzie's shoulder.

"Where is it?" Hew demanded, his voice low and tight. "Where is she?"

"West of the city." Ozzie pulled up a wide-angle view of the site where the van was parked beneath the tarp. "It's that old bottling plant we pinpointed as a possible location. It's been abandoned since the seventies. Nothing much left of the place but busted brick, broken concrete, and a few outbuildings."

The eagle-eye view showed the bottling plant was a ghost of a building. Isolated. Forgotten. A perfect place to hide a hostage.

"Can we get infrared on the site?" Hew asked, feeling his nerve endings itch. It was like his skin struggled to contain the adrenaline ballooning inside him. "See if she's bein' held in the main building or one of the smaller ones? See how many unfriendlies we're dealin' with?"

"Not using *this* satellite." Ozzie shook his head. "We need to wait for a military eye-in-the-sky to swing back around." He checked his watch. "Another forty minutes, give or take."

Forty minutes.

It might as well have been forty *hours* the way time was creeping.

"Forty minutes it is," Graham chimed in. "In the meantime, we learn everything we can about that site. Entrances. Exits. We need blueprints, if they exist."

"I'll make the call for the bird." Hew was already turning, already moving. Finally, *finally* they had actionable intel, and he could stop twiddling his dick. "If we fly in fast, we can hit 'em before they know what's comin'."

He bolted up the stairs two at a time, his phone already in hand. The instant he hit the third floor, his thumb flew over the screen until he found the contact information for the private airport where the Black Knights housed their Black Hawk.

He was about to press the call button when his boots turned into cement galoshes outside Sabrina's open bedroom door. The small lamp atop her dresser glowed a soft yellow. But the quiet inside the room thundered louder than any battle zone he'd ever flown over.

A bright rug covered the floor, woven in a dizzying pattern of coral, teal, and sunflower yellow. Novels lined the shelves of the two low-slung bookcases she'd pushed under the windows. And the phone stand and ring light she used to film her social media posts sat beside the little armchair angled into the corner.

It was so *her*.

So vibrant. So thoughtful. So…*warm*.

Every square inch of the space carried her fingerprint, carried her fruity/floral smell. And the sudden, choking thought that she might never step foot inside—

That's not goin' to happen! he silently swore.

Motion flickered in his periphery. He turned his head sharply, his heart leaping—

But it wasn't Sabrina emerging from the mound of pillows atop her bed. Of course it wasn't. It was Peanut.

The cat's gray fur was rumpled. His big yellow eyes blinked up at Hew with feline reproach, seeming to say, *How could you let this happen? How could you let them take her?*

Hew's throat tightened around a knot.

"I know, buddy." He moved to crouch beside the bed. "But I'm goin' to bring her back. Just ya wait and see."

Peanut stepped toward the edge of the mattress, pressing his whiskered cheeks against Hew's knuckles. Hew buried his calloused fingertips in the soft fur, drawing comfort from the only thing in the room that still carried a hint of Sabrina's gentle warmth.

Then, he stood abruptly. Hit call. And listened as it rang and rang.

The airport's ground crew rarely worked in the office. They preferred spending their time in the hangars or in lawn chairs by the fueling truck. Eventually, however, a deep, familiar voice barked, "Lake Michigan Aviation."

"Larry," Hew said without preamble. "We need the chopper fueled and ready to fire up in forty minutes."

Larry Eastman didn't miss a beat. "I can have her good to go in thirty."

"Even better."

Hew moved with purpose then, trotting into his own room.

It didn't smell nearly as nice as Sabrina's.

Unless you think gun oil, leather, and Downy dryer sheets make a good combo.

Crossing to his dresser, he snatched up the ridiculous lobster plushie beside his dopp kit. It was red, soft, and stuffed with buttery-smelling cotton.

A gag gift from the team.

A wink at his Maine roots.

Sabrina's go-to when she needed comfort.

She liked to rub the claws like worry beads, and he'd tried to gift it to her. But she'd refused. Saying it gave her an excuse to visit him.

As if she *ever* needed an excuse.

Clutching the stuffed lobster until his knuckles blanched white, he stared at the silly thing and silently promised, *I'm comin', Sabrina. And heaven help the bastards who took ya, 'cause I'm bringin' hell with me.*

CHAPTER 16

Old bottling plant west of the city

Gone was the adrenaline-charged clarity that had sharpened Sabrina's mind when she lunged for Hummer's throat. Now, only clawing thirst, relentless fatigue, and the stink of death remained.

The big man's body lay at her feet, spread out like a slab of discarded meat at a butcher shop. His blood was already turning dark and gelatinous as it congealed atop the cracked concrete. And flies drifted in lazy spirals above him, drawn by the sharp tang of rot.

He hadn't been dead that long. Only a few hours. So why was he already starting to stink?

But she knew why. The heat inside the old building pressed down like a second skin. The ancient bricks held onto humidity the way old bones held onto pain. And the thin veil between what animated a human body and what made it nothing more than a pile of flesh and bone for the maggots and the carrion beetles didn't stand a chance against those elements.

She turned her head away and tried to breathe through her mouth. But that was worse. The air tasted like rust and mildew mixed with the fetid, coppery echo of a life extinguished.

She'd taken a life.

And it didn't matter that he'd have happily killed her. It didn't matter that any right-minded person would say, in a situation like this, it was self-defense. What mattered was that she'd aimed, shoved the shard deep, and then twisted slightly to ensure she did as much damage as possible.

What mattered was that she'd live the rest of her life with the memories of how hot his blood had been when it spilled over her hand. How he'd staggered and bellowed and fallen to his knees. How his throat had gurgled, how his lungs had rattled, how his boots had scrabbled against the concrete as his body fought to hold on to the last vestiges of life.

She squeezed her eyes shut to block out the sight of the dead man. But behind her lids, the image only sharpened. Dark, bloody pool. Pale, mottled skin. *Flies.*

She'd have to ask Hew how he did it. How he went on living after knowing he'd been the end of someone else and—

What am I thinking?

I won't need to ask Hew how he goes on living because I *won't go on liv—*

"Take your rifle and get to our prearranged spot," Black Widow's voice, oddly crisp and cold compared to the stifling air, cut into Sabrina's thoughts.

Her eyes flew open, and she found the platinum blonde at the far end of the room. Night had fallen some time ago. Now, the only lights inside the space came from the two kerosene lanterns Diesel had lit.

One burned on the table of weapons. The other burned by the entrance to the old office space. They both caused long, trembling shadows to writhe across the cracked floor, crumbling walls, and Hummer's body until it looked like the man's restless spirit had stuck around to haunt the place.

"And Vance?" Black Widow barely turned her head toward the man standing at the table full of weapons, arming himself to the teeth. "You sure we sealed everything off? These guys were trained by the best of the best Uncle Sam has to offer. If they can find a back door, they'll use it."

"After you make the call, they won't have time to do much more than a preliminary examination of the site," Vance replied, tightening straps on his tactical vest. "That's why we planned it this way. But even if they had all day to do recon, there's only one way in thanks to those old derelict shipping containers we stacked out front."

He jabbed a thumb toward the metal cargo door that groaned on its rusting tracks anytime the wind blew. It was frozen open halfway, like it'd been caught mid-scream.

"Once they drop the cash with you," Vance continued, "they'll head out the way they came in. And that's when we'll light 'em up. Like shooting fish in a barrel."

"It's never that easy," Black Widow muttered.

"Kurt'll take care of any Diesel and I miss. What our boy lacks in height, he makes up for in marksmanship."

Sabrina's stomach churned. Her thirst, her exhaustion, the dried blood caking her fingers…all forgotten as she listened to the plan.

One by one, they were going to pick off her friends. Her family. The people who were willing to risk everything to bring her home.

The Black Knights would be forced into a gauntlet of bullets and betrayal, and she couldn't stand the thought of it. Couldn't stand the thought of being the reason—

"What if they don't have the money?" Kurt asked as he shouldered a wildly evil-looking weapon with a scope that belonged on a *National Geographic* photographer's camera.

"Then I tell them to bring what they can and come anyway," Black Widow explained. Her pale skin looked luminous in the faint, flickering light of the nearest lantern.

Sabrina studied the woman across the expanse, thinking she was elegant in the way vipers were elegant. Then, she turned away when a fly landed on Hummer's face, crawled across his cracked lips, and disappeared inside his open mouth.

Why hadn't they thrown a tarp over the body? How could they stand to look at it? How could they stand to *smell* it?

Didn't they *care*?

"Bishop's paying us plenty," Black Widow went on, and Sabrina glanced back over to find the woman eyeing her phone's screen. "Especially now that it's split four ways. So whatever the Black Knights bring to us is just icing on the cake."

The blonde looked directly at Sabrina then. And just like that, Sabrina no longer felt the heat in the air.

She was chilled to the bone. Goosebumps rose along her arms, the little hairs lifting like they were trying to pull out of her skin and retreat from the assassin's cold, emotionless gaze.

"Remember, she's mine," Black Widow hissed.

"How are you planning to keep her from warning the others?" Vance asked.

"Don't you worry." Black Widow's eyes were still locked on Sabrina as she pulled a syringe from her hip pocket. The capped needle still looked wicked. And when Black Widow winked, Sabrina couldn't help but shiver. "I've got a plan for that. I'll dose her again right before they get here."

After that portentous announcement, she waved a hand. "Now, go take up your positions. I have a call to make in ten minutes, and I don't want any distractions."

Weapons rattled as they were shouldered or stowed. Boots echoed around the crumbling walls. Then, one by one, the men disappeared through that yawning metal door and slunk into the night.

Sabrina was reminded of mountain lions vanishing into a tree line.

And now she was alone with Black Widow.

Somehow, that felt even more dangerous than anything she'd suffered yet.

The blonde sashayed across the floor with that feline precision Sabrina had first seen when she'd raced down the muddy embankment after Sabrina plowed into the tree. When Black Widow made it to Hummer's body, Sabrina expected her to pause.

She didn't.

She stepped over his corpse like he was a fallen branch in her path. Like he was nothing.

Then, she bent, and Sabrina flinched—she couldn't help it—when the woman's fingers clamped around her jaw like a vice.

"I'm not going to knock you out," Widow whispered, her voice like acid. "I'll give you just enough to make walking and talking tough for you. But I won't knock you out like before. I wouldn't want you to miss the show."

CHAPTER 17

12,000 feet up

The outskirts of Chicago glittered like someone had dumped a bucket of diamonds over black velvet. Red brake lights on the roads and highways were gridlocked arteries. The streetlights shone in straight, even rows like ribbons of gold.

But none of it mattered.

None of it drew Hew's gaze.

Only one point on the map below meant a goddamned thing to him, and that was the dark square sitting at the edge of it all.

No light penetrated the bottling plant or its surroundings because no one paid the electric bills. The city had written off the whole place long ago. And, seen from above, it resembled a strangely geometric black hole in a sea of twinkling stars.

Somewhere in the middle of that black hole…Sabrina.

The Roman river goddess.

Hew handled the controls without conscious thought. His left hand gripped the collective, and his right hand was on the cyclic. The pedals under his boots adjusted the tail rotor output and yaw. And every movement was fluid, precise, and automatic.

This was where he truly felt alive. High in the sky, rotors chewing through the air like steel teeth, the smell of old grease and newly burned transmission fluid mixing with the faint scent of ozone.

Except tonight, there was none of the usual exhilaration. None of the usual euphoria.

This wasn't a joyride.

This was Sabrina's life he flew above, and he felt every inch of the thousands of feet that separated them.

Night-vision-compatible gauges cast a dim green glow across the dash. The headset was snug over his ears. And the rain of the past few days had finally moved on, leaving the sky dark and moonless.

But it felt like a storm gathered inside him.

He didn't remember buckling into the harness. Didn't remember going through the pre-flight checks. Hell, he didn't even remember making the flight to the city's west side.

I'd say the bird flew herself if I didn't know better.

What he *did* know was that he'd been pedal to the metal and balls to the wall since they'd pinpointed her location.

Ozzie had made good on his promise. He'd hacked a military satellite and pulled up real-time infrared. Before the team had left for the hangar, they'd seen the heat signatures inside the bottling plant, knew they were dealing with four unfriendlies, and had decided they liked their odds.

While they'd been in the air, Ozzie had relayed that three of Sabrina's captors had taken up positions outside the old factory, one in sniping position on the roof of an adjacent building, and two of the others squirreling themselves inside dilapidated outbuildings.

"That leaves just two inside the bottling plant," Ozzie had said over their FHSS comms.

The handy frequency-hopping spread spectrum system, utilized by intelligence agencies and contractors worldwide, jumped between multiple frequencies per second. Even if someone *tried* to intercept it, they'd hear only random noise unless they had the exact encryption key and hopping sequence.

"Send the infrared images to Hunter's tablet. We need their exact locations," Hew had directed, flying high, fast, and far from the regular commercial jets' flight paths.

They were running dark. No navigation or anti-collision lights. No tail numbers. They'd turned off their transponder—the electronic ID that aircraft broadcasted to local air traffic control and surrounding aircraft.

All completely illegal, of course.

But for the Black Knights, it was just another day on the job.

When Hunter brought his tablet to the cockpit, Hew blinked at the infrared images on the screen, noting especially the two people left inside the old bottling plant.

It hadn't taken his years of service to realize the seated figure, glowing orange and yellow against a background of deep blue, was Sabrina.

She'd been slumped like a marionette with her strings cut. Her head dipped forward, her hands bound behind her back, her body curved in on itself as if she was trying to disappear.

Something in him had cracked at the sight. A soundless shatter that had left him bleeding out internally.

He had been ready to rain down hellfire on that entire bottling plant and everyone who'd dared lay a hand on Sabrina. Just land the chopper in the middle of the plant's decrepit parking lot and go in balls out and guns blazing.

Cooler heads had prevailed, however. And he'd been talked out of his plan.

He'd desperately wanted to join his teammates in storming the castle and saving the princess. But they'd quickly reminded him in true Liam Neeson form that they each had a very particular set of skills, skills acquired over very long careers, and *his* were to drop them in, haul their asses out, and be ready to rain pain down on their enemies on the ground should things go pear-shaped.

"Makin' my way to the rooftop." Graham's scratchy voice rasped through Hew's headset, wrenching his mind back to the moment.

The whole team had fast-roped out of the chopper six blocks from the plant. Close enough to make hoofing it easy. Far enough away to keep the noise from the big bird's rotor wash to a minimum.

Graham's objective was to ghost toward the sniper's perch and take the bastard out of play one way or the other. For such a large man, the ex-SEAL was surprisingly stealthy.

"Making contact now," Graham said lowly. Then, louder, "Hands up where I can see 'em!" A pause followed by a grim, "Don't do it! Don't—"

Crack!
Crack!
Crack!

Three shots echoed through Hew's headset. Graham's signature move. Two rounds to the chest. One to the head.

Hew held his breath and waited for the sound of return fire.

None came.

Graham had introduced the fucker to the Reaper before he'd even had time to aim.

Graham verified this a heartbeat later when he relayed simply, "Target one neutralized."

No sooner had the words been transmitted than Hunter's voice boomed over the shared connection. "Move in! Go, go, go!"

While Graham had gone for the sniper, the other four—Hunter, Britt, Sam, and Fisher—had flanked the perimeter. They'd cut through the high chain-link fence surrounding the property, quiet as church mice. And now they surged through the darkness.

Hew didn't need to see them to know their blades were drawn and their guns were ready.

He wasn't breathing so much and bracing, and then—

The scrabble of bodies moving quickly. Shouts over the comms. The concussive *boom, boom, boom, BOOM* of suppressed rounds slicing through the darkness.

"Target two neutralized," Sam reported, sounding only slightly breathless.

"Target three neutralized," came Hunter's immediate follow-up.

"Moving toward the plant's front door now," Britt added and Hew tightened his grip on the cyclic.

"Ozzie?" He stared unseeing through the windshield. "You got eyes on that last hostile?"

Ozzie's reply was immediate. "They must've heard the gunfire. They're moving toward Sabrina." Their resident hacker watched it all play out in infrared from his post on the second floor back at BKI. "Get in there, guys, before they do something to hurt h—"

Whatever he said next was lost in the hell that exploded in Hew's ears.

Shouts. Static. Sabrina's name and then her scream cutting through the chaos like flares through fog. Followed by...

Silence. Silence. *Silence.*

Seconds beat by. Interminable ticks of the clock that had sweat sliding down his temples, had his heart shuddering inside his chest. He heard only the roar of the rotors, the rush of his own blood between his ears, and the sound of his breathing. Which, despite his training, was too fast. Too shallow.

"I'll blow her brains clean through the front of her skull!" The voice—shrill and far away—was picked up by the teams' comms.

It was the woman who'd called in the ransom demand—although the device no longer distorted her voice. The same woman who'd made the call giving them the location of the drop just five short minutes ago.

Ozzie had kept her on the horn, playing the part of concerned and attentive sucker. Little had she known that the Black Knights circled high above her head and slithered around the outside of her perimeter, preparing to flip the trap she'd laid for them back onto her.

"Your team is dead," Hunter's voice, low and deliberate, was crystal clear through the connection. "Unless you want to join them, I suggest you lay down your weapon."

"You must be out of your goddamned mind!" The woman's laugh echoed hollowly. "She's my only ticket out of here."

Hew imagined a muzzle pressed to Sabrina's skull. Imagined the woman slicing through Sabrina's restraints and forcing her to stand and become a human shield.

"The only ways you're leaving this place," Sam's harsh snarl matched the menace burning at the center of Hew's heart, "is with us or in a body bag."

"You've gone to a lot of trouble for this one," the woman snapped, and Hew imagined her pushing Sabrina in front of her as she made her way toward the door. "Something tells me you'll do whatever it takes to keep her six feet above ground. And that means the two of us are walking out of here together."

"Target four lined up." Graham's voice was as cold and as hard as stone. "Gimme the go-ahead and I'll take her down."

"Hold," Hunter ordered lowly. Louder, he said, "Ma'am, take a peek over your left shoulder, if you would."

Hew didn't need eyes on the ground to know what was playing out far below.

Sabrina's captor was turning. He saw in his mind's eye the moment the woman noticed the laser dot slicing through the broken window, aimed at her head. He imagined the look on her face when she realized she was seconds away from having her gray matter atomized by a lead round traveling three thousand feet per second.

Graham had taken over the sniper's perch. And he was one hell of a marksman.

One and a half pounds of trigger pressure was all it would take for it to be game over for the last remaining hostile.

A pause stretched and stretched and stretched until it felt like Hew's last nerve might fray and break. Then…

"Moving to secure the final unfriendly." Sam's words were like a benediction. "Hunter, you and Britt help Sabrina."

Hew sat up straighter in the dimly lit cockpit, his eyes on the black hole below as if he could see her if he squinted hard enough.

"Help Sabrina?" he barked. "Why does she need help? Is she hurt?"

No answer except for the *whomp, whomp, whomp* of the rotor blades cutting through the air.

"Check in!" he roared, not caring about anyone's eardrums. "Is she okay?"

Hunter's voice was grim. "She's been better. But she's alive and kicking. Headed to the exfil location now."

"Roger that." Hew shoved the collective forward. "Comin' down hot."

He dropped the chopper like a goddamn rock, nose tipping at a precarious angle as he headed for the pre-arranged spot in the crumbling parking lot outside the bottling plant, welcoming the G-forces that pushed him back into the seat.

Within minutes, his skids kissed the busted concrete, and he immediately turned his attention to the hole his teammates had cut through the high, chain-link fence.

One Mississippi.

Two Mississippi.

Three Mississippi.

Come on. Come on.

And then…shadows.

At first, only dark blobs of undulating black inside the stygian darkness. Then, the amorphous shapes became familiar figures.

He was used to seeing his teammates clad in all black, balaclavas covering their faces. What he *wasn't* used to was seeing Sabrina stumbling between two of them.

The moonless night didn't reveal much. But it was enough.

He could see that she hung between Britt and Hunter like her legs barely worked. Her head bobbed loose on the stem of her neck. And was that…

Blood on her face?

Red-hot fury replaced his momentary relief at finding her in one piece. He knew exactly where to aim it.

Her.

Sam and Fisher frog-marched a woman between them. Despite her perilous position, her eyes were flinty, her expression was remorseless, and her chin was up at an arrogant angle.

Hew had never hit a woman. Had never *wanted* to hit a woman. But he was more than tempted to hit *her*. Right on that pointy, imperious chin.

As always, the Black Knights loaded into the waiting chopper in short order. Weapons were stowed. Gear was secured. Every movement was muscle memory.

But Hew only had eyes for Sabrina.

She had a cut on her cheek above a bright purple bruise. Her lush lips were cracked and split. Her hair was soaked through with sweat and matted with grime.

She'd never looked more beautiful.

Especially when her chocolate eyes met his and seemed to melt.

"You're okay, sweetheart! We gotcha now!" He tried to yell above the turbine's roar, but his words barely came out in a rasp.

She must've read his lips, though, because she nodded, her eyes welling and her chin trembling.

Hunter slapped the back of Hew's flight helmet. "Go, go, go!" he yelled.

Hew hated to drop Sabrina's gaze, but there was nothing for it. He whipped around and hopped the big bird back into the sky.

BKI's Blackhawk was old. But she'd been meticulously refitted with radar-absorbing coating and sound-dampening rotor blades, giving her a low infrared signature. And she handled like a dream.

Soon they were zipping through the humid night air as the swirling black waters of Lake Michigan yawned below. Once he reached altitude, he kept one hand steady on the controls. With the other, he reached between his knees and pulled out the ridiculous, well-loved, stuffed *lobstah*.

Stretching his arm behind his chair, he held out the toy.

Didn't matter to him if she saw him do it or if someone passed it to her. He just needed her to *have* it.

A second later, he felt a tug and released his hold. He went to pull his hand back, but something stopped him.

Sabrina…

Her fingers slipped between his, cool, trembling, and unmistakable. She didn't let go even after half a dozen heartbeats. Neither did he.

Her touch was a tether, binding him back to the moment. Back to certainty. Back to her.

He couldn't turn and take her in his arms like every cell inside him begged him to do. So, instead, he flew her toward safety. Flew her toward *home*.

And for the first time since he woke up to find her gone, he drew in a full breath.

Then, he exhaled.

CHAPTER 18

Black Knights Inc.

Consciousness returned slowly, like sunlight creeping over the horizon. Sabrina liked sunrises. But she didn't like this.

She wanted to stay in the cool and dark. In the dreamless void where there was no thought, no pain, no cruel reality.

She tried to hang on to the oblivion. Tried to will her mind back to nothingness and her body back to numbness. But the more she struggled to stay asleep, the more wakefulness tugged at her.

Sound was the first thing to return…the low, slow rhythm of someone's breaths. Sensation came next…the smooth, cool sheets beneath her fingers, the faint stitch at the bend of her elbow. Her nose twitched at the scent of her favorite laundry detergent, clean linen and crushed lavender. And then she smelled something richer, something that reminded her of earth and woods and safety and man.

Hew.

Her lids were heavy, but she forced them open.

The golden glow of the lamp on her dresser spilled dim light across the room, showing her all her favorite things.

There was the bedspread she'd ordered from Etsy. There were the books she'd borrowed from Hew sitting next to the ones she'd picked up from the secondhand bookstore after she regained her freedom. There was the man who'd made it all possible because he'd been the shoulder she leaned on and the ear she spilled all her grief and trauma into when her whole world had been turned upside down.

He was still in his flight gear. Black tactical pants. Fitted black thermal shirt that stretched tight across his wide chest. Combat boots that had seen better days.

He looked…lethal.

He *was* lethal, she supposed. But he rarely *looked* lethal. At least, not to her.

Because he was her Hew. Her quiet, gentle, generous Hew.

When he was teasing her or talking to her or tenderly brushing away her tears, it was hard to remember that he was also a trained killer. A man who dropped bombs and pulled triggers and bested bad guys.

He'd dragged beside her bed the armchair she usually kept shoved in the corner. And somehow, he'd curled his massive frame into the thing.

His big arms were folded across his chest. His long legs were stretched out in front of him and crossed at the ankle. His head was tilted back into the corner so that his Adam's apple bulged in the tan column of his throat.

There was that hollow at the base of his neck. That vulnerable dip in a body that was otherwise hard and honed.

It had fascinated her from the start. And after she'd begun to heal, she'd spent her days fantasizing about flicking her tongue into it and her nights dreaming of what it would be like to taste his tough skin *right there.*

He was asleep.

But only just.

She'd learned from all her nights curled against his back that, even at rest, he remained vigilant. The tiniest sound could pull him straight into action. The slightest movement had him lifting his head and asking, *"Everything okay?"*

Something about that, about the thought of him never fully resting, made her throat tighten.

She could have gone on watching him forever. Memorizing the exact shape of the whorl of dark hair over his forehead, the inky shadow his thick lashes cast on his high cheekbones, and just how plump his lips looked when his mouth was relaxed. But her gaze was drawn across her room to the tall, leaded glass windows and the muted, golden light pressing against them.

Daytime? She blinked in confusion. *How long have I been sleeping?*

The chopper ride to the private airport east of the city was a blur. She remembered choking back tears at Hew's thoughtfulness when he handed her the plushie. She remembered being hustled into a dark car for the ride back to BKI. And, to her chagrin, she remembered losing it.

When Hew had slid into the back seat beside her, throwing an arm around her shoulders and pulling her close, all the spunk and spirit that had kept her going for the last day had deserted her. Silent, hiccupping sobs had wracked her chest and burned her lungs. And no matter how hard she'd tried, she couldn't stop them.

He had whispered comforting words that had blended and blurred together in her brain as they mixed with snippets of conversation from the front seat.

"—dangerously dehydrated. Call Ozzie and make sure—"

"What are we gonna do with—"

"—get some damn answers about—"

She remembered the car nosing out of the Bat Cave—the tunnel dug beneath the Chicago River that was BKI's secret entrance. And she remembered the concern on the faces of the people around her as she attempted to smile and reassure everyone she was all right.

She *vaguely* remembered being helped up the stairs and coaxed into bed as Peanut purred and curled into her side. And there was a fuzzy memory of Hew bending over her before…

Oblivion. That sweet, dark, dreamless void.

When she shifted slightly now, Peanut blinked at her with sleepy yellow eyes. Then, having determined he'd done his duty by her, he yawned, stretched, and hopped off the bed with a solid-sounding *thud*.

No doubt going in search of breakfast, she thought fondly.

She went to stretch, but stopped when she saw the tube snaking up from the crook of her arm. She followed it to its source. A clear plastic IV bag hung from her headboard.

It was nearly empty, explaining the urgency building in her bladder.

"You're awake." Hew's voice was rusty from disuse. But his green eyes were as sharp as ever when her gaze darted to his face.

"How long was I out?" Her eyes flicked again to the window. The light flooding in was brighter now.

He checked his watch. "Nearly seven hours."

"*Seven.*" She blinked. "Did y'all give me something?"

"With the level of dehydration you were suffering, disorientation and extreme fatigue are normal. We didn't *need* to give ya anything. You went out like a light as soon as your head hit the pillow."

He leaned forward, elbows on his knees, big hands dangling in the void between them. "Didn't know if we were goin' to have to haul ya to the ER." He pointed to the IV bag. "That's your third one. Your poor body's been soakin' it up like a sponge."

"Well *that* would explain why my bladder's about to burst." She grimaced. "How do I—?" She waved vaguely at the needle and the tubing.

"Here." With careful, practiced hands, he peeled the tape free, withdrew the needle, and pressed a cotton swab to her arm.

Then…*poof*…a Band-Aid miraculously appeared from the first aid kit on her nightstand. Hew pasted it over the injection site.

"You're a deft hand at that," she murmured, only slightly surprised. He was a man of many talents.

He winked and reiterated her thoughts. "Just one of my many talents."

A few months ago, she might have thought he was flirting. Now? She knew better.

"Thank you." Her throat went tight. "Thank you for coming for me. I was so afraid y'all would walk right into her trap and—" She blinked as a hundred questions bloomed to life inside her brain. "Wait. How *did* you avoid her trap? Did someone tell you what she was planning? Did you know that she was hired—"

"Hey." He stopped her flood of words and worry. "Take a beat. Take a breath. We're okay. You're okay. And we have all the time in the world to talk about what happened."

Her relief at being back at BKI with everyone safe and sound mixed with the remnants of her fear to have a sob bursting from the back of her throat. It shocked her with its suddenness.

In an instant, Hew was there. Pulling her against the solid wall of his chest.

No questions. No hesitation. Just him offering her everything she needed while silent tears fell and her soul emptied out the last of the terror she'd carried since the black van rear-ended her and sent her careening off the side of that country road.

"It's over now," he murmured against the top of her head. "You're safe. You're home."

Home.

Such a simple word. Just four little letters and one little syllable. But its meaning was immense.

Home was a windy exhale after a long-held breath. It was where she could shut away the world, and no one would ask her to be anything but herself. It was the familiar creak of door hinges. The light pooling in certain corners at sunset. The scent of strong coffee and old paperbacks and fresh-baked pastries.

It was where her name sounded right, even when spoken in a whisper. Where silence didn't feel like absence but acceptance.

And she'd never truly had any of that until BKI. Until Hew.

She wrapped her arms around his shoulders as gratitude swelled inside her. It took over all the space horror had left behind.

Hew…

With his tender heart and lopsided half-smiles and love of books, with his courage and loyalty and steadfastness, *he* had become her sanctuary. Her shelter.

And she *wanted* him.

All of him.

She wanted his quiet words and his unpredictable wit. His silly jokes and his soft silences. His heat and his hardness. His warm breath and his firm lips. His calloused hands and his hot—

Blame it on her recent near-death experience. Blame it on the lasting effects of the drug her abductors had given her. Hell, blame it on the long months she'd gone without knowing the feel of a man inside her.

Or blame it on me, she thought as she inhaled deeply, sucking his scent all the way down into her toes before…

She did it.

The thing she'd been dreaming of doing since the moment she reclaimed the part of herself Eddy Torres had taken. She opened her mouth over the hot skin of his neck, over the pulse that beat strong and steady, and flicked out her tongue to taste him.

Hot and dark. Sweet and savory. The flavor of him hit her tongue with the eye-crossing joy of melted sugar.

The hand that had been smoothing her hair stilled. But his heart raced against the tip of her tongue. And the low growl at the back of his throat seemed to reverberate in the achy spot between her legs, making her keenly aware of its emptiness.

"Sabrina." He spoke her name like a warning.

But who was he trying to caution? Her? Or himself?

Definitely me, she decided, regaining her senses and realizing the unambiguous boundary she'd crossed.

He'd been *very* clear about what he felt for her. And what he *didn't*.

Shame at having taken advantage of his comfort rolled through her, burning and bright.

What are you doing? A voice of reason screamed in her head. *Do you want to ruin everything you've found here at BKI? The trust and friendship you've built with Hew?*

Her heart suddenly felt fiery and full, a hot air balloon threatening to rise out of her chest.

You fool!

You idiot!

You absolute asshole*!*

She pulled her mouth from his throat and jumped up with a blurted, "Sorry! I have to pee."

"Uh…"

She didn't look back as she raced for the bathroom. But she knew he stood from the bed. She heard the mattress springs squeak.

"Sabrina." He said her name with such softness, in that Mainer accent that would always bring to mind lobster boats, winter boots, and maple syrup.

She was almost to the door of her ensuite, almost to freedom. But she forced herself to turn and face him.

She'd already proven she was a boundary-crossing jerk. She couldn't add *coward* to the list of her sins.

She blinked in astonishment when she realized he'd followed her across the room. The man could move with a quiet precision that was disconcerting to the layperson. And when she tilted her chin back to look at him, she found the light that always lived in his eyes had flared into a flame.

She quickly dropped her gaze to that delicious divot in his throat. She couldn't stand to look at him directly.

It was like looking at the sun. He was too bright. Too beautiful.

"I'm hungry," she whispered hoarsely, grabbing the first thing she could think of to distract him from what she'd just done. "Do you think Eliza baked this morning?"

She felt his hesitation more than she saw it. Then she saw it when he slipped his fingers into his hip pockets and rocked back on his heels.

Holding her breath, she waited for him to call her out for the line she'd crossed. Waited for him to say out loud what he'd been silently saying for months.

She blew out a shaky breath when, instead, he took pity on her and said only, "Want me to run down and check?"

"Would you? I need sustenance before I face everyone."

She chanced a glance at his face and saw the speculation in his eyes. There were questions there. Questions she wasn't ready to answer. Thankfully, in the end, he didn't push.

That wasn't his way.

"Ayuh. I'll see what I can scrounge up." He turned on his heel and headed for the door.

She watched his retreat. Watched the easy way he moved. The breadth of his shoulders, the narrowness of his waist, and the hard, round bulge of his glutes in those black fatigues.

Stop ogling the poor man, Sabrina! the voice of reason scolded. *Haven't you done enough to the poor man?*

Right, she thought with a determined dip of her chin. *No more ogling. No more stolen kisses. No more trying to force something that isn't there.*

After she relieved herself, she washed her hands and made the mistake of glancing into the mirror above the sink.

Holy shit.

Her waterproof mascara had not lived up to its advertisement. The bruise on her face was a kaleidoscope of colors. And the cut on her cheek had a thick, untidy scab.

And don't even get me started on my hair.

She might need to borrow Boss's clippers. The only solution to her rat's nest might be a buzz cut.

Turning on her shower, she waited for the water to heat and steam to fog the glass before slipping out of her filthy clothes. Her nose wrinkled when she smelled what twenty-four hours of sweat, grime, and fear had left on her.

No wonder Hew wanted nothing to do with me, she thought as she pushed her clothes into the corner, determined to burn them in the fire pit the first chance she got.

That pesky voice of reason piped up again.

It really was incredibly annoying.

That had nothing to do with the way you smell, Sabrina. And everything to do with the fact that he spent months making his intentions clear and still *you had to push it.*

"Ugh," she grumbled as she stepped into the shower. "What an absolute *asshole* I turned out to—"

A knock had her poking her head through the glass door. "Yeah?" she called above the loud *shush* of the water spraying against the tiles.

"You're in luck," came Hew's voice, smooth and deep. "Eliza whipped up those cream Danishes ya like. I snagged the last two. And I brought up a mug of coffee. Full of milk, just like ya like it."

Full of milk because the coffee at Black Knights Inc. was strong enough to wake up her ancestors if she didn't dilute it by half. And…*just like you like it.*

Lord, the man was a dream. She'd molested him, ogled him, *ran* from him so he wouldn't say aloud the words she didn't want to hear. And still he treated her like a queen.

Or, better yet, like a *friend.*

"I don't deserve you!" she shouted.

When he didn't respond, her earlier shame and embarrassment increased tenfold. *She* had created this awkwardness between them.

"Just leave it on the dresser!" she yelled, wanting to fill the void and also wanting to shoo him away so she could suffer in silence and solitude. "And thank you!"

Again, no answer.

Not that she expected one.

Closing her eyes, she tipped her head under the hot spray and hoped it would wash away the memory of how good he'd felt against her. How good he'd *tasted* on her tongue.

It was a losing battle, of course. What she'd felt in Hew's arms wasn't something that could be sent down the drain. It wasn't just friendship or comfort. It wasn't even passion or lust.

It was love.

She loved him.

She was *in* love with him.

And god help her.

CHAPTER 19

Hew heard the shower cut off. Heard the soft whir of Sabrina's toothbrush. Heard the rhythmic hum of her hairdryer.

Such sweet, domestic sounds. Feminine sounds. *Sabrina* sounds. They should've comforted him. *Warmed* him.

She was home. She was whole. She felt well enough to go about her usual morning ablutions.

Except…a war raged within him.

On the one side was the part of him that was *sure* he'd felt her warm lips on his skin. Felt her hot breath as she opened her mouth and the wet, tentative, *testicle-tightening* touch of her tongue over his pulse point.

On the other side was the certainty that his brain, fried from twenty-four hours of fear and adrenaline, had hallucinated the whole damn thing. And what he'd thought was her wet tongue was just one of her tears sliding against his skin. What he's mistaken for her lips opening was just…

What?

He scrubbed a hand down his face and dragged in a deep breath that contained plenty of oxygen but, unfortunately, didn't contain any answers.

The sound of the bathroom door creaking open pulled him from his battling thoughts. Looking up, he decided it was a good thing his last breath contained plenty of oxygen. Because, suddenly, he forgot how to breathe.

Sabrina stood framed in the doorway like a goddamn vision. Damp hair clung to her throat, curling at the ends like chocolate ribbons. Steam kissed her skin, making it glisten. And her little pink robe molded itself to her lithe frame like it was trying to decide if it wanted to be completely immodest or just slightly immodest.

He felt his self-control fray and barely refrained from marching over, cupping her sweet face in his hand, and kissing her cross-eyed.

That would tell him if she'd really kissed his neck or if he'd imagined it all.

"I thought you left." She pulled the two halves of the robe tighter, interrupting his heated thoughts.

Good thing. Too much more of *that* and he'd need to pull one of the pillows from her bed over his lap.

"Sorry." He stood from the chair, suddenly aware of how inappropriate it was to linger in her bedroom uninvited. "Didn't mean to— I'll head downstairs and—"

He saw it then.

The dark bruise blooming just above the robe's lapel. Deep. Angry. *Fresh.*

His body moved before his brain caught up. One second, he was standing beside her bed. The next, he was there, chest-to-chest, fist in the silk of her robe, fury singing through his veins.

Before he could stop himself, he pulled the material aside to examine what it covered.

"What—?" Sabrina squeaked and blinked up at him in shocked astonishment.

He barely noticed. He was too distracted by the rage that rolled over him as quickly and as densely as a New England fog bank.

This wasn't cold, though. It was white-hot.

"What did those motherfuckers *do* to you?" His voice was gunpowder soaked in gasoline. He barely recognized it as his own. "I'm goin' to *kill* her." He turned toward the door, determined to march downstairs and wrap his hands around the throat of the blonde. "I'm goin' to put three holes in her skull and turn her head into a fuckin' *bowlin'* ball—"

"Hew. *Stop.*" Sabrina had somehow beaten him to the door. She used her body—her arms spread out to grip the doorframe—to keep him from leaving. "It wasn't Black Widow."

He swallowed, fighting for control. "*That's* what she calls herself? Jesus. What an arrogant—"

"Doesn't matter," she cut him off. "What matters is that it wasn't her. It was the one they called Diesel. And you can't turn *his* head into a bowling ball because he's already dead."

"Good riddance." If he'd been outside, he would've spat on the ground. "Although I wish he weren't. 'Cause I'd like to kill him again. I'd like to rip him limb from limb for touchin' ya. For markin' ya. For—"

He couldn't finish past the bile that spurted into his throat. His stomach heaved. His fists curled. He had to force his next question through his clenched jaw. "Did he ra—"

"No," she assured him swiftly, shaking her head, bravely holding his violent gaze. "I was groped." She tilted her chin toward her poor, bruised breast. "Hit." She pointed to the cut on her cheek. "But that's it."

The fury in his blood cooled to embers. But it wasn't doused. Because… *groped. Hit.*

Hurt.

They'd hurt her. And he hadn't been there to protect her from them. He hadn't been there to—

"Wait." She suddenly frowned. "Black Widow is *here*? I remember her being in the helicopter, but…" She trailed off, shaking her head.

"She's down in the Bat Cave," he informed her, jaw still tight with barely leashed rage. "We need to interrogate her. But first, we're lettin' her stew in her own juices. No food. No water. A little quid pro quo for what she put you through."

He caught her chin between his fingers, forcing her to look at him.

She blinked, wide-eyed, and he could see the little flecks of gold floating in the creamy brown of her irises. The flutter of her pulse in her long, pale neck was like a hummingbird's wings.

"Are ya *sure* they didn't—"

"I did more damage to them than they did to me," she assured him, chin trembling. "I—I killed one of them, Hew. The one they called Hummer."

The words came out raw, ragged. Like they'd been torn from somewhere deep inside her. Hearing them made something inside *him* rip open, too.

"They were going to kill me," she explained unnecessarily. "They planned to take the money and kill all y'all, and so I shoved a glass shard into Hummer's throat because I thought if I could help you guys then…"

She stopped and shook her head, her breath going thready. "I *felt* it go in, Hew. His blood was hot on my hand. And I watched him struggle until—"

Her fingers jumped to her mouth. Her other arm curled around her midsection like she was trying to hold herself together.

Hew didn't hesitate. Didn't even *think*, really. He did the only thing he knew to do. The only thing he *could* do. The same thing he'd *been* doing since she first arrived at BKI.

He picked her up, carried her to the bed, and rocked her gently in his lap as her tears fell.

Hunter had reported on the corpse that'd been at Sabrina's feet when the Knights stormed the bottling plant. But none of them had thought *she* had been the one to slit the man's throat. They'd all assumed it'd been a tiff between teammates. Assassins turning on one another.

But it was our brave Sabrina.

Our Roman river goddess doin' all she could to even the odds for us.

"I didn't know what else to do," she whispered into the crook of his shoulder. "I couldn't stand the thought of being the reason y'all walked into a trap. And so I—"

"You did *exactly* what ya had to do." His voice was low and rough. It had to work past the lump in his throat. "You were fightin' for your life. For *all* our lives. And there's not a soul on this planet who'd blame ya for that."

"But I—"

He pressed his thumb under her chin so he could see her pretty face. Then, he silenced her words by tapping a finger over her lips.

Of course, when he felt her warm breath bathe his skin, he had to remove his hand because it made his dick twitch.

Stupid bastard, he silently admonished. *Now's not the time.*

With Sabrina, it was *never* the time.

Or was it?

Had she opened her mouth over his throat? *Had* she flicked out her little tongue to taste him?

"You didn't *choose* to be taken." He pushed all other thoughts aside. "You didn't *want* to be put into the position to save yourself and give the people ya love like family a fightin' chance. And the fact that you're feelin' anything but vindication right now? Well, that just means ya have a heart. A big, brave, beautiful heart. And I couldn't be any prouder of you than I am."

A fresh tear slipped down her wounded cheek. He gently caught it with his thumb and brushed it away.

"I'd take it from ya if I could," he swore vehemently. "All the grief. All the fear. I'd carry it so you don't have to."

"You *have*, Hew," she declared with a determined dip of her chin. "I couldn't have gotten through all these months without you."

Her full, lower lip trembled, and it took everything he had not to duck his head and pull it into his mouth. Soothe its motion. Instead, he leaned in until their noses touched.

Her breath smelled of her minty toothpaste. Her skin smelled of her fruity body wash. And her hair smelled of her flowery shampoo.

"Why does life have to be so hard?" She sniffed pitifully.

The smallness of her voice had every protective instinct inside him roaring and beating its chest Tarzan style.

He pushed back so he could see her face when he told her, "It's a rule. What? Don't look at me like that. I wasn't the one who made it up."

She laughed, just as he'd meant her to. But it sounded brittle, like glass breaking.

"Sorry about earlier," she whispered, immediately sobering.

Everything inside him stilled.

Except for his heart.

That beat against the cage of his ribs like it was doing its level best to escape his chest.

"What d'ya mean?" he asked carefully.

Her mouth flattened. "Come on, Hew. Don't play dumb."

"I *am* dumb," he insisted. "Most times I just go around playin' smart."

She scrambled off his lap, and he had to fist his hands to keep from pulling her back. After she flounced into the chair, adjusting her robe over her silky thighs, she turned a sullen frown on him.

Snatching the *lobstah* off her pillow, she worried its claws before finally saying, "I took advantage of your friendship, and I shouldn't have. I don't know what I was thinking. You've made it very clear where you and I stand."

He shook his head. Then nodded. Then asked, "I have?"

"On *many* occasions," she emphasized. "I finally caught a clue." She tapped her temple. "Even though I was a little slow on the uptake."

He nodded again. In fact, he couldn't seem to *quit* nodding. It was like his body's attempt to comprehend what they were talking about because his brain had completely given up on the task.

"So earlier I…" She shrugged and shook her head. "Earlier, I was an idiot. And I apologize."

"Right." Nodding. Nodding. Nodding some more. "And what, exactly, are ya apologizin' for?"

She thrust out her chin at an angle. "You're going to make me come right out and say it, aren't you?"

Still nodding. "You're goin' to have to. 'Cause I'm lost."

"I'm apologizing for kissing your neck." She waved a vague hand at the neck in question, and he felt his lungs collapse. "I know you don't like me like *that*."

Now he couldn't stop blinking.

He thought maybe the nodding was better. At least he was contributing to the conversation that way.

"I don't?" he finally managed to ask.

She rolled her eyes. "You've made it obvious."

"I have?"

She sighed heavily. "Remember when you showed me the yearbook with your parents' pictures?"

He nodded.

Great. Back to contributin' to the convo.

"I grabbed your thigh when we were flipping through the pages, and you jumped up like you were snake bit and said you were going to go get us something to drink. And remember when we took Freedom for a ride and stopped at the beach?"

You guessed it. He nodded.

"Remember how, when we were walking back to the bike, I faked a trip and you caught me? Our mouths were this close together?" She held two fingers an inch apart. "But instead of kissing me, you set me back on my feet and brushed the sand off my jeans like I was a toddler. And *then* there was the first night we all went to Red Delilah's."

His voice sounded raw when he managed, "What happened there?"

"Not there." She shook her head like he was ten kinds of idiot. Honestly? He was beginning to think she was right about that. "When we came back. I was teasing you about getting the brunette's phone number, giving you a hard time about having a *type*. Basically, leaving the door wide open for you to tell me if *I* was your type. But did you walk through it? *No.* You just said you didn't *have* a type and—" She stopped and tugged the halves of her robe together. "Hey, Boss. What's up?"

"Uhhh." Frank Knight stood in the open doorway and glanced awkwardly between them. "Martin's on the phone for you. The *business* phone," he stressed. "Said if you're ghosting him, that's okay. He understands that's how things work in the modern world. But he asks that you let him know. Or that you tell *me* to let him know. Because he's been trying to get a hold of you ever since you missed the show last night. And he's worried."

"Oh, my god!" Sabrina jumped up. "I can't believe I forgot Martin!" She put a hand to her head and threw the stuffed lobster back on the vacated chair. Hew felt like maybe that was a metaphor for something he didn't like in the least. "We were supposed to meet at the Lyric Opera House. What must he think of me?"

Hew dumbly watched her slip out the door, his eyes clinging to her the way dew clings to flowers on a spring morning.

After her footsteps sounded on the stairs, Boss turned to him and lifted an ash-gray eyebrow. "Y'okay?"

Hew nodded. It seemed to be the only thing he was capable of. Then he shook his head and admitted, "I actually have no idea."

CHAPTER 20

The White House

Lura sat perched on the edge of her desk chair, fingers hovering uselessly over her keyboard, eyes gritty from lack of sleep.

She'd stumbled into her D.C. apartment at 1:42 A.M., hair a mess, deodorant long-since worn off, and head pounding from the flight.

Air travel always left her with a headache. Something about the rapid change in pressure.

She'd kicked off her shoes and gone straight to bed, hoping to catch a couple hours of sleep before her alarm screamed its wakeup call and she was forced to shower and head for the office.

Alas…sleep had eluded her. Her mind had been far too full.

She would've liked to say her thoughts had been dominated by the Black Knights. By the electric hum of their shop, by the steady discipline belied by their cocky swaggers, by the sheer *thrill* of rubbing elbows with the president's very own covert fast response force.

She would've liked to say her brain had been preoccupied with thoughts of the rescue operation underway when she took off from Chicago. With Sabrina Greenlee, and whether or not she'd made it home safely. With Kerberos and their unlikely insertion into the whole mix.

And, sure, all of that *had* crossed her mind. But what had kept her staring at the ceiling all night as headlights painted undulating shadows across the drywall was…

Graham Coleburn.

Heaven help her, she hadn't been ready to run into him.

Not just because he was a blast from the past in the middle of a present-day fiasco. Although that was enough to throw anyone for a loop. But because she'd been unprepared to feel…

What?

What exactly was it that Graham made her feel?

Attraction, of course. But that was no surprise.

Before his mother's death, he'd been a walking advertisement for testosterone. Bravado and a Southern charm had spilled off him in syrupy waves, and he'd had every girl in grades nine through twelve swooning.

But now, she felt…

What?

It was more than remembered attraction. More than nostalgic lust. More than mere enchantment over a pretty face and a Vin Diesel voice and body that looked as solid and as immovable as fortress walls.

Intrigued, she decided.

She was *intrigued* by him.

By how he had the same slow drawl despite having spent almost twenty years hell and gone from Rabun County. By how his once laughing green eyes now held deep shadows. By how he was so much the same and yet so…*different.*

It'd been a long time since she'd been intrigued by a man.

On second thought, had she *ever* been intrigued by a man?

Much to her Southern momma's chagrin, Lura had spent the last fifteen years focused on college and her career instead of marriage and providing grandbabies. She hadn't been a nun, by any means. But men had come and gone out of her life as easily as houseplants.

One minute, they were there and thriving. The next, they'd meet their inevitable end because she couldn't be bothered to tend to them like they wanted or needed.

C'est la vie.

She had more important things to do. More important things to think about.

But Graham Coleburn felt…different.

More than once, she'd caught herself watching him too closely. More than once, she'd wondered how time could turn a small-town boy who'd loved fishing and football into a man who was basically the real-life version of James Bond. More than once, she'd—

"Miss Dougherty!"

Leonard Meadows's voice cracked like a whip through Fiona Apple's husky voice crooning, *I've been a bad, bad girl.*

"Coming!" Lura called, pulling out her AirPod and grabbing her tablet. She held it in front of her like a shield as she scurried across the small room.

"Yes, sir?" After she pushed into the chief of staff's office, she forced a bland smile and thumbed on her device, ready to take notes.

"Close the door behind you."

She blinked. That was…unusual. He seldom asked for privacy when it was just the two of them.

After easing the door shut, she faced him again with what she hoped was a calm, composed expression.

His desk was organized chaos as usual. His posture was military straight as usual. But there was something new in the set of his jaw, in the sharpness of his eyes behind the glint of his glasses.

The hairs on the back of her neck lifted and she had to grit her teeth to keep from rubbing a hand over them.

"How was it at Black Knights Inc.?"

It was said breezily. But something about the weight of the question seemed to fill all the space in the room.

"Uhhh." She had to stop and clear her throat. "It was…enlightening," she finished carefully.

"Enlightening." He rolled the word around in his mouth like he was tasting it. "How so?"

"The Black Knights are even more impressive than I imagined."

"Impressive in what way?"

Okay, this is getting weird.

Didn't he know more about them than she did? Hadn't he been with the president when she handpicked the men on the team? Didn't he send his own *daughter* to work for them?

She was tempted to cover her hesitation with another *uhhh*. But that would make her sound dumb and make *him* annoyed at the delay. Instead, she cocked her head and twisted her mouth as if trying to find the right words to capture her thoughts.

"They're more cohesive and tight-knit than I thought they'd be. Not just cohorts and colleagues, but *family.*"

His eyes narrowed. It was slight. But she saw it. And it deepened her discomfort.

He was probing her.

But for what?

What was he after?

"And were they successful in bringing their social media guru home?"

She blinked in surprise. "I…don't know. I thought *you* would know. Haven't they checked in?"

A muscle twitched in his jaw. Again, it was slight. But again, she saw it. "They have not."

"Is that…um…*unusual* for them?" she asked carefully.

He didn't answer. Instead, he leaned forward, voice low. "Did anything odd happen while you were there?"

She swallowed. But the spit stuck in her throat.

"I think the entire concept of a private security firm working directly for the president while hiding their identities behind the façade of a custom bike shop is pretty odd. Are you looking for something more specific than that?" She forced a small smile to lessen the tension in the air.

He didn't return the gesture. "Did they determine *why* the woman was taken?"

She thought of the message sent from Kerberos. But something in her gut warned her not to mention it.

"She was taken for the money, I assume. Why else?"

His frown deepened.

"Sir, is there something in particular you're driving at? I feel like   "

"Call them."

"What?" Her chin jerked back so quickly she nearly gave herself whiplash.

"Call them and ask them if their mission was successful. You spent the day with them. It'd be natural for you to want to know how things turned out."

"I…" she faltered. "I don't know any of their numbers. I don't have—"

"Call their business line." He waved a dismissive hand, as if that made everything so simple.

"But I thought you didn't want any correspondence coming from the White House? Isn't that why I had to fly—"

"Don't get into *specifics*." He cut her off, clearly exasperated that he needed to explain himself. "Just ask if they were successful and leave it at that."

Lura nodded jerkily and slowly backed out of the office, but her mind was absolutely spinning.

Why ask *her* to call and demand details when they reported to him… er…the president, but also him by proxy? Why not just pick up the phone himself?

Of course, part of her didn't care what his reasons were. Because part of her was glad for any excuse to reach out to BKI. Glad for any excuse to hear Graham Coleburn's voice again.

She hurried to her desk and quickly set aside her tablet. But before she could google BKI's business number, a whisper of doubt curled around her heart.

What am I missing here?

CHAPTER 21

"How do you think she'll explain her absence last night?" Boss asked.

Graham stood just outside Boss's office, arms crossed, shoulder propped against the wall like it might fall down without him.

The familiar hum of the War Room buzzed behind him. Ozzie clacked on his keyboard. Eighties music blared at a surprisingly reasonable level. From below, the sounds of the shop echoed. The soft *shush* of a blowtorch. The harsh whine of a metal grinder.

It was business as usual at BKI.

Funny, considering they had an assassin tied up in the tunnel hidden behind the shop wall.

Graham and Boss had been in Boss's office discussing interrogation techniques when Martin Massey's call came in. All the men of Black Knights Inc. had been through SERE training. It was the military's standard course for spec-ops soldiers—regardless of their branch—and it was meant to prepare them should they ever find themselves captured by the enemy.

But teaching a guy how to survive, evade, resist, and escape was not the same as teaching him how to get information from someone who didn't want to talk. Whose very life likely depended on them *not* talking.

That was the CIA's purview. Those soulless shitbags had a whole training module covering enhanced interrogation techniques.

A handful of SEALs in each unit spent six weeks at Langley learning the ins and outs of torture from spooks and spies. Boss had been one of the unlucky bastards in his unit. Graham had pulled the short straw in his.

This meant it'd fall to them to devise a game plan for getting the blonde to cough up information. Like who'd hired her. And, more importantly, *why*.

Of course, they'd taken a break from discussing their plan to let Sabrina have some privacy for her call with the rich hedge fund manager. And now, instead of throwing around phrases like *sleep deprivation* and *stress positions*, they were talking about the love life of their resident social media maven.

Life is weird, Graham thought idly.

Aloud, he said, "Dunno," in response to Boss's question. "She'll need to get creative."

Sabrina had swung the door shut behind her when she'd raced to take Martin's call. But it hadn't latched. Now, they could hear the hum of her voice through the crack in the doorway, although they couldn't make out her words.

"I don't know how someone can build a relationship on lies." Boss frowned, a line digging deep between his bushy eyebrows.

Graham gave a philosophical shrug. "She can't tell him the truth. So I don't reckon she's got another option."

Boss's nod was slow, thoughtful. "I guess there was a part of me, at least when she first got here, that hoped she and Hew might start something. You know, once she'd healed enough to want to."

"You ain't the only one."

Boss slid him a quizzical look. "He ever tell you why he never made a move? Sometimes I catch him looking at her like he can't decide whether he wants to eat her whole or wrap her up in cotton so no one can touch her."

Graham barked out a laugh. "And sometimes I catch *her* lookin' at *him* like she wants to climb him like a cat climbs a tree."

"So what's the problem?" Boss's frown deepened. "Why's she in there making plans with another man?"

"I think our resident Nightstalker doesn't know which end is up when it comes to romance. Poor Sabrina would probably hafta sit on his face before he'd catch a damn clue and—"

The tone of Sabrina's voice changed. What had sounded low and apologetic suddenly turned businesslike and cautious.

Graham exchanged a look with Boss. Then they both straightened when the door swung open, and Sabrina stood there blinking, surprised to find them waiting outside.

"There's a Lura Dougherty on the line," she said, and Graham felt his heart hammer. "She called in right as Martin and I were saying our goodbyes. She says she wants to talk to you."

"To me?" Boss cocked an eyebrow.

"To *you*." Sabrina pointed a finger at Graham's chest.

Boss slapped a firm hand on his shoulder. "Well, what are you waiting for, son? There's a tall, smokey-eyed redhead on the horn for you."

"Right." Graham firmed his shoulders as he traded places with Sabrina in the doorway.

"Who's Lura Dougherty?" he heard her ask as he palmed the knob.

"Yesterday was a helluva ride. We have a lot to catch you up on," Boss said before Graham closed the door and the world outside faded away.

Boss's office was sparse. Severe. Like the man himself.

The air held the faint tang of blade oil. The walls were lined with practical metal shelves—the kind you could get at any home improvement store. And every item on them was meticulously placed.

Except for the photos of his wife and his two kids that he kept on his desk, there was no clutter. No distractions. Just pure, utilitarian focus.

Graham appreciated that now. Since it was just him and the black handset waiting on the desk. Him and his quiet thoughts that cautioned him not to jump to conclusions.

She's not callin' to tell ya she's missed your face for the last two decades.

She's not callin' to say she can't stop thinkin' 'bout ya.

She's not callin' to ask ya out, dipshit. Get it together.

"Hello?"

Damnit! His voice cracked like a pubescent boy's.

By contrast, Lura's voice was soft and smooth. "Graham?"

Despite losing her accent over the years, something about how she made his name into two syllables reminded him of the Appalachian foothills.

For the first time in a long damn time, he ached for the hush of the holler, the creak of a porch swing, and the peace of those thick, slow summer nights that never seemed to end.

He had to clear his throat. "None other." He hoped it sounded breezy and only faintly curious.

"I know it's strange, me calling you like this," she replied quickly. "But I wanted to see if everything…" She trailed off, searching for the right words.

He appreciated the pause. It gave him a second to rein in the stampede of his heart.

"Did everything turn out okay last night?" she finally finished. "Is everyone good over there?"

Right. Unsecured line.

"Everything's great. Everyone's fine. And everyone's home," he told her, and thought he heard a small sigh of relief.

"Good. That's really good, Graham."

There it was again; his name in her mouth making him miss home.

Silence stretched then. He wanted to fill it. Wanted to hear more of her voice. But he couldn't think of a damn thing to say. And…*how's the weather in your neck of the woods?*…would only make him sound like an idiot.

"Okay, then." *She* was the one to fill his awkward pause. "I won't keep you. I know you're busy."

A sudden sense of desperation gripped him. He couldn't let her go. Not like this. Not when it felt like she'd just cracked open a door he hadn't dared knock on in years. "Lura?"

"Yes?"

"It was…" He had to clear his throat again. "It was really nice seein' ya again. I'm glad to know ya grew up to be such a badass."

He could hear the smile in her voice. It wrapped around his ribs like silk. "If we're handing out trophies for being badasses, I think you take first place."

"Speaks volumes for Rabun County, huh? Producin' *two* of us?"

That made her laugh. "I guess that's better than being known for being the place they filmed *Deliverance*." She thickened her accent, dropped her voice, and quoted, "You got a real purdy mouth, boy."

"Ya know, I never saw that movie."

"What? I thought everyone in Clayton had to watch it. It was, like, a requirement or something."

"My momma told me it wasn't fit for little ones. And by the time I got old enough, I reckon I wanted to forget where I came from. Too many bad memories."

Another pause.

Damnit Graham! Way to spoil the moment.

"They say home is where our stories start," she finally said, her voice soft and low. "Good thing *we* get to decide how they end."

For some reason, that made a lump form in his throat. He couldn't get a word around it.

"Well, okay then." Again, she was forced to fill the void he left in the conversation. "I'd better get back to it. You take care, Graham."

"You too, Lura," he managed. His usually gritty voice sounded like crushed gravel.

The *click* of the line disconnecting hit him in the chest like buckshot. It was sudden, surprising, and oddly final.

He'd gone nearly twenty years without seeing, talking, or even thinking about her. So why the hell did returning to that status quo make him feel so…*unsettled?*

Nostalgia, he told himself as he stepped away from the desk. *Sentimentality and a touch of homesickness. That's all it is.*

Somewhere in the back of his brain, a little voice whispered…*bullshit.*

CHAPTER 22

"Hey," Hew said quietly as he caught Sabrina on the bottom tread of the stairs leading up to the third floor. She was still barefoot. Still wearing that short silk robe that was doing its damnedest to kill him by inches. And her cheeks were flushed a pretty pink.

Flushed because of her conversation with Martin?

He could feel a muscle twitching in his jaw. The one beneath his right eye tried to follow suit, but he stilled it by briefly glancing away from her expectant expression toward the short hallway leading to the offices.

It'd taken every ounce of self-restraint he possessed not to eavesdrop on her call with the vertically challenged hedge fund manager. And *maybe* he'd even started down the hallway before turning on his heel because Boss and Graham had been posted up outside the door like a couple of goddamn bouncers.

Now, he hadn't a clue what she'd said to Martin. Where she stood with Martin. Whether her confession upstairs to *him* had changed everything or nothing between them.

He was flying blind.

He *hated* flying blind.

"Hew?"

Her voice drew his attention back to the moment. Back to her quizzical expression.

After clearing his throat—too noisily if her rapid blink was anything to go by—he finally managed, "We need to talk about—"

"All right, everyone!"

Boss's deep voice boomed across the mezzanine, slicing clean through Hew's words and his rapidly fraying nerves.

For fuck's sake! Can't a guy catch a break?

"Team meeting!" Boss marched to the railing and hollered down to the shop floor. "Let's gather in the War Room!"

The windy blast of the blowtorch quieted. Whoever had been using the metal grinder switched off the tool. And the only sound left in the whole place was Ozzie's music. But a second later, Black Sabbath's "Iron Man"—*RIP Ozzy Osbourne*—was silenced in the middle of the third verse.

"Do I have time to change?" Sabrina asked over Hew's shoulder. When he glanced back, he saw her tug at the belt on her robe.

He wanted to tug it.

With his *teeth*.

Ayuh. He'd spent nine months *refusing* to allow himself to have thoughts like that. Or, at the very least, shutting them down quickly when they reared their ugly heads. And all it'd taken was a few words from her and suddenly he was all Horny McHornerson.

Then again, he couldn't chastise himself too much. Because, at the end of the day, he was just a man. And she was a beautiful woman who—

"Two minutes." Boss dipped his chin toward Sabrina. "You're a major player in this discussion."

She gave a curt nod, squared her shoulders like the trooper she was, and ran up the stairs.

Don't watch her go. Don't watch her go. Don't—

Hew watched her go.

Loving the flash of her smooth, bare legs. Loving the way her peach-shaped ass pressed against the silk. But he managed to wrench his eyes away when she climbed high enough for him to sneak a peek beneath the hem of her robe.

He might be just a man, as debauched as the next—*probably more so*—but he drew the line at Peeping Tom.

After dropping into a seat at the long conference table, he frowned when Fish slid into the chair beside him. The chair usually reserved for Sabrina.

After a quick glance his way, Fish's eyebrows drew together over his nose. "You okay, bruh?"

Hew refrained from sighing heavily. "You're the second person to ask me that question in the last ten minutes."

"Probably because your face is screaming even though your mouth is clamped so tight I can almost see your teeth through your cheeks."

"Don't you usually sit over there?" Hew hitched his chin toward the seat across the table.

Fish craned around to look at his chair. He bent side to side and then used his hand to feel around beneath the seat.

"What are ya doin'?" Hew finally asked in annoyance.

"Seeing if someone pinned a sign with their name to this chair."

"Oh, haha. Very funny. You plannin' to take your show on the road sometime soon?"

Fish just smirked as he settled back into place. "Who ate your bowl of sunshine this morning, thundercloud?"

Hew dragged a hand down his face, hoping to wipe away his expression. He realized he was only slightly successful when Fisher continued to study him with narrowed eyes.

"Is Sabrina okay?" Fish finally asked. "No lingering effects from her abduction or the dehydration?"

All the jealousy Hew had felt since she flounced downstairs to take the hedge fund manager's call came out in his clipped tone.

"Seems fine. She certainly raced down here, quick as her legs could take her, to talk to Martin Massey."

"Ah."

It was a single syllable. But it held a wealth of meaning.

None of which Hew liked.

He opened his mouth to say…he wasn't sure. Probably something that would make him sound like an even *bigger* asshole. Thankfully, Sabrina saved him the embarrassment when she stepped off the last tread onto the second floor and announced, "Okay. I'm here." She checked the old-fashioned analog clock on the wall above Ozzie's bank of monitors. "With fifteen seconds to spare."

She wore jeans and a plain white T-shirt. No frills. No nonsense. Just her.

It was a wonder Hew's jockey shorts didn't burst into flames.

Just her was everything he hadn't allowed himself to want. Everything he'd told himself he couldn't have.

She'd swept her hair into that messy bun she wore when she wanted it off her neck. And lord help him, that pale strip of skin from her collarbone to her delicate jawbone made his mouth go dry.

Her cheap, plastic flip-flops clacked on the floor as she made her way to the chair across from him. And he couldn't help noting her toenails were painted a dark, sparkly purple.

He'd never had a thing for feet. Never really got the appeal.

But *Sabrina's* feet?

They were long and graceful, with high arches and smooth skin and—

Damn, man. You've spent months convincin' everyone—includin' yourself—that all ya feel for her is friendship. Then she tells you that there for a while she wanted more, and suddenly you're waxin' poetic about her damned feet?

After she sat, pulling her rolling chair close to the table, he tried to catch her eye. But she was either refusing to look at him, or she simply had no idea he was still stuck on their conversation from upstairs.

More than stuck. Mired. *Cemented* there until it was impossible to think about anything else.

Boss stood behind the chair at the head of the table. He cleared his throat once Graham, the last of the Knights to wander into the War Room, grabbed a seat.

"All right." Boss folded his big arms over his even bigger chest. "We got ourselves a hostage downstairs who's probably going to need some gentle persuading to answer a few questions."

"Gentle persuading." Ozzie snorted, but there was no humor in it. "That's one way to say *waterboarding*."

"We're hoping it won't come to that." Boss's face was grim. "We're hoping that after nearly eight hours in the damp and the dark, she's ready to pony up some answers."

"She won't be."

There was quiet certainty in Sabrina's tone. It had every head in the room turning in her direction.

"She's slick," Sabrina went on. "She had every man on her team eating out of her hand. If y'all want her to talk, you're going to have to find the chink in her armor, the thing she wants above all else."

"Tell us about her," Boss said, no doubt hoping to build the arsenal of information that he would use against the woman during interrogation.

Sabrina hesitated. Then, slowly, steadily, she laid it all out. Everything she'd gleaned during her time as a hostage. From the tone of Black Widow's voice when she spoke to each man in her crew to the glint in the blonde's eye when she allowed the one they called Diesel to abuse Sabrina's breast.

By the time Sabrina finished, Hew's breath was ragged. He white-knuckled the edges of his chair to keep himself from flying down to the Bat Cave and throttling the hired assassin with his bare hands.

"Hummer, Diesel, and Black Widow are probably code names," Boss muttered, rubbing a hand under his chin. "And given what you just told us about them, I'd say they're either ex-military, ex-fed, ex-spook, or some combination of the three. Which means there are records. See if you can find anything on them, Ozzie."

"Already on it." Ozzie's fingers flew over his laptop's keyboard.

"And then there's the one who hired them," Sabrina said.

Boss's bushy eyebrow arched up his forehead. "They *told* you who hired them?" he asked incredulously.

"Not directly." Sabrina shook her head. "But I heard them talking. And the only time I saw Black Widow look unnerved was when she spoke to the guy."

"Guy," Fisher said. "So it was a dude who put them up to the job. A single entity and not some group."

"I mean—" Sabrina twisted her fingers together. It was her habit when she was unsure of herself. She saw what she was doing and quickly hid her hands under the table. "I *think* it was a guy. They referred to him as a him."

She wrinkled her nose. "But now that I think about it, the name isn't gender specific. I mean, depending on the denomination, women can be bishops, right?" She frowned. "Or maybe Bishop refers to a chess piece?"

The name dropped like a two-ton anchor through the hull of the War Room.

Silence. Followed by a collective intake of breath. Then Sam uttered a curse not fit for mixed company.

"What?" Sabrina's startled gaze swept around the table. "Who's Bishop? Someone y'all know?"

"Someone we know *of*," Hew told her gruffly.

And just like that, her eyes landed on his and held for the first time since she'd returned downstairs.

He wasn't sure if *finally* having her full attention made him feel steadier… or like someone had yanked the floor out from under him. Was it possible to feel both?

"Who is he?" she asked warily.

"That's the million-dollar question." This from Fish.

"And we know just who to ask for the answer." Boss angled his gaze out over the second-story railing toward the shop's unremarkable brick wall.

Nothing special about it. Just a chunk of old factory façade…unless you knew about the button behind the rolling Craftsman toolbox. The one that activated the hidden door that pulled back to reveal the yawning black mouth of the Bat Cave and the evil bitch being kept on ice inside it.

"Graham and I have some work to do," Boss said.

"You need our help?" Sam asked, a muscle ticking under his eye.

Boss shook his head. "We have it covered. The rest of you go about your day. We got code names to trace, bikes to build, and at some point, we'll have to apprise the lady sitting in the Oval Office of our situation."

Hew didn't envy Graham or Boss. Not for one millisecond.

It took a special breed of man to stand before a prisoner and strip away their lies without losing sight of the line between justice and vengeance. Without losing a little piece of his soul to the hellish work that was enhanced interrogation.

As the group started disbanding, chairs scraping across the floor and boots thudding toward the stairs, Hew rose. His feet carried him around the table toward Sabrina like they had minds of their own.

"Hey." He caught her wrist gently.

She turned expectantly. Despite her seven hours of shut-eye, weariness left dark smudges beneath her eyes.

He wanted to rewind time and return to the moment she announced she was going for a drive. He'd *insist* on going with her. Chain himself to her back bumper if that's what it took.

"Either I'm suffering a severe case of déjà vu," she cut into his thoughts, "or we just did this song and dance over there." She tilted her head toward the staircase.

Right.

He cleared his throat. "We need to talk about—"

"Hew?"

Boss's voice. *Again.*

Damnit it all to hell!

Hew clenched his jaw so hard his back teeth ached before turning toward the head of Black Knights Inc. He made sure to temper his tone when he said, "Ayuh?"

"You got a minute?" Boss jerked his thumb toward his office door.

No, Hew wanted to snarl. *I don't have a minute. I don't have a friggin' second to spare until I talk to Sabrina about what she said upstairs.*

Instead, he reminded himself that the Black Knights had bigger fish to fry than his *will they/won't they/does she even still want to* relationship with their social media maven.

"I'll be right in," he told Boss, then turned back to Sabrina, ready to finish the sentence he'd started and stopped twice now.

However, the words slipped to the back of his tongue when he saw the look on her face. It was…worried? Distressed?

No, he decided. *It's pained.*

"I know you want to talk about what I told you upstairs," she said in a sudden rush. "But you really don't have to say anything. I really *do* understand where you stand. Where you've *been* standing. And it's okay, Hew. I'm a big girl. I've been rejected before and bounced back from it." She offered him a small smile that twisted in his heart like a blade. "When one door closes, another opens. Isn't that what they say?"

She did something then that damn near knocked the breath from his lungs. She patted his chest. A light touch. A simple touch. A *friendly* touch.

"I'm moving on." She nodded determinedly. "I've got Martin now. So there's nothing for you to feel bad about. Let's chalk up what happened earlier to sheer lunacy brought on by the stress and horror of the previous twenty-four hours and forget it ever happened. Can we do that? Can we go back to the way things were *before* I licked your neck like—" She glanced around to make sure no one was listening in. "Like a Push Pop on the Fourth of July?"

He couldn't speak. He couldn't breathe. In his mixed-up, muddled-up state, all he could do was nod.

He'd gotten damn good at nodding at her.

"Great." Her smile widened, taking up her whole face and crinkling the corners of her eyes. "Thank you, Hew."

She immediately turned for the stairs leading to the ground floor and left him staring after her with his mouth half open and his stomach hitting the soles of his shoes.

Moving on.

Got Martin now.

Forget it ever happened.

His fingers flexed, but he wasn't sure whose neck he wanted to throttle this time. He finally settled on his *own* because he'd been a damned fool. A *blind* fool.

She'd hinted. She'd tried. Hell, looking back, she'd stood right in front of him countless times with her heart in her eyes, and he hadn't seen it.

Or he'd been too chickenshit to act on it.

Or more likely, he'd been too Maine-stubborn to believe it.

He recalled one night months ago when they sat beside the fire pit, and she turned to ask him, *"Do you believe there's one person for everyone?"*

He'd laughed off the question, giving her some flippant reply about how he *hoped* not because that would mean some of his foster folks had been fated to find each other, and that just seemed too awful to contemplate.

God, what a jackass.

He'd missed the boat entirely. And now he'd be forced to watch her sail away in it with someone else.

When he remembered Martin actually *had* a boat—a real one, not a metaphorical one—he laughed. Or choked. He couldn't tell the difference.

"Hew!" Boss's voice echoed. "Time's a-wastin'."

"On my way." He turned on stiff legs. But he'd only taken three steps before a thought occurred that stopped him in his tracks.

He hadn't missed the boat. He'd shot a hole in the damn thing, sinking it himself.

CHAPTER 23

Vivian wasn't a stranger to fear.

She could chart the sensation like a map. Fear pinched behind the ribs. Sat cold and heavy in the gut. Crept into the dark hollow of the throat like a swallowed scream.

Fear was a part of her job.

But this?

This was different.

This wasn't fear of bullets and bombs. This wasn't fear of danger and destruction. This was fear of—

Stop it!

The words thundered through her head.

Stop it right now!

Letting herself fall prey to panic was a sure-fire way to lose her damned mind. And she needed her wits about her. Needed to keep sharp. Stay steady.

How long have I been here? she wondered, knowing it had been hours. But how many? *Two? Twenty?*

It was impossible to tell.

Also…*where is here?*

She'd been blindfolded and handcuffed in the chopper. Chopper! The

Black Knights had a motherfucking *helicopter*, and Bishop hadn't bothered to tell her about it.

He hadn't bothered to tell her about a lot.

She'd been flown…somewhere. She'd counted twenty minutes before she'd lost track. Her ears had popped twice during the descent.

But where had they landed?

O'Hare airport?

No. Somewhere smaller. More private.

There'd been no roar of jet engines. No *beep, beep, beep* of cargo trucks backing up. Just the distant buzz of the city and the occasional muffled conversation.

Then came the trunk. She'd fought to keep from being shoved inside. She'd kicked and screamed. But all that had gotten her was a sweaty length of fabric shoved into her mouth and a strip of duct tape slapped over her lips.

In the end, she'd been folded into the cramped space like human origami. Every bump in the road had jarred her bones. Every breath had seemed to lack enough oxygen to feed her brain. She'd kicked at the enclosure until her thighs ached. But…again…she'd gained absolutely nothing.

And now…*this.*

She sat strapped to a metal chair. Ankles bound. Wrists cinched tight behind her back.

At first, her nostrils had flared at the scents pressing in on her. Wet concrete. Musky mildew. Fish? But she'd long since gone nose-blind to the smells. And now, the only thing that reached her nose was the slightly chemical odor of the duct tape beneath it.

A soft *plip-plip-plip* told her water dripped nearby. It reverberated. Echoed into empty space.

But it wasn't a *large* empty space. She could feel the cold, hard presence of rock walls—or maybe concrete?—hovering around her. Over her.

Had they left her in a cave? An old bomb shelter? A bunker?

She was underground. She was certain of that.

Somewhere deep. Somewhere hidden. Somewhere where silence echoed, but there was no light. No time. No certainty.

Just…thoughts.

That was always the worst part of capture, of confinement. Not the pain. Not the thirst or the hunger. Not even the not-knowing.

It was the *thinking*.

Thinking about the mission. Thinking about where and how they'd gone wrong. Thinking about her team. Dead. All of them down to the last man.

It'd taken her four years to gather and train them into a unit she could depend on. Starting over would be a pain in the ass.

If she *lived* long enough to start over.

Because even if she managed to escape this place, she'd failed. Failed in her mission to kill the hostage. Failed in her job to shine a light on the true nature of Black Knights Inc. Failed in the task Bishop had set before her.

Bishop.

From the beginning, she'd known he didn't do forgiveness. Didn't believe in second chances. Measured lack of success in ounces of blood and pieces of bone.

He was the true source of her fear and—

Motorized movement cut into her thoughts. It was a mechanical growl. Like a garage door, but bigger. Thicker. Heavier.

She'd heard it once before, after they'd pulled her from the trunk and secured her to the chair. And now, just like then, she blindly turned toward the fresh air that poured across her face. Her nostrils flared at the smell of motor oil and molten metal.

The motorcycle shop?

Was the cave/bomb shelter/bunker attached to the old menthol cigarette factory?

Bishop hadn't mentioned that either.

The sonofabitch. This was all *his* fault. If he'd told her—

Footsteps echoed and interrupted her thoughts. They were heavy. Booted. Coming closer with each heartbeat.

One man? Two?

She caught a faint whiff of aftershave mixed with laundry detergent. Beneath all that was the familiar scent of gun cleaner.

The air around her shifted, grew warmer. He was close. *They* were close. Within arm's length.

She braced for the slap. For the punch. For the bullet or the blade.

None came.

And then…there it was again. The grinding sound of metal on metal as the garage door that wasn't a garage door swung shut, taking the fresh air with it and sealing her back inside the damp and the dark.

She could hear the breaths of those who'd joined her. The soft sound of air filling lungs. Then…something clicked. A flashlight?

Yeah. A flashlight.

Dull light filtered through the fabric of the blindfold. A second later, the cloth was pulled away, and she was left blinking against the darkness.

But it wasn't a true black now. The pale glow of the handheld lamp carved out just enough contrast to paint shadows across the concrete walls and show her the long, dark tunnel that seemed to dip down into nothingness.

The road to hell, she couldn't help thinking.

She'd always assumed it would be hot and sulfurous, not cold and fishy-smelling.

She tried to see the end of it, the orange glow of a sulfur fire. But the blackness was complete. And she was left to swing her attention to the man who stood directly before her.

He looked as solid as a mountain. His face was just as craggy.

Beside him towered another man. Younger. Prettier. But just as big. Just as dangerous-looking.

The eyes they fixed on her were unreadable. And the lack of emotion on their faces made her skin feel like it was crawling with bugs.

It occurred to her then…

She'd been focused on what Bishop would do to her when she *should* have been focused on what the Black Knights could do.

CHAPTER 24

Graham wasn't a fan of confined spaces. And the damn tunnel dug down beneath the Chicago River always seemed to close in on him when he set foot inside it.

Too much weight pressed against the walls. Not enough sky showed above his head.

A tomb.

The hairs on his neck rose, but he refused to shudder. Instead, he kept his stare hard and mean and locked on the woman tied to the metal chair.

He might not be a fan of confined spaces. But he absolutely *hated* interrogation.

The entire process was antithetical to anyone who valued their humanity.

It took all that was good and sacred inside a man and stomped on it, leaving him wondering if what he'd pulled out of his interrogee's mouth was worth the pieces of himself he'd lost in the process.

He'd only done it once before. Back in Syria. Back when he'd been a wet-behind-the-ears baby SEAL. Cocksure and cavalier. Still convinced his trident pin made him ten feet tall and bombproof.

His prisoner had been some mid-level terrorist with info Graham's unit needed *yesterday*. And Graham…well…he'd followed orders. Played the hard-ass just like he'd been trained to do.

He'd gotten the intel.

But he still sometimes saw that man's eyes at night. That broken look. That hollowness that said that prisoner's soul had fallen through the cracks in his flesh while Graham had used his fists on him and…whatever else it took.

The thought of having to do the same to this woman, this…Black Widow, or Vivian Drake, or whatever she wanted to call herself, made his stomach heave until he regretted that fourth cream Danish. And the three that had preceded it.

Eight hours in the Bat Cave had left the blonde's hair limp and clinging to her face. There was a smudge of dirt on her jaw. And, despite the coolness of the cavern, sweat dotted her brow.

But her chin was up like a queen sitting on her throne. And he'd swear her nostrils flared like she was breathing in hellfire.

Not that he was surprised by her bravado.

Ozzie had used his hacker magic to conjure up the intel on her and her team. Which meant they now knew the woman wasn't your average, everyday hired gun.

Vivian Drake, aka Black Widow, had spent ten years with the CIA working as a swallow, a female agent trained to seduce information out of foreign marks. But somewhere along the line, seducing had turned to killing. And she hadn't stopped, even when the agency had ordered her to.

Which is when they'd given her the boot.

Now…she was Graham's problem.

Boss's problem too.

They needed to drag Bishop's identity out of her. Unfortunately, she'd been through the same course on advanced interrogation techniques that they had. And *that* meant this would be more difficult than it might have been otherwise.

Unless they could find the right button to push. The right leverage to use.

"So," Boss finally drawled after they'd exhausted their intimidation technique of looming and glowering. "How would you like us to proceed, Miss Drake?"

Graham saw it. A flicker. Just the barest tick of her lashes when Boss used her real name.

"Oh, yes." Boss stepped closer, deep voice thick and edgy, like honey dripping over a sharpened blade. "We know all about you. Recruited straight out of college. Top marks at Camp Peary. Worked in Moscow, Kyiv, Damascus, and D.C."

Graham saw her jaw tighten behind the duct tape. But that was the only indication she gave that Boss's words hit a nerve.

"Struck out on your own after the spooks cut you loose," Boss continued. "Been doing wet work for anyone willing to pay your fee for the last six years. And now, here you are, because Bishop promised you a paycheck."

Bishop.

The code name that kept popping up when they least expected it.

The ghost in the machine.

Without warning, Boss ripped the duct tape off Black Widow's mouth.

She didn't scream. Didn't so much as flinch, even though a bead of blood welled on her bottom lip where the tape had taken skin with it.

Graham's gut revolted.

He knew what she was. A stone-cold killer who didn't care about the line between right and wrong. Who saw no difference between murdering those who were guilty or innocent. But…still…

She spat out the soggy handkerchief Sam had shoved in her mouth the night before. Then, she licked the blood on her lip.

Slowly.

Deliberately.

Her eyes locked on Graham like she was challenging him to speak up.

"You boys want me to talk?" Her voice was hoarse from hours of suffering with the gag. "Then you better be prepared to make me bleed worse than this."

Graham stepped forward. Showing her the steel in him. Hiding his disgust with the entire business.

"One way or another, we *will* hear everything ya have to say 'bout Bishop." He kept his voice low and steady but ensured she could hear its honed edge. "How much ya bleed before that happens is entirely up to you."

She smiled then, her teeth tinged pink in the low glow of the flashlight in Boss's hand.

"Well, now," she cooed. "A Southern boy with a violent streak. You're just my type, sugar."

Something twisted in the center of his chest. Revulsion, maybe. Or just the echo of his mama's voice saying, *"Don't ya never raise a hand to a woman, Graham Coleburn."*

"Why did Bishop hire you? What was his endgame?" Boss's tone was as flat as West Texas.

She shrugged like she wasn't tied up and two bad minutes away from this interrogation moving on from the *talking* phase to the *fear and pain* phase.

"Who cares? I failed. Which means, when it comes to your merry little band of brothers, all's well that ends well, right?"

Graham leaned his shoulder against the concrete wall like he had all the time in the world. Like he was ready to settle in and really draw this thing out.

"Like ya said." He kept his voice casual, conversational. "You failed. So there's no reason ya can't just come out and tell us what it was you were hired to accomplish in the first place."

Her mouth twisted, and he saw the cruelty and callousness behind her beauty. "What's in it for me?"

"What do you want?" Boss asked.

She turned from Graham and leaned forward as far as her restraints would allow. Her face was only three inches from Boss's big thigh as she grinned up at the man.

"I want you to tell me how you found us. You knew where we were long before I called to give you the location of the money drop."

"You're not as smart as you think you are." Boss shrugged and took a casual step back. Graham didn't blame him. He wouldn't want to be that close to the viper, either. "And we're a whole helluva lot better than Bishop led you to believe. Obviously."

Graham saw it then. The subtle narrowing of her eyes. The quick flex of her jaw.

Bishop was their ticket to getting her to talk. She blamed him for her current predicament. And a woman like her wouldn't take kindly to losing her team *or* her freedom.

"Let me guess." Graham kept his easy-like tone. "He told ya this'd be a simple job. Grab one of the women, hold her hostage, demand ransom, and then…what? Kill all of us who showed up for the drop?"

"He didn't care how many of you I killed," she hissed. "He just wanted me to leave enough of a mess so the authorities would have to investigate, and the clues would lead them back here. *I* was the one who decided to end all of you after that brunette bitch stuck a glass shard in my guy's throat."

Gotcha.

One part of the mystery was solved. Bishop wanted to expose Black Knights Inc. to the world.

But why? Did he have a vendetta against the president? Was he simply tired of the Knights showing up at inopportune times to throw a wrench in his works?

Also…*Sabrina* slit the big guy's throat?

Well, what'd'ya know, Graham thought. *Our resident social media pro has more gumption than I gave her credit for. Good for her.*

The blonde blinked when she realized all she'd revealed. He could see her wheels spinning, looking for ways to turn her confession to her advantage.

"So maybe I didn't fail after all, huh?" She was back to projecting bravado. "That chopper you shoved me into was surely picked up on radar. The authorities are bound to find my men's bodies. Will ballistics lead them here, I wonder?"

"Come on," Boss snorted. "Our chopper's got no tail numbers, no transponder. We flew completely dark." He let that shoe hang in the air for a beat before dropping the second one. "And your men's bodies? Two FBI agents have already disposed of them."

Graham saw the shock that flashed through Black Widow's eyes.

He latched onto it.

"Ah." He pasted on a sympathetic expression. "Another of Bishop's omissions, huh? He didn't tell ya we have an in with the local feds? He really *did* send you into the seventh circle of hell without any warnin', didn't he? Your assignment was pretty much doomed from the get-go."

Hunter and Britt had drawn the short straws when it came to doing the dirty work of corpse cleanup back at the bottling plant. Their partners, Grace and Julia, had run cover for them. So Boss had only fudged a *little* when he'd said two FBI agents had handled the problem.

All four of the Black Widow's henchmen were now food for the fish at the bottom of Lake Michigan.

"Tell us who he is." Boss's tone shifted. It was almost…*gentle* now. "You don't owe him anything. Hell, him holding back on you is what got your crew killed and what got *you* into *this* mess." He waved a big hand around at the shadows undulating on the weeping walls.

She bared her teeth. "You don't know who he is? You seem to know every other goddamned thing."

Graham stepped in, exploring that chink in her armor. Looking for just the right leverage to split it wide open. "We can protect ya from him, if that's what you're worried about."

She laughed, sharp and humorless. "I can protect myself."

But he saw it then. The subtle eye-twitch. The tiniest hesitation.

She feared Bishop. And fear—real fear—was just the crowbar he needed.

"Then how's about, once we find him, we make sure he can't do to anyone else what he did to you and yours?"

That got her attention.

Her eyes fired like silver bullets. Cold. Fast. Straight into him. "What did you have in mind?"

He smirked. "Use your imagination."

"I can imagine some *very* unpleasant things," she assured him.

"Multiply that by ten and you'll begin to scratch the surface of what we're capable of."

Boss leaned in. "Who is he? Can we use *this* to contact him?" Boss pulled from his pocket the cheap plastic flip phone they'd taken off her when they first apprehended her. "There are only two phone numbers on this thing. One is BKI's. Is the other one his, Vivian?"

He'd used her given name on purpose to create a sense of intimacy, of shared intention.

Damned if it didn't work. Her eyes softened. Just a hair. But it was enough.

There was no more bluster in her tone when she said, "If I tell you what I know, you have to promise to go after him. The only way he won't come for me is if you get to him first."

"We've been anxious to expose Bishop for what he is for *years* now," Boss admitted. "Believe you me, our number one priority from here on out is to find the fucker and deal with him the only way traitors *can* be dealt with."

The assassin hesitated a second longer, looking for the truth in Boss's eyes. When she saw it, she opened her mouth and ponied up everything she knew. The first time Bishop had contacted her. All the things she'd gleaned during their conversations. The *hints* he'd inadvertently dropped.

The more she spoke, the higher Graham's heart climbed into the column of his throat because…

It sounded like Lura Dougherty might be in grave danger.

CHAPTER 25

All things considered, Sabrina decided it was a good day.

She was fed and watered—maybe overwatered, since she'd peed twice more following that initial time. She'd apologized to Martin for missing their date, and he'd been heart-wrenchingly kind about it, saying he was just glad she was okay before asking her to meet later for a drink. And she'd cleared the air with Hew after that whole neck-kissing debacle.

So, yeah, a good day.

Four men are dead, the voice in her head chided. *Black Widow is tied up in the Bat Cave. And some dude the Knights don't know wants them all six feet under and pushing up daisies.*

A good day?

Okay. Fair enough. Maybe *good* was pushing it.

But those four men were fully prepared to kill me and everyone I care about, she reminded the voice. *Black Widow is evil and deserves whatever she gets. And, if we're lucky, Graham and Boss will soon know Bishop's true identity and—*

The Bat Cave door ground slowly open, halting her thoughts and her feet at the base of the stairs leading to the second floor.

That was fast, she thought. And she wondered if *fast* was a good thing or a bad thing when it came to interrogation.

She braced herself for the sight of Graham and Boss. She had a hard time envisioning either man raising a hand to a woman. But apparently, they'd been trained to do just that.

To her relief, though, they both appeared in the yawning mouth of the tunnel looking none the worse for wear. No bruised knuckles. No hints of horror in their eyes.

Her relief was short-lived, however, when she saw the grim cant of Boss's jaw and the hard fists Graham kept curled at his sides.

Something Black Widow said has them spooked.

She craned her head, trying to catch a glimpse of the assassin before the brick wall slid shut on its tracks. The tunnel looked empty. No platinum head in sight. Which meant Black Widow was being held farther down, probably past that first steep bend.

Sabrina shuddered at the thought.

Before last night, she'd only been in the Bat Cave once before. And once was enough.

The place put the *eep* in creepy.

Boss waited for the brick wall to seal shut with a solid-sounding *thunk* before circling his finger in the air. "Back upstairs, everyone. We need to talk."

Sabrina's stomach balled into a fist as she quickly made her way to the War Room. She was the first to grab a seat at the conference table, and she placed her second cup of coffee in front of her, watching it cool because her stomach was suddenly too jittery to take a sip.

Hew slid into the chair beside her, his expression unreadable. But his arm touched hers atop the table.

She almost pulled away. After what happened earlier, it felt odd to touch him.

Then again, *she'd* been the one to ask *him* to forget about it, to go back to the way things were. So it'd be the height of hypocrisy if she couldn't do the same.

To keep from concentrating too much on how good he smelled, on how warmly his body heat wrapped around her, on the stark contrast between the pale skin on her forearm and the tan skin on his, she offered him a wan smile and grabbed her mug.

Yes, it was an excuse to stop touching him.

Yes, she was a coward who couldn't even play by her own rules.

Yes, she had to steel her stomach for what was about to enter it when she tipped the mug to her lips.

Just as she'd suspected, her belly revolted by twisting and threatening to bring up what she'd just sent down to it. But she refrained from gagging and instead chanced a glance over at Hew to see if he'd picked up on her discomfort.

God, she loved his profile.

Loved how his jawline was highlighted by his close-cropped beard. Loved how dark and thick his lashes were. Loved *him*.

It hit her now as suddenly as it'd hit her upstairs. And the urge to blurt out her feelings was nearly overwhelming.

But she couldn't burden him with the truth. It wasn't fair after all he'd done for her. After all she owed him.

So she'd concentrate on what they *did* have.

Affection. Understanding. Friendship.

It was enough. She'd *make* it enough.

And besides, Martin deserved better than to have her pining for another. He was thoughtful and sweet. He planned dates and never missed a chance to tell her she was smart and funny. He was clear about what he wanted from her and what he wanted to give her.

In short, he was perfect. He just wasn't…*Hew*.

But, god willing, if there's a way to take all the love Hew doesn't want from me and transfer it to Martin, I'll find it.

"Black Widow couldn't give us a name." Boss's booming voice cut across the conference table and into her thoughts.

A disgruntled groan rolled through the room.

Boss lifted a calloused hand, palm out. "Because she doesn't *know* the name," he clarified. "But she knows enough."

Every head was suddenly pinned in his direction, every eye glued to his face.

"She's certain Bishop is someone high up in government. Near the top. And if just half of what she told us is true about the things he said to her, the things he *knows*, I believe her."

"High up in government." Fish scratched his chin. "So, who are we talking about? The VP? Speaker of the House?"

"Maybe the head of the Joint Chiefs?" Ozzie offered. "The former head knew about the OG operation here, so maybe…" He made a rolling motion with his hand.

"Could be anyone close to the president," Boss agreed. "Anyone she trusts enough to tell about us."

Eliza leaned forward, her dark eyes worried. "I thought the whole point was that Madam President didn't tell *anyone* about us. I thought the whole point was the secret was kept between her and my father."

Sabrina winced.

Leonard Meadows was the first person to come to mind when Boss said the words *high up in government.*

Something about the man had never set right with her. He always sounded so cold. So…*transactional.* Like his daughter was just another one of his employees. Like BKI was nothing but a tool to be used and tossed aside if it ever stopped serving him.

Fisher squeezed Eliza's hand atop the table. "His assistant found out about us. Which means there could be others who know."

"I can think of maybe a half-dozen folks who might fit the bill. Who the president might've felt obliged to enlighten," Hew added, because he was just so…Hew.

For a kid who'd grown up fending for himself, his ability to empathize with others amazed her.

"Yes." Eliza nodded, her expression still stricken. "And one of those folks is my father." She glanced around the table. "But why? Why would he want to kill all of you or expose any of this?" She held her hands wide. "What would that gain him?"

Boss shook his head. "We won't know the *why* until we figure out the *who.*"

Ozzie nodded, his unkempt hair waving in the breeze of the overhead vents. "So that's step one. Figure out the who. It's a short list. It shouldn't be too hard."

"And maybe this will help." Boss pulled a black burner phone from his hip pocket and shoved it into the middle of the table. Sabrina recognized it. The last time she'd seen it, it had been in Black Widow's hand.

"It's the phone she used to contact us and to contact him," Boss told the group.

Ozzie reached for the device. Thumbed it open. Glanced at the screen.

"The number is probably encrypted." He hastily typed something on his laptop. Squinted. Typed again. "Definitely encrypted."

"We could call it," Sam suggested. "At the very least, we'd have his voice on record when he answers. We could run it through Ozzie's voice recognition software."

"Black Widow says he always uses a voice modulator," Graham said. "And if we call him, he'll know we're onto him."

"Exactly." Ozzie frowned. "I'll do some more work on tracing the number, but I—"

He stopped abruptly when Peanut launched his fat, furry body onto the table, landing on the edge with a solid-sounding *thump*.

"Jesus." Fish caught his coffee mug just before the old tom could tip it.

The cat sauntered across the table like it was his own personal runway, flicking his tail into Ozzie's face, sniffing Sabrina's coffee, and then—with the deliberateness only cats possess—sitting down in front of Hew to lift a leg and thoroughly clean his butthole.

"How are we supposed to have a serious conversation with *this* goin' on?" Graham gestured toward the former alley cat.

"You're just jealous because you can't lick *your* butt," Fisher quipped.

"True." Graham shrugged. Then, when he saw Boss eyeing him closely, he demanded, "What's with your face?"

"Ozzie's right." Boss nodded, not joining in the joking, keeping squarely attuned to business. "Bishop could only be a handful of folks. He shouldn't be hard to find if we have a man inside the West Wing."

"A man inside the West Wing?" Graham blinked uncomprehendingly.

"Maybe I should've said a *woman* inside," Boss stressed. "You think your friend Lura's up for the task?"

Sabrina lifted an eyebrow at the muscle that started ticking in Graham's strong jaw.

Boss had given her the skinny on Lura Dougherty. But Graham's reaction said maybe there was more to the story than she'd been told.

"She's not my friend," Graham insisted. "She's an acquaintance from back home. And she's an assistant, not an operator. She doesn't have the trainin' for—"

"She doesn't need training to keep her ear cocked and her nose to the ground," Boss interrupted.

Graham's nostril flared and Sabrina lifted an eyebrow. Her curiosity was well and truly piqued.

Boss's next words came out slow and deliberate. "Graham, my man, how do you feel about a trip to D.C.?"

Sabrina didn't hear Graham's response because Hew suddenly slung an arm across the back of her chair. His forearm warmed the back of her neck. His fingers brushed her shoulder.

It was nothing he hadn't done a hundred times before. It was friendly. Unceremonious.

Ha! Tell that to my nervous system, she thought hysterically.

Every synapse in her head short-circuited. All the oxygen had been sucked from the room, and even though her lungs worked, she couldn't get enough air.

He squeezed her shoulder. Offering casual comfort just as he'd been doing since the day they met. Except her skin tingled like champagne bubbles ran beneath it.

She knew what it was to taste him now. Knew how warm his skin was against her lips. Knew how his pulse felt as it beat against the tip of her tongue.

She crossed her legs against the ache in her sex. Refused to look down for fear she'd see her nipples pearled against the front of her T-shirt.

She could *feel* Hew looking at her expectantly. Besides being observant, he was incredibly perceptive to the slightest change in her breathing. Undoubtedly, he'd clocked her subtle gasp and wondered what had caused it.

Ignoring him would be proof that even though she'd asked *him* to forget what happened upstairs, *she* was the one who, despite talking the talk, couldn't walk the walk.

So she risked a glance.

Determination glinted in his gorgeous green eyes, and his expression told her he still wanted to talk. Still had something to say about that kiss.

Shit.

Swallowing jerkily, she desperately looked for a way to avoid the coming catastrophe as the meeting broke up. Chairs scraped. Coffee mugs clunked. Individual conversations sprang up.

Aha! she thought as Fish pulled Hew aside. *Just the distraction I need!*

After quietly slipping away from the conference table, she took the stairs to the third floor two at a time.

Coward, that little voice chided.

Fine. She was a coward. But she needed a second to breathe. A second to *think.*

She might just blurt out the truth if he started grilling her, pushing for a more thorough explanation.

And if she thought kissing his neck had changed things between them, that was nothing compared to what admitting that she was in love with him would do.

She'd barely closed her bedroom door, leaning against it in momentary relief, when a sharp knock sounded.

Oh, god.

Remember when she said she was having a good day, all things considered?

She retracted that statement.

CHAPTER 26

Sabrina opened the door, and Hew narrowed his eyes.

She'd bolted upstairs after the meeting, and he hadn't missed the tight set of her jaw or the pale cast to her face. It was clear that all the talk of Black Widow and Bishop had shaken her.

"Y'okay?" he asked.

"Fine." Her voice was thin. Not brittle, exactly, but close enough to have him arching an eyebrow.

"I hate callin' bullshit. But…bullshit."

Her sigh was theatrically breathy. "Come in."

She stepped back, holding the door wide.

His boots sank into the plush rug as he crossed the threshold. He blinked when she shut the door behind him with a solid *thud*.

She never closed the door when they were together in her room. He'd always thought it was because she didn't want the others to get the wrong idea about them.

"Okay." She lifted both hands in a come-on gesture. "I'm ready. Give it to me. Lock, stock, and two smoking barrels."

"Huh?" His pulse kicked hard enough to have him blinking rapidly.

"Let me have it," she said. "I'm ready."

Surely, *surely*, she didn't mean what it *sounded* like she meant. Although images of him *giving it to her* and *letting her have it* crashed through his brain like a rogue wave in Penobscot Bay.

"I…uh…" He swallowed. Or tried to. Mostly, he just made a strangled sound.

Her beautiful mouth turned down. "I know I haven't given you a chance to say your piece. So here's your shot. Give it to me."

Ayuh. *That.*

He didn't know if he was relieved or disappointed she'd shut the door because she thought he needed privacy for a conversation instead of privacy for—

He put the brakes on that line of thinking hard enough to throw sparks. It was that or his jeans were going to start feeling two sizes too small.

It took him a moment to gather his wits. And even after two deep breaths, he still struggled with where to start.

Should he tell her he hadn't bolted the night they flipped through his parents' yearbook because he was nervous about her hand on his thigh, but because he'd sprung a hard-on like a goddamn teenager and needed a minute to cool his jets?

Or maybe he should admit that when she'd asked about his type after Red Delilah's, it'd been *right there* on the tip of his tongue to say, *My type's five-foot-six, has a smile as bright as sunlight, and answers to the name Sabrina.*

Or he could simply fess up that the day she'd tripped on the beach and landed in his arms, he'd wanted to kiss her so badly that his teeth had hurt, and the whole brushing-sand-off-her-jeans thing had just been a ploy to hide the lust in his eyes.

In the end, he went with, "You're wrong."

She blinked. Then, she nodded slowly. "I'm wrong about a lot of things. But what specific wrong are we talking about here?"

"I'm attracted to ya," he said, seeing her expression blank, as if his words didn't compute. "You're a beautiful woman. Any man with blood runnin' through his veins would be."

"Yeah, okay." She scoffed, waving a hand like she was shooing a fly. "But there's attraction… and then there's *attraction.* There's the *oh, she's pretty* sort of attraction. And then there's the *holy shit, I want to see her naked* sort of attraction."

She crossed to the chair beside the bed and dropped into it with a tired little huff. After picking up the stuffed lobster, she stroked its silk claws between her fingers.

He nearly groaned because damned if his body didn't react like she was rubbing *him.*

Jesus, son, he silently told his unruly dick. *Get a hold of yourself.*

He imagined his dick replying, *I'd rather* she *get a hold of me.*

Great. Now, he was having a made-up conversation with his own penis.

He cleared his throat once. Then again before stiff-legging it to sit on the bed because, despite his best efforts, his jeans had shrunk.

Sabrina didn't seem to notice—*thank god.* She was too busy frowning down at the toy as she continued to rub, rub, *rub.*

For fuck's sake.

He had to look somewhere besides her hands.

His eyes dropped, and he immediately knew it for the mistake it was. Her sparkly purple toenails winked up at him like they knew what they were doing.

Teasing him.

Taunting him.

Putting images in his head of how they'd looked resting in the crooks of his knees as he thrust into her or hooked over his shoulders as he buried his face in her sweet, wet—

Damnit all to hell!

Okay. Shirt.

Just look at her shirt. Plain white cotton. A safe zone. Nothin' to see there.

Except…he caught the faintest outline of the lace that edged the cups of her bra. Delicate. Sweet. *Deadly* to his ability to think or breathe or keep from having to sit funny.

Fuck it!

He gave up and focused on her face. On her eyes. Except…those sweet, brown pools weren't soft and warm. They were wary. Guarded.

Get on with it, dickhead, he told himself. *Stop torturin' the poor woman.*

After raking in a deep breath, he blurted, "When ya first came here, I thought ya were the sexiest woman I'd ever seen."

She rolled her eyes. "When I first came here, I was terrified, malnourished, mourning my brother, and so traumatized I could barely see straight."

"Exactly." He pointed at her nose. That straight, perfect nose he'd stared at dozens of times when she didn't know he was looking. "You were *all* of that. Which is why I made myself *not* see how sexy ya were. You didn't need some big, hairy guy lustin' after ya. You needed a *friend.*"

Her face softened. "Your friendship means everything to me." Her tone was so earnest it hurt. "I don't think I would've made it without you."

"You'd have made it. You're tough."

Her eyes melted then, like molasses warming on a stove. "And you're tender. Tender is what I needed. I'm not sure I've ever thanked you for that."

"I'm not *always* tender," he assured her. "I've got impulses and instincts like any other man. But I got used to white-knucklin' it. I think maybe I got too used to it. I didn't notice when things changed for you." He watched the pulse flutter in her neck as delicately as a butterfly's wings. He wanted to cover it with his lips to soothe its rhythm.

"It's why I didn't realize you were hintin' ya wanted more," he finished, lifting his hands in a helpless shrug.

Her words about one door closing and another opening whispered through his head. *I have Martin now.* He dropped his hands so he could curl them around the edge of the mattress.

"It wasn't like a switch flipped one day," she explained, still caressing the lobster's claws. "It happened slowly." She made a sad face. "Because I was scared."

"Of me?" He hated the very thought.

"Of *me.*" Her voice cracked, just a little. "The idea of being intimate with someone terrified me. What if I freaked out in the middle of it? What if I couldn't relax and enjoy myself? What if I found out that the part of me that…Eddy took"—she curled her lip like saying the man's name made her sick—"was gone for good?"

He pictured Eddy Torres's face. And he hoped there was a hell, because he hoped the bastard was burning in it.

Her expression turned sheepish. "I figured who better than my good friend Hew to see me through it?" Her chuckle sounded self-deprecating. "But now I realize that was unfair of me. I was being unfair to *you.*"

Unfair? he wanted to shout. *In what world?*

Then, her words sank in. *My good friend Hew.* She wasn't confessing to romance or love. She was confessing to comfort and convenience.

He was her *friend*. He was *safe*. He wouldn't judge her if things went pear-shaped in the thick of it.

What was that feeling tumbling around behind his ribs?

Disappointment?

"And now you have Martin." Could she hear how the words dripped like bitter bile from his tongue?

"Maybe." She nodded, and he felt a small kernel of hope lodge under his heart because *maybe* wasn't a definitive *yes*. "He's definitely expressed interest."

"I'm sure he has," he grumbled, his jaw working back and forth.

"But I haven't told him about…" She swallowed. "What happened to me. And I'm going to have to before we…" Her cheeks heated, and she dropped his gaze. "Before we do anything."

He made a decision then.

It was an irresponsible, hasty, *reckless* decision. It was a decision that might very well break his heart in the end. But the words were out of his mouth before he could think about the consequences.

"Or you could still let me be the one."

CHAPTER 27

Sabrina's brain chose that moment to stop comprehending English.

She knew the look she gave Hew was the same one she might give a guy who'd suddenly sprouted corn cobs from his ears. And as soon as she opened her mouth, she closed it again because the words caught in her throat. She had to press a hand to her chest to make sure her heart was still beating.

Yup. More than beating. Racing out of control.

"I'm sorry. I think I took one too many raps to the ol' noggin' in that bottling plant." She tapped her temple. "Could you repeat what you just said?"

"I don't think it should be Martin." His delicious accent made it sound like *Mahtin.* "I think it should be me."

"But...but..." she sputtered, blinking. "Don't you hear those alarm bells?" She pointed into the air. "The ones screaming that this is a bad idea between friends?"

"Historically, when it comes to alarm bells, I'm tone deaf."

He looked so calm. By contrast, her emotions were breaking through her bloodstream and making her feel high. Or drunk. Or oxygen-deprived.

Didn't he worry about what would happen after? Didn't he realize that if they had sex, she'd probably grow to love him more, and that might ruin her for any man in the future?

That was all he was offering, right? Sex for the sake of making her feel safe? Sex for the sake of helping her heal? Sex for the sake of sex, without any conditions or expectations?

Her heart twisted into a hard knot.

But her ovaries? Oh, they cartwheeled, begging her to forget about hearts and consequences. Telling her she should focus instead on the promise of slick tongues and hot skin and tangled sheets and—

"I…I…" She tried to form words, but her whole body betrayed her. Her vocal cords included.

His green eyes glittered in the soft yellow light of her dresser lamp. That look—dark and daring—urged her to trust him. To trust *this*. To admit it was a good idea.

But was it?

She didn't know. She couldn't think.

That little voice of reason sure had an opinion, though. It shouted at her in big capital letters. *SAVE YOURSELF! SAVE YOUR HEART!*

When he leaned forward to take her hand, she sucked in a ragged breath.

How many times had he touched her? Too many to count. How many times had she curled her fingers through his? More than she could remember.

So why did *this* touch feel so different? So unfamiliar and titillating?

Of course, she knew.

All those previous touches had been platonic, done out of a need to comfort. He had something besides comfort in mind now. Something that curled her toes and dried her throat and made her skin feel too tight.

When she dared to look at him, there was no denying the set of his square jaw. The resolution in his expression.

"Have ya changed your mind?" His voice slid into her like smoke—curling, teasing, slipping through all the cracks in her good sense.

She glanced down at their joined hands. At the sheer *maleness* of his long, knobby-knuckled fingers compared to her pale, slim ones. Images of what it would be like to have those fingers tracing over her body, flicking her nipples, pushing inside her in a steady rhythm bloomed to life in her mind's eye.

"Did I miss my chance?" His voice was even softer now. A *bedroom* voice, and heaven help her. "Would ya rather it was Martin?"

"God, no." The two words burst out of her before she'd even formed them in her head.

His chuckle was low and delicious. *Sinful.*

"Look at me, Sabrina."

Not a request. A demand.

And she thought, maybe for the first time in nine months, she was getting to see the *real* Hewitt Birch. The man behind the mask of amiability and understanding.

She braced herself for the impact of his eyes. But the look in them, the *lust* in them, blew past her fortifications. Burned away her apprehension. Scorched through the last of her caution.

She'd always thought Hew was handsome. But Hew in seduction mode was like nothing she'd ever seen.

His beauty became that of the sea he loved so much. Dangerous. Intimidating. *Primal.* And the look in his eyes, so dark and hot? She couldn't help thinking he knew countless ways to make her gasp and moan. Endless tricks to have her writhing and begging.

"I want to do this with you if ya still want me to." He used his free hand to rub a thumb over her bottom lip. Her mouth opened on an involuntary breath.

The smile that stretched his beautiful lips was male and triumphant. Like she'd answered a question she hadn't even known he'd asked.

"Do ya trust me?" His deep voice reached an even lower register.

"You know I do." Her own words were rough, raw, dragged from the very heart of her.

"Then trust me with this."

She couldn't think with him touching her. Couldn't reason with his eyes going all dark and seductive.

She pushed to a stand and paced to the other side of the room.

It hardly helped. Especially when he followed her.

His fingers wrapped hot around her wrist as he spun her to face him. He was all height and heat and *him.* The moment he stepped close, his boots bumping the toes of her flip-flops, goosebumps scattered up her arms.

"What do ya need me to say, Sabrina? What promises do I have to make?"

Promise to love me! Promise this is more than two friends indulging in some benefits!

But she took the coward's way out and whispered, "Promise me this won't change anything. Promise me we'll still be friends after. Promise you won't hate me if I need to stop, or—"

He tapped a finger against her mouth to quiet her.

"I promise."

She felt the words more than she heard them because, once again, she was lost in his eyes. In the *look* in his eyes that said he was everything she needed, everything she wanted, everything she'd ever dreamed of, and more.

Am I really going to do this?

She didn't wait for the voice of reason to give its opinion. Instead, heart hammering, she said, "So we agree to terms then?"

His lopsided grin had her core clenching around its own emptiness. "Where do I sign?"

The inches between them felt like a fuse. And her next words? They were the spark.

"Here." She pressed a finger to her lips. His gaze sharpened on her mouth. "And here." She opened her lips and touched her tongue.

A low growl rumbled at the back of his throat like she was the source of all pleasure and pain.

Then, he sealed the deal by kissing her.

CHAPTER 28

Hew was lost.

Lost in the feel of Sabrina's hands tangling in his hair, pulling him closer. Lost in the way her lithe body pressed tight to his, her nipples scraping his chest, her hips rolling in a slow, needy rhythm. Lost in the sweet, breathless heat of her mouth as she licked and laved, sucked and stroked, tasting him like she was starving and he was an all-you-can-eat buffet.

Her hunger was contagious. Ball-tightening. Desperate.

Too desperate?

Like she needed it fast and furious because if they slowed down, even for a second, there'd be room for doubt? For fear? For her demons to come clawing back in?

No.

He didn't want it to be like this.

He wanted *her*. Fully present. Fully aware. Fully willing—not just in body, but in heart and mind, too.

He wanted to claim her. Of course he did. Wanted to make her tremble and moan and cry out his name. But more than that, he wanted to help her *heal*. Wanted to take away every memory that had ever made her flinch and replace it with something that would make her sigh.

But Jesus, Mary, and Joseph, she's hot as hell.

She tasted like strawberry yogurt and sugared coffee. And it took every ounce of inner strength he possessed—truly, were there medals for this sort of thing?—to gently curl his hands around her upper arms and ease her back.

"Wha—?" she breathed. Eyes heavy-lidded. Lips already kiss-swollen.

He swallowed hard. Told himself to *focus, ya dumbass.*

Easier said than done with her sweet little nipples poking through the fabric of her bra.

"We gotta slow down, sweetheart." His voice sounded like it had been dragged behind an Abrams tank down twenty miles of bad road.

"Why?" She blinked in confusion.

He didn't have the words to explain why a quick, hard fuck wasn't what she needed. So he said the only thing that mattered.

"Trust me."

Her breath released in a shaky sigh. "Okay."

Lacing their fingers together, he led her to the bed.

But he didn't lay her down. Not yet.

Instead, he turned her to face him and reached for the hair tie holding her messy bun atop her head. Pulling it free, he watched, awestruck, as a waterfall of dark hair tumbled over her shoulders.

A sound of appreciation rumbled in his throat. "So beautiful," he murmured.

"It's brown." She wrinkled her nose.

"No." He shook his head. "It's milk chocolate and midnight. Shiny as sea glass. Soft as velvet."

He buried his fingers near her scalp, loving the contrast of warm skin and cool strands.

His mouth tugged into a smirk as he held her gaze. "I've dreamed about it, ya know. Dreamed of what it would look like spread out over my chest." She blinked. "Over my lap."

Her lips parted. "You dreamed of me?"

"More nights than I ought to admit."

"I dreamed of you, too," she conceded, the hot look in her eyes making his cock twitch behind his fly.

"What did ya dream?" He traced a fingertip over her injured cheek, down her jaw, pausing on the fluttering pulse in her throat.

"I dreamed of you kissing me."

He bent and replaced his fingertip with his lips, opening his mouth to press the tip of his tongue to her hammering heartbeat. Her hand cupped the back of his head, holding him close, silently asking for more.

He gave her more. Sucked gently. Savored the way she shivered.

"What else?" He knew the words were hot against her skin. "What else did ya dream of me doin'?"

"Touching me," she whispered.

"Where?"

"Everywhere."

His mouth curved into a victorious smile.

"I like your dreams."

He straightened and pulled his shirt over his head, tossing it into the chair atop the discarded lobster.

His hair stuck up in all directions, but she wasn't looking at that. Her eyes were locked on his chest. On his scars.

He wasn't shy, not by nature. His body was solid and hard-packed with muscle from years of training and flying and…yeah…fucking. Still, when her eyes traced the roadmap of old wounds across his skin, he felt exposed in a way that had nothing to do with nakedness.

"You're gorgeous," she breathed, her hands landing lightly on his chest, making his stomach muscles contract.

Her fingers were cool, *erotic* as she traced the lines of his pecs, brushed his ribs, stroked his abs like she was memorizing him.

He'd been called hot plenty of times. *Sexy* was the adjective he was most used to hearing out of a lover's mouth. But gorgeous? Never.

He was too big and battle-scarred to be gorgeous.

She wasn't blowing smoke up his ass, though. Sabrina looked at him and saw beauty. And *that* was more sensual than any dirty talk he'd ever heard.

"What happened here?" She pressed a finger to a round mark on his flank.

"Spent six months in a foster home with a woman who smoked," he admitted, although it was hard to think with her hands on him. "She made use of the old-fashioned cigarette lighter in her sedan."

Sadness flickered in her gaze, but she didn't offer hollow sympathy. He appreciated that more than he could say.

She moved on to the long scar slicing up his side. "And this?"

"I'd just turned sixteen," he admitted. "By that point, I was an old hand at the game of foster care roulette. I could size up a new house within two minutes of walkin' through the front door with my trash bag full of worldly possessions slung over my shoulder."

Even now, all these years later, he could still remember the tang in the air from the prayer candles, the prurient gleam in the man's eyes when he'd let his gaze roam over Hew's form.

"Folks who were willin' to take on a teenager were usually either religious nuts or perverts who wanted to shove their hands down my pants," he went on, his tone devoid of emotion because he'd worked through that trauma and could now view it with the disgust and derision it deserved. "*That* particular place was both. So I turned and ran. Caught myself on their barbed wire fence and nearly spilled my guts into their yard."

Her hand stilled. "Jesus, Hew."

"Mmm." He nodded. "My social worker was more pissed that I ruined a *perfectly good placement* than anything else. Didn't even take me in for stitches. Just patched me up with butterfly bandages."

He glanced down at the mess of poorly healed skin and shrugged. "Ain't pretty, but it did the job."

Her chin trembled. Her eyes shimmered.

It wasn't exactly pillow talk. But maybe talking about his scars, his old hurts, helped her to forget about hers for a minute. Maybe showing her how he'd survived what happened to him helped her believe she could fully recover, too.

She touched the clean white scar beneath his right pec but didn't ask the question.

He answered anyway. "Stab wound. Africa. 2019. Dropped in to extract my team. Got overrun by rebels. It was messy as hell."

Her gaze moved to the ragged line cutting through the meaty part of his right shoulder.

"Colombia. Firefight. Dodged when I should've ducked."

"Hew." There was a catch in her throat. "I—"

"Shh." He cupped her face in his hands, careful of her injured cheek. "It's okay. Bodies heal. So do heads and hearts."

She nodded, knowing he wasn't talking about himself anymore.

He caught the single tear that spilled over her cheek before it could drip from her chin.

"I'm gonna take off my pants now," he told her quietly.

She blinked, startled by the sudden change in topic.

"We need to make sure you're comfortable with me bein' naked. I know the last time ya saw a man's…" He left the sentence unfinished. "I should be the vulnerable one. If ya want me to stop, say the word."

He made fast work of his boots and the buttons on his fly. After stepping out of his tactical cargos and boxer briefs, he straightened and let her see exactly what she'd signed on for.

Hair spread in a mat across his chest, arrowed down the centerline of his stomach, and spread out again at his groin. He was tall and muscular and…*male.* His erection was long and thick, standing proudly from his body.

She'd been hurt by someone who was all of that. Abused and assaulted. Had had her autonomy stripped from her.

He was fully prepared for the sight of his naked body, particularly the sight of his *aroused* naked body, to be triggering.

She stepped back slightly, fixing her gaze on the part of him that would either make or break this experiment. The part of him that promised pleasure but might remind her of too much pain.

"Holy shit." Her voice was husky. "Do you get lightheaded when you get hard?"

He blinked. Then he laughed as relief rushed through him.

Laughing caused his cock to bounce. She reached for him, her face filled with fascination, and he immediately sobered.

"No." He caught her wrist before her fingers wrapped around him. "Not yet."

"When?" She pouted.

"When you're ready."

"I'm ready."

"Well, *I'm* not."

She gave him the side-eye. "You look pretty ready to me."

"Sabrina." His tone was beseeching.

"Hew." Her tone was seductive.

"You're goin' to kill me, woman."

Her eyes bounced around to his various scars. "I won't be the first to try. I think you can handle it."

He dropped his head back and groaned.

Jesus. He'd known it would be like this. Sweet, sensual… damn seductive. But somehow it was even better than the fantasies that had tormented him. Because she was still *her*. Still his friend. Still teasing and taunting, making him laugh between throbs of unspeakable lust.

When he looked at her again, she caught her bottom lip between her teeth. *He* wanted to do those honors.

But first…

"Can I undress ya?"

Her eyes took another trip down his length, stopping at his dick. It flexed as if she'd touched it, and her grin was positively feline.

"Seems only fair," she purred.

He took his time peeling her T-shirt over her head. Her skin was so pale and perfect. Her belly button was pierced. And her waist tucked in tightly before flaring at her hips.

Woman.

In every sense of the word.

He slid a finger beneath the strap of her bra and used his thumb to trace the delicate lace at the edge of the cup that covered her bruised breast.

He was determined to replace her pain with pleasure. Determined to make her forget any heavy hand that had ever touched her.

"You're so goddamned beautiful." His words were barely above a whisper.

She shook her head. "My boobs are too small."

"Fuck that." He snapped the front clasp of her bra open, quick and sure, then tossed it aside.

When she moved to cover herself, he caught her wrists and pinned them at her sides. "Let me look."

And look, he did.

Truth was, he could have stared at her small, plump breasts—those perfect molasses-colored peaks—for the rest of his natural life and still not gotten his fill.

Too small? In what world?

They fit her lean form perfectly. Two gorgeous, round globes rising above her ribs. Smooth. Firm. *Mouthwatering.*

"Flawless," he hissed and used both hands to prove it.

Cupping her gently, he flicked his thumbs across her nipples and watched them pucker and pinch. Her body was so responsive. And seeing her react to his touch was all it took to have a hot drop of precum beading on the tip of his cock.

"God, Hew." She sucked in a ragged breath. "That feels good."

"That's the name of the game, sweetheart. Makin' ya feel good."

He could've spent a week worshiping her breasts. Could've made a home there, happy as a clam. But he had another plan in mind for this first time. An undertaking he hoped would give her everything she needed, everything she wanted, while resurrecting none of her old ghosts.

His fingers slipped down to the button of her jeans.

"Yes," she whispered, and he quickly decided that was his favorite word. Especially when *she* said it.

He worked slowly, not just to avoid spooking her but because…hell, this was like Christmas morning. Half the pleasure was in the unwrapping.

Goddamn teasing toes, he thought when she stepped out of the pool of jeans and panties he'd left at her feet.

After straightening, he allowed himself the honor of seeing her.

All of her.

All her delicate curves. All her pale, perfect skin. The little triangle of hair at the top of her sex. The small mole on her right hip and the tiny scar on her left thigh.

Her breath caught when he touched it.

"Caught it on a nail on the dock of our neighborhood swimming hole," she whispered. "I was eight."

"Mmm," he hummed, stepping into her space. Not stopping until they were skin to skin.

Her breasts brushed his chest, nipples dragging in the most delicious way. Her cool belly cradled the hot, aching length of him. And when he slid his thigh between hers…

Christ.

She was wet. Slick. *Ready.*

He groaned, deep and helpless.

She did, too, when he kissed her with determined precision, stealing the air from her lungs and replacing it with his own.

She rose up on tiptoe, fisting one hand in his hair, tugging him close like she never wanted to let go.

He let go. Just a little. Let the reins on his restraint slip just enough to teeter there on the edge. Testing his limits.

And hers.

She didn't flinch when he deepened the kiss, charting her mouth with long, languid strokes of his tongue. She didn't pull away when he ground his thigh into her damp heat, holding her hip in one big palm so he could guide her sex in tight little circles.

That keening moan she gave him? Oh, it threatened to undo him.

Mine, growled the part of him that had no patience, manners, or mercy. *My woman.*

It begged him to lift her, to seat himself inside her, to let all that wetness and softness and warmth swallow him whole before he thrust and thrust and *thrust* until she clamped around him. Until she spasmed with pleasure. Until she went limp and sated in his arms.

He bridled it just in time. Just before reason was torn to shreds and instinct took over.

She whimpered at the loss when he stepped back.

"I'll get ya there, sweetheart," he promised.

Then he yanked back the covers, propped the pillows against the headboard, and sat down.

"C'mere, Sabrina." He patted his chest in invitation. "Let me hold you. Touch you. Edge ya 'til you scream."

CHAPTER 29

Sabrina didn't move.

She couldn't.

Lust had melted her bones. Passion had turned her muscles to mush. The sight of Hew, so long and strong and so very, *very* naked, had scrambled her brains.

She'd known he would be beautiful. But she'd never imagined the sheer grandeur of so much sun-warmed muscle. Every inch of him was dusted with a golden tan. And his body hair was two shades darker than the hair on his head—a deep, coffee brown.

His nipples were flat brown disks atop the heavy squares of his pectoral muscles. Impossibly broad shoulders tapered down into lean hips. And his thighs were thick and corded with muscle.

There was a rawness to him. It was in the way his scars marked him, visual reminders that he'd lived and fought and bled. It was in the way his dick jutted unabashed from the crux of his thighs, thick and long and looking like it'd been carved in a wilder century.

There was no artifice or polish to him. Just the sheer unapologetic truth of a man built for strength and sex and sin.

He grinned like he knew what the sight of him did to her. Then he grabbed her fingers and pulled her onto the bed with him.

"Face away from me and lean against my chest," he instructed.

She frowned. She wanted to look at him. Wanted to kiss him and touch him and spread her legs around his hips and—

Edge ya 'til you scream.

His words echoed through her head, making her blood run thick. Making her sex pound.

She wasn't an innocent. She knew what edging was, although she'd never experienced it herself. Had never had a lover who'd expressed any interest.

She hadn't known *she* had an interest until now. Until Hew.

Then again, if he asked me to stand on my head and recite the alphabet backward, I would.

She was completely caught up in the spell he'd woven. Certain that doing everything he asked would end in the kind of pleasure that shook her, body and soul.

So she settled between his thighs. His dick wedged against the top of her ass and lower back. He splayed her hair across his chest—just like he'd dreamed—then cupped her chin so her head rested against his shoulder.

"Now." He nipped at her exposed neck. His breath was hot. Sultry. Seductive. So were his words. "Relax and let me learn all the ways you like to be touched."

Hooking his hands beneath her knees, he bent her legs until her feet were planted on either side of his thighs, her sex spread wide.

"Hew," she whispered, exposed in a way she'd never been before.

"Trust me, sweetheart." He turned her head so he could claim her mouth.

She did trust him. She trusted him more than she'd ever trusted anyone.

She *loved* him more than she'd ever loved anyone.

And if this was the only time they would be together, if he was doing this because he'd been the one to walk beside her on her healing journey, and this was the last step, then she would revel in it. Indulge in every sweet sensation. Bask in every brush of his fingertips, savor every kiss from his lips, and delight in every pleasure he pressed on her.

Would that ruin her for any man in the future?

Probably.

But it's better to have loved and lost than never to have loved at all.

Didn't someone smart say that?

She couldn't remember. Probably because his kiss melted her brain.

His lips were warm and searching. His tongue was hot and carnal. He tested her, teased her, *learned* her. And only when she was completely caught up in the play of his mouth did he use his big hands to cup her breasts.

His palms were so large and warm. His fingers so rough with calluses. But he was careful as he brushed them over her distended nipples. Gentle and thorough and *studied* as he found just the right amount of friction. Just the right amount of pressure.

She gasped and pulled her mouth from his so she could arch into the sensation, wanting more of it. *Needing* more of it.

But he was in no hurry. So she leaned her head against his shoulder, screwed shut her eyes, and enjoyed the ride.

"Touchin' ya like this has me so hot I'm shakin'," he murmured against her temple, playing with the tips of her breasts until they were so hard they hurt.

Time and space ceased to exist. There was only him. Only her. Only the way he pinched and stroked and plucked and plumped.

By the time he drifted one hand down the centerline of her body, both of her hands were fisted in his hair. Holding on for dear life against the agonizing pleasure of his ministrations.

He was slow as he teased her open. Gentle as he slid fingers over her distended clitoris.

"Oh, god!" she gasped when he set up a delicious, strumming rhythm that created a torturous friction.

"That's it," he encouraged, pressing and rubbing, pressing and rubbing until her whole body was as taut as a bowstring and vibrating with need.

"Hew!" she cried out when his fingers suddenly stilled.

He cupped her then, his palm hot compared to the air in the room. Claiming her mouth, he silenced her pleas, swallowed her objections, and gently ground the heel of his palm against the part of her that ached the most.

It settled the sensation. Tamped it down from a fiery ache to a soft, needy want. And through it all, he kissed her. Deeply. Thoroughly.

When she finally quieted, when the edge of orgasm receded and she stopped twisting and turning against his hand, he began to play with her again.

Just like the first time, he softly, slowly, *gently* tormented her clit to the point of pain. Only, this time, when she was close to the top of that steep slope, he dipped his fingers into her quivering center, stroking and beckoning in a come-hither motion.

Her back arched. Her womb pulsed. She reached for orgasm but—

Again, he stopped. Again, she protested. And again, he expertly brought her back down until the terrible tension eased and her clenched muscles relaxed.

It was heaven.

It was hell.

It happened over and over again until she lost count of the number of times she'd almost, *almost* slipped over the edge.

At one point, she didn't know if she should beg him to stop or tell him to keep teasing her forever. She wanted both. And so she let him do as he pleased until she was mindless to anything that wasn't his magical hands and talented mouth.

By the time he whispered, "Okay, sweetheart. Cum for me," she was incapable of doing anything other than he commanded.

Her eyelids slitted. She could see his profile from beneath her lashes. The determined clench of his jaw. The subtle flare of his nostrils. The prurient intensity of his gaze as he watched what he was doing to her.

She might have been embarrassed, exposed to him like she was, *vulnerable* and *submitting* to him like she was. But he'd pleasured her past the point of caring about anything other than her body's desperate need for release.

When she came, it was so sudden that it surprised her. She didn't know if she cried out his name or whimpered in relief as her body clamped down tight around his marauding fingers.

A kaleidoscope of colors exploded behind her eyelids when wave after wave of painful pleasure crashed through her. Her hips worked. Her heart thundered. Her sex shuddered and clasped and gripped in greediness for more, more, ever more.

He gave it to her. Teased her. Stroked her. *Worked* her until the last ripples of release faded away and she was left sated. Languid. Collapsing against his chest as his heart raced against her back, and his breaths came harsh and heavy.

"Holy hell. That was hot," he grumbled after he'd given her time to recover.

She murmured her disapproval when he slipped his fingers from inside her. But then he rubbed her own wetness around her areola, and it was enough to have tiny aftershocks shaking her core.

She wasn't sure how long they stayed like that, her coming down from the throes of the hardest orgasm she'd ever had. Him continuing to lazily play her body as expertly as a master musician plays his instrument.

Eventually, though, reality returned.

Her eyelids fluttered open to reveal he was still avidly interested in the length of her splayed out in front of him. His hands continued to skate over her skin with the kind of hot hunger that had her stretching and murmuring and smiling like the Cheshire Cat.

"I was right." She turned her face to nip at the skin of his neck.

"About what?" His voice was ragged with unquenched lust.

"You *do* have secret ways to make me gasp and moan, endless tricks to make me writhe and beg."

He growled his satisfaction. Before she could think, she was flat on her back with him looming above her.

She bit her lip at the passion in his eyes. "Is it your turn now?" she teased, lifting her head to nibble at his lower lip, loving the scrape of his beard against her chin.

"Not quite yet." And then his mouth landed on her breast, and his hot tongue stabbed at her nipple.

CHAPTER 30

Hew was *more* than ready for a turn.

In fact, he'd been so worked up from watching her body reach for orgasm time and again—from feeling her growing softer and hotter and wetter by the minute—that by the time he'd *finally* pushed her over the edge, by the time her inner walls had clamped down on his fingers with enough force to rub his knuckles together, he'd nearly lost it.

Had nearly blown his passion all over her back.

Now? He could so easily pull her beneath him. So easily plunge inside her wet, willing body. He'd more than made sure she was prepared to accommodate him.

And if he was being honest, a huge part of him was tempted to do exactly that. But a bigger part of him, the part that had spent months fantasizing about this moment, dreaming of everything he would do to her, demanded he take his time.

Besides, even though he'd touched her in ways that had left a brand on his brain, he had *yet* to taste her.

And good god! I need to taste her!

He used the tricks he'd learned while teasing her breasts with his fingers to tease them with his tongue. He swirled. He flicked. He sucked—always careful of her bruised flesh—until she was once again mewling and wiggling and begging.

Her bucking hips rubbed her hot juices along his length because she'd wrapped her pretty legs around his waist. And by the time he moved down her body—skating his lips along her ribs, dipping his tongue into her belly button, nipping at the jut of her hip bones—he had to press his dick hard into the mattress to find some relief for the ache she'd built.

His nostrils flared at the scent of her. Warm, healthy, recently sated woman. His mouth watered in anticipation when he hooked her knees over his shoulders. And his gaze narrowed at the sight of her so close. So swollen and pink. So ready and willing.

Her clitoris was engorged, peeking past its little hood and begging him for more attention. With a feral growl, he obliged, covering it with his mouth.

She was sweet and salty. Tart and tangy. Everything a woman should be.

He wanted to rub his lips all over her, bury his face so deep that her scent and essence slicked his entire face. Instead, he settled in and slowly feasted.

Just like with her breasts, he'd learned how she liked to be teased. Liked to be rubbed. And he used his tongue to torment her, to push her back up the mountain of passion until she teetered at the brink.

He didn't delay her gratification this time. Instead, he slipped two fingers deep inside her core, rubbed his tongue gently against the hard nub at the top of her sex, and let her fling herself over the edge.

Her flavor exploded in his mouth at the same time her body exploded in pleasure.

She was a goddess taking her fill after being worshiped the way she was meant to be. And he was the lucky bastard, the mere mortal, she'd deigned to let please her.

The harsh sound of her rapid breaths met his ears when her thighs finally fell away from his face. The hold she had on his hair loosened. And the hard pulse of her body around his fingers settled to mere flutters.

He kissed the inside of her thigh. Nipped her hip bone. Swirled his tongue into her belly button. And gently laved her nipple on his journey back up her body.

Then, he lay beside her, watching her breasts rise and fall, memorizing the way her belly quivered, and loving the pink flush that tinted every inch of her skin.

His dick flexed in entreaty. But honestly, if she'd said she was done, if she'd told him she couldn't continue, he'd have been satisfied. Because pleasing her was better than any orgasm he'd ever had and—

"Now it's *definitely* your turn," she declared, her eyes languid and hot when she shoved him onto his back and straddled him.

Oh, thank god.

"Ya don't have to—"

"Maybe I should've said it's *my turn* to have my way with *you*," she growled as she claimed his mouth.

If he'd thought having her splayed out in front of him was heaven, then there wasn't a word for what it was like having her on top of him.

Her breasts brushed his chest. Her thighs cradled his hips. And he couldn't help spanning her waist before slipping his hands around to grab the full, round globes of her ass.

He grumbled his disappointment at having to let go when she started mapping his torso with her mouth. Then he groaned with pleasure when her lips found his nipples, his ribs, his belly, his…

She stopped an inch above the head of his cock. It flexed toward her, begging when her breath sent licks of heat over him.

"Touch me. Lick me. Suck me," he wanted to tell her. But he wasn't sure she was ready for demands.

Instead, he held his breath and waited, his hand cupping her cheek, his thumb smoothing along her jawline. Not coaxing. Not cajoling. Simply accepting whatever she wanted to take. Whatever she wanted to give.

"Can I touch you?" Her words sounded ragged.

He let out a harsh breath he hadn't even known he was holding. "God, yes. Please."

Without delay, she wrapped her fingers around his needy dick and tugged.

His toes curled. His hand fisted the sheets. And now *he* was the one gasping and whimpering and unable to stop himself from bucking into her grip because it brought such sweet relief. Such unimaginable pleasure.

She made everything so much better—or worse?—when she swallowed his head and he was lost in the hot haven of her mouth. In the wicked flick of her tongue. In the hard suction of her lips.

His eyes rolled back so far it was a wonder he couldn't see his own brain when she set about her task in earnest. Stroking his shaft as she bobbed and sucked and bobbed and sucked.

He'd known pleasure. He'd known passion. But he'd never known anything to compare to the sensation of Sabrina's hands and mouth on him.

He couldn't help himself. He looked down to see her pale hand working his turgid length. Her wide mouth stretched tight around his girth. And her hair spread across his thighs like a dark curtain.

It was better than his fantasies. Because she didn't tease. She didn't torment. She simply sucked and stroked with a determined tempo that had him groaning and begging.

Too soon he was slipping toward the point of no return.

"Sabrina." He fisted a hand in her silky hair to stop her delicious ministrations. "Ya gotta stop, sweetheart, or I'm—"

He gritted his teeth when the head of his cock popped free of her mouth. It was so swollen it was nearly purple. Shiny from the hot lash of her tongue.

"Do you have a condom?"

He blinked at the question. Then cursed when reality hit.

When he'd followed her upstairs, he'd had no idea this was where they'd end up. He hadn't thought. Hadn't come prepared.

"In my room," he rasped, the need for release making his words ragged.

"Do you want me to stop so you can go get one?" She shook her head. "Because I don't want to stop."

"But—"

"I want you in my mouth." She continued to stroke him languidly. "I want to feel you straining against my tongue. I want to taste you when you cum."

"Sabrina…"

He'd pleasured her with his fingers. He'd pleasured her with his mouth. He wanted to finish her off with his dick, but he couldn't think with her hands still working him. He could hardly *breathe* from the thought of her sucking him off.

She must've taken her whispered name as acquiescence. Because her mouth was on him again. The hot, slick, *sucking* wonder that was her lips and teeth and tongue.

He tried to hold on. Tried not to let the beast in him take over. But it was too late.

His self-control shattered, and he was thrusting up into her firm fist, into her magical mouth.

She hummed her pleasure. Almost purring in feline triumph. And it reverberated through his shaft until—

He groaned her name. Half sitting up as hot jets of pleasure poured from his body and into her mouth.

She took him. Worked him. Wrung every last drop from him as he shuddered and shook. As his orgasm seemed to stretch on forever and ever. As the world disappeared and all that remained was her and him and bliss like nothing he'd experienced before.

He didn't remember collapsing back against the mattress. He didn't recall when she released him and crawled up beside him. He didn't come back into himself until a long time later, when he felt her leaving little kisses on his shoulder while her talented fingers played with the hair on his chest.

"Will you sign my ass?" she asked when the blood rushing between his ears had quieted to a dull roar.

Blinking open his eyes, he watched as the ceiling slowly came into focus. Surely, he'd misheard her.

"Hmm?"

"Will you sign my ass?" she said again. "I want to get a tattoo to remember this moment."

He chuckled and pulled her close. Kissing the top of her head. Loving that she could still tease after what they'd just done together.

"Sure thing," he told her. "As soon as I remember my name."

She pushed up on her elbow and blinked down at him in mock confusion. "What *is* your name, by the way?"

"After that?" He motioned to where his cock lay against his thigh, happy and spent. "You can call me anything ya want."

She giggled and tucked her head into the space between his chin and his heart. It seemed perfectly made to fit her cheek. "I think I'll call you Mr. Eighth Wonder of the World."

He was grinning ear to ear, gently running a fingertip up the delicate divot of her spine.

"You've got a great ass," he told her. "But I'm not sure it's big enough for a tattoo that long."

"You're probably right. How disappointing."

"God, woman, I—"

He stopped mid-sentence, the words shriveling up in the back of his throat like slugs hit by salt.

He'd almost said, *I love you.*

CHAPTER 31

Vivian had lost track of time since the men exited the tunnel.

The pitch-black hole slinking beneath the earth had swallowed the minutes, stretching each one into eternity. Only the gnawing hunger in her gut and the dry fire in her throat kept her tenuously tethered to reality.

The cold, once a welcome reprieve from the bottling plant's sweltering heat, had turned on her like everything else. Her clothes hung damp and heavy, plastered to her skin until goosebumps crawled up her arms, and the back of her neck felt like raw meat laid on ice.

She couldn't stop shivering. But pride kept her from letting her teeth chatter audibly.

The blindfold was gone—the two men had left it off—but it made no difference. The darkness was complete. And yet…

She swore she saw movement sometimes. Shadows slithering at the edges of her sight. Shapes that coiled and circled and seemed to…*breathe.*

Tilting her head, she strained to catch any sound beyond the steady *plink…plink…plink* of dripping water. But the only other noises to reach her ears were her own ragged breaths and the occasional squeak of the metal chair when she moved.

Her shoulders burned from having her hands tied behind her back. Her feet were numb from being strapped to the chair legs.

It didn't escape her notice that the Black Knights had secured her in the precise position she'd secured Sabrina Greenlee.

Coincidence?

Hell no.

She began to understand that the Black Knights did nothing by accident.

Whirrr.

The low mechanical groan of the large sliding door was familiar now. She turned toward the ever-widening opening, desperately grasping for some light amidst the darkness. But that was a mistake.

The bright white glow pouring in through the breach sliced into her unprepared eyes like blades. She blinked rapidly, hating the tears that sprang into her eyes as the wedge of light on the sloping ground grew wider and two figures stood silhouetted in the gap.

The *same* two figures who'd stood before her earlier, demanding answers.

The door reversed course on its tracks, groaning in its journey. Then it sealed shut, and darkness once more swallowed her down its black throat.

Afterimages of the silhouettes danced in her vision. Her breath picked up as her eyes fought against the return of the blackness.

Snick.

She heard the flashlight snap on before seeing its thin beam.

Heavy boots fell on damp concrete and echoed off the curved walls as the two men approached.

"So?" she demanded when they stopped beside her and shone the light on her face. "Were you able to trace the number? Do you know his identity?"

Her voice was too dry, too brittle from lack of hydration. But it was still steady. And that mattered.

The one with the buzz cut answered. "If it were possible to trace the call, *you* would've done it already."

She couldn't stop the self-satisfied smile that curved her lips. It was nice when one professional recognized another and gave them their due.

"True," she admitted with a little shrug. "So that's that, then." She wiggled her feet against her ankle restraints. "Time to let me go. I'm no more use to you."

"What happens to ya now isn't our decision to make," said the one with a voice like Sam Elliot.

Vivian froze. "Then whose is it?"

"Sabrina's," the man with the buzz cut muttered. "She suffered in your hands. It's only fair to let your fate rest in hers."

No.

A lump of dread thickened Vivian's throat.

She remembered the brunette all too well. Remembered the woman's banshee yell. The shocked but victorious gleam in her dark eyes after she rammed the shard of glass into Hummer's throat. The absolute *loathing* on her face when Vivian promised to kill everyone she loved.

Sabrina Greenlee had every right to hate Vivian. And if she had even *half* the fire Vivian remembered…

Plus, Vivian knew what *she* would do in the woman's place.

A single thought ran through her head and chilled her to the bone.

I always knew I'd die at the hands of someone I was sent to kill. I just didn't think it would happen so soon.

CHAPTER 32

"**G**od, woman, I—"

Sabrina sat up when Hew's words cut off like a sword had sliced through them. His expression was…

What?

Stunned, maybe? Shocked?

She couldn't quite put her finger on it. But then he blinked and returned to his old, stoic self, and she thought maybe she'd imagined everything.

"You what?" she prompted, holding her breath in anticipation.

"I need to go next door for the condoms." He threw back the covers and stood in one swift move. "'Cause I'm not done with ya. Not by a damn sight."

It was strange. His words tickled her—what woman wouldn't be pleased to have a handsome man ravenous for her?—but also disappointed her because she'd thought…

It doesn't matter what I thought, she told herself sternly.

What mattered was that there would be more of Hew's talented ministrations. More of his touching and kissing and teasing. More of his big naked body and—

Speaking of his big naked body…

She shamelessly admired the firm curve of his ass when he stepped into his boxer briefs and tactical pants. He straightened to do up his fly, and when his gloriously broad chest caught the warm light of the lamp, she bit her lip as renewed lust fired through her blood.

Donning her sultriest grin, she told him, "I'm not done with you either, flyboy."

Without warning, he ripped the bedding away and tossed it unceremoniously at the end of the bed. She gasped as the cool air caressed her skin. Then she blushed at being completely bare beneath his heated gaze.

Her first instinct was to cover herself. But that seemed silly considering she'd been splayed out in front of him just a little bit ago, mewling and bucking and begging as his talented hands and magical mouth did unspeakably naughty things to her.

Besides, it was *beyond* gratifying to watch the way his hot stare raked over her body. To feel the path of fire his gaze left behind.

She bent a knee and slowly trailed one fingertip between her breasts. It was a challenge. An invitation.

It was *successful*, apparently, because his nostrils flared like a predator scenting prey.

"You're a damned temptress." His voice was so rough with need that it raised goosebumps on her arms.

"Me?" She blinked innocently. "I was just lying here, minding my own business, and then you—"

"That's all it takes." He sounded irritated that her mere *existence* was enough to make him want, to make him lust, to make him *hard*.

As quickly as he'd yanked them away, he flicked the covers back over her and stalked from the room.

She lay there stunned, laughing softly at the power she wielded. Overjoyed at the memories of what they'd already done and anticipating all they were *about* to do together and—

The door slammed open, and he strode back in. There was a definite gleam in his eyes as he kicked the door shut behind him and proudly held aloft a long strip of condoms like they were a blue ribbon from a county fair.

"Wow." She blinked, counting at least a dozen square, foil packages. "You have a lot of faith in your sexual prowess, huh?"

His lopsided smile was pure sin. "No. But I have *all* the faith in yours. Ya make me ravenous. Ya know that, right?"

She glanced down at the bulge straining his fly. "Oh, I think I have *some* idea—"

Bam, bam, bam!

The heavy knock barely gave her time to pull the covers up to her chin before the door flew open.

Hew half-turned, Sabrina squeaked her surprise, and Graham slowly took in the scene before lazily propping his massive shoulder against her doorframe.

"Well, well, well," he drawled, lifting an eyebrow at the strip of condoms Hew still held in the air. "So much for *just bein' friends*." He made air quotes. "Caught ya red-handed." He turned to grin at Sabrina and the blush burning her face. "And red-cheeked."

That had her blush extending to the roots of her hair.

When he returned his attention to Hew, he lifted a challenging eyebrow. "Why are ya starin' at me like I'm a festerin' sore on your ass?"

"Is there something you need?" Hew crossed his arms, the strip of condoms still dangling from his fingertips. "'Cause, in case it escaped your notice, we're a little busy here."

Instead of answering, Graham chuckled and waved a magnanimous hand. "I approve, by the way."

"Approve of what?"

"This." Graham wagged a finger between Hew and Sabrina.

Hew scowled. "I wasn't aware we needed your approval."

Graham shrugged. "It never hurts, right? So what finally pushed ya over the edge?" He pinned Sabrina with a knowing look. "Was it seein' him all suited up and helmeted and piloting the chopper like a sky god?" He hooked a thumb in Hew's direction.

"It was, wasn't it?" Graham whistled through his teeth. "I don't blame ya. He *is* a handsome devil when he's mannin' those controls. All square-jawed and with that eagle-eyed concentration. There's been times I've been tempted to—"

Hew interrupted. "Ya realize your presence here's about as welcome as an itchy asshole."

All the teasing fled Graham's face and was replaced by a look of apology.

"Unfortunately, there are times when the only options are bad ones."

"Meaning what?" It was clear Hew's annoyance was growing by the second.

"We need Sabrina. It's time for her decision."

"What kind of decision?" Sabrina frowned, feeling her heart kick up a notch. And *not* in a good way.

Instead of answering, Graham simply told her, "Take a coupla minutes to get dressed. I'll meet ya downstairs."

He dipped his chin before disappearing down the hall.

Hew closed the door behind him with maybe a *smidge* more force than was necessary. When he turned back to Sabrina, his whole demeanor had changed.

Gone was the tease. Gone was the flirt. In his place was the guy who kept his blades sharp and his powder dry. The guy who acted as an umbrella when bullets started raining down.

"I can tell 'em all to fuck off," he offered, the tightness of his jaw highlighting its angularity.

"No." She pushed the covers away and reached for her discarded clothes. "If Graham says I still have a part to play, I'll play it. It's the least I can do.

"Come here." He issued the command from between clenched teeth. "I need one more kiss."

She dropped her clothes and walked to him naked, uncaring of what jiggled or sagged or swayed. All that mattered was *him* and how he made her feel beautiful and safe.

Made her feel…*loved.*

Going up on tiptoe, she framed his face with her hands—reveling in the scratchy feel of his beard against her palms—and kissed him.

God, the freedom to kiss him…

She still couldn't believe it. Had spent months dreaming about it, only to realize her fantasies didn't hold a candle to reality.

His body was a wall of unyielding strength. His mouth was fire and velvet, kissing her like…well…like he kissed her. Which was unlike anyone else.

When she finally pulled away, she was pleased to see his eyes were hot with a lust that mirrored her own. That was *just* the impetus she needed to hurry up and get dressed.

The sooner she did whatever needed doing, the sooner she could return to him. The sooner she could pull him back into bed. The sooner they could start making a dent in that strip of condoms.

"Now I want to tell 'em to fuck off for purely selfish reasons," he admitted hoarsely.

She donned a coquettish smile as she pulled on her panties and jeans. "How about instead of that, you promise to fuck *me* when this is over?"

He grabbed her hips before she could snap her bra shut and hauled her against him. His wide chest was hot against the hard tips of her breasts. His lips were warm and hungry on her throat.

"Deal." He nipped at her earlobe. "Where do I sign?"

She grinned and backed up a step so he could see her point to her left nipple. "Here," she told him, her voice dropping an octave as her hand slid lower, past the waistband of her jeans to disappear inside the denim… "And here."

He shuddered. Actually *shuddered*. And then groaned like his want of her physically hurt him. When he reached down and adjusted himself, she realized maybe it did.

Feeling beautiful in a way she never had before, feeling powerful in a way she never had before, feeling…like her old self, but even better, she told him seriously, "Thank you, Hew."

He clocked the change in her mood and blinked in confusion. "For what?"

"For reminding me how nice it can be to be wanted. For helping me find that part of myself I worried was lost forever. For being patient and gentle and…" She searched for the right word. "*Thorough*," she finally finished with a teasing grin.

"And we haven't even scratched the surface," he promised before pulling her back in for another kiss.

It was more than a couple of minutes before she made it to the War Room. Graham's slow, smug smile said he knew *exactly* what had kept her.

"So?" She tried to act nonchalant—and failed if Graham's low chuckle was anything to go by. "What can I do to help?"

"No Hew?" he asked.

"He'll be along. He was lacing up his boots when I left."

"We'll wait."

She narrowed her eyes, her curiosity piqued. What in the world did they need her for? She couldn't begin to imagine.

From below came the grind of some sort of rotary tool and the staccato *hiss* of an air compressor. Ozzie sat at his bank of computers, his fingers going *rat-a-tat-tat* over a keyboard as lines of code flew by on a monitor. His speakers weren't blaring eighties tunes. Instead, he had his earbuds plugged in and his head bobbed in rhythm to whatever hairband played through them. She could hear Becky in her office, half-laughing as she negotiated over the phone with someone about a shipment of V-twin engines.

It was all so…normal.

Eerily so considering that just yesterday, she'd been tied to a chair in an abandoned bottling plant, feet numb from her restraints, mouth a desert from dehydration. Not to mention, *today* they had a platinum-haired assassin tied up in the tunnel dug down beneath the river.

"So…" Graham eyed her curiously. "Is Hew your lobster?"

She thought of the stuffed lobster on the chair upstairs. "Huh?"

"Ya know." He nudged her. "From *Friends*?"

When she only blinked, he rolled his eyes. "Phoebe Buffay?" He donned a terrible falsetto. "It's a known fact that lobsters fall in love and mate for life. You can actually see old lobster couples walking around their tank, holding claws." He made a circle with each thumb and forefinger, linking them to imitate joined claws.

A hard seed of longing lodged beneath her heart.

Hew was certainly *her* lobster. Problem was—and despite everything they'd just done together—she wasn't sure *she* was *his*.

"What are you doing watching, and *memorizing*," she emphasized, "*Friends*? Isn't that show about two decades too recent for you?"

He shrugged. "The seventies were better than all others when it comes to sitcoms. And *M*A*S*H* was the best show of all time; I won't be acceptin' any arguments to the contrary. But *Seinfeld* and *Friends* definitely rank in the top ten and therefore deserve my time and attention." He pointed to her nose. "And don't think I didn't notice ya changed the subject. I was talkin' about you and Hew and—"

He was cut off—*thank goodness*—when the familiar cadence of Hew's boots sounded on the stairs. The instant Hew appeared on the second floor, Sabrina caught her breath.

Literally.

She'd read that phrase many times in books and had always thought it was hyperbole.

Then she'd met Hew.

When he entered a room, it was like the temperature changed. Like he sucked out all the air. Like he stopped time.

It was all that dark auburn hair paired with all that height and breadth. It was those sparkling green eyes paired with that lopsided smile. It was all that tan skin paired with that easy, athletic grace.

Graham elbowed her as Hew ambled toward them. "Close your mouth, darlin', or you'll start drawin' flies."

She scowled, but then caught her breath *again* when Hew automatically took her hand in his and squeezed her fingers.

He glanced between Sabrina and the big SEAL and lifted a thick eyebrow. "So what did I miss?"

"Nothing," she was quick to say. Then, just as quickly, she asked Graham. "The Avengers have now assembled. What can I do to help?"

Graham's teasing expression pulled back like a curtain, revealing a hard-set seriousness beneath. "Come with me." He hitched his chin toward the stairs leading to the bottom floor.

She didn't realize the Bat Cave door was wide open until her flip-flops landed on the last tread. She couldn't shake the feeling that the gaping black throat was waiting to swallow her whole.

"Hang on." Her stomach high-jumped into the back of her mouth as her feet stuttered. "Why do I have to go in *there?*"

Graham glanced over his shoulder. "'Cause that's where Black Widow is."

She bit her lip. "But I don't—"

Hew draped a heavy arm around her shoulders. His breath was warm against her cheek. His voice was a velvet growl in her ear. "Ya got this. But say the word, and we'll stop it before it starts."

A part of her wanted to let him do exactly that. But a *bigger* part of her realized he was right.

She *did* have this.

She wasn't the same wounded, wide-eyed woman who'd first walked through BKI's front gates. She'd found her footing here. Found her voice and her courage here. Found *herself* here.

Found *Hew*.

Her shoulders were square and her chin was high as she marched across the shop, nodding to the men working at the bike lifts. But the moment she stepped into the Bat Cave, her bravado seeped out of her, leaving her skin prickling and her hair standing on end.

She didn't realize she'd reached for Hew's hand again until his warm, wide palm kissed her own and his long, strong fingers wrapped around hers.

That's all it took.

Just his presence, just his *touch*, and she could take on the world.

Careful, the little voice cautioned. *Because what happens when he's gone?*

If *he ever goes*, she mentally argued. *There's no guarantee he will.*

They'd only gone a few feet inside when the heavy metal door rumbled behind them. When it closed with a solid-sounding *thunk*, it sealed them in the darkness and sealed *out* the sounds and the safety of the shop.

She blinked. Blinked again as she willed her eyes to adjust. When they finally did, she realized the tunnel wasn't pitch dark. It was more like a shaft of shadows.

In those shadows…him. Standing beside a chair. Silent. Looming. Broad shoulders lit by the narrow beam of a flashlight.

Boss.

Tied *to* that chair…her. Chin up. Eyes glinting in the gloom. Sharp jaw and cruel mouth spotlighted by the beam.

Black Widow.

Sabrina flinched like a bolt of electrical current had hit her. Even bound, even *beaten*, the blonde still exuded menace.

Boss turned to them when they approached. She couldn't see his eyes but could feel his attention on her face.

"We've gotten all we'll get out of her." His voice echoed before being swallowed by the curve of the tunnel. "It's up to you what happens next."

"Me?" Her brow furrowed. "What do you mean?"

"You're the one who suffered at her hands," Hew said softly. "So ya get to decide her fate."

Her mouth opened. No sound emerged. Then, when it did, it was jerky. "I…I don't understand. I…I'm not—" She stopped and shook her head as she stared at Hew. "You knew this was what Graham wanted?"

He looked only mildly chagrined. "It was discussed." She remembered Boss asking him to step into his office. "I said I couldn't speak for ya. You'd have to speak for yourself."

"Right." She dipped her chin, although she wasn't sure what she was agreeing to.

"What are her options?" Hew's grip on her hand was firm, supportive as he asked the question.

"We hold Black Widow here," Graham said, his voice flat. "Indefinitely. Or at least until we're confident she's no longer a threat to us."

"I *said* I'm not—" Black Widow began.

"Shut up," Boss's voice snapped out, cold and dangerous. It reminded Sabrina of walking across a frozen lake and suddenly hearing the ice cracking beneath her feet.

Black Widow's mouth twisted into a spiteful sneer. But she didn't utter another word.

"She'd live here? With us?" The notion sickened Sabrina.

"She'd be *kept* here," Graham corrected, and Sabrina understood what he *wasn't* saying. They would feed and house and clothe the woman, but it wouldn't be any kind of life.

"Or?" she pressed hopefully. "What else?"

"We let her go and hope she takes seriously our warnin' to tuck tail and run," Graham said. "Because if she so much as *blinks* wrong in our direction, we'll find her and turn her into fertilizer." He paused before delivering the coup de grâce. "Or we turn her into fertilizer now."

Sabrina let loose a ragged breath.

She wasn't an idiot. She knew the Black Knights could be ruthless. But it felt different to be presented with that truth so undeniably.

She turned to Boss, voice barely more than a whisper. "How would you do it?"

"The easy way." His tone was purposefully devoid of emotion. But she knew him well enough to know he was a far cry from unfeeling.

This act was for Black Widow's benefit.

"One tap to the brainstem." He pressed two fingers to the back of his head. "Lights out before she knows what hit her."

"*Fuck you!*" Black Widow shrieked, spittle catching the flashlight's beam. "You know I told you what I told you because I thought you'd let me go!"

Sabrina's pulse hammered as she stared hard at the blonde. "A quick, painless shot to the brainstem is better than you were going to do to me. If I recall, you promised I would watch them all die." She waved a hand to indicate the men gathered. "That I would smell their blood, hear their screams, see their final, rattling breaths."

A muscle twitched in the woman's cheek. Her nostrils flared with feeling when she snarled, "One bad turn deserves another, I suppose. We're all just animals scrabbling for scraps in the end."

"You're wrong." Sabrina shook her head. "Some of us take no pleasure in ending a life. Some of us have a heart."

"Spare me your self-righteous bullshit, Sabrina. You killed Hummer without a second thought."

"I will use this knife to cut her name off your tongue if ya speak it again," Hew snarled, having produced a short blade from…

God only knows where.

"Do it! Show her the truth about yourself! Show her you're all just as bad as I am! You just wrap it up in the flag!" Black Widow's rage revealed cracks around her edges. Through those cracks, Sabrina saw it.

Fear.

The assassin was afraid.

And *that* was enough to have her lifting her chin and staring boldly down at the woman.

"If we keep her here, she'll poison the air," she mused aloud. "She'll ruin all sense of safety and security. Plus, it's a pain in the ass to hold a hostage long term."

Not that she knew from experience. But logic said she was correct.

"True." Boss dipped his chin.

"Killing her would mean safety and peace for all of us," she continued. "A guaranteed end to any danger she poses."

Again, that chin dip. Again, that single answer, "True."

She swallowed and felt a line appear between her eyebrows. "But it would also mean blood. Death. A life, however twisted, ended by our hands. And we're better than that. Better than *her*."

She crossed her arms and regarded the assassin. Black Widow's eyes were gray. But in the tunnel, they looked black.

"Your team is dead," she told the assassin coolly. "Your mission has failed. So if we let you go, what's to stop you from trying to exact your revenge on us? On *me*?"

Black Widow's throat worked. Sabrina could hear the note of hope in her tone when she said, "Grudges give you wrinkles. Besides, until you guys bring Bishop down, I'll be too busy finding a deep hole to hide in from him."

"And when Bishop is no longer a threat?" Sabrina pushed. "What then?"

The blonde's eyes danced desperately around the group. Her chest rose and fell with rapid breaths. "What do you care? I'll be well and truly out of your hair by then."

Sabrina closed her eyes, thinking of all the ways this woman had wronged her, thinking of all the ways this woman could wrong her *still*.

Then, she thought of Hew's lips on hers. Of how it felt to finally *live* again. To finally feel *whole* again.

She didn't want to sully all that with Black Widow's blood.

"I don't want to put any of us in danger," she admitted quietly to the men. "But I also don't want another life on my conscience. So, I say we cage her or free her. And I'm leaning toward the latter."

Hew exhaled, his forehead coming to rest briefly against her temple as if he'd been right there with her, suffering the same turmoil she'd suffered in having to make her choice. Now that she *had*, he could breathe.

Black Widow stared hopefully up at Boss. His brow ridge cast his eyes in deep shadows, making them unreadable.

"Reckon we should flip a coin?" Graham offered, and Sabrina thought he was only half-joking.

"Just let me go," Black Widow pleaded. "I'll disappear. You'll never see me again."

The only indication Boss struggled with indecision was the subtle flex of his jaw. When he finally spoke, the threat in his voice was sharp enough to make Sabrina wince.

"Remember how easily we thwarted your little operation," Boss said. "Remember that we have resources you could only dream about and a reach far beyond anything you could fathom. There's no corner of the world you can go to where we can't find you. There's no amount of protection you could pull around yourself that we can't penetrate. Don't mistake our clemency today for an unwillingness to put a lead round between your eyes."

CHAPTER 33

Hew pressed a palm over the red button on the brick wall and watched as the motorized door to the Bat Cave moved along its tracks.

The sound of it, a deep, resonant rumble, always reminded him of the earth grinding its teeth. And with it closed, the bricks fitted together so tightly that the seams in the mortar were impossible to see.

He'd watched the phenomenon dozens of times. Each time, he was amazed at the completeness of the illusion.

Graham and Boss remained in the tunnel with Black Widow. They would handle what came next regarding how, when, and *where* she would be released.

And thank god for that.

Hew had agreed with Boss that Sabrina deserved a say in the assassin's fate.

But Christ on a snowmobile!

It'd been torture watching her struggle with the choice.

If she'd agreed to pull the trigger, she'd have been haunted. If she'd decided to imprison the Widow illegally, she'd have been haunted. And letting the woman walk? Well, that might *still* haunt her, depending on how things played out but—

"So?" Becky's voice cut through his thoughts. "What's the verdict?"

Dum-Dums stuck out of the bib pocket on her pink coveralls. And the look on her face was…

A little more than concerned.

She tried to cover her anxiety by nonchalantly tucking her blond bob behind her ears. But she wasn't fooling anyone. Her fingers shook.

She wasn't *scared*. Not in the traditional sense. She simply didn't want her husband back in the killing game.

And, really, who can blame her?

"We're letting her go," Sabrina said with a staunch dip of her chin.

Becky's shoulders slumped like someone had stuck a pin in her, letting out all her air.

"And we're hoping that choice doesn't come back to bite us on the ass," Sabrina added, her mouth twisting with distaste.

"If it does, we'll deal with it. I've got a salve that usually works." Becky winked.

Sabrina laughed, and Hew wanted to hug Becky for adding levity to such a tense situation.

"Now." Becky slung an arm around Sabrina's shoulders, steering her toward the stairs. "Couple of things for you. One, the Wisconsin highway patrol called. They've towed your car. I wrote down all the info on a sticky note and stuck it to your bedroom door. They say you can come get it whenever you're ready or call to have it sent to a mechanic."

Sabrina wrinkled her nose. "I hope it isn't totaled. I haven't even changed the oil in it yet."

"Mmm." Becky nodded in commiseration. "I once had a client total a bike within ten minutes of taking it for its maiden ride. He got sideswiped by a taxi and lived to tell the tale. But the chopper?" She shook her head sorrowfully. "I actually cried when he called to tell me."

"All that hard work straight down the drain." Sabrina shook her head sympathetically before prompting, "And that second thing?"

"Martin called." Becky smiled broadly. "Said he'll be out front in fifteen minutes."

Sabrina skidded to a stop at the same time Hew's heart quit beating.

"My god!" Her hand shot to her messy bun. The one he'd watched fall down around her shoulders before he'd undressed her. The same one she'd retied atop her head before meeting Graham in the War Room. "I forgot about Martin. *Again!* I'm such an asshole!"

Hearing the man's name in her mouth made Hew's chest feel hollow, like someone had carved him open with a dull spoon.

Becky, oblivious to the change in circumstances, smiled at Sabrina. "You have just enough time to wash your face, brush your teeth, and comb your hair. Better hop to."

Sabrina turned to Hew, her expression caught somewhere between guilty and apologetic. "I made plans with him this morning before—"

She stopped and swallowed, cast a furtive glance at Becky, who was all ears.

What? She didn't want Becky to know what had transpired upstairs? Why not?

"Before what?" Becky blinked between them.

"Never mind." Sabrina waved her off, and Hew slowly curled his hands into fists.

Becky narrowed her eyes. "Curiouser and curiouser." Then she shrugged. "Back to the grind for me, though. Literally. I have a new gas tank to shape."

Hew didn't move until Becky disappeared behind a rack holding parts and tools. Then he turned, slowly, feeling like his bones were made of concrete, to find Sabrina watching him closely.

"Sorry." She twisted her fingers together, her expression stricken.

"For what?" He forced mortar through his veins, hoping it would harden his resolve and shore up his walls. "No one would blame ya for keepin' the plans you made first. Least of all, me."

"So you're…okay with this? With me going to meet Martin?" Was that hope in her tone? Or worse…*anticipation*?

He huffed out a dry laugh. "Why wouldn't I be?"

Her dark eyebrows pulled together over her perfect nose. "I know we planned to put those condoms to use, but—"

"But now you've gone and proved ya *can* be with a man without fallin' to pieces," he cut her off. His desperation had gotten tangled up with his jealousy and uncertainty until he couldn't tell which part was eating him alive. "So, mission accomplished, ayuh?"

She didn't speak. Didn't move. Simply stared at him. Seeking. Searching. Wanting. Needing something from him.

But what?

His permission? His absolution? His endorsement?

Was she waiting to see if he could keep his promise to remain friends? To ensure nothing changed between them?

But everything *had* changed. *He* had changed.

There was the Hewitt Birch who had existed before he made love to Sabrina Greenlee. And there was the Hewitt Birch who existed now.

He could tell her. Admit his feelings. But one of the first lessons he'd learned in life was that vulnerability equaled hurt.

And Sabrina? She had the ability to slice him clean to the bone.

"I mean, we did what…we did"—he waved a vague hand in the general direction of the upstairs—"because ya wanted to test the waters, right? Because, as you put it, who better than your *good friend* Hew to see ya through your first time since Torres? I don't think it's premature to say ya passed with flyin' colors."

He winked at her.

He wanted to kick his own ass the instant he did it.

Fuck!

"Right," she said slowly. "Right," she said again and firmed her chin. "So, I'll go get ready?"

"Is that a question or a statement?"

Her jaw sawed side to side as she firmed her shoulders. "I'll go get ready."

"Sounds like a plan." He shoved his hands deep into his pockets so she wouldn't see his fingers clenching.

She hesitated another beat. Searching his face. Searching his eyes.

But he'd donned the mask he'd gotten good at wearing back when he was just a kid. In all the years since, it'd become impenetrable.

"Right," she said for the third time before slowly heading for the stairs. He watched her walk away. Waited for her to turn back.

She never did. And when she jogged up the treads, her footsteps pounded out a rhythm that sounded…*final?*

He had the sudden, nearly overwhelming, urge to chase her. To catch her up and pull her close. To tell her to forget Martin and—

He could still feel her, damnit! Under his hands. Under his skin. The touch of her fingertips. The taste of her mouth. The way she'd cried out his name like it had been pulled straight from her heart.

He ran a hand over his head like he could scrape out the memory of her and all they'd shared.

But she wasn't going anywhere.

Except for out with Martin.

Fuck, fuck, fuck!

CHAPTER 34

Tired.

Cranky.

Confused.

Sabrina was all those things four hours later as she crossed the blacktop stretch from BKI's front gate to the front door of the old menthol cigarette factory.

Sweat slid between her shoulder blades despite the sun finally tapping out. What was left of the big, orange orb sent long, lavender shadows crawling over the compound. And the humidity in the air clung to her like wet denim.

Winter in Chicago could be miserable. She'd expected that when she'd first moved from Charleston. But what she had *not* expected was for summer to be so…*summery*, for the heat to compete with the sultry southern sun she'd lamented her whole life.

Don't wish your life away.

She'd read that somewhere. But here she was, dreaming of autumn. Dreaming of falling leaves and cool breezes, scarves and hot chocolate and evenings out by the fire pit in deep conversation with Hew.

Hew…

It always came back to him, didn't it? Although at the moment, she had no desire to converse with him and every desire to whack him upside the head because he was the cause of the current state of her tiredness, crankiness, and confusion.

Behind her, Martin waited in his car, engine idling. A gentleman to the core.

When she reached the front door and turned to wave at him, to assure him she was safe—as if she wouldn't be inside a ten-foot-tall razor-wire-topped brick wall with a security guard posted out front—he gave her a huge smile. Waved back. And then slowly let his Mercedes crawl away from the curb.

Such a good man, she thought as she dejectedly opened the door. *He deserves better than me. Better than someone who's in love with someone else.*

The familiar smells inside the big, brick building wafted over her. Motor oil, burned coffee, and that faint tang of scorched steel that always tickled the back of her throat.

Usually, the scents settled her. Lent her a sense of security she hadn't felt since…

Actually, she'd *never* felt it.

Her childhood home had been a den of neglect and poverty, and the apartment she'd rented in Charleston once she'd moved out of her parents' house had been susceptible to tidal flooding and palmetto bug infestations.

It wasn't until she'd taken up residence inside the big-shouldered building that was Black Knights Inc. that she'd enjoyed true, unassailable safety.

Today, however, the three-story factory seemed to mock her. Seemed to whisper in her ear, *Home is where* your *heart is. But where's* Hew's *heart?* eHew

She didn't know. Couldn't begin to guess because the mixed signals were mixed signaling, and she was too tired, cranky, and confused to sort through them.

The way Hew had touched her, so reverent and worshipful—like she was fragile and holy—had convinced her what they'd done together was more than obligation on his part. More than just him helping her over that final hurdle in her healing.

No man fakes that kind of care, she'd told herself as she lay naked in his arms.

Now? She wasn't so sure.

He'd been so *unbothered* by the thought of her meeting Martin. So uncaring that they wouldn't get to go upstairs and finish what they'd started. But more than that, he'd seemed…*relieved?*

That *had* been relief she'd seen in his eyes, right?

His body wanted her. There was no denying that. But physical attraction didn't equal romantic intention. It *certainly* didn't equal love. And she wasn't fool enough to believe it wasn't possible she'd projected all of her own feelings—her own wants and desires—onto him.

Was it reasonable to believe that what she'd *thought* was reverence and worship was just her good friend Hew giving her his all? Giving *it* his all? Because the man didn't know how to do anything by half-measures?

Unfortunately, the answer to that question was *yes.*

So, where does that leave us now?

Then she remembered his promise.

Friends.

He'd vowed that, no matter what, they'd remain friends.

Unfortunately, now that she knew how much more was possible between them, now that she knew the joy of sharing her body with him on top of already sharing her heart and soul, the thought of going back to *just friends* felt unsatisfying. Depressing even.

With a dejected sigh, she shut the door behind her. Then, she straightened her shoulders and willed herself to get it together.

Any disappointment she felt was of her own making. Any awkwardness or confusion or heartbreak was hers and hers alone. *She* had been the one to offer up the arrangement. *She* had been the one to make the deal.

Grin and bear it.

That's what she'd do. She'd put on the proverbial happy face. Suck it up and bury it deep, and then pave over it with two feet of asphalt.

The smile she forced was so fake it made her cheeks ache. But it faded quickly when she realized the shop was empty. No clanking tools. No revving engines. No humming machines.

She'd spent more time than she'd meant to with Martin at the pub down the street. But it had been good to sit on the barstool and forget the horrors of the past two days. Forget the hurricane of emotions making her heart swirl and her head twist. Forget that in the space of one afternoon, everything and nothing had changed.

There at the pub, surrounded by regular people enjoying regular lives, she'd been able to pretend she belonged to a world untouched by violence and fear.

And despite the foul taste it had left in her mouth, she'd lied to Martin about how she'd sustained her injuries, telling him she'd gotten them in the wreck.

Martin, who was so kind and concerned. Martin, who gave her the opposite of mixed signals. Martin, who was smart and funny and handsome and…*not Hew*.

That was the kicker, wasn't it? He wasn't Hew.

And although she *tried* not to compare the two men, she couldn't help herself. Martin's charm was polished and polite. His confidence was borne of personal achievement and financial success—and having a face that belonged on billboards. Whereas Hew? Hew was raw edges and callused hands. He had the kind of confidence that came from feeling more at home in a cockpit or a mechanic's bay than in a boardroom.

Where Martin dazzled with easy conversation, Hew spoke in a few words that somehow carried more weight than entire TED Talks. Martin's smile impressed her. Hew's smile unraveled her.

Damnit, *why* hadn't she told Martin that her heart belonged to someone else?

She could have brought it up when he took her hand and held it beneath the bar. She could have confessed it when he softly cupped her cheek to stare deep into her eyes. She could have blurted it out when he pulled up beside the curb next to the front gate and leaned over to kiss her lips.

But she hadn't.

Lord, help her; she hadn't because it had been *nice* to sit next to a handsome man and know how he felt about her. Nice to feel wanted because she was *her*, Sabrina Greenlee, a strong, independent, successful woman, and not because she was some damsel in distress who needed saving. Or *worse*, some sort of final obligation.

She hadn't told him. But she *should* have. She *would* the next time she saw him because it was only fair. Only right.

Sighing heavily, she turned for the kitchen. But she stopped in her tracks when she heard voices floating down from the second floor.

"—made it back with no one the wiser—"

"—bodies won't be found—"

"—no record of our involvement—"

The Knights were in the War Room doing a sit-rep. Considering she'd been at the heart of their recent troubles, she should go up and chime in where appropriate.

But first? Water.

The gin and tonic she'd nursed at the pub should have been refreshing. But all it had done was leave a bitter taste in her mouth and make her stomach feel queasy.

Or maybe that's just my mixed-up, messed-up emotions, she admitted dolefully as she resumed her journey toward the kitchen.

Half the can of lime sparkling water was gone when she stepped onto the second-floor landing. And she hid a silent burp behind her fist when she realized it wasn't only the Black Knights discussing the events of the past two days.

A laptop sat open at the end of the table, facing Boss. Its display threw a cold glow over his stony expression.

On the screen, Sabrina could see Madam President, looking as stately and poised as ever in a blue blazer and a brown bob that could've passed for a bicycle helmet. Beside her was Leonard Meadows. He looked like he'd just bitten into something sour.

"How did you find the abductors?" Meadows was asking.

Boss answered smoothly, "Ozzie matched CCTV footage of the van that followed Sabrina out of town to images we later captured at an old bottling plant. The Knights were ready to drop in the second Sabrina's abductors called to reveal the location of the drop."

Given what the Knights had learned from Black Widow regarding Bishop and his position in government, they'd decided not to inform Madam President or her chief of staff about Kerberos's involvement or Black Widow's capture.

The Knights no longer knew whom to trust. And perhaps *that* was the most disturbing thing to come from the events of the last two days.

Sabrina skirted around the table, careful to avoid the laptop camera's line of sight because she'd never been comfortable talking to two of the most important people in the country. And now that one of them might actually be a traitor? She was even *less* inclined to show her face.

She dropped into the first open seat, next to Fisher. He greeted her with a downward jerk of his chin, and she nodded back. Then she slid her gaze around the table, looking for…

There you are, you sexy, confusing, infuriating thing, she thought when her eyes landed on Hew's profile.

She *willed* him to look at her. To give her some clue about what he was thinking. What he was feeling. What he wanted to do going forward.

He didn't. He just stared straight ahead, expression unreadable.

"And I'm assuming the cash is back with the treasury?" the president asked.

Boss nodded. "Signed, sealed, and delivered by our two favorite G-women."

Meadows's voice was as sharp as a tack. "And the abductors? Were you able to ID them?"

"They were all ex-military. Except one, who was ex-CIA."

"You don't think that's…coincidental?" Meadows pressed.

Boss's insouciant shrug was award-worthy. "If there was more to it, the people who could tell us about it are dead."

"Okay." The president's strident voice sounded through the laptop's speakers. "What's done is done. We've kept you long enough this evening. Go home to your families."

"Sorry, Madam President," Meadows cut in just as Boss was about to shut the laptop. "But I have one more thing to ask before we sign off."

Even though Sabrina couldn't see the screen from where she sat, she imagined President Sandra J. Stevens nodding her head regally.

"Do you all still feel equipped to continue this work?"

Meadows's question hung in the air like a lead anvil. And for long moments, it was met by silence. Deep, resounding, soul-sucking silence.

"Sorry, sir," Boss said carefully. "What, exactly, are you asking?"

"You were all confronted with a situation wherein the promise Madam President and I made to you years ago was put into play. The promise that we wouldn't intervene, for good or for bad. The promise that we would protect the president's plausible deniability at all costs." There was another pregnant pause before he finished. "I suppose I'd like a little reassurance that this most recent incident hasn't changed our working relationship."

"Leonard." The president's tone held a note of reprimand.

Meadows didn't budge. "We need to know, Sandra."

The easy way they used each other's first names felt oddly uncomfortable. Sabrina shifted in her chair.

Boss glanced around the table, locking eyes with each of the Knights before once again facing the screen. "The Black Knights continue to serve at your pleasure, Madam President. Nothing's changed."

Except…everything had. Because the White House had a conspirator walking its hallowed halls.

"Good," Meadows said. "Then, we'll let you all head home for the night. Thanks for the update."

And then, mercifully, Boss shut the laptop lid with a satisfying *snap*. Multiple people around the table exhaled like they'd been holding their breath.

"Is it just me?" Becky looked around. "Or does everything they say now sound shady as shit?"

"I hate being paranoid," Fisher muttered.

"Try being the daughter of a maybe-traitor," Eliza grumbled, and then gave Fisher a wavering smile when he lifted her hand to kiss her fingers.

"Sorry, darlin'," he told her quietly. "I hate this for you."

"I hate this for *all* of us," she countered.

"Here's a silver lining," Ozzie interjected, looking at his phone. "Graham just landed in D.C. He'll spend a couple of weeks shadowing Lura Dougherty. If she's clean and clear, he'll ask her to be our eyes and ears inside the White House, and Operation Find Out Who Bishop Is will officially be underway."

Becky wrinkled her nose. "Let's workshop that title. Doesn't quite slide off the tongue."

Despite the seriousness of the situation, Sabrina chuffed out a laugh.

That was the thing about the Black Knights. They could joke even when they were knee-deep in shit.

"Black Widow?" she asked, looking at Boss. "Is she…?" She didn't finish the question.

"Gone," he assured her, and her shoulders sagged with relief.

"Hopefully for good," she muttered, still unsure if she'd made the right call. Still worried about what would happen to them if she hadn't.

His rugged face softened. "Mercy is never the wrong move, Sabrina."

She gave him a weary nod but couldn't keep the skepticism from her expression.

"It's been a helluva couple of days." Boss rapped his knuckles on the table and then pushed to a stand. "I need my kids, my wife, and a large meat lovers' pizza." He offered Becky his hand. "Take me home, Goose, or lose me forever."

And that was that.

The room broke into motion, chairs scraping, conversations starting and stopping as goodbyes were said. Those who lived off-site headed for the exit, and those who didn't scattered into other parts of the building.

Which left…Hew.

He was *finally* looking at her, although his expression was unreadable.

If the Guinness Book of World Records *ever decides to open up a category for Best Poker Face, Hewitt Birch is a shoo-in*, she thought irritably.

She had *just* convinced herself to grin and bear it, to suck it up and let things go back to the way they were pre-multiple orgasms. But screw that.

She needed more than his taciturn expressions and vague commentary. She needed answers. Actual *words.* The unvarnished truth straight out of his mouth.

Only *then* would she be able to bury her feelings deep and pave over them.

Her fingers twisted together beneath the table. But above the table, she firmed her chin and blurted, "Can we talk?"

CHAPTER 35

Hew wanted to roar. He wanted to rage. He wanted to stomp around like a gorilla and beat his chest. But he made sure his expression was devoid of that when he lifted an eyebrow and said, "About what?"

"About what happened between us earlier." Sabrina's tone was the equivalent of *well, duh.*

He carefully slipped his hands beneath the conference table so she wouldn't see him curl his fingers into fists. "Thought we covered that already. *Mission accomplished.* That's what ya said, right?"

"That's what *you* said," she countered quickly.

He tipped his head. "You tellin' me the mission *wasn't* accomplished? You still need more of my hand-holdin' before ya jump in the saddle with your boyfriend?"

"I—" She faltered, mouth open, eyes wide.

He pounced on the pause because he couldn't stop himself.

"Ya sure were gone a long while," he declared.

She sat back and crossed her arms. Her expression was cautious. *Guarded.* "Time got away from us," she admitted.

It flies when you're busy swallowin' each other's tongues, he thought, feeling his nostrils flare.

Aloud, he said casually, "He's a good talker. Noticed that about him right off."

Her jaw worked side to side like she was searching for words. Finally, she settled on, "He's lived an exciting life. That helps to keep the conversation lively."

"Mmm." He nodded like he gave a fiddler's fuck about Martin Massey's exciting life. Then he leaned back in his chair and asked, "Did ya share the good news with him?"

Her brow furrowed. "Good news?"

"That you've cleared the last hurdle in your healin' journey and you're ready to jump back into life and all its…*pleasures*." The last word came out slicker than he meant. Even *he* wanted to recoil from it.

What the hell was wrong with him?

But he knew. He was possessed. Possessed by that green-eyed monster. Possessed by the little boy in him who never got picked. Possessed by the need to lash out and protect himself.

"That…uh…didn't come up." Her throat worked over a swallow.

"No?" He cocked his head. "Funny. Given the way ya kissed him out front, I figured it was the lead story."

Her chin jerked back. "How did you—" She glanced over the railing toward the big TV mounted next to the shop's front door. It had switched from showing daytime's full-color security feed to night's black-and-white images.

"You saw that?" She turned back to him.

"Happened to be walkin' by," he admitted through a jaw that ached from clenching. "Kinda hard to miss."

She leaned forward a little, her voice…what? What was her tone? "How did that make you feel? To see me kissing another man?"

It had made him want to rip the whole damned security system out of the wall before breaking Martin Massey's perfect jaw.

"How *should* it have made me feel?" he asked carefully, painting a fresh coat of confusion on his face like he painted on fresh oil camo before each op. "We're friends, right? If Martin's the man for you, I'm happy." He softened his tone. It was the only crack in his armor he would allow. "All I've ever wanted is your happiness, Sabrina."

Her eyes were bright in a way that made him want to look away. But he forced himself to hold her gaze. Forced himself to listen and believe when she whispered, "It's all I've ever wanted for you, too, Hew."

"So, we're good, ayuh?" His heart pounded out a terrible rhythm.

Why couldn't he just tell her he wanted her?

Why couldn't he just say he'd been waiting his whole life to feel about anyone the way he felt about her?

Why couldn't he admit he loved her?

He *did* love her, by the way. That fact had become crystal clear to him in the hours since she'd left. In the hours he'd spent envisioning her in Martin's arms and then fantasizing about all the ways he could rip apart the hedge fund manager limb from limb.

He loved her, and yet...

She'd given him no indication she felt the same.

She liked him, of course. And her body certainly liked the things he'd done to it. But she'd never said a thing about having feelings for him beyond friendly affection. She'd raced to her date with Martin. And then she'd spent four *hours* with the sonofabitch.

It didn't take four hours to apologize for missing their date. And it *certainly* didn't take four hours to tell a guy she didn't want to see him anymore because she was in love with someone else.

"We're good," she finally said, slowly standing from the table before walking purposefully across the room.

When she disappeared up the stairs, he was left alone.

As usual.

CHAPTER 36

Washington D.C.
15 days later…

Graham sat tucked in the shadowy back booth, his long legs stretched under the table. He nursed a lukewarm beer while his eyes tracked Lura across the room.

He'd been tailing her for two weeks and had learned two things. One, work wasn't just her nine-to-five. It was her oxygen. She lived and breathed her job. And two, she was a creature of habit so predictable he could set his watch by her.

That's how he knew she'd be at this particular bar in D.C.'s Capitol Hill Neighborhood tonight.

Wednesday night, barring a White House event, she went for sushi. Thursday evening was set aside for hot yoga followed by frozen yogurt. And Friday night? Beers at The Pug on H Street.

The joint was a dim little hole-in-the-wall decorated in whatever leftover junk had lost a bidding war at a yard sale. Christmas lights drooped across the ceiling in sagging rainbow strands despite being months past the holiday. And the cushion he sat on was ripped and digging into his ass.

An odd choice for her.

Or so he'd thought at first.

After some observation, it had become clear that Lura's buttoned-up façade was just that. A façade.

Off-duty Lura preferred Costco-brand joggers and New Balance sneakers. Her apartment was cozy and colorful, but her furniture was purchased for comfort instead of fashion. And when she went out for a night of fun, she didn't choose a nice restaurant or any of the fancy cocktail bars frequented by the government elites. She chose *this* dive that made him feel like he might contract hep B from the toilet seat.

It was amazing.

She was amazing.

She was also perfect for the job he'd been sent to offer her.

She was well-connected because she was the right-hand woman to the president's right-hand man. Since she was single, no boyfriend drama would steal her focus from the mission. And she was equally well-liked by her superiors *and* her peers, which meant folks tended to let their guard down around her.

No one gave her a second glance when she walked into a room with the likes of the president, the vice president, or the Joint Chiefs. She was important enough to warrant a relatively high security clearance, but not important enough to need a security detail. And everyone was used to seeing her at the office at all hours, so if she happened to stick around after all the others had left for the day, no one batted an eyelash.

Which meant…survey says?

It's time.

He drained the last of his beer, set his jaw, and slid to the edge of the booth.

Before he could stand, however, some jackass sidled up beside her at the bar.

The shitbird looked like all the other shitbirds in Washington. Tall, square-jawed, hair styled like he'd just walked out of an ad for overpriced cologne. His suit jacket was pulled tight over a set of gym-built shoulders, and his grin…

Yeah, he practices that in the mirror.

Lura didn't return the man's smile. At best, her expression was what might be called *politely interested.* And when she bent to pick up the earring that dropped on the floor after she brushed her hair behind her ear, Graham would swear the asshole smacked her ass with his eyes.

Graham's hands stayed loose on the tabletop, but his right boot shifted, crossing over his left knee just enough to bring the pistol strapped to his ankle into easy reach.

Accuracy depended on a shooter's skill and the range to the target. Graham was a skilled shooter. But even a kindergartener could hit a man fifteen feet away. Also, with twelve in the clip and one in the throat, he had thirteen tries to get it right.

His focus narrowed to the point of a pin in the center of the douchecanoe's forehead. He couldn't help thinking how good that spot would look with a neat little hole drilled through it.

Not that Graham could really blame the guy for ogling. Lura Dougherty was five feet eleven inches of boom and pow. She had it all in all the right places. And all of it was explosive to a man's senses.

Deciding he'd seen plenty—and letting go of the fantasy of putting a lead round through the asshat's brainpan—he slid from the booth and threaded his way through the crowd, boots tacky against the beer-soaked floor.

He wasn't sure how he'd expected Lura to receive him when he stepped up beside her. But he certainly wasn't prepared for her to squeal his name and throw her arms around his neck.

CHAPTER 37

What the ever-loving hell are you doing, woman?

The thought ripped through Lura's head the instant she launched herself at Graham Coleburn.

Her only excuse? She'd been thinking about him pretty much nonstop since leaving Chicago. Plus, she was grateful for the easy out when it came to Bryan. *Or did he say his name was Ryan?* And also, Graham smelled really, *really* good. Like charred vanilla and warm leather and…

Okay, so fine. Those were *three* excuses. But still.

Stepping back, she carefully arranged her features and tried to cover her blunder by quickly asking, "What in the world are you doing here?"

"Came to see ya." His growly voice cut clean through the hum of clinking glasses, bluesy music, and the chatter of three dozen conversations.

"Me?" Her chin jerked back in surprise.

"Mmm." He nodded once, his green eyes sliding toward Bryan/Ryan/Whoever.

"Right. Uh…Graham Coleburn, this is…" She wrinkled her nose at the guy in the Brioni suit. "I'm sorry, I didn't catch it earlier over all this noise. Did you say your name was Bryan or Ryan?"

"Doesn't matter now, does it?" The guy's eyes flicked between her and Graham like a man conceding the field.

"Sorry," she offered, but the apology in her smile was wasted on the back of the guy's head as he ambled away.

She took a quick swig of beer to drown the butterflies in her belly before her gaze locked back on Graham.

Graham, who was looking way too yummy in jeans that hugged his tree-trunk thighs. Graham, who towered over everyone else. Graham, who was attracting the notice of every single female eye in the room—and some of the male eyes, too—simply by existing.

He'd always had an outsized presence, even back in high school.

"Is this a personal or professional visit?" she asked with a teasing grin.

He didn't return her easy expression. In fact, he looked as grave as a battlefield. "Can we step outside for a minute?"

The butterflies in her belly grew lead wings and plummeted. Apprehension tickled the hairs at the nape of her neck. But she nodded. "Of course."

She headed for the front door, but his hand closed around her wrist. It was so big and callused that it made her forget her name for a half-second.

"This way." He steered her toward the back of the bar. Past the people lined up for the bathrooms. Past the little storage closet. Past the pyramid of empty beer kegs.

Outside, the back alley was dim and close, smelling faintly of spilled liquor and crumbling concrete. The brick walls trapped the thick night air until she felt like wet hands pressed against the back of her neck. And somewhere above, an AC unit rattled like it was about to give up the ghost.

He scanned both ends of the alley, making sure they were alone. Then, he turned back to her. "How ya been?"

She blinked. Small talk? From Graham? "Uh…fine?"

"Is that a question or a statement?"

"Fine." She shook herself. "I've been fine. You?"

"Right as rain."

"Good."

They stood there for a beat, the silence stretching between the faint thump of the jukebox inside and the wail of a siren a few blocks away.

Eventually, she lifted an eyebrow. "Are we just going to stand here staring at each other all night? Not that I mind. You're not hard to look at. But I feel like we could do that inside, away from eau de dumpster."

That got a twitch of his mouth. Then, in a low voice, he told her, "We'd like you to be our eyes and ears inside the West Wing. We want your help uncoverin' Bishop's true identity."

Her breath stuttered. The beer in her stomach turned sour, and she deeply regretted that last sip.

"You think he's someone in the White House?"

"We think he's more than that. We think he's someone very close to the top."

A cold shiver slid down her spine despite the sticky heat. "My boss?"

A slight pause. Then… "We haven't ruled him out."

She pressed a hand to her forehead as her mind raced.

Could Leonard Meadows be Bishop?

But why? What did he gain by the subterfuge? And why would he try to set up the Black Knights?

Aloud, she said, "My god. What does Eliza think?"

"She's devastated by the idea. Naturally." He shrugged one massive shoulder. "But if Bishop ends up bein' her dad, she'll help us take him down."

"I always thought they had an odd relationship," she muttered.

"It might not be him," Graham cautioned. His bearded jaw was cut close enough that she could still appreciate the depth of his dimples when he firmed his lips.

Those dimples had launched a thousand lady boners back in Georgia.

She suspected they did the same in Chicago.

"*Why* do you think it's someone close to the president?" she asked carefully.

And then he told her. All of it. About the assassin they'd caught. About the intel they'd pieced together. About the chaos Bishop had been orchestrating from the shadows for years. Chaos that could only be set up by someone with a top-notch security clearance and knowledge of things only someone intimately acquainted with Sandra J. Stevens would know.

By the time he was finished, the fine hairs on Lura's arms stood on end.

"I'm not a spy," she breathed. "I have no training."

"That's why I'm here." He looked down at her, all solid muscle and quiet determination. "And I'll be here with ya the whole way through if you say yes. But ya should know…this is a dangerous game. Secrets have weight. The more you keep, the longer you keep 'em, the heavier they get."

"Like pushin' a wheelbarrow full of shit up a steep hill, as my daddy says." She purposefully thickened her accent to impersonate her father.

His expression was grim. "You can say no, Lura. Ya probably *should* say no."

He was right. She should. She wasn't cut out for this sort of thing. And yet…

"There's no fun in that. Plus, playing the detective has been my dream job since I read my first Nancy Drew novel at age eight."

She'd meant to lighten the mood. She failed.

A muscle ticked in Graham's jaw when he stressed, "Bishop, whoever he is, is a powerful man. A dangerous man. A *murderous* man. One with a lot to lose."

A ghostly hand of apprehension trailed cold fingers up her spine.

"All the more reason to unmask him," she declared staunchly, hoping she looked more confident than she felt.

His gaze flicked down the alley before zeroing back to her. "Okay. Then let's get started."

"Now?" She blinked rapidly. "Tonight?"

"Ya got somethin' better to do? Ryan/Bryan maybe?"

She pressed her lips into a thin line. "Don't be a dick."

He grinned. And he was standing close enough that she could smell that impossible mix of leather and vanilla. It made her knees go weak.

It occurred to her then that *Bishop* wasn't the only danger she faced. Working so closely with the likes of Graham Coleburn might be her ultimate undoing.

CHAPTER 38

"Where ya headed?"

Hew leaned a shoulder against the doorjamb outside Sabrina's room. Trying like hell to sound casual, *friendly*.

She stood before her dresser, clad in a forest-green gown that cinched in her waist. It held her breasts high and flirted with her ankles and the black patent leather heels strapped to her feet. She tugged a brush through the waterfall of her hair, and it looked so shiny he thought he could see his reflection in the long, dark locks.

He loved it when she wore it down, when it cascaded over her shoulders and curled around her clavicles. Then again, he loved it when she wore it up, too, when it showed off the softness of her neck, highlighted the delicate line of her jaw, and exposed all the lovely, pale, perfect skin.

His throat went tight with the memory of what it'd been like to run his hands through the strands. They'd slipped through his fingers, as soft as seafoam, as cool and clean as a spring morning. And she'd sighed at his touch, tipping her head back. Trusting him. Letting him in.

In that moment, he hadn't felt unloved or unwanted. He'd felt like he finally, *finally* belonged somewhere. Belonged *with* someone.

And then it had all come crumbling down.

As castles built in the sky tend to do, he told himself.

Then, with a silent curse, he did what he'd been doing for the last two weeks. He shoved the memory into a mental closet, turned the key, and told it to stay put. To stay hidden. To please, please, *please* have mercy on him.

"Martin's finally back from his business trip." Her South Carolina drawl swirled delicately inside his ears. "He's taking me out to dinner," she finished without turning from the mirror.

Martin Massey. Great.

After meeting her for a drink the day after her abduction, the shiny hedge fund manager had hopped on a red-eye flight. Which meant Hew had been granted a blessed reprieve while the man was overseas.

Apparently, though, the clock had run out. And there was no more denying the fact that Sabrina had a boyfriend and Hew had…nothing.

Nothing but the image of Martin stepping out of his expensive Mercedes in a suit tailored to within an inch of its life, with shoes so shiny they could blind a man, and wearing a 100-watt smile that had won over the hearts and minds of investors, boardrooms, and social media mavens from Charleston.

What did Hew have in comparison? A tragic childhood, scars across his knuckles, and a wardrobe full of T-shirts that smelled faintly of aviation fuel.

You were lucky she deigned to let ya—

What was he supposed to call that singularly glorious afternoon? A tryst. An encounter? An all-too-brief sexual rendezvous?

The day that wrecked me and changed everything I thought I knew about my feelings for her?

Whatever name he gave it, it all boiled down to the same truth.

He'd been a damned fool to promise he could make love to her and then act like nothing had changed. Like *he* hadn't been fundamentally changed by the act.

He'd done his best to hold to his word, though. To keep things easy between them. To act no differently than before.

But he had to admit, his pretense was cracked six ways from Sunday.

Things between them no longer felt like a comfy blanket on a cold winter's night. Now, they walked around each other like the space between them was a minefield. Every step was cautious, careful. Every word was honed with an edge of tension.

She no longer sought the seat beside him at the conference table. Didn't catch his eye from across the room to share a conspiratorial smile that told him they were in on the same inside joke. And hadn't once come knocking at his door to talk or to swipe the stuffed lobster off his dresser…even though he'd left his door ajar in invitation. Even though he'd kept an ear cocked and his fingers crossed. Waiting. Hoping.

He couldn't say if it was him or her creating the awkwardness between them. What he *could* say was that he missed the easy way she used to laugh around him. Missed how she would touch him without reluctance or tell him what was in her head without him first having to ask.

Lying awake at night the last two weeks, he couldn't help but wonder if it might not have been better had he kept his damn hands to himself. If it might not have been better had he never known the gentleness of her touch or the sweetness of her lips.

Then he'd remember the glory of loving her, of *making* love to her, and he couldn't bring himself to regret having experienced that one perfect thing. That one perfect moment.

Even if he took nothing else with him to his grave, he could take that.

For one blissful afternoon, Sabrina Greenlee—the Roman river goddess— was mine.

She set aside the brush and turned to him. Just like always, her big brown eyes sucked him in like whirlpools. He wanted to drown in them. He *did* drown in them all day, every day, because he was helpless to do anything else.

When she walked over to stand with him in the doorway, her perfume drifted around him like sweet morning mist. That pear and lavender scent would always remind him of their time together, because it lingered in the space between her breasts, in the hollow of her belly button, and in the crook of her knees. All the places he'd explored with his hands and his mouth. All the places he wanted to explore again. A million times over.

"What's on the agenda for you tonight?" she asked, her voice polite. Too polite.

This was how they were around each other now. *Too polite.*

"I'm goin' to hunker down with that dragon book you were pestrin' me to read."

Her smile flickered, but it didn't light up her face like it used to. "Be prepared for fast flying, sword fighting, and wars between realms. There's also romance. Which, in my humble opinion, is what takes a book from good to great."

"Mmm," was all he said, because she didn't want to hear what he *wanted* to say.

Romance is what takes a life *from good to great. I love you, Sabrina. Say ya love me, too, and I promise ya more adventure than either of us will ever find in a book.*

They stared at each other then, each waiting for the other to speak. To say something *real*. To find the one word or phrase that would return them to how they used to be.

Neither of them did.

Neither of them could.

And that silence…that chasm of everything unsaid…was the most desolate place on earth.

"Right." She finally nodded. "Guess I'll see you later, then."

For the briefest second, he saw sadness flicker in her eyes. Or maybe he was projecting his own thoughts and feelings onto her—*hoping* to see his own melancholy mirrored back to him—because she quickly turned, and he was left to listen to her heels tapping down the hall.

With each echoing footfall, he would swear she dragged a piece of him with her. And the farther she went, the hollower he became until he was nothing but an empty shell standing in the hallway.

He waited until he heard her step off the last tread before he trudged into the TV room. With a defeated sigh, he sank onto the couch, picked up the damned dragon book from the coffee table, and opened it to the first page.

No matter how hard he focused, though, he couldn't stop the words from blurring. He kept imagining Sabrina sitting across a candlelit table from Martin Massey, laughing that laugh and smiling that smile that Hew hadn't heard or seen in days.

That he feared he might never hear or see again.

CHAPTER 39

North Cherry Avenue, Chicago

Two hours later, Sabrina pointed to the curb. "Here's fine."

Martin's fingers tightened on the steering wheel. A line appeared between his perfect eyebrows. "I'll take you to your gate."

"I'd like to walk. It helps clear my head."

His jaw sawed back and forth in indecision. *Clearly*, he hated the idea of leaving her to her own devices in the middle of the city.

Ever the gentleman, she thought with a dejected twist of her lips.

"It's only a few blocks to the compound. I'll be fine," she assured him softly.

"If you're sure." There was still hesitation in his voice.

"I'm sure," she said. Then she waited for him to execute a perfect parallel park between two SUVs. He made the move look easy when, in fact, she knew it wasn't—hence the dent in the side panel of her Prius.

Truly, the man had no flaws.

Except for the fatal flaw of not being Hewitt Birch, she thought sadly.

After he put the Mercedes in park, she turned in her seat and placed a hand on his arm. His suit was made of the finest French linen, smooth and cool beneath her fingers. It slid over his forearm like water over iron, doing little to disguise the strength of the man beneath it.

"Thank you, Martin. For tonight. For everything," she whispered, meaning every word.

Her smile was a quiet curve of lips that she hoped spoke of the things she couldn't bring herself to say aloud. Things like how they might have stood a chance at something rare and remarkable if life had been different—if *she* had been different.

His expression was sweet. Kind. His tone was both when he said, "I've enjoyed your company, Sabrina. More than I expected to."

She let out a breath that was half a laugh. "I don't know whether to be insulted or flattered."

"Flattered," he assured her, his dark eyes sparkling in the dim interior lights. "One of the drawbacks of being as well-schooled and well-traveled as I am is that I've seen it all and done it all. I rarely meet anyone who truly intrigues me."

She shook her head and stared at him in wonder. "Seriously, do you have *any* flaws?"

He joked about it being easy to appear flawless when he had a therapist, an on-call chef, and a personal trainer determined to iron out his wrinkles. Then, before she could brace herself, he leaned across the console and kissed her cheek.

His lips were warm. Solid. His expensive cologne reminded her of fine leather and rare woods. And masculine confidence radiated from him in the very best way possible.

Most women would have swooned to have him so focused on them. *Kissing* them.

She didn't.

She couldn't.

Her heart belonged to one man, and Martin Massey wasn't him.

You're an idiot, the little voice that lived at the back of her head declared.

I know, she silently agreed.

After he pulled back, she whispered, "Thank you for being so kind about everything."

"Thank you for being honest with me."

Her expression turned self-deprecating. "You must think I'm ten kinds of crazy, huh?"

He shook his head. "Crazy or not, the heart wants what the heart wants."

"Unfortunately, just because the heart wants something, that doesn't mean it'll get it."

"He's a damned fool if he doesn't grab onto you with both hands and never let go."

She made a face and then shrugged dejectedly. Her last words to him were, "Good night, Martin."

"Goodbye, Sabrina."

His cultured voice followed her as she stepped out into the night. She gave him a little wave and watched as he slid his sleek car back into traffic. Then, she dragged in a deep breath and let herself be surrounded by the city.

Summer still had its cloying, clutching hands around Chicago's throat. But a blessedly cool breeze was blowing in from the lake.

The evening had turned soft as silk against her exposed skin. Warm enough to keep her from shivering. Cool enough that the air tasted crisp and clean instead of hot with baking blacktop and car exhaust.

She didn't turn toward Black Knights Inc. Instead, she headed toward the river, searching for quiet. For solitude. For a moment to gather her thoughts and shore up her walls before returning home.

Neon reflected off the pavement. Laughter and honking horns floated in the air from the direction of downtown. The smell of fried onions and Garrett's popcorn created a strange perfume. And a couple hurried past her, arm in arm, their voices bright with tipsy happiness.

The city was vibrant. *Pulsing* with life.

In contrast, she felt like a ghost drifting through it. A dark specter of melancholy amidst all that gaiety and frivolity.

She'd tried.

Tried to go back to the way things were before that one glorious afternoon. Tried to act the same and talk the same and *feel* the same.

But nothing was the same.

She wasn't the same.

So now what?

She didn't know, but she wanted to know. With her car still in the shop, she was forced to walk instead of driving to let her mind work through the problem.

It wasn't long before her destination appeared in front of her. A tiny city park that was little more than a manicured patch of grass, a small stand of trees, and three cement benches planted in a neat row.

She descended the steps from the street, gazing intently at the river rolling by. Its glittery surface caught the city's lights and refracted them into shards.

There's a metaphor there, she thought with a sad snort. *Something about how things can be whole and broken at the same time.*

After sinking onto the bench closest to her, she sighed and let the tension slump out of her shoulders.

Two weeks. That's all it had been.

Two weeks since her life had been upended, rearranged, ripped open, and stitched back together again into something new. Something she didn't recognize. Something she didn't even really *want*.

But it wasn't like this was the first time she'd had to start over. It wasn't like she'd never had her illusion stripped from her, never stared into a future that was a foggy unknown.

She'd survived the upheaval before.

She'd survive it again and—

A sudden shiver raced down her spine despite the perfect weather. The hairs on her arms lifted. Her pulse stumbled.

She raised her chin slowly, deliberately. Hoping she appeared casual as she scanned the grass, the trees, the deep shadows that avoided the reach of the lampposts' lights.

A couple kissed beside a parked car up on the street. A jogger passed by in neon shorts and a reflective vest. A private pleasure boat glided across the water, lit up like a floating bar and bumping with club music. *Utz, utz, utz.*

Ordinary.

All perfectly ordinary.

And yet…

Someone was watching her. The sensation clung to her like spider-silk, fine and cloying.

Automatically, her hand dipped into her purse. Pulling out her phone, she thumbed on the screen and brought up Hew's contact.

Two weeks ago, he'd been her safe place. Her rock.

Now? There was caution in his eyes when he looked at her. Wariness in his voice when he spoke to her and—

There it is again.

That crawling awareness. Stronger this time. Pressing hard against the back of her skull so that her spine snapped straight and her shoulder blades hitched together.

She started to stand, but stopped when someone slid onto the bench beside her and the cold, unmistakable kiss of a gun barrel jabbed into her side.

"Easy," came a low voice. Feminine. Deadly. *Familiar.* "I'm not going to hurt you. I just need you to be quiet."

Sabrina bit her tongue to keep from screaming.

The hair color was different. Platinum blond had been replaced by a deep, cherry red. But there was no mistaking that jaw's cruel angle or that tone that was always edged in ice.

Black Widow.

Sabrina's phone was still in her hand, still open to Hew's number. Keeping it low, hiding it from the assassin, Sabrina tapped out a single word in the message field.

The only word she could think of.

The one word that mattered.

Luckily, she'd silenced her phone's alerts while having dinner with Martin. She'd wanted no interruptions, no distractions when she ended things between them. Now, she was able to send the text without the telltale *woosh*. And a few more quick taps on the screen meant she was sharing her location.

Her lungs felt like they were coated in cement. But she forced herself to inhale. To oxygenate her body and brain just in case she got the chance to run.

"You shouldn't have come back here," she whispered. "The Black Knights told you what would happen if you did."

The gun pressed harder into her ribs, making them ache. But Sabrina refused to flinch.

"Is this about what I did to Hummer?" Sabrina was pleased to hear that her voice sounded steady, conversational even. She was getting good at keeping her cool in life-threatening situations, and she wasn't sure if that was a good thing or if it simply meant her trauma response had been blunted by, yeah, you guessed it, too much trauma. "I thought you said grudges give you wrinkles."

"I don't give a shit about Mark Kesslar," Black Widow hissed. "I give a shit about *me*. That's why I'm here."

The pressure of the gun vanished from Sabrina's side. It was replaced by the cold, metallic *snap* of something slamming around her wrist.

She blinked in astonishment. Black Widow had…handcuffed them together? Why on earth?

"Get up," the woman snarled, her eyes darting restlessly around the park. "We're going for a walk."

CHAPTER 40

Black Knights Inc.

Hew didn't realize he'd nodded off until someone cleared their throat.

His eyes cracked open, heavy with sleep, and the world tilted a little before he got his bearings.

Sleep had always been hit or miss for him. But the last two weeks had been a lot more misses than hits. And when he *did* manage to catch some Z's, he still felt groggy and unrefreshed upon waking.

A quick squint toward the tall, leaded glass windows told him the sun had bid this side of the world adieu for the day. Darkness pressed against the windowpanes. And, in the distance, the Chicago skyline glowed white and gold.

He stretched and yawned wide enough to make his jaw crack. Then, he searched for the source of the noise that had pulled him from sleep and found Boss sitting on the love seat across the way.

The man's broad shoulders filled the piece of furniture like a king sitting on a throne. His expression was anything but magnanimous, however.

A cocked ear told Hew the shop was quiet. And empty. Except for… Boss.

"Where is everyone?" Hew swung his legs over the side of the couch and sat up to run a weary hand through his hair.

"Gone home for the day," Boss said evasively. "And Fish and Eliza are at Red Delilah's. He's been doing his best to keep her busy so she won't worry so much about the possibility of her dad being Bishop."

"Right." Hew nodded. Then, he tilted his head. "You workin' late?"

"Nope." Boss bent to scratch Peanut's cheek. The cat sat between his legs, yellow eyes half-closed in feline ecstasy at the attention. "Waited until everyone left so I could tell you privately that you're an idiot."

"Sorry?" Hew blinked and shook his head.

"You're right about that." Boss dipped his big chin. "Sorriest sonofabitch I've seen in quite some time."

Hew carefully set the dragon saga back on the coffee table.

Boss wasn't the type to run a man down just for the hell of it. So if Boss was calling you out, it was because he thought you needed to hear it.

"Mind elaboratin'?" Hew made a rolling hand motion.

"Glad you asked." Boss leaned back, the picture of composure, ankle crossed neatly over one knee. Peanut meowed his displeasure at the withdrawal of Boss's affection, but quickly flopped onto his side to satisfy himself with cleaning his whiskers. "You're in here sleeping like a baby and reading a damn dragon book"—Boss flicked a blunt finger at the gold-embossed cover on the table—"when the woman you love is out with another man."

Shock slapped Hew so hard he almost reeled. He could feel his pulse banging in his temples. "Is it…that obvious? That I love her?"

"Yes!" Boss exploded, tossing his hands skyward. "And also…Graham told me before he left for D.C. that he found you guys in flagrante. I think he assumed things would naturally progress from there. But here you are doing jack shit to move anything along."

Hew was excellent at camouflage. Unfortunately, he didn't have the face grease or the gilly suit required to blend into the sofa. So all he could do was close his eyes and will himself to disappear.

"Who else knows?" he asked through gritted teeth.

"Everyone," Boss said without a hint of mercy.

Sometimes, Hew wished Boss wasn't such a straight shooter. Just once, it might be nice if the man sugarcoated things.

He opened his eyes and shook his head. "Never would've pegged Graham for a gossip."

"No." Boss jerked his chin to the side, making the gray in his buzz cut catch the light. "Graham told me. I was the one who told everyone else."

Hew's eyebrows shot up. "Now, why the hell would ya go and do a thing like that?"

"I was hoping one of your damned teammates would take it upon himself to talk some sense into you. But, like always, I'm left holding the bag."

Hew dropped his head into his hands, searching for a way to stop this conversation in its tracks.

Feign a seizure?

Jump out the window?

Pretend to be possessed and start gnawin' on the coffee table?

"What the hell are you two doing?" Boss demanded. The guy was as relentless as a howitzer.

Hew lifted his head. He knew his expression was bleak. "What do ya mean?"

"You're walking on eggshells around each other and making the rest of us feel like we have to walk on eggshells, too."

Damnit! Hew hadn't even considered that his misery was leaking out of him and onto everyone else. He'd been so wrapped up in his self-pity that he hadn't noticed how conversations dimmed when he and Sabrina walked into a room. Or how the guys looked at him like they were bracing for an explosion that never came. Looking back, though, he could see it.

Hindsight bein' twenty-twenty and whatnot. Fuck!

Embarrassment slid under his skin like grit, raw and uncomfortable.

"You care about each other. You get each other. You're obviously *attracted* to each other," Boss went on. "So I don't understand why you're not doing it on every horizontal surface in this place." He spread his big hands wide.

"Because she doesn't *want* to do it with me on every horizontal surface!" Hew snapped, his temper briefly pushing aside his self-pity.

To no one's surprise, Boss didn't flinch. He simply cocked an eyebrow. "How do you know? Have you asked her?"

Hew laughed, but the sound was so dry and sharp that it scraped his throat on the way out of his mouth. "Ya make it sound so easy."

"Because it is." Boss slapped the arm of the love seat like a judge banging a gavel. "You just walk up to her and say, "'Sabrina Greenlee, I'm crazy about you. I think you're crazy about me, too. Let's give this thing a go; you want to?'"

The lump in Hew's throat swelled until talking felt like breathing around a boulder. "That's the thing. I *don't* think she's crazy about me. She's never said as much. And if I tell her how I feel and she doesn't feel the same, where does that leave us? Even *more* uncomfortable and awkward around each other?"

Boss's sigh was slow and heavy. When he dragged a finger under his chin, his stubble rasped against his nail.

Finally, he said, "Here's the thing, son. There are no guarantees in life or in love. But there's one thing I know for sure. If you love someone, you have to be brave enough to tell them. Otherwise, you have to be brave enough to watch them be loved by someone else." Sympathy slid into his tone. "I know which kind of brave I'd rather be. Do you?"

"I'm *trying* to be the latter," Hew insisted with an exasperated toss of his hands.

The move made Peanut stop his whisker-bath and blink annoyed yellow eyes at Hew.

Ayuh, he thought, *join the club and go on and judge me.*

"That was the wrong answer." Boss gave a sorrowful shake of his head.

Before Hew could say anything else in his own defense, his phone buzzed in his pocket. He tugged it out, glanced at the screen, and—

Nearly shit his own heart.

Sabrina. She'd typed one word.

Help.

CHAPTER 41

Three blocks from Black Knights Inc.

"**C**areful!" Black Widow hissed when the toe of Sabrina's patent leather pump caught on a crack in the sidewalk, nearly sending her sprawling onto her face. The assassin jerked their joined wrists so hard the metal handcuff bit into Sabrina's skin and bruised the bone beneath. "If you go down, I go down."

There's a thought, Sabrina mused. *I could end all this by jumping in front of the next city bus.*

She would be dead, of course. But so would Black Widow. And that might make it all worth it.

She regretted her shoe choice with every step. The narrow back straps were cutting deep furrows into her heels. She regretted the underwire bra she'd put on since it was doing its damndest to puncture a hole clean through her armpit. But what she regretted most of all, what she cursed herself for, was not going full rabid raccoon on Black Widow the moment the assassin sat next to her on that park bench.

Should've punched her square in the mouth, she thought, her temper flaring hotter with each passing second and each painful step. *Should've scratched her eyes clean from her head. Should've ripped out her newly dyed hair by the roots.*

Then she reminded herself that she hadn't had the time. The unforgiving press of cold steel against her ribs had precluded any chance of going on the offensive.

A pistol trumped punishment any day.

But, oh, the fantasy was nice.

Surprise—and no small amount of wariness—slammed into her once they turned a corner and she realized where they were headed. "Why are you taking me back to BKI?"

"Shut up," Black Widow snarled. "You'll find out soon enough."

Possibilities pinged around in Sabrina's skull like pinballs.

Did Black Widow plan to use her as a ticket inside the compound? If so, to what end? Sabotage? *Revenge?* Carnage for the hell of it?

Or maybe she planned to march Sabrina up to the big, wrought-iron gate and pull the trigger there…knowing one of the Connelly brothers would be in the guard shack to witness the murder, knowing security cameras would catch it all.

She didn't put it past the assassin to be cruel for cruelty's sake. Or for her to mete out retribution for Hummer even though she claimed the contrary. But neither did Sabrina peg the woman for a fool.

Black Widow had to know what it would mean if she killed Sabrina. The Black Knights would never stop hunting her.

Sabrina could still hear Boss's deep voice. *There's no corner of the world you can go to where we can't find you. There's no amount of protection you could pull around yourself that we can't penetrate.*

It wasn't bravado or bluster. The truth had rung clearly in his words, shone fiercely from his eyes. *Surely* Black Widow had seen and heard it the same way Sabrina had and—

Where the *hell* was Hew?

It was impossible to keep track of time when her blood raced with high-octane adrenaline. Each second stretched, warped, and extended until she would swear it'd been an eternity since she'd thumbed out that text.

Of course, *logically*, she knew no more than a few minutes had passed. The little park was only a few blocks from BKI and—

A terrible thought suddenly occurred.

What if he hadn't received her text?

What if he'd left his phone charging on his nightstand? What if he'd ignored the alert, figuring it was nothing important? What if he was in the shower, water pounding over his broad shoulders, while she was being frog-marched by a psychopath? What if—

And then she heard it.

A sound like rolling thunder. It filled the ears and reverberated in the chest. A motorcycle engine, throttled high and coming fast.

Relief burst through her so hard she had to fight to keep her knees from buckling.

He's coming! Hew's coming!

Of course, terror immediately piggybacked on the heels of her brief reprieve.

Dragging Hew into this meant putting him squarely in the center of Black Widow's sights. She'd never forgive herself if anything happened to him.

Why hadn't she let Martin drop her at the gate? She should've ignored her need for fresh air, her need for space outside the shop, and done the *smart* thing. The *safe* thing.

If she kept bringing danger to BKI's door, the Black Knights might very well decide the revenue she brought in through her social media accounts wasn't worth the trouble she made and—

Her racing thoughts ground to a halt when she realized what she'd thought was one motorcycle was actually two. Two huge, custom-made miracles with souped-up engines and hand-tooled exhaust systems.

They were close.

And then they were there.

Hew was the first to blaze around the corner, his big body bent low over Freedom's handlebars. Man and machine were one. Wild. Raw. Yet somehow tightly controlled.

And right behind him came Boss. His pearly white motorcycle roared like the beast it was. The bike was every bit as massive and intimidating as the man who straddled it.

Sabrina nearly laughed.

Black Widow was insane to think she could square off against guys like these. Guys who'd been forged in blood and battle. Scarred warriors who dealt with danger and death as easily as other men dealt with breakfast.

A feral grin pulled at her lips. It was petty, maybe even a bit childish, but she couldn't stop herself from saying, "You're in for it now."

Black Widow didn't bother answering. Instead, she cursed and shoved Sabrina in front of her, forcing Sabrina's cuffed wrist behind her back at a painful angle. The gun barrel moved from her ribs to her spine, and the assassin pressed hard enough that Sabrina thought she was trying to bore a hole clean through the vertebrae.

"How the hell did they find us?" Black Widow hissed. "You got a panic button hidden on you somewhere?"

"Something like that," Sabrina admitted evasively, congratulating herself on her quick thinking. She hadn't been able to go full rabid raccoon on Black Widow. But she *had* been able to call in the big guns.

Literally.

Boss had a piece strapped to his ribs while Hew's weapon was cinched to his thigh. Neither man had bothered to conceal their carries.

A calculated decision, no doubt.

When Hew hit the brakes, Freedom skidded sideways, tires screaming. Rubber burning. Smoke curling.

The maneuver should've dumped him onto the asphalt. It *would* have dumped most men. But with a big, booted foot braced hard against the pavement, he muscled the bike under control and came to a rocking stop.

By contrast, Boss was all precision and calm. The huge, white motorcycle rolled to a dignified halt a split second before his biker boots landed on the roadway.

The smell of melted rubber and hot cement hit Sabrina's nose before Hew's wonderful voice hit her ears. "Sabrina!"

The three syllables were ragged, filled with equal parts urgency and fury. And maybe a pinch of fear?

"I'm okay!" she shouted, throwing her free hand in the air as proof, her purse dangling by the strap from her fingers.

The thunder of the bikes' idling engines ricocheted off the buildings and rolled down the street. Black Widow had to lift her voice to be heard above the racket. "I don't want to hurt her! I just want to talk!"

"Ya don't need a hostage if all ya wanna do is talk!" Hew bellowed, his voice like a battle cry as it carried over the short distance. "Let her go as a show of good faith!"

Black Widow's hot breath scalded the back of Sabrina's neck when she hollered, "If I let her go, what's to stop you from loading her up and riding away? Or sending a bullet through my brain?"

"That's why it's a show of good *faith*!" Hew shot back, his accent clipping the words like an ax striking wood. "There aren't any guarantees. You either trust us or ya don't!"

A taxi passed by, the driver craning his head at the scene. Sabrina had to appreciate the situation from his point of view. Two women were huddled on the sidewalk while two huge, intimidating men on motorcycles yelled and gestured.

Great. The last thing we need is the authorities showing up, she thought.

She was close enough for her voice to float across the inches between her and the assassin without her having to raise it. "The Black Knights aren't liars. To a man, they hold true to their word."

A ragged breath sawed in her ear. Then another as Black Widow ran through her options.

"Promise you won't kill me!" the assassin finally demanded. Her voice cracked. Barely. But Sabrina heard it. "Promise you'll hear me out!"

Sabrina caught the flick of Hew's eyes toward Boss. For the span of two heartbeats, the men communicated without words. Then, Boss gave a dip of his chin, and Hew raised his voice again.

"Ya have our word! Now, let Sabrina go!"

Five interminable seconds ticked by. And Sabrina counted each one. Then, miraculously, the gun barrel pulled away from her spine, and the cuff around her wrist popped open with a muted *shnick*.

She immediately rolled her shoulder forward, working out the familiar tension. If she never had to spend another second with her arms wrenched behind her back, it would still be too soon.

"Come here, Sabrina." Hew motioned with a big hand, keeping the other casually wrapped around the butt of his gun. "Come to me."

Gladly, she thought, bolting toward him.

It wasn't dignified. It wasn't careful—not that there was a way to do either in the heels or form-fitting dress. It was like her soul depended on it. The warm air whipped her face. Her pumps *clacked* a quick rhythm against the pavement. And she never once looked back to see what Black Widow was doing.

When she made it to Hew, relief blew through her like hurricane-force winds. His jaw was set at a hard angle. Danger seemed to shimmer off him like heat from the sidewalk in the middle of August. And he only spared her a quick glance, a half-second to scan her face and search for injuries, before his focus snapped back to the assassin.

"Get on." His voice was urgent and only for her ears. "Careful of the exhaust pipe."

"I remember," she assured him, tossing her purse strap over her shoulder so she could hike her skirt high enough to swing a leg over Freedom's seat.

She had to keep the hem bunched indecently high across her thighs to straddle the bike and Hew's hips. But she didn't give a rat's ass about decency. All she cared about was wrapping her arms around his waist and pressing her chest flush against the broad wall of his back. And going *home*.

"Toss your piece into the gutter!" Boss barked, pointing toward the storm drain hole that was cut into the curb.

Black Widow's eyes rounded. "You're crazy if you think I—"

"You're not coming anywhere with us armed!" Boss's voice cut her off as cleanly as a guillotine's blade, just as a city bus rumbled by.

Sabrina caught a glimpse of a half-dozen faces in the windows. Only one was turned toward her. But she saw the woman blink in confusion and then frown in concern.

Come on, come on, she thought. *We need to take this thing off the street!*

"You got something you want us to hear?" Boss continued. "You'll do as I say!"

Sabrina saw the hesitation in Black Widow's face. The sawing of the jaw. The twitch of the cheek. For a moment, she wondered if the assassin might decline to see this thing through.

Whatever this thing is, she thought.

But desperation won out in the end.

After a sharp jerk of her head, Black Widow strode toward the curb with that familiar feline grace. Then, with expert aim, she tossed her pistol into the storm drain's yawning black mouth. It fell into the waiting abyss and landed at the bottom with a satisfying *thunk*.

"There!" the assassin snarled. "Happy now?" She nervously scanned the road and buildings around them. "Can we get off the goddamned street?"

Boss angled his head toward Hew. "You two go on. I'll follow this one to the compound."

"Ya sure?" Hew's voice was reluctant. "She'd rather shoot a man than blink." He hitched his chin toward Black Widow.

Boss's answering wink was quick, confident. "I've dealt with far worse than her. And besides"—he patted the bulging grip of the pistol riding high in his shoulder holster—"if she tries anything hinky, I'll drop her."

The words were for Hew, sure. But Sabrina knew they were *more* for Black Widow's benefit.

Hew dipped his chin, decision made. Then he turned slightly, his voice a growl. "Hang on."

Don't gotta tell me twice, Sabrina thought, and tightened her arms around his waist.

When he gunned the throttle, Freedom leaped forward like the two-wheeled monster it was, eating up the pavement in great, roaring chunks. The warm wind whipped tears into her eyes until the city blurred around her.

She didn't care. She didn't need to see. Not when every ounce of her being was focused on how *good* it was to touch Hew again.

She hadn't put even a fingertip on him in two weeks, and holding him now proved how much she'd *missed* the feel of him. The solidity of him. The unimaginable warmth of him.

In what felt like mere seconds, the wrought-iron gate of BKI loomed. Manus Connelly was quick to hit the switch that sent it rattling open. But even after Hew guided them into the compound, Sabrina couldn't fully relax.

Black Widow was coming.

And she couldn't shake the feeling that the assassin was bringing something sinister with her.

CHAPTER 42

Black Knights Inc.

"**H**e's found me. He's following me," Black Widow declared staunchly, and Hew fisted his hands so tightly he could feel his blunt nails leaving crescent moon marks in the skin of his palms.

They were sitting at the scarred kitchen table inside the cottage in the far front corner of the property. It was a squat little house with creaky floorboards and lace curtains left over from another lifetime.

Back when BKI had been a menthol cigarette factory, the foreman and his family had bunked here. Nowadays, the place only got dusted off for rare occasions. Holiday shindigs, birthday bashes, or the odd wedding when the OG Knights and the current active members all gathered and extra space was needed to house everyone.

Or when we need a spot away from the shop to talk to someone who isn't welcome within spittin' distance of our main operation, Hew thought.

After Boss had followed the assassin into the compound, he'd pointed them all toward the cottage. And even though Hew had damn near barked himself hoarse telling Sabrina she should stay inside the old factory building where it was safer, she'd firmed her stubborn chin, crossed her arms, and declared, *"I'm as much a part of this as any of you. Probably more so since she's abducted me* twice. *So I'm coming with you."*

Ayuh. He'd wanted to point out that Black Widow had abducted her *twice.* And since no one wanted the assassin to have a chance at a *third* go 'round, all the more reason for Sabrina to keep herself behind locked doors.

But Hew hadn't reached the ripe old age of thirty-six without learning a few immutable truths. And right at the top of that list?

Arguin' with a woman once she gets that look in her eye is about as practical as breathin' underwater.

So he'd swallowed back every *no,* every *don't,* every *for Christ's sake stay put.* And had settled for plunking her down across from Black Widow while he and Boss kept their pistols hidden beneath the table and trained on the assassin.

"I'm assumin' by *he,* ya mean Bishop," Hew said now, squinting at the woman, looking for even a hint of subterfuge.

He saw no deception, but her expression *did* seem to scream, *Duh.* Her words just reiterated the sentiment. "Who else would I mean?"

Boss kept his voice even when he asked, "How do you know he's following you? Have you seen him? Has he contacted you?"

Black Widow tucked a strand of hair behind her ear. Hew didn't know why she'd dyed it that god-awful shade, but if her goal was to look even *more* lethal…well, then…mission accomplished.

The color reminded him of clotting blood. The kind that dried under your fingernails and ruined your clothes.

"Of course I haven't seen him." Her tone was the epitome of exasperation, and Hew was finding it difficult not to pull her up by her ear, march her to the front gate, and toss her out on her ass.

"Or maybe I *have* and just didn't know it, since I have no clue what he looks like," she continued. "As for contacting me? I told you before, the way Bishop will contact me is by sending someone to slit my throat in my sleep."

"So how do you *know* he's followin' you?" Hew pressed.

The assassin's lips flattened. They were painted the same shocking red as her hair. And since the lamplight in the cottage was dim, it cast her face in sharp planes and deep shadows.

The whole effect was like one of those campfire tales where the storyteller shines a flashlight up under their chin. Eerie. Ghoulish, even.

Fittin' for an executioner.

"I *know*," she insisted. "I can feel it. And you both understand what I mean by that." She wagged a finger between Hew and Boss. "People like us *know* when we're lined up in the center of somebody's crosshairs."

Hew balked at the idea of being lumped in with the likes of *her*. But he didn't say as much.

What would be the point? People like Black Widow did not distinguish between pulling the trigger for pay or patriotism.

And, ayuh, some might argue there was a fine line there. But the devil was in the details, and, for Hew, *that* little detail meant the difference between being able to look at himself in the mirror every morning and…*not*.

There'd only been one time when he'd ended a life outside the line of duty. It had been for justice. And if he lived to be one hundred years old, he wouldn't spend a second regretting it.

"Maybe you'd better start from the top." Boss leaned back in his chair, head cocked.

Black Widow laid it all out. How she'd spent the last half-dozen years scattering safe deposit boxes across the country, each one stocked with cash in case she ever needed to vanish. How she'd spent the last two weeks working her way through the states, emptying the boxes one by one.

"It was at the fifteenth up in Wisconsin I realized I was being watched," she said. "I pulled every trick in the book to lose the tail, and when I was sure I'd shaken them, I came here."

"Why?" Boss asked, one dark brow arched high. "Why come back to the place, why come back to the *men*, Bishop asked you to expose and kill?"

"Because I can't go to anyone in my circle. I can't *trust* anyone in my circle." A muscle in her jaw jerked. "Someone gave Bishop my contact info to begin with. Who's to say they're not still working for him? Helping him?"

She took a deep breath and admitted through clenched teeth, "I need a way out of the country. And if anyone can secret me across the pond, it's you guys."

Hew snorted. *The absolute audacity of this woman.*

But it was Sabrina who voiced aloud his thoughts. "And you thought abducting me, *again*, was the way to gain our favor?"

Black Widow hitched one shoulder. "I knew you all wouldn't listen to me unless I had leverage."

Sabrina's tone remained incredulous. "We already did you the ultimate favor by letting you go." Her eyes didn't shine like melted chocolate now. Oh, no. They flashed like fire on glass. "Why the hell would we give you additional aid?"

Hew looked at her then. Really looked. And saw no hints of the fear that had been in her face when he first blazed around the corner to find her arm-in-arm with the assassin.

Fuckin'-A. It had felt like it had taken forever to strap on his sidearm and fire up Freedom after her text came in. And by the time he'd actually reached her, he'd been nearly out of his skull with worry and dread.

But all of that had been forgotten the instant she climbed onto the back of his bike to slide her arms around his waist. Her touch after two weeks of absence lit up every nerve ending in his body like downed power lines. For a few beats of his heart, he'd thought of no one else. Not Bishop. Not Black Widow. Just her.

Just Sabrina.

"Because if Bishop *doesn't* want me dead"—Black Widow's voice cut through his thoughts—"if he wants me alive to question, then you can bet your ass I'll tell him everything I know. About you. About this place. About your plans to hunt him down. If it means saving my own skin, I will gladly throw you guys under the bus."

She let her eyes ping around the table before delivering her final volley. "So keeping me out of his psychotic clutches? Well, that behooves all of us, now doesn't it?"

The irony of an assassin calling someone else a psycho nearly made Hew's eyes roll into next week.

"Where do you want to go exactly?" Boss's tone was still calm. Still emotionless.

Hew shot him a look. He wasn't surprised Boss was considering helping the woman—she had a point about it being better for all of them if she was kept away from Bishop. But he *was* surprised Boss would even consider giving the woman a say in where they shipped her off to.

"Glad you asked." Black Widow smiled, and it reminded Hew of a viper baring its fangs. "I've got the perfect spot."

Hew only half-listened as Black Widow laid out her plans. His mind kept drifting to questions that refused to settle.

Why the hell didn't Martin drop Sabrina at the gate?

Why does Sabrina keep lettin' her arm rest against mine when she hasn't touched me in two weeks?

Did that motorcycle ride remind her of how good things are when we aren't tryin' to keep each other at arm's length?

"If we do this, I don't ever want to see your face again." Boss's words interrupted Hew's ruminations. "In fact, if you *ever* come within ten miles of BKI , then you'd best be prepared for us to get real inhospitable."

"I'd say you have my word." The assassin lifted her hands. "But something tells me my word won't mean much to you."

Boss snorted. "That's the understatement of the century." Then he smacked the table—his standard gesture when the meeting was over and it was time to make tracks. "Okay. I've got some calls to make. Hew? You mind staying here and keeping an eye on her while I do that?"

Hew wanted to say, *I do mind.*

The simple act of sitting across from Black Widow made his skin crawl. She tainted the air around her with her villainy.

But, of course, he dipped his chin and replied, "Ayuh."

"I'll stay with you," Sabrina volunteered.

Hew was quick to correct her. "You'll go with Boss."

Her chin tilted stubbornly. "In case you missed it, I'm not a kid. You can't tell me what to do."

"I can insist very vociferously," he countered as their gazes clashed and their wills warred.

She wasn't a kid. She was a *woman.* All woman, emphasized by that damn dress that left little to the imagination and hugged her curves.

Never in his whole life had he been jealous of a piece of clothing.

He was jealous of that dress.

"Kinky," Black Widow purred, glancing between them with a smile that could only be described as lascivious.

Sabrina's gaze snapped to the assassin, her upper lip curling in disgust.

Hew could barely resist the urge to strangle Black Widow because she'd ruined a…

What?

What had just passed between him and Sabrina? If he didn't know better, he'd say it was sexual tension. But that couldn't be right. Could it?

She was with Martin. She'd put on that damned dress for *Martin.*

"Don't forget we still have a second option," Hew snarled at the assassin. "We could kill ya and all our problems would be solved."

Black Widow's greasy smile faded as her eyes narrowed into slits.

"Come with me, Sabrina." Boss's tone brooked no argument as he stood from the table.

Sabrina still tried to argue. "But—"

"Hew doesn't need any distractions," Boss interrupted. "And you're *definitely* a distraction."

Sabrina's expression turned sullen as she glanced between Hew and the assassin. Then, her gaze softened, and Hew didn't miss the worry in her eyes when she said, "Will you be okay?"

Ayuh. He'd *definitely* been imagining things earlier. What he'd mistaken for sexual tension was just her concern for him. Just her trying to be his *friend* and show her solidarity by remaining with him to guard Black Widow.

Fuck.

The little flame of hope that had flared to life in his chest guttered and died.

"I'll be fine," he assured her. "Go on, now."

She hesitated a few seconds longer but eventually pushed up from the table and followed Boss out of the cottage and into the night.

He continued to stare after her even after the door closed. In his mind's eye he could still see the swish of her hips, the sway of her long, dark hair.

"Damn, man, you got it bad, huh?" Black Widow drawled, her gaze glinting with crude speculation. "Bet it drives you crazy that she's dating some guy who drives a Mercedes and wears Gucci cuff links."

Obviously, she'd been spying on the place. Obviously, she'd seen Sabrina with Martin.

"Bet you want to feed that fucker his own teeth. Bet you dream about her wrapping that lithe little body around you, moaning your name and—"

Hew transferred his pistol to the top of the table, barrel angled straight at the assassin's chest. He slowly, deliberately slid his finger from the trigger guard to the trigger itself.

She snapped her mouth shut.

And that suited him just fine.

CHAPTER 43

Sabrina came awake with a start.

Which was when she realized she'd fallen asleep.

She'd *tried* not to. After Boss and Hew had left with Black Widow, she'd promised herself she'd wait up for them, no matter how long it took.

Sleep is for normal people, she'd told herself. *Not people who spirit assassins out of the country in the middle of the night.*

But her traitorous body hadn't gotten with the program.

Even sitting upright in the chair she'd moved back into the corner of her bedroom hadn't been enough to keep her from succumbing to bone-deep exhaustion. The blanket she'd pulled up around her chest had fallen to her waist. The paperback she'd been determined to read lay facedown in her lap, pages crinkled from where it'd fallen from her lax fingers.

She blinked, trying to get her bearings, trying to determine…

How long have I been out?

It'd been midnight when Fish and Eliza trudged up the stairs from their date night at Red Delilah's. She'd spent half an hour bringing them up to speed on what they'd missed, and then another fifteen minutes answering the frantic questions they lobbed at her head. Afterward, voice hoarse from recounting the nightmare, she'd padded downstairs to make tea.

She'd hoped the heat and the caffeine would be enough to stave off oblivion, but…

No such luck.

The last thing she remembered was checking her phone and seeing it was half-past two. Then…nothing. Not even dreams.

Now, her gaze slid to the window. To the light leaking in through the thin crack of her curtains. It was pink and muted gold. That first blush that heralded the dawn.

For heaven's sake, the little voice chided. *You slept half the night away.*

Had Hew come home without her hearing? She'd left her door wide, knowing he'd have to walk by her room to get to his. But she didn't sleep with one eye open like he did because she hadn't grown up attuned to danger the way he had. It was very possible he'd slipped by while she was zonked out.

She picked up the book, did her best to smooth its crinkled pages, and set it on the bookcase beside her. Then, she pushed the blanket to the floor, ready to stand, before—

She froze.

There it was again. The sound that had jerked her from sleep. Heavy boots moving down the hallway.

His boots. *His* stride.

She'd recognize it anywhere, even when he was clearly trying to tiptoe.

Her pulse tripped over itself like it did whenever he entered a room.

And then he was there. Entering her room.

Or, rather, he stopped on the threshold, his green eyes pinging to her bed before sliding around the space and stopping once he found her tucked into the chair in the shadows of the corner. She would *swear* it felt like a physical touch when his gaze collided with hers.

"You're awake." Surprise had one eyebrow arcing up his forehead. That fabulously wide forehead with that knee-weakening whorl of hair and that faint, crescent-moon scar.

"You're home," she whispered back, and the words sounded too soft, too…*something*, even to her own ears.

He leaned a broad shoulder against the doorjamb and crossed one booted ankle over the other. Then, he ran a hand down his face. And that's when she got a proper look at him in the soft glow of the lamplight that reached across her room and framed him in the doorway.

He was exhausted. It was there in the neck stubble that sprouted beneath his neatly trimmed beard. There in the new lines carved into the corners of his eyes. There in the wild riot of hair that looked like he'd either raked his fingers through it a hundred times or rode with his head out the window.

Heaven help me, all I want is to pull him into bed, smooth the line from between his eyebrows, and hold him until he falls asleep.

A few months ago, she would've done exactly that without thinking twice.

Now? She couldn't find the words to bridge the distance that'd opened up between them. Couldn't find a way to go back to how things had been… *before.*

"Ayuh." He nodded. "I'm home. And none too soon, either. I feel like a man who's been draggin' lobster traps with no gloves on."

Her lips tugged at the corners. Only Hew could compare exhaustion to Maine fishermen and make it sound miserable and endearing all at the same time.

"Bit of a whirlwind, was it?"

"When Boss puts together a quick escape package"—his tone was wry—"he doesn't mess around."

"No, he does not," she agreed. "You should've heard him barking orders and calling in favors over the phone." She tilted her head. "How is he, by the way?"

"Back home with Becky and the girls. Said he'd catch a few winks and then come in later to give everyone a sitrep on our most recent adventure."

She turned her head to peer at him from the corners of her eyes. "Does that mean *I* have to wait to hear how it went?"

He hooked his thumbs into the front pockets of his jeans, letting his hands dangle loose. She stared helplessly at the veins tracking the backs of his hands. At those long, knobby-knuckled fingers.

The same fingers that had once taken her apart piece by piece until she'd been nothing but shaking, shivering, screaming surrender in his arms. The same fingers that had expertly put her back together again.

"We flew her low and fast over the border into Bumfuck, Ontario," he said. "Landed in someone's hay field where one of Boss's old combat buddies was waitin' in a mud-splattered pickup truck to take her from us."

He stopped, one corner of his mouth tilting ruefully. "Ya think Boss looks like he's seen some shit? Should've seen this guy. I swear he was carved from driftwood and rawhide. More scars than skin. But he had a firm handshake and trustworthy eyes. So even without Boss's endorsement, I would've been tempted to like him."

Her own lips twitched at the vivid picture he painted. Despite being reticent by nature, when he *did* speak, it could be almost…lyrical. Or maybe *literary* was the better word.

All that reading, no doubt.

"Apparently, he had a little float plane parked at the dock on a nearby lake. He agreed to fly her up to Alaska, where a friend of his will load her up on a rusted-out fishin' boat and sail her to Russia. After that, she's on her own."

"Good riddance." Sabrina made a face. Just the thought of Black Widow was enough to leave a bad taste in her mouth.

"To bad rubbish," Hew finished with a dip of his chin.

Her brow creased. "And these guys…they just volunteered to do all this? Because Boss asked them to?"

That's when Hew smiled.

Not his usual half-smile. Not the guarded, fleeting tipping up of one corner of his mouth.

Oh, no. This was a *full* smile.

The kind that lit up his face like the sunrise and made his eyes glint like sea glass.

Her breath caught.

"Did I leave out the part where we stopped to pick up the bags of money she stashed under an overpass before she grabbed ya?" He winked. "Boss made sure she paid for the trouble she was puttin' these guys through. Ya should've seen her face…red as a beet when she realized her great escape came at the cost of a quarter of her cash."

Sabrina laughed. *Really* laughed.

And Hew? He laughed too. The easy, comfortable kind of laughter she hadn't heard out of him since that fateful afternoon when everything changed.

It was the most beautiful sound. It wrapped around her like a blanket fresh from the dryer. Warm. Reassuring. A little scratchy in the best possible way.

She'd missed it.

And lord, she'd missed him.

It was bone-deep and visceral. A feeling that curled around her soul and sank into her heart until there was no her without him. No part of Sabrina that didn't include a part of Hew, too.

She'd plucked the stuffed lobster off his dresser earlier, placing it on her lap before settling in for the night. Imagining it was her tether to him. A silly, red, overstuffed stand-in for the man himself.

His eyes tracked the toy as she fiddled with it now, and all the humor drained from his face. He grew so still it wasn't easy to distinguish him from the long shadows that held sway in the hallway.

"Ya finally took the lobster." *Lobstah.*

"I *borrowed* it," she emphasized, giving the plush claws a gentle pet. "Just for tonight."

His Adam's apple made a slow trek up the tan column of his throat. She thought he'd again try to convince her to keep it. So she was blindsided when, instead, he asked, "Why didn't Martin leave you at the gate?"

Her mind quickly sifted through the two outcomes should she answer his question.

If she admitted the truth, the awkwardness…the yawning chasm that already stretched wide between them…would grow. But if she lied, she'd feel the guilt like a stone in her chest, and it would become an obstacle between them in every conversation they had.

She realized she'd been quiet for too long when he quickly said, "If it's too private, all ya got to do is say."

"Nothing's too private between us, right?"

Why was her voice so hoarse all of a sudden?

Oh, right. Because her heart was sitting in the back of her throat.

"So why didn't Martin leave ya at the gate?" he asked again, his gaze fixed firmly on hers.

She rubbed the lobster's claws, using the motion to steady her trembling hands. It didn't really help the tremble in her voice, though, when she admitted, "Because I asked him to. Because I needed some space and some time to think."

"About what?"

"About my life. About my feelings. About my future."

He straightened from the doorjamb, all traces of his earlier exhaustion vanishing like fog hit by the sun. His gaze flicked to her left hand, sharp and assessing.

"Did he propose?"

The question startled her so badly she nearly dropped the lobster. "What?"

"Did he ask ya to marry him?"

"God, no! Why would you think that?"

"Life and feelings and future." He made a rolling motion with his hand.

Despite the impediment of her heart having found a new home in her throat, she laughed. Shook her head. "Oh, right. I hear how that sounds now." Then she sobered. "No. He didn't ask me to marry him. I broke up with him."

Hew didn't move. And his voice was so soft and low she was reminded of the barest whisper of wind when he asked, "Why?"

Ah, she thought. *And here we are.*

The two paths stretched before her, neither one more traveled than the other. Both full of possibilities and possible pitfalls.

She chose her course, the *truth*. And didn't look back.

"Because it wasn't fair to keep dating him when I don't love him," she admitted, watching her fingers fiddle with the stuffy because she couldn't bear to face him when she spoke the words. "When I *won't* love him."

Her heart hammered in the momentary pause. Finally, his voice floated across the space between them. "How do you *know* ya won't love him? Eventually?"

Her voice cracked under the weight of her confession. "Because I'm in love with someone else."

She couldn't breathe, couldn't move, could only sit there. Waiting. Hoping.

Just ask it, Hew, she silently begged. *Please ask it so the truth can set me free.*

And then he did.

"Who?"

The lobster fell from her fingers when her hands flew out wide. The gesture was one of helplessness. One of surrender.

"You, Hew. It's only ever been you."

CHAPTER 44

Sabrina's smile was soft. Sad. But it was also fierce in the way broken things were fierce.

As Hew stared at her, he couldn't help but wonder who had reached a hand inside his chest to squeeze his heart until it threatened to explode.

He was dreaming. Or hallucinating. Or hell, maybe he'd crashed and burned on the flight home, and this was heaven.

He'd never believed in heaven.

He wanted to believe in this.

She bit her lip and twisted her fingers together. "I know that's probably not what you want to hear." Her voice was raw with emotion. "Intimacy has already strained our friendship, and now I go and tell you this. But I couldn't keep lying to you."

A line appeared between her eyebrows. "That's not true. I *could* keep lying to you, but I don't want to. Because if we can't hold on to everything else we've built together all these months, then at least we can hold on to the truth. To always being honest with one another and I—"

She stopped abruptly when he kicked the door shut. The sound cracked like a gunshot in the quiet, and Peanut—nestled like a fat, furry sultan in the pillows on Sabrina's bed—lifted his sleepy head and loudly meowed his displeasure.

Hew barely noticed.

And he certainly didn't pause. Didn't think. Just moved…halving the distance between them with long, prowling strides until his boots touched the tips of her bare toes as they poked out from the bottom of the blanket.

They were still purple. Still sparkly.

Still perfect.

The lamp on the nightstand cast her face in a golden glow, glinting off the mussed strands of her hair, painting her cheeks a tender pink.

"Say it again," he growled, his hands flexing at his sides to keep from grabbing her up, tossing her onto the bed, and devouring her like he was a starving man dropped into the middle of a clambake.

"S-say what?" she stammered, blinking at his sudden intensity. "Th-that I didn't want to lie to you? That I—"

"No." His chin jerked sideways. "Before that. Repeat what ya said *before* that."

Understanding bloomed in her eyes, and she gave him that sad, fierce little smile.

"I love you, Hew. I think maybe I've loved you all along. I just didn't know it was love because it didn't feel crazy or scary. It just felt warm and easy and…*right*. But please don't feel like you have to—"

He didn't let her finish. He *couldn't* let her finish.

He couldn't go another second without touching her. Without kissing her. Without showing her everything he'd been keeping locked inside his head and heart for days, weeks, *months*.

He caught her wrists and pulled her up from the chair like she weighed nothing. The blanket tumbled to the floor, forgotten, and she gasped right before his mouth crashed down on hers.

Sweet Christ.

Her lips…

Soft and full. They tasted of peppermint tea sweetened by honey.

He'd kissed her before, but not like this. Not with his whole soul poured into it because he no longer had to safeguard his heart.

She hesitated for a fraction of a second, momentarily stunned by his ardor. But then she was there. All in. Meeting him lick for lick. Suck for suck.

Her hands fisted in his hair and tugged him closer, *closer*, until there was no daylight between them. Until her entire length was pressed tight to his.

He lost track of time. Lost track of reality. Two weeks since their last kiss felt like twenty goddamn years. And relearning her mouth, her body, was decadence itself.

Her soft whimper when he nipped at her lower lip went straight to his cock. Her nails scraping across his scalp and the ankle she hooked behind his knee as she tried to better align their bodies nearly undid him.

And then…chaos.

Needy, desperate, frenzied chaos.

Buttons were popped. Boots were unlaced and toed aside. Clothes were shoved off shoulders, peeled down hips, and dragged over heads.

Each layer lost meant more skin. More heat. More of *her*.

He only came back to himself, back to reality, when there was nothing left between them but panting breaths and unquenched passion.

Despite her protest, he stepped back to look at her. To admire her. To delight in the way the lamplight washed over every curve, every plane, every dip and whorl and inch of pale, perfect skin.

Goddess, he marveled, still reeling with the idea that she had chosen him. Wanted him. *Loved* him.

How was it possible?

He didn't know. But he wasn't about to spend another second questioning it.

The bruise on her breast had faded away, leaving only plump skin. Her belly button piercing winked at him, as sexy as a warm whisper in his ear. And that tiny mole on her hip still charmed the hell out of him because it matched the one beneath her eyebrow.

"Hew?" Her forehead creased at his sudden, breathless stillness. "Is there…something wrong?"

Wrong? His gaze snapped to hers.

The scant inches between them felt like both a gift and a curse. A gift because he wasn't sure he could trust himself not to ravish her if he closed the gap. A curse because it physically *hurt* not to be touching her, tasting her, *loving* her in all the ways he'd dreamed.

"Nothing's wrong, sweetheart." His voice was gravel and grit. "In fact, nothing has ever been more right."

He couldn't hold back another damn second. He scooped her into his arms and kissed her like he was a drowning man and she was oxygen itself as he carried her the few steps to the bed.

She loves me. She loves *me. She loves* me.

The refrain matched each beat of his heart as he marveled at his luck. At the miracle of being loved. *Finally.* But most importantly, being loved by *her.*

Sabrina Greenlee.

The Roman river goddess.

A woman who was braver than she knew. Kinder than was probably wise. And smarter than she'd ever admit.

If his heart had been a balloon, it would have burst from the sheer magnitude of the happiness filling it.

Peanut hissed when Hew lay Sabrina on the bed. The tom thudded onto the floor with an irritated flick of his crooked tail, but Hew gave him little more than a fleeting glance.

He was too busy stretching out beside Sabrina, gathering her close, reveling in the feel of her breasts crushed to his chest, her thighs twined with his, her soft belly cradling the hot, hard evidence of just how badly he wanted her. How much he needed her.

She needed him, too, if her busy, *busy* hands were anything to go by.

As he reclaimed her mouth, she touched him everywhere. His back. His buttocks. His chest. His nipples. Reaching between them to fist the length of him in her hand and make him groan.

"Ya keep doin' that," he whispered against her wet, wanton mouth, "and I won't be able to go slow."

"I don't want you to go slow. We went slow the first time. Now, I want you inside me." She wiggled her hips and angled him toward her core, swiping the head of his swollen cock between her lips so he could feel the searing heat of her. The sopping wetness of her.

She was ready. She was so, so ready.

And they'd barely even begun.

His groan turned into a growl. "Sabrina," he warned when she thrust forward. Just a little. Just enough to dip his tip into her hot, honeyed center.

His toes curled. His eyes crossed. He had to stop kissing her and grit his teeth to keep from shoving into her. To keep from seating himself to the hilt. To keep from thrusting deep and grinding hard against the swollen nub of her little clit.

"Don't. Move," he rasped. His thumb found her nipple, rolling it as tight as a stone.

"I can't help it." Her hips jerked, and he slid in another fraction. Just enough so that her sweet pussy surrounded his head, his rim enclosed inside her gripping, milking entrance.

He screwed his eyes shut and fisted his hands into the covers behind her. Nothing had ever felt so good. So wet. So soft and tight and—

"I'm on the pill," she whispered, her voice husky with wantonness. She leaned in to nip his chin. "And I was tested…after…after…" She didn't finish. Didn't want to spoil the moment by speaking of the monster who'd shattered her life in Charleston.

That was it. That's all it took.

She was protected from unwanted pregnancy. And he was clean. And that meant…

He rolled her onto her back so quickly she squeaked her surprise.

The move disconnected their bodies. But she was quick to spread her thighs wide. And he was quick to grab the base of his cock.

Within a breath, they were chest to chest, nose to nose, and he was once again nudging his tip into the very heart of her.

Her breath was warm and sweet against his hungry lips. Her nipples scraped through his chest hair as they both struggled with each ragged breath. And her brown eyes were melty and warm as she held his gaze.

Something flickered briefly across her face.

Hesitation? Uncertainty? *Unease?*

He could barely speak past the pounding of his heart, past the begging of his cock. But he managed, "What is it, sweetheart?"

"I—" She bit her lip. He could see her pulse fluttering furiously in her throat. "I don't know what this means, Hew." She shook her head, her silky hair rustling against the pillowcase. "Does it mean you—" She swallowed, and a line formed between her eyebrows. "What do you feel for me?"

He blinked. Confused that she would ask. Confused that she didn't know.

"Isn't it obvious?" His voice was rougher than usual, breaking around the edges of his words. "Hasn't it *been* obvious?"

She licked her lips. "I don't know. I—"

"My heart refuses to beat unless you're with me," he interrupted, pressing his forehead to hers. "I can't breathe when you're not near." He lifted his head and framed her beautiful, beloved face with his hands. "I love you, Sabrina. River goddess. I've loved you since the moment ya walked through the front door and fainted into my arms."

Her nostrils flared, eyes filling until a single tear slipped from the corner of each.

He used his thumbs to gently brush them away, still unable to believe he was here. With her. And that there was nothing between them but love.

"I wanna make love to ya now." He bent to nibble at the gentle curve of her bottom lip. "Is that okay?"

"God, yes." Her immediate reply made him smile.

Lifting his head so he could watch her face, he entered her. Slowly. Gently. Easing in inch by inch because even though she was slick with desire, she was small and he was…*not*.

His vision dimmed at the edges and coalesced on the pleasure he saw in her expression as he pushed inexorably forward. Feeling her silky walls close tightly around him. Feeling her hands on his hips urging him onward. Feeling her heels hook into the bend of his legs for purchase as she arched and finally, *finally* seated him fully.

His swollen head pressed tight against the barrier of her cervix. His balls smashed gloriously against the curve of her ass.

It was all too much. Too pleasurable. Too decadent.

And yet it wasn't enough because his shaft ached for friction, testicles begging for release.

She had gasped at the feel of him fully embedded inside her, her eyes screwing shut. But now, she framed his face and held his gaze.

"I love you." The words were said softly, sincerely. They fell into his ears, overflowed his heart, and filled all the empty places inside him left behind by a lifetime of loneliness, neglect, and rejection.

His throat was full. There was a terrible burning behind his eyes. But he managed, "I love you, too, Sabrina," before he claimed her mouth and began to move.

Hew had had sex in backseats and bedrooms. In quick, sweaty bursts of need. And, sometimes, in slower, heated tangles that left him sated but still somehow empty. He'd even been blissfully passionate before. Had lost himself in the pleasure of the body beneath his. But this…

This was different.

Different in the way a ham sandwich was different from filet mignon.

Because this was the first time he'd made love to a woman. The first time he'd bared his whole heart while sharing his body. The first time every thrust carried not just lust and hunger, but devotion and reverence.

Short, fast thrusts that ground his pubic bone against her swollen clit. *That's* what his Sabrina liked. Which was lucky, because that's what he liked, too.

It was a rocking, rolling motion that kept them locked tightly together, body to body, heart to heart.

The sounds she made were low, raw, unbearably sexy. Not the kittenish mewls or the keening whimpers of women who performed how they thought men wanted to hear. Oh, no. Sabrina's groans of pleasure and gasps of need were all natural, pulled out of her by desire and the uninhibited way she worked with him toward her own release.

"Yes, Hew," she whispered. "Yes, just like that."

She moved with him like they'd done this a thousand times before. Like this was a dance they'd practiced over and over again.

They'd been made for this.

Made for each other and—

His thoughts stopped because he felt it then. The little flutter inside her as her orgasm rushed closer.

Thank Christ. Because he was hanging on by a goddamned thread.

Forcing himself to keep the same pace, the same angle, he worked to push her past the point of no return. And then her body clamped down hard around his, rippling, milking, sucking him deep as her orgasm hit with the force of a lightning strike and she screamed his name.

That did it.

Hearing his name ripped from the back of her throat at the same time her body was ripped by wave after wave of delight had his own release tearing through him.

"Sabrina! I love you!" he groaned as jet after jet of molten heat shot out of him and spilled into her.

The pleasure wracked him, flexing his hips tight as a bowstring as he held himself deep. Emptying all that he had. Feeling her taking it. Welcoming it.

CHAPTER 45

Hew abruptly fell asleep.

It was like he'd been waiting for that orgasm so long that it'd been intense enough to fell him like the proverbial tree.

Sabrina laughed. She couldn't help it. She was so happy, she could have levitated.

If I weren't pinned down by 220 pounds of pure sex, sinew, and muscle, she thought.

Her shaking chest startled him awake. He pushed up on his elbows, his hair wild from her fingers, his eyes dazed and bleary.

"Did I fall asleep or pass out?" he rumbled, lazily pressing a kiss to the corner of her mouth, his lips warm and firm and so wonderfully familiar now.

"Pretty sure they're the same thing in this instance."

"Mmm." He rolled off her and then hissed—they both did—when his softened body slid from hers. "I'll grab a washcloth."

"My knight in shining…*nudity,*" she finished with a devilish grin, watching his firm, bunching backside as he stalked across the room to disappear inside the bathroom.

When he reemerged, he had one of her fluffy washcloths in hand, and his spent member bobbed between his thick thighs. Even flaccid, he was… *impressive.*

She lifted her hand for the washcloth, then drew her eyebrows together when he shook his head. "I made the mess." He winked. "I'll be the one to clean it up."

Before she could object, he whisked the covers aside and gently pressed the washcloth to the center of her.

She hissed, and a line of worry creased his brow. "Sore?" he asked.

"Mmm." She nodded as he softly wiped away the evidence of his desire. "But in the best possible way."

Hew was a big man. He'd stretched her to the limit. But she'd reveled in every inch of him.

"It'll get easier," he assured her. "Your body will become accustomed to mine."

"Spoken from experience?" She lifted a teasing eyebrow.

His expression blanked. "No. I was a virgin before this."

The laugh that exploded out of her had Peanut, who'd curled up in the chair in the corner, lifting his head and blinking judgmental yellow eyes at her.

"It's a good thing you're not Pinocchio. Your nose would've grown three feet with that whopper of a lie."

His eyes dragged over the length of her naked body, stopping at the points of her breasts before traveling south and then stopping again at the apex of her legs. She knew she was pink and swollen. Still dewy from their combined orgasms.

"If I stand here starin' at ya for ten more seconds, *something* is certainly goin' to start growin'."

On cue, his dick jerked. He gestured to it. "See?" he said unnecessarily.

"Toss that cloth in the tub and then come back to bed," she instructed. "I miss you next to me."

He marched to the bathroom door, lobbed the washcloth like a basketball player lobbing a shot, and then hopped into bed so quickly she couldn't help but laugh.

"I do like a man who's quick to follow orders," she teased.

"I do like a woman who knows what she wants and isn't afraid to ask for it," he shot back.

She snuggled next to him, finding that place between his heart and his chin that was perfectly made to fit her cheek. "Well, then, we're going to get along just fine."

He chuckled, and she pushed up on one elbow so she could see his face.

His green eyes glowed with a happiness so pure it made her heart expand in her chest. For a heartbeat, she got a glimpse of the boy he'd once been. Unguarded, untouched by neglect and rejection.

"Why didn't you say anything?" she asked, not realizing the question was sitting on the tip of her tongue until it'd fallen out of her mouth.

"Hmm?" One dark eyebrow arced. "When?"

"That afternoon two weeks ago. After we…" She made a motion with her hand. "Why didn't you tell me how you felt then? Why did you act like you were anxious to foist me off onto Martin?"

Something flickered across his face. Shame, maybe? Embarrassment?

"Self-preservation, I reckon," he finally admitted, his voice pitched low. "I was so used to bein' rejected that I tried to beat ya to the punch."

Her heart cracked for him then. For the sweet, little boy who'd never been chosen, never been anyone's first pick. For the kid who'd grown a tough skin as he'd been shuffled from foster home to foster home, group house to group house. For the man who'd learned to armor himself in stoicism because no one had ever loved him.

Until now.

Until her.

And she would love him until her final breath.

She was rarely sure of much. But she was one-hundred-percent convinced of *that*.

"Is it too soon to tell you that I want to spend the rest of my life with you?" she asked quietly, her heart in her throat as she watched his face for any sign of shock or misgiving that she'd already jumped ahead to happily-ever-after.

None came.

"No." He shook his head, his mouth pulling into a wide smile. "It's not too soon. I've been waitin' my whole life for someone to say that to me."

She kissed him then. She'd meant for it to be quick and comforting. And it started that way to be sure. But it soon turned into so much more when he pulled her atop him so he could cup the back of her head and slide his talented tongue between her teeth.

As it always did when they were together, time lost all meaning. She had no idea if it was minutes later or an hour later when she reached between their bodies to grab him.

Even though she knew him intimately now, it was still a surprise to find him such a delicious, ridiculous handful. And if he hadn't spent the last…however long…kissing her nipples and tickling her clit and readying her body, she might have hesitated. Might have wondered how the thick, veiny, throbbing column of flesh that she stroked in her hand could *ever* fit inside her body.

But, as it was, she didn't pause. She placed him at her opening and then slowly, *slowly* sank onto his length. Rejoicing in the way he filled her up and stretched her tight.

The first time had been fast and furious and filled with ravenous kisses and hungry hands. This time was slow and sweet…a dance of patience and reverence. Each glide down his length was a worshipful offering, each rise a silent promise that she wasn't going anywhere.

The world beyond the bed ceased to exist as they rocked together in unhurried rhythm, two hearts speaking fluently in the oldest language known to man until they couldn't hold out anymore, and they both gave in to delicious, decadent completion.

After the final throes of release subsided, they assumed the position they'd perfected when Sabrina was freshly traumatized and needed someone to hold onto, and when Hew was happy to provide her with the anchor she needed.

"Little backpack," he murmured happily as she curled against him, the big spoon to his little spoon, her nose pressed into the sweet-smelling skin of his neck, and her fingers splayed wide against his ribs.

She could no longer fight the fatigue brought on by the past day's adrenaline, excitement, and emotional upheaval, so she let her last conscious thought be this…

I finally found a home. And it's not a place. It's a person. A man. A warm, brave, funny, wickedly sexy man.

And I'll never, never *let him go.*

CHAPTER 46

Brooklawn Memorial Cemetery, Portland, Maine
Two months later…

Hew zipped his leather jacket as far as it would go under his chin in an attempt to keep the cold Maine wind from tunneling down the collar of his thick, wool fisherman's sweater.

It was only the end of October. But fall was on the way out and winter was quick on its heels. The trees were still festooned in their autumn finery, burnt orange, fiery red, and cheery goldenrod. But the branches grew barer with every gust. And soon they would be completely naked.

Stick season.

When the tourists fled to warmer climes, and the locals buckled down, hibernated, and dreamed of when the spring daisies would push through the frost in…five to six months.

"She should be here," Sabrina said as she studied the map the cemetery manager had printed for them when they stopped in to get directions.

Hew halted his slow trudge and glanced around.

The place where his parents and grandparents were buried wasn't like other cemeteries. There were no mausoleums or headstones. Each grave was denoted by a simple, in-ground marker, which made the whole area appear like a well-manicured park rather than a graveyard.

There was nothing to block the view of the green, rolling hills or the brightly seasoned trees. And the hush of the wind through the dry leaves, the rustle of their boots on ground, as well as the distant cry of a gull riding the current…it all lent the place a serene stillness. A tranquil kind of beauty.

He'd only been there once before.

He'd asked his social worker to bring him on his sixteenth birthday. After a few eye rolls and much huffing and puffing, she'd loaded him up to make the short drive.

He wasn't sure what he'd expected to find, what he'd been looking for. Connection, maybe? A sense of self and belonging?

He'd found none of that. Just cold stones and the chiseled names of people he'd never met.

Maybe that was why he'd balked when Sabrina had originally suggested they make a trip. He hadn't wanted a repeat of the disappointment he'd felt the first time.

Although, as he watched her walk down the row of markers in her navy coat with a plaid scarf looped snug at her throat and her gloved hands clutching two riots of bright flowers that seemed to defy the gray day, he couldn't help thinking this time might feel different.

He felt different.

Sabrina had done that. She'd changed him. Her *love* had changed him.

"Here she is." She breathed reverently, staring down at the grave marker that read simply: *Natasha Smith, April 2ⁿᵈ, 1972—May 28ᵗʰ, 1990. Beloved Daughter. Loving Mother.*

There were tears in Sabrina's big, brown eyes when she glanced up at Hew from where she'd crouched to lay one of the two bundles of brightly colored mums next to the marker. Her voice sounded watery as she reached for his hand and whispered, "Her parents made sure the world knew she loved you even though she never got to meet you."

All the emotion he hadn't felt before, all the gratitude and love for the woman who'd harbored him safely inside her body for nine months, welled up and filled his eyes.

"Tasha…" Sabrina whispered reverently. "I promise to give him all the love you never got the chance to. I promise to spend the rest of my life making up for the time that was stolen from you."

Hew couldn't speak past the lump clogging his throat. And a single tear slipped from the corner of his eye, carving a cold track down his cheek. But he didn't brush it away.

There was no reason to hide with Sabrina. No reason to tuck his feelings deep where no one could see.

With her, he was safe. Safe to feel every sharp edge of grief and every warm swell of love without judgment or ridicule.

He squeezed her hand, feeling the shape and solidity of the ring on her finger. The ring he'd placed there just last week.

Not a diamond.

Sabrina had wrinkled her nose at every clear, flashing stone they'd looked at in the high-end jewelry shop on Chicago's Magnificent Mile. Instead, she'd chosen a square-cut emerald.

"To match your eyes," she'd said. *"And it's your birthstone. It symbolizes renewal and hope and loyalty. If that's not you…not us…I don't know what is."*

Now, he managed only, "I love you, Sabrina."

She let go of his hand so she could go up on tiptoe and swipe the cold tear from his cheek. Cupping the side of his face, she pulled him down for a kiss.

Her nose was chilled from the biting wind, but her lips were warm. Her lips were always warm. Just like her heart.

He could've gone on kissing her all damn afternoon, losing himself in her. In them. But all-too-soon she leaned back, pulling the folded map from her coat pocket.

She squinted toward the horizon. The clouds hung heavy and low, their gray bellies threatening freezing rain later in the day. "Your dad's over there." She pointed. "Let's go visit him."

They started toward the little rolling slope. But before they'd gone two steps, she turned back and called over her shoulder, "Goodbye, Tasha. For now. We'll be back."

After Sabrina laid her second bundle of flowers on his father's marker and said, "Thank you, Tommy, for giving me this man. I promise to take care of him," they made their way across the lush green grass that was just beginning to lose its luster to the waning growing season. As they turned down the little footpath that wound toward their rented car, Sabrina took a deep breath before she blew it out on a long sigh.

He tossed an arm over her shoulders and gave her a little squeeze. She had that look in her eye. The one she got when she was thinking of her brother.

And no wonder. Cemeteries had a way of making those who'd passed feel closer.

"Thinkin' of Cooper?" he asked, even though he knew the answer. "We can make a trip to Charleston, too. Visit his grave."

"I miss him at odd moments," she admitted, twisting her gloved fingers together. "Inconvenient moments, it seems, when I least want to because I'm in a crowd of people. Or I'm here." She splayed a gloved hand wide. "In this place where I should be focused on *your* family."

"There's no *should* about any of it," he assured her. "No right or wrong when it comes to the how, why, and when of grief."

Her smile was wobbly. "How did I get so lucky to find you?"

He snorted. "*I'm* the lucky one. I keep waitin' for ya to come to your senses."

"Never." She vehemently shook her head. "If loving you is crazy, I don't want to be sane."

After bundling her into the passenger seat, he buckled himself into the driver's seat and listened to the rental's engine rumble to life. They had reservations at a B&B. And tomorrow morning, he planned to take her to the local library that'd been his refuge and the lighthouse that'd been his safe place.

Before he could put the car in gear, however, she placed a gloved hand on his forearm. "I think I *would* like to make a trip to Charleston to visit Cooper. I want to introduce him to you. Show him he doesn't have to worry about me anymore."

"Ayuh." He nodded. That pesky lump was back in his throat because neither of them had living family to visit, so it only felt right that they made the rounds with the dead. "I want to meet him, too. Tell him how grateful I am that he rode ya to the hospital on his handlebars to get that broken arm set. It's attached to your right hand, which is my favorite, since it's the one that gives the best—"

She slapped his shoulder before he could finish. "Pervert," she grumbled, but her eyes were bright and sparkling. Then, a cloud passed over her face, as dark and heavy as the ones hanging outside the windshield.

"What is it?" he asked.

"Eddy Torres and Cooper are buried in the same cemetery." Her upper lip curled. "Maybe I'll find his grave and spit on it."

He tapped his finger against the steering wheel as he thought of the pudgy, dark-eyed man. Hew had learned to identify evil by seeing past a too-slick smile or too-bright eyes. But he hadn't needed to use his years of experience to recognize the vileness that had lived inside Eddy Torres. It'd been obvious.

"Might I suggest ya piss on it, too?" he said flatly.

She chuckled. "As long as you promise to stand lookout while I drop trou."

"Deal." He jerked his chin down.

As he pulled down the little lane, headed toward the front gate, she wrinkled her nose and said, "Does it make me a terrible person to hope he was terrified in his last moments?"

Hew considered his next words carefully. He could continue to keep her in the dark. Or…

He could tell her the truth and bring into the light the only secret that still remained between them.

"No, it doesn't. And, ayuh, he was." He waited in the silence that filled the car's interior as his words sank in and realization dawned.

He expected her to bombard him with questions, expected her to demand the details of the night he'd pulled Eddy Torres out of his car at gunpoint before marching him to the edge of the marsh.

She did neither.

She simply swallowed, nodded once, and then stared out the windshield as the rolling landscape of the cemetery slipped by. When she finally spoke, her voice was calm, quiet. "Thank you, Hew."

He hadn't realized he'd been holding his breath until it leaked out of him in windy relief. "I'd do anything for you, Sabrina. Surely, ya know that."

She reached for his hand, twining her fingers through his, and squeezed. "And I'll do anything for you. Everything for you."

His heart swelled so big and wide he thought it a wonder his chest managed to hold it.

After a while, she laughed and said, "Graham was right. You *are* my lobster."

He frowned and pictured the red stuffy that now lived on her bed along with her pile of pillows.

"Apparently, lobsters mate for life," she explained. "And Graham says you and I will still be walking around our tank holding claws"—she made interlocking circles with her thumbs and forefingers—"even when we're old and gray."

He smiled at the imagery. "I like the idea of bein' your forever lobster, stuck together until our shells are crusty and our claws are cracked. Sounds like the perfect life."

"Spoken like a true Mainer."

As Hew drove out of the cemetery and into his future with Sabrina, he remembered something he'd read once.

The universe has three answers to any question you might ask. The first is 'yes.' The second is 'not yet.' And the third is 'I have something better in store for you.'

He'd spent his life asking the universe…*when will I be loved?*

It had answered with Sabrina.

And she was *more* than worth the wait.

CHAPTER 47

Stockholm, Sweden

Vivian Drake lounged at a corner table in the little café she'd been frequenting since her move, a steaming coffee cup between her hands. She wasn't a fan of the cold. It sank into her bones and made her joints feel stiff. And she hated the long, dark nights of a Scandinavian winter.

But Sweden had one thing she craved more than warmth and sunshine. *Privacy.*

The Swedes were big on individual rights. They didn't believe in omnipresent CCTV cameras or government drones tracking the steps of every citizen. Stockholm was a city full of people minding their own goddamned business. And *that* was exactly what she wanted.

It'd been nearly two months since she landed in the new country she was determined to call home. She'd spent that time renting a flat, learning the back alleys and side roads—*just in case*—and waiting for the paranoia that had dogged her back in the U.S. to find her here.

It hadn't.

Thankfully.

Her shoulders were beginning to relax. The hairs on her neck were beginning to stand down. The sense that she was lined up in someone's crosshairs was beginning to fade.

She took a slow sip of her coffee and smiled in appreciation.

It was stronger than the dishwater the Americans brewed. Thicker. Darker. With an earthy bitterness that clung to her tongue.

Outside the frosted window, the narrow street bustled with pedestrians covered in chic coats and flowing scarves. Bicycles weaved between tiny hatchbacks. A food cart steamed in the cold air. And pastel building fronts leaned into each other across the road like gossiping old friends.

Bishop, I hope whoever you are, wherever you are, you're feeling the heat of the Black Knights' breath on your n—

She didn't finish the thought.

A man slid into the empty chair beside her in one fluid motion. A charcoal overcoat was expertly draped over his shoulders. But it was open to reveal a suit worth more than her rent. His silver hair was barber-perfect, and his face was familiar in a way that had her cocking her head.

It took a heartbeat too long for recognition to hit.

Then it did.

And her blood iced over.

"You." She set down her coffee with deliberate care. Her right hand slipped into her coat pocket, fingers curling around the butt of the pistol she'd purchased out of the back of a van less than twenty-four hours after stepping off the train at the Stockholm Central Train Station.

"Hello, Vivian." His voice was deep, smooth, every syllable polished like he'd been born behind a podium. "I've been anxious to meet you."

The Swedes around them continued chatting over their coffees and pastries, oblivious to who sat among them. In fact, she'd be surprised if any of them even knew his first name.

Being half a world away from U.S. politics had its advantages.

"Where's your security detail?" she asked, aiming for casual.

"Outside." He winked like they were sharing a private joke. "I wanted to meet you alone to discuss your failure. You never called." He tsked. "You could have at least told me you managed to survive. For too long, I thought you perished alongside your crew. Imagine my surprise when I discovered you in Nowhere, Wisconsin."

"I *knew* you had eyes on me." A muscle twitched in her cheek. "How did you find me there?"

"Oh, Vivian." He chuckled. "As careful as you were, you weren't careful enough. Surely you realize someone with my resources would know about your cache of safe deposit boxes. And surely you realize I would put eyes on them after your death. Just in case."

She swallowed thickly.

Stupid, stupid, STUPID!

She should've left her cash behind and fled the country immediately after the Black Knights cut her loose. But she was used to a particular kind of lifestyle. And the thought of being on the run without a red cent to her name hadn't interested her.

"You evaded me in the States." His expression was slightly puzzled. "What happened after you left that Airbnb in Sheboygan?"

"What does it matter? You found me anyway."

"Not without some effort." He frowned like he was annoyed she'd had the audacity to run from him. Then he cocked his head. "How *did* you survive the Black Knights, by the way? They don't tend to leave loose ends."

The Black Knights…

Why hadn't they found this fucker? Identified him? Splashed his name and his backdoor dealings all over the front page of every newspaper?

"They're not as ruthless as we are." She gave a breezy flick of her fingers despite her thundering heart. "They let me go."

His eyes narrowed slightly. But no lines appeared beside them.

Botox?

That made her snort. She'd always thought he was a bit of a peacock. Smiling for the cameras. Wearing bespoke suits. But the Botox meant he was even more vain than she imagined.

"Why would you hire me to expose them?" She ensured her tone was conversational, even though her lizard brain told her to fight or fly. Or maybe fight and *then* fly. "I thought your—"

"What did you tell them?" he cut her off. And his eyes looked as sharp as his words sounded.

"What *could* I tell them? I didn't know anything," she was quick to point out.

"You knew *some* things," he countered, and her mind raced with her options.

Lie? Or tell the truth?

In the end, she settled on the truth. It was more satisfying.

"I told them you're connected. I told them your position had to be somewhere near the top."

His smile looked carnivorous. He licked his teeth before whispering, "Bad, bad girl."

Despite her pounding heart, she arched an eyebrow and let her lips curve into a smile she'd used to disarm more powerful men than him.

She traced one fingertip along his gloved hand where it lay open atop the table. "And what did you have in mind for my punishment, sir?"

She'd always used her sexuality as a tool, a weapon. She used it now even as she curled her finger around the trigger on the *real* weapon in her pocket.

His stare was flat. His tone even more so when he said, "Your death."

Her heart stopped for half a beat, then slammed into motion. She began to draw the gun, but he clicked his tongue and gave a small shake of his head.

"Don't bother. It's already done."

"What is?" Why did she suddenly sound so breathless?

"You're already dead."

The words crawled up her spine like a cluster of spiders.

He flicked a gaze to the fork beside her plate. The tines glinted in the soft, gray light filtering in through the window. On her plate, only crumbs from her cinnamon bun remained.

"Poison?" she rasped, though she wasn't sure if the tightness in her throat was fear or something much more sinister.

"Curare," he said casually, like he was ordering a coffee. "New formula. More potent than the previous incarnations. No injection required. Just ingestion. I sprayed it on your fork."

Curare.

She knew of it, of course. Had used it herself once. It started with muscle paralysis and ended with suffocation.

She yanked out the gun, determined to take him with her. But her arm refused to move. And that's when she realized her heart was stuttering, its beat erratic.

She tried to suck in a breath, but her lungs refused to work.

Bishop smiled again. Not happily. Not smugly. Just…satisfied.

Her watering eyes locked onto his. She poured every ounce of venom she had inside her into that one final glare.

"BKI's…coming…" She forced the words past a tongue that felt carved from stone.

Then, her head fell forward on a neck that no longer supported it. Her heart struggled to beat once…twice. It forgot what came next.

"Sweet dreams, Vivian." Bishop's politician's voice reached her ears, and she remembered saying those exact words to Hummer. Had he heard her on the other end of the call? Was he mocking her now?

It was the last thought she ever had.

EPILOGUE

Bishop handed paper cups to the two men in his security detail. Both accepted with murmured thanks, their fingers curling around the heat.

"Did anyone inside recognize you?" the dark-haired agent asked as the younger agent strode toward the black government sedan idling by the curb.

"No one." Bishop feigned a sigh. "My pride is well and truly pricked, if you must know."

Richard Jarvis had spent the past five years on Bishop's detail, and he shook his head affectionately. "You and your sojourns, sir. I've never had a protectee who loves to ditch us more than you do."

"A man needs his privacy, Agent Jarvis." Bishop clapped a hand on the agent's shoulder and felt the strap of the man's body armor beneath his overcoat. "Even if it's just to sit in a café and enjoy a quick hit of caffeine in solitude."

"It's all about life's little joys, I suppose."

"Mmm." Bishop smiled. "And I appreciate you allowing me mine."

Jarvis scanned the street before motioning for Bishop to precede him across the sidewalk. "Just don't tell the director, sir. He'll have my head and my gun if he ever hears how often we let you sneak away."

"Your secret is safe with me, Agent Jarvis." When the agent opened the car door, Bishop added, "*All* your secrets."

Jarvis froze for a fraction too long. A small, delicious tell.

Bishop was good at gathering around him the people best suited to serve him.

Despite having a loving wife and three school-age kids, Richard Jarvis hired sex workers from D.C. all the way to Bangkok. The man was an addict. And his predilections meant he knew not to ask too many questions about the private lives of others.

It also meant he was easily persuaded to look the other way when Bishop asked him to.

Once inside the sedan, the younger agent turned from the driver's seat. "The flight back to D.C. leaves in two hours, sir. Should we head to the airport?"

"This little café was my last stop," Bishop assured him. "It's back to the land of the free and the home of the brave, boys."

"Was the trip a success, sir?"

John Snyder was fresh-faced and earnest enough to make Bishop feel every one of his quickly advancing years. Snyder was also still green enough to take his cues from Jarvis without question.

"The king has agreed to continue dedicating Sweden's time and resources to our joint UN peacekeeping missions," Bishop said. "Madam President will be pleased."

Not that the Swedish king's opinion meant much in parliament. His role was ceremonial, but their meetup was perfect for a glossy photo op.

"Very good, sir." Snyder slid on his seat belt once Jarvis folded himself into the passenger seat.

Bishop's gaze drifted across the sidewalk. Through the fogged windowpane of the little café, he caught a glimpse of her silhouette…

Vivian Drake.

The infamous Black Widow.

She looked so peaceful sitting there with her head tilted toward her chest. To the casual observer, she appeared to be resting or scrolling on her phone.

Someone would discover the truth in a few hours, of course. And there would be questions.

What could cause the death of such a young, vibrant woman? Why was she packing heat in a country with restrictive gun laws? Who was she *really*?

By then, though, the poison would be out of her system. The autopsy would simply show her heart had stopped. And her death would be one of those mysteries put on a shelf and quickly forgotten.

One problem down, he thought with a secretive little scowl. *One to go.*

If the Black Knights thought they were hunting him, they'd soon learn that wolves fare poorly against a man determined to set the forest on fire.

AUTHOR'S NOTE

As time and society progress, we become aware that certain words and phrases in our everyday lexicon have problematic origins or can be used to further marginalize vulnerable readers.

As a writer and a language lover, I strive daily to educate myself on outdated, offensive terms and stereotypes, and work to eliminate them from my novels. (We're not talking swear words here, people.) But I'm still learning. And if I screw up, I'd love to be educated and allowed the opportunity to correct any mistakes. Because I truly believe the pen is mightier than the sword.

Or, in simpler terms, *words matter*.

ACKNOWLEDGEMENTS

Major thanks to "The Asheville Crew" for keeping me hiking, laughing, and karaokeing. You all save me from atrophying behind the keyboard by forcing me (sometimes unwillingly) out of my pajamas and into the real world. Glad to be on this part of the journey with all of you.

As always, props to the people who do the unsung work of getting a book into readers' hands: Marlene Roberts, proofer extraordinaire, Jennifer Johnson, formatter for the stars, and Erin Dameron-Hill, talented cover artist.

And last but certainly not least, thank YOU, dear readers, for coming back for more Black Knights Inc. I hope you all had as much fun jumping back into the world of motorcycles and mayhem as I did.

OTHER BOOKS BY JULIE ANN WALKER

ABOUT THE AUTHOR

A *New York Times* and *USA Today* bestselling author, Julie loves to travel the world looking for views to compete with her deadlines. And if those views happen to come with a blue sky and sunshine? All the better! When she's not writing, Julie enjoys camping, hiking, cycling, fishing, cooking, petting every dog that walks by her, and... reading, of course!

For more information, please visit:
https://julieannwalker.com

facebook.com/julieannwalkerauthor

instagram.com/julieannwalker_author

tiktok.com/@julieannwalker_author

@julieannwalker.bsky.social